# Will Rise
# from Ashes

## by

## Jean M. Grant

This is a work of fiction. Names, characters, places, and incidents are either the product of the author's imagination or are used fictitiously, and any resemblance to actual persons living or dead, business establishments, events, or locales, is entirely coincidental.

**Will Rise from Ashes**

COPYRIGHT © 2019 by Jean M. Grant

Cover Art by *Debbie Taylor*

The Wild Rose Press, Inc.
PO Box 708
Adams Basin, NY 14410-0708
Visit us at www.thewildrosepress.com

Publishing History
First Mainstream Women's Fiction Edition, 2019
Print ISBN 978-1-5092-2511-8
Digital ISBN 978-1-5092-2512-5

Published in the United States of America

Even from far away, I recognized the man's plaid long-sleeved shirt and the large backpack, but now he was walking alongside a bike on his approach.

"Hey, look! It's that guy you drove past this morning!"

I shuddered inwardly. Well, karma just bit me in the butt.

"How did he catch up with us?" Motherly instinct took over as I rose, my legs wobbly. "Will, stay there. Here, take this," I said, handing him the tire iron.

"We already tried that, Mom."

"Not for that, Will."

He scratched his brown hair, which was overdue for a cut, and looked at me, confusion wrinkling his brow.

"Be my wizard, Will. It's your sword."

"Wizards have wands."

"Will…"

The circuit connected. "Oh…yes, Mom, I'll protect you!"

I smiled faintly. "Thank you, honey." I didn't want to explain further that it was me protecting him. I didn't want to say that if something happened, to run and hide in the woods. Because he *would* run and hide. Then what? Who would come help?

I shoved my hand into my front jeans pocket to nestle my fingertips around the pocket knife I had given Harrison for our wedding anniversary. The man slowed his bicycle as he drew nearer. He gave me an understated, yet significant, nod. The nod of understanding, of kindness. I didn't buy it.

"Hello, again," he said.

*Ouch.*

## Dedication

To my husband Christian,
my partner and my heart on this life journey.
To my sons,
Ewan, whose gentle spirit
flows from him like sweet honey, and
Henry, whose exuberance brings joy to my day.
I love you all.

# Acknowledgments

I write and live by the three P's: patience, perseverance, and putting in the time. Writing is a coffee-laden, research-heavy, hone-the-craft, dust-yourself-off, and try-again kind of career. And I love it. Through college, graduate school, job changes, parenting, and all the nooks and crannies I could find, writing has been my constant. I'm grateful for my husband's support as I shifted to full-time dream-realizer. My children have been patient and now are at the age where they ask more about my books with genuine interest: The volcano book, Mom? Yup, honey, that one (again, still…).

Every journey is filled with bumps and bruises, but there are also friends beside us helping each step of the way. I could not be where I am without the friends and fellow writers who've supported me on all levels. Beta readers, critique partners, and writing groups…thank you to all who've helped me by giving your time and providing feedback with this book and others past or future: Lorraine, Rachel, Jill, Barbara, Briar, Miranda, Keri, Jen, Piper, Marte, Stefani, Christine, Natasha, Alex, Allison, Jess, and the Central Massachusetts Christian Writers Fellowship. I'd also like to thank the authors and the editors of The Wild Rose Press, especially my editor, Eilidh MacKenzie, who took a leap for this new(er) author and helped me chase down that dream a wee bit more!

Chapter One
Inception

A gray column of ash exploded on the screen. The plume darkened the sky.

"Mom, come look!" Will said, without turning from the TV.

She fidgeted with the mail on the kitchen counter. Then said a bad word. The metal trash lid clanged open, and she grumbled. He tapped a finger on his thigh as he listened to the newscaster.

A few minutes passed. "Mom…"

"One minute," she called. He turned. She dragged the basket of dirty laundry from their vacation to Yellowstone down the basement steps. Thump, thump, thump.

"But it's the *volcano*! On TV!" His pulse flickered. This was important. She needed to see.

"Hang on a sec, Will."

The clock read 9:03 p.m. Eastern Time, but it still felt like Mountain Time and he wasn't sleepy. He counted to one second. He knew she didn't mean that. Her "a sec" or "a minute" could be way longer.

She returned from the basement and opened the window over the kitchen sink. The metallic, vibrating hum of the foghorn sounded in the distance. He rose and added a tally mark to the chart on his clipboard. Soon, he'd need to make his snow charts, too. But it was only August.

"Where are they?" Mom said.

She came through the doorway to the living room with her mug in one hand. It smelled like burnt stinky milk. He covered his nose.

"Mom, watch out!" She almost stepped on his eight red volcano cut-outs lined in a row in front of the TV. His heart kerthumped. He straightened one, so the bottom edge realigned with the rest. *There, better.*

"So, honey, what is it? Find an interesting documentary to watch?" she finally asked, drawing her gaze to the TV as she stumbled. "Will, the tape and scissors. I need you to pick them up, okay?" She yawned. "We need to go to bed soon." She leaned over the coffee table and clicked her laptop shut with another curse. "I can't even track their flight. Where are they?" she repeated to herself.

Her brown eyes were shiny, holding that sad look she got when she thought about Dad. Some expressions confused him, but Mom was easier to understand than others. She was sad *a lot* these days. Was she sad about his little brother Finn not returning home yet? He approached her and hugged her around the waist. He nudged the top of his head against her ribcage. "It's okay, Mom. Finn and Uncle Brandon will be here. Maybe their flights were delayed again?"

She exhaled. Coffee breath. His stomach squeezed. Delays. Yuck, he didn't like delays either.

She said in a whisper, a raspy grating sound, "They should've landed by now…the traffic north to Maine from Boston isn't awful this time of day. Finn's going to be so wired."

*But he's not a robot,* Will wanted to say, but he

knew it was just one of Mom's weird phrases. The commercials ended. He grabbed her hand. "Look, Mom. Yellowstone! Maybe Finn and Uncle Brandon saw it erupt since we were all *just* there! How lucky of them to see that, huh?" He pointed to the LIVE symbol in the bottom right corner.

Her mug slipped and fell in a crash, spilling all over his volcanoes.

****

I stared at the open laptop. My brother's flight was still listed as "pending departure" on the airline's website. The airplane icon was frozen in time. It had not budged in the past twelve hours. I powered the laptop down.

Drumming my fingers on the counter, I heaved a sigh and picked up my phone. Again. I hit redial, hoping against hope Sarah would answer this time. The news had not shown California affected by the ash cloud yet.

Hell, an ash cloud.

A volcano.

It was the morning after, and I still couldn't say those words aloud.

The click of her picking up on the other end shut that pervading thought down.

"Hello, AJ?" she breathed into the phone.

"Sarah! Thank God. Please say you've heard from Brandon."

Silence. Crackles.

"Sarah?" *Dear God, don't let me lose her, too.* She was the only connection I had to my brother Brandon…and to my sweetheart, Finnie. My mother-in-law had already called me in a panic last night. Even

Patsy's rock-solid attitude wavered in the wake of mankind's largest volcano...and I didn't need it to add to my anxiety.

"...closing roads north of us near Sacramento and San Francisco...last I heard from him was before he boarded..."

"He's not called at all?" I tried again. A few more crackles.

Will trudged into the kitchen, toting a large clear bin of Lego bricks. "No, not all those, honey. Please. Pick your favorites. We won't have room in the car," I said.

"Car?" Sarah said, her voice clearer. "You're not planning to drive out there, AJ? No, no, don't do that! And that's a long car ride for you—you know, since...Can you handle it?"

My pulse raced and head buzzed from minimal sleep and a high dose of caffeine. Jitters shook my hands. "My son's out there." I choked on my own words. I tucked the phone between my ear and shoulder as I unscrewed my pill bottle. I popped a pill. I tossed the recapped bottle into my open handbag. "No call or text?"

"Not yet. But he will."

Always the optimist, my sister-in-law. Well, I supposed she had to be, with a husband who had spent the better part of the last twenty years in the air force. Now that they'd settled into a routine in southern California, he had grown restless in his early retirement. He was the one who had insisted on our trip redo, coming in Harrison's place. And now he was...oh, Jesus, no. *Stop that, AJ!*

Will raked through the bin, the sound of bricks

clacking against each other both jarring against my swelling migraine and a squeezing of my heart. Finn wasn't here to dig through them with him. My seven-year-old baby was out there. Somewhere. With my brother. "Will, please, take that to the living room. And get your bag from upstairs. We leave in five minutes."

"Okay, Mom. I have the list here, on the clipboard. Make sure we double-check that we have it all." He handed it to me with a pencil. I forced a smile. "I'm going to say goodbye to Snow."

Sarah's voice poked in. "AJ, please, give him more time. He'll call. He'll get through. You can't possibly be thinking of driving all the way from Maine to…" Her words faded but not from the poor connection.

"Exactly. We don't even know where they are! He could still be in Salt Lake City," I said, a lump rising in my throat.

Will perked up from the living room. "That city's not there anymore, Mom."

The knot in my stomach tightened. *Thanks for the reminder, honey.*

"Well, it is. Just in bits and pieces," he corrected, while stroking the cat. "Don't be sad, Mom. We'll find them."

He turned on the TV.

Sarah's voice held a higher note of affirmation. "No, stop that. I'm sure he *got* on the flight to Denver. I ran through the timing, the delay, and the eruption. He caught the flight. *They* got on. They got out of there, okay?"

She neglected to mention the earthquake that had also hit Denver shortly after the eruption.

Earthquake.    Eruption.    Either    way,    their

5

whereabouts were unknown.

"Dear God, Sarah. The Yellowstone supervolcano erupted."

"I know, honey."

Silence.

Will's channel-surfing emanated into the kitchen. Click, click, click.

"I can't talk you out of this, can I?" she said.

"Nope."

"Then please detour to Virginia and drop off Will with Patsy and George. Or with a neighbor by you," Sarah offered.

The commercials on the TV ended, and the newscaster's voice streamed into the kitchen.

*"Governments of multiple states including Idaho, Wyoming, Colorado, Montana, Utah, South Dakota, and Nebraska have issued State of Emergency orders and have requested federal aid. Over 70,000 National Guard personnel are now activated and have been deployed to the hardest hit areas where they'll assist with search and rescue, evacuations, and relief operations including delivering packages of water, food, and medical supplies. Highway driving is now strictly prohibited in the states aforementioned unless escorted by National Guard or specific military convoys. Mobile relief and medical units are being set up in surrounding regions."*

Will flipped through the channels. He stood two feet in front of the TV, stock still and engrossed.

My pulse drummed in my head. I paced the kitchen, fingers fluttering over the checklist again. Belatedly, I countered, "Sarah, driving south to Patsy will take too long and with the bottlenecks on the beltway around DC, I may never get to Colorado. I can't leave him here with a neighbor." What if it got worse here? What if he had an episode or meltdown? I didn't say that aloud, as Will's ears were always on listening mode.

More clicks.

*"The president will be addressing the nation this evening. The death toll has risen to over 50,000, with estimates projected at over 250,000..."*

"Will, please, turn that off. Gather your bags."

Click.

*"...the mandate on freezing all prices of gas, food, home utilities, and many more goods. See our website for the complete list. Price gouging will be handled by—"*

Click.

Tingles rippled from my fingertips to my palms. I opened my mouth to yell at him, but I clamped it shut.

"Finally. Some weather!" Will said.

*"Early measurements are in, although not verified. The region around Yellowstone has seen extensive damage from earthquakes, ground drop, lava flows, and ash in measurements of inches. Bordering states have unverified levels of ash ranging from centimeters to inches. We've confirmed earthquakes in Washington, Idaho, Arizona, and Colorado, with the quake near Denver registering a 7.4 magnitude on the Richter scale. Ash clouds have already been observed in Kansas, where recordable amounts of ash have fallen. Jennifer joins us from..."*

I tuned it out, the images from watching TV all night already burned in my memory. I hurried down the basement steps again, nearly tripping on my weak ankle.

Sarah's pleading came back to me. "Oh, AJ, honey, please just be careful, okay? Check in with me when you can? If I hear from him, you'll be the first to know."

I nodded, not responding as the line cut out and tears brimmed in my eyes. I swiped them away and bustled around the basement, collecting what was left on my packing list.

I could do this.

I lugged the last of my things to the car.

*The car is not my enemy*, I repeated three times.

I plodded upstairs to the living room. "Let's go, Will."

\*\*\*\*

Jolted awake from a nightmare, I sat up in my sleeping bag. I shuddered and rubbed my throat.

It wasn't real, yet I swallowed ash, my tongue parched.

Predawn light crept across the meadow and rocks as I scanned the surroundings. Thick evergreens encircled the clearing where we'd set up our makeshift camp. The sharp scent of pine shifted me from the haze of sleep to awareness. I blinked a few times and turned to Will's sleeping bag.

It was empty.

*Shit.*

I stood, grabbed the lantern, and croaked, "Will!" as if his name were stuck in my throat.

*Not him, too.* One child's unknown whereabouts and now Will…where the hell was he?

Will hated camping, despite his love of the outdoors. Will grew scared if left alone. Will wandered.

I recovered my voice and searched shoeless around the clearing. "Will!" I shone the light into the bushes.

Someone's scream still rang in my ears. Had I screamed, or dear God, had it been Will?

He must've had to pee. But Will didn't like to pee in the woods like his brother. He could hold it for twelve hours if needed. He preferred bathrooms, with toilets. No standing for him.

A cold drizzle began to patter the ground, and my socks were already soaked. I shivered as I hurried along a narrow dirt path through the trees toward the nearby pond.

I held the lantern in front of me to deflect errant tree branches. "Will!"

No answer.

Why had I stopped by a pond, of all places? Will was drawn to water in any form, but he wasn't a proficient swimmer yet. Dammit, why hadn't I pitched the tent? A zipper would've woken me sooner. Because I had been exhausted, that's why.

My chest tightened as worst-case scenarios assaulted my brain. Getting lost. Drowning. Kidnapping.

A moment later, the placid pond lay before me.

There he was, at the water's edge, hunched over something.

"Oh, my God, Will. Why are you here?" Tingles prickled my fingertips, and the lantern teetered in my hand. My mind wrestled itself over what I was more concerned with: my sweet Finn, stuck somewhere in the ravages of Colorado, or my quirky nine-year-old Asperger's Will, who loved water too much.

What if I hadn't awoken? He'd slithered away

without me knowing. There were countless what-ifs these days.

He prodded the mud with a stick, crouching like kids do, his prominent spine poking through his thin, wet pajama top. His backside hovered close to the ground, and his legs were tucked beneath him.

"Will!" I said too sternly. "Why—"

"Because we stopped here last night, Mom. Don't you remember?"

I loosened my hand. Fingernail marks peppered my palm. I set the lantern down and squatted the best that my approaching-forty-year-old body could beside him. I blew a forceful breath. Now was not the time for my palpitations to return. Mental note: take my pill when I returned to our camp. "I asked why you came to the pond...*now*? You know the rules with camping. It's..." I paused and looked at my watch...the one Harrison had given me on our first anniversary. "It's only five in the morning." Not like that was early for him.

He turned to the mud after a brief glance at me. "I followed these frogs."

I shook my head with a muffled curse. I was hopelessly failing with my efforts to stop swearing around the boys.

"Mom, why did you scream?"

"What? I didn't scream."

"Yes, you did. You scared the frogs. Did you have a nightmare?" Will asked with his usual earnest, no-nonsense tone.

"I—" Numbness returned to my fingertips. I *had* been screaming. The nightmare flashed across my memory. *The scream burned. Panic raced through my veins as chunks of volcanic rock tore down the hillside, heading straight for my Finn. I tried to call to him, but fear halted me. My legs wouldn't move. Then, he was gone, swallowed by the rush of mud and rocks.*

I stifled a sob.

"It's okay, Mom. Good thoughts, remember?" Will stuck a spindly pine twig in the mud.

I nodded. "Yes, good thoughts."

A sudden movement across the pond caught my eye, and I shifted the lantern behind Will. There it was again. Campers on the shore farthest from us. Were they traveling west, too? Muted voices. I grabbed Will by the shoulder. I wondered if they'd heard me scream as well.

"Ouch!"

"Shh! Come back to camp. Let's pack and go."

"But the frogs!" he whined.

"They're happy there. Let's go."

"You're right. No ash has come this far yet."

*Yet.*

I rubbed my throat, the scream still burning and the fears of where my brother and youngest son could be, still paralyzing.

****

"Mom, how long will it take?" Will asked, not looking from his clipboard drawing, which I knew to be another map. All he drew these days were geographical maps. Correction: not even these days. He'd been drawing them since kindergarten. How many hundred had he drawn since then? Accurate enough to plug into any map software program.

"I'm not sure, honey." I drove the car in a sleepy daze, my body longing for caffeine. Coffee had not been on the essentials list, and Will hated too many stops. *Triple mocha latte*, Harrison used to say as our inside joke. I'd grab my java fix at the next gas station stop. Two nights of disjointed sleep and too much worry plagued my overworked mind.

I tightened my grip on the wheel, my chest tightening. I'd forgotten to take my pill this morning. I reached into my handbag and dug out the bottle. Half looking at the road, I twisted the cap off, grabbed a small white pill, and popped it in my mouth with a chug of water. I knew on this trip, of all trips, I would need to stay on top of them if I didn't want my anxiety to halt me in the days ahead.

"I can do this," I whispered for the umpteenth time since we'd departed.

Will pondered aloud. "Grandma drives from Virginia to California every year to see Aunt Sarah and Uncle Brandon and that takes her five days, right? So, it should take us maybe four days to get to Colorado?"

"Uh-huh," I said, mid-yawn, distracted by a few stopped cars ahead. At least they were pulled off to the side. Gray-black smoke curled from the crushed hood of one vehicle.

"Well, that's if Colorado is still there," Will said matter-of-factly.

Dammit. Tears blurred my vision. Not now, not again. His wheels always churned. "It's there, honey. The news said southern Colorado is not in the impact ring." Oh my God, was I really talking about this?

The accident's smoke triggered yet another memory flash of the newscasts. The eruption column of the volcano billowed miles into the sky, suffocating all light, like the shroud of a nuclear blast. I had spent all night by the TV and phone, idle, helpless. Brandon had never called. Denver Airport was unreachable, sustaining irrevocable damage from earthquakes.

"Can you feel earthquakes while in a plane? The earthquakes were reported all the way south into Arizona!" Will said.

The people by the cars waved their hands at me to stop as I accelerated around them, without a look behind.

"Mom, why are those people waving?"

"I can't stop to help them, Will."

"I know, Mom. We need to get to Finn and Uncle Brandon."

I pursed my lips. "Yes, honey, we do."

****

"Please, Mom, can we stop?"

I sighed. The dashboard clock read five p.m. "Yes, we'll stop," I said in response to Will's third plea as I glanced back at his face. His furrowed brow immediately softened.

At least we had reached New York. I suppressed a moan. Gone were the days of naps and snoozes in the lulling motion of a moving vehicle. There would be no all-night driving on this journey. Will couldn't sleep without a bed; well, minimally he needed a sleeping bag.

A short while later, I relented and pitched the tent at a campground, having learned my lesson with his early morning rising to see the muddy pond and frogs. We were both quiet through dinner. At bedtime, Will asked, "Mom, do you have my sleepy spray?"

*Shit.* I'd intended to reorder his homeopathic melatonin spray after our Yellowstone vacation.

"No, honey. I have glow sticks and your special

blanket." I lifted the blue and red seven-pound weighted blanket and spread it across his torso and legs.

Worry flickered in his eyes. "Okay, Mom. I'll try those." He cracked a glow stick and held it like a wand.

"Thanks, honey." I kissed him and snuggled beside him until he fell asleep.

Tomorrow I had to make better time, push the speed limits. We had gotten around the congestion of southern Maine and Boston without a hitch and were now halfway across upstate New York. If I'd had my way, we'd be in Ohio by now, but Will...

*Dammit, AJ, why didn't you leave earlier?*

I scratched my head. My fretting would not help us. I had to stay strong for him. I had been forced to do a lot of things in the past year for the sake of my children.

A few minutes later, while Will snored and probably dreamt about volcanoes, I sat up, grabbed my pen, and opened my journal, its virgin pages stiff and aromatic. I snapped on my headlamp, glanced sideways at my snoozing son once more, and began to write in the late evening darkness of the tent.

I wasn't sure how to start the journal. I rewrote the first few lines before I found something I approved. Nobody was going to read it anyway. This was for me. Writing was way cheaper than therapy. Not sure it helped as much as my anti-anxiety med did though. And it wasn't like an agent had picked up any of my previous work. My mind was a whirling mess of thoughts. *Why* was I writing now of all times? If anything, I could hold on to my sanity during our journey. I scribbled about the eruption as much as I wanted to avoid it. Yet writing about it didn't make me feel better right now.

I paused, fighting the tears when I thought about my missing son and brother. Seriously. A journal? Writing had gotten me through much of my life…escapism at its best. I couldn't stop now. This time it happened to be nonfiction. This was for me, and me alone. Audrey Jane Sinclair, aspiring writer, former scientist, and part-time working mom. Oh, wait, no-longer-working mom.

I snorted. If only Harrison could see me now. Seriously.

The Finn-ism made me think of him. He always said, "Seriously, Mom…" Never apart from my sons for longer than the occasional weekend at Patsy's, my heart ached more than it usually did. My Finn. Where was he?

I directed the headlamp to the side and turned to Will. My fingers itched to snuggle with him more, the heat of his nearness already having dissipated. What was I thinking? I closed the journal for a moment. All those cheesy Hollywood movies could not compare to what had happened.

It had really happened.

No, not an asteroid hitting the planet, although Finn would have loved that, but rather, the earth had opened, an unbridled wrath of ash, mud, lava, and havoc raining on a third of the country. So many dead. So much destruction. Our country forever altered. The goddamn supervolcano beneath Yellowstone National Park had erupted, and here I was, writing in a journal somewhere in the sticks, New York.

I ran my fingers over the gold-embossed and lily-speckled cover. My friend Siobhan had given it to me for my thirty-seventh birthday. The notebook had spent far too many months sitting beside me on the passenger seat in my car and had slowly worked its way to the back of my SUV, eventually becoming buried beneath a soccer ball, karate bag, books, jumper cables, and artwork crafted by the boys.

I must have asked myself the same painful questions a hundred times in the past two days. Why had I left them there? Why hadn't we stayed with Brandon and Finn at the airport so the four of us could leave Salt Lake City together?

Why?

One word: meltdown. Well, two words: autism meltdown.

I'd left my seven-year-old son at the airport with my brother Brandon.

The memory begged to be replayed as I overanalyzed it for moments of failure. I clicked off the headlamp and closed my eyes.

\*\*\*\*

*Two days earlier*

"Will, come out. Will, honey, please." I reached to touch him as he hugged his legs against his body while wedged behind a row of airport seats at our gate.

He snarled and sobbed. "Tell me when the flight's ready!"

"Please wait over here with me, okay?" I tried again. He wormed as far back as the corner would allow.

Finn spun the carry-on suitcase around with a whoop behind me. The suitcase smacked into a woman nearby, and she released a surprised curse. I stood, heat stealing my voice. "Finn! Control your wiggles!"

"See!" Will's cheeks flushed, and crinkles appeared under the dark smudges beneath his eyes. Those were not his happy dimples. Red splotches formed on his forehead. I recited the abbreviated version of a tranquility prayer in my head.

"Mommy, there's nowhere to sit," Finn countered. He kept spinning the suitcase around. Sure, those fancy 360-degree spinning wheels were great for navigating an airport, but now, I wanted to rip the wheels off. I grabbed the handle to prevent an injury to another innocent bystander.

Brandon returned from the bathroom and squeezed my shoulder. "I've got it. Finn, let's get hot chocolate."

Finn dropped the suitcase on my foot. "Okay!"

I sucked in a steadying breath.

Brandon righted the wayward suitcase. "We'll check at the counter again, okay?"

My okay held far less exuberance than Finn's.

I shot a look to a reproachful old woman who was mumbling about "bad parents and bad kids" as I reached for Will in the corner. My fingers made contact.

I wanted to holler, "He's autistic! Let him be!" I bit my tongue. I hated labels. There was no perfect label to describe my Will, who hung on the Asperger's syndrome and high-functioning fringe of the autism spectrum. Even Asperger's was an obsolete term with both negative associations and preconceived notions. He was "too normal" to be autistic, but "too quirky" to be normal.

Instead of voicing my rebuttal, I turned, tucked the suitcase beside our other carry-on bags, and squeezed beside Will on the carpeted area around the seat. I

17

ignored the paper wrappers beside me, the glares of bystanders, and the grumblings of disgruntled passengers who were not pleased about our two-hour delay.

"Come, honey." I coaxed him from his hiding place, my fingers gentle on his arm.

He thumped his forehead against a seat a few times before I could stop him.

"Will, we can't hit our head. Come here," I said, placing a hand on his forehead.

Even at age nine, he didn't think twice about sitting in my lap. I stroked his hair and wiped tear-stained cheeks as he leaned against my chest. "It's noisy here. You're tired. We had a great trip though, right?"

He sniffled and replaced head thumping with hand tapping—against his thighs, against the seat.

"Tell me about your favorite thing." I rubbed his cheek, and he closed his eyes.

"I want to go home."

Tap, tap, tap.

"I know," I said, brushing aside errant brown hairs from his forehead. "I liked Jenny Lake. You and Finn enjoyed stacking those rocks into cairns."

"Yeah." He peered into the throng of briskly moving bodies, the moaning conversations, the shuffling of impatient feet. His gaze was glassy, and his mind was certainly processing it all. Well, *over*processing it all. He touched the tears on his cheeks and licked his fingers; then repeated it. I let it go. A kid could do a worse thing than lick their tears and stim a little. Stimming helped him cope and relax.

"How many parks did we see? We went to Seattle, Olympic National Park, Mount St. Helens, Crater Lake,

Craters of the Moon, the Tetons…Yellowstone…"

"Seattle isn't a national park."

"Ah, you're right. Remember how I used to do this when you were a baby?" I cupped his cheek.

"Uh-huh."

His hands fluttered.

Tap. Tap.

I held him quietly. He allowed it. Always my love bug, he wouldn't refuse physical comfort.

A few minutes later, my brother returned with a smiling Finn. "Got you tickets!" Finn said, a hot chocolate mustache tracing his upper lip and his blue eyes glimmering with excitement.

"Huh?" I asked.

Brandon angled his dark brown gaze to me, pleased with himself. "You and Will. You two are on the flight to Portland that leaves in thirty minutes. They're boarding now."

"How did you manage that? What about you two? I can't leave Finn."

"We'll stick to the already scheduled flight to Denver in two hours and then from there we catch a connecting flight to Dulles, then on to Portland. We'll be a few hours behind you. It will be our own adventure, right, Finn?"

"Yup!"

"I can't leave you. What about your flight to California? You can't come all the way back to Maine with us."

"Yes, you can, and you will, and I will, too. I switched my ticket," he said with a subtle head nod to my weary son, who lay crumpled in my lap now, his head burrowed into my thighs. At least his crying had ceased, and the looks of judging passengers had moved on to more interesting things.

"I haven't been around enough for you, AJ, since…" He pulled off his ballcap and ran a hand through his receding hair line. "It'll be okay. Sarah's off work for a few weeks. She's cool with me staying with you guys for a week or two. I'd love to see Maine again. I just called her. If that's okay with you?" Brandon plopped the hat on his head.

And so I'd left my seven-year-old son at the airport in Salt Lake City with my brother.

\*\*\*\*

*Present day*

Rage boiled within me. Damn you, Harrison. "Why did you have to leave us?" I said into my hands. The headlamp illuminated the worn lines on my palms in the darkness of the tent.

"Mom?"

I wiped my mouth on my sleeve and snuffed my tears. "Go back to sleep, Will."

"Mom…"

"Yes, honey?"

"Mom…," he moaned. He sat upright and whimpered. He pushed the sleeping bag away and squirmed.

"Go to sleep, Will," I said as gently as I could, though my voice trembled. I removed the high-powered headlamp from my forehead and laid it in my lap, the beam pointing away from his face.

He released short bursts of cries, frantically looking around. He scrunched his face and tried to stand in our short two-person tent, panting.

"Down, honey." I laid a gentle hand on his

forearm.

He fluttered one hand, while the other was tightly gripped on a glow stick.

I took his hands in mine while saying, "Sleep, Will. Think good thoughts." It's what I always told him when he had night terrors. "Think about jumping in puddles or playing in your sandbox or your cool Lego constructions or—" I stopped short from saying volcanoes. Good thoughts. I snorted. What good was left now?

"Try to block it, honey. Happy thoughts. Think about..." Stillness hung over me. All that came to me was a toad's ribbit in the nearby woods. "Here's Douglas." I nestled his favorite plush dog into his hands.

I murmured soothing words, rubbing his cheek. His eyes were dark in the low light, wide, distant, and staring off beyond the closed tent flap. He was in another place. Will never remembered the terrors come morning. Although he appeared awake, he was locked in a sleepy world with his spinning thoughts. I often wondered what was going on in his brain during the terrors. They had begun when he was three, and now at age nine, he continued to have them, but they were rare and occurred in clusters, usually triggered by stress or lack of sleep. In uncommon cases, the terrors could be seizures, a condition I knew sometimes went hand in hand with autism, but in Will's case, the symptom profile was not there so we'd never investigated it further.

His eyelids danced as he fought and eventually succumbed to sleep, my hand never leaving his cheek. It had become our new normal. Will joined me most nights in bed—that is, when I decided to sleep there instead of on the sofa. He was comforted when beside me and would fall asleep instantly. Then, I would carry him back to his room. I hated to admit that I was equally comforted with a warm body beside me instead of an empty spot once occupied by my husband.

Soon again, it was my journal, the headlamp, and me. I picked up the pen to write.

I could do this. I had to.

Chapter Two
Bumps in the Road

Early dawn had become my reliable companion, and I rose to the subtle sounds in the campground: a birdcall, the rustle of leaves from a breeze, the occasional cough from another tent. I emerged from our tent, quietly zipped it closed, and began to gather our things. Will was also an early riser, but I gave him a few more minutes to rest.

There wasn't much to pick up in our campsite. Most was in the tent or car. A neatly stacked pile of rocks sat beside the extinguished fire. They looked just like a cairn, with the larger flat rocks on the bottom, angling up to a pointed small topper. It reminded me of our trip. Finn had loved Jenny Lake in the Tetons just as much as Will. They had stacked smooth rocks into cairns while Brandon and I sat on the shoreline taking it all in. It had been beautiful. It had been my first enjoyable time in a year.

I fell onto the bench at the picnic table and hung my head in my hands.

My mini-geologists had been delighted beyond words as we traveled around Grand Prismatic Spring and Old Faithful, explored old lava tubes, and participated in ranger-led programs to experience the geothermic marvel that is—or was, I thought, as a sharp taste rose in my throat—Yellowstone National Park.

Dear God, we had just been there. *There*. Where it all happened. There, where my brother Brandon and my son Finn remained. My spunky Finn. Salt Lake City had been on the edge of the "central ring" of devastation. The city had been decimated. However, per news reports, the eruption had begun after their scheduled flight boarding. After. Had they been in the air when it happened? What if they had been delayed further?

I had kissed Finn goodbye on his cheek, given his plush animal, Otter, a squeeze, said my love-you, and boarded the plane with Will.

Three days ago. Just hours before the eruption.

Oh, my sweet, enigmatic, energetic, give-me-gray-hairs son, Finn. My brother Brandon had wholeheartedly come along with us on the trip we were supposed to have taken last year with Harrison before the accident. Brandon's experience from his years in the Air Force Special Ops and an overseas deployment abated some of my worries. Some. What if he'd been hurt though? Where were they now? Were they alive? Had they caught their scheduled flight from Salt Lake City to Denver? Even if they had…Denver Airport had been rocked by a horrible earthquake. Tears blurred my vision. I shook and fought the urge to vomit. I was on a hamster wheel with my obsessive thoughts and, for the life of me, could not get off.

I pleaded with the air, an invisible force, or God, I didn't know which. "Please, I swear I'll never complain again about searching for a damn toy or count the minutes until bedtime or ask Finn to take a talking break." I gulped, I sobbed. "Please," I said in a pathetic whisper, reeling it in to control my tipping into hysteria.

They must have boarded the plane before the eruption. I refused to believe anything else. I'd received Brandon's text message after we landed in Portland once I turned my phone back on after landing. They had been on schedule to get on the flight to Denver. *Boarding in thirty minutes*, his text had read. Yet I'd heard nothing else from him after that. They couldn't have been in Salt Lake City when the devil's fingers rose from beneath Yellowstone.

Nope.

I continued to reason with myself, threading hope with logic as my pulse grew erratic. Details invaded and kept me spinning on the hamster wheel.

Early reports indicated tremors in the West, from Spokane south to Albuquerque. The newscast had said Denver had been devastated by earthquakes during the actual event and was in the outer ash ring. The city was in shambles. Not leveled, but dire. I reviewed my options.

Volcano near Salt Lake City.

Earthquake in Denver.

Or they were in the air. Somewhere else. No word. No call or text. Nothing. My brain told me they were in Denver.

*Finn buried under rubble, suffocating. Brandon knocked unconscious.*

I nipped that train of thought with one fell swoop.

Although we were well-informed on the supervolcano's history courtesy of Will's fixations, while we'd meandered through the meadows and mountains of Wyoming's most famous park, we thought that type of eruption was thousands of years off. No warnings or alerts had been posted. *We* had felt no tremors. Did the scientists know? Of course they did. They'd learned the hard lesson after the eruption of Mount St. Helens. I scratched my head, pulling documentaries from memory. Yellowstone was an active bubbly volcanic wonder with daily tremors or spurts. If there had been concern, officials would've closed the park. None of the visitor centers had postings on recent seismic activity despite news reports saying there were earthquakes during the twelve hours leading to the event.

My mouth grew dry. I rose, lumbered to the car, and located my water bottle.

The thought of what-if coiled my stomach. We'd escaped, unknowingly, and barely by a day. But my brother and Finn…

I had to stop debating. Denver it was. That's where I was going.

My heart did a flip-flop. Even my body told me to stop this madness. The usual nausea that no amount of antacid could fix had already crept in. It had joined its pals, the aching prickle that wrapped around the back of my head and the tingles in my fingertips. They were my daily trio these days.

My calls to Brandon were greeted with no answer or a dial tone. Regardless, I had to try again. I pulled my phone from my back pocket. The glow of the screen on my phone sneered at me. I dialed.

Nothing. Not even a ring.

I dialed the airline number, which by now I had memorized.

Nothing new.

An automated message referred people to a website that had no useful information, of course. Internet service had already become fragmented and slow, too. I'd emailed Brandon several times, hoping email would work, even if texts and calls didn't. I had to do *something*. The laptop sat in the front seat of the car, ready and waiting to be used once we checked into a hotel along the way.

I slammed the car door.

I approached Will's cairn and touched the smallest rock, which glistened with striations of pink feldspar, seemingly out of place with the rest of the granite and gneiss rocks he'd used to build it. I pocketed it for Finn.

It was time to go.

****

To the passerby, life appeared unchanged as we drove on a quiet stretch of highway in northern New York. Chaos had not yet broken out on the East Coast. Governments were intact and people went to work; yet I'd felt the rumblings of early unrest as we had left town. People were pissed off about lack of cell coverage, and the stores were hectic in prewinter storm mode as people emptied shelves. A few radicals had been touting about end of the world crap on the corner near the bank, but thankfully they hadn't gotten much airtime. I wondered if people were glued to their televisions the way our country had been post 9/11. I hadn't been able to tear my eyes from the screen the entire first night. When I did, I slipped into terrible dreams about Finn. I imagined him being swallowed by great chasms in the ground that opened with razor-sharp teeth.

Disorder trickled across the country at the same rate as the ash cloud. Slowly and certainly. It was happening. I was crazy to drive straight into it, but I couldn't lose another person. Not my baby. I had loaded the car, got cash, and grabbed my weapons of choice.

*Bring it.*

To suppress the tangled thoughts that clawed at me, I clicked on the radio. I yearned for Finn's chatty questions. Will was lost in his back seat oasis.

News reports. I kept flipping. Not one damned music station.

I steadied my hands on the steering wheel. Once again, I'd forgotten to take my morning dose. I changed the station again and then thumbed through my handbag on the passenger seat.

*"Now a message from Governor Benitez."*

The governor of Colorado rattled off her condolences and assured the public that the government had created shelters and mobile hospitals in immediate areas including southern Wyoming, southern Idaho, and northern and central Colorado. Unless people were injured, they were to stay put and wait for recovery packs to be delivered.

"Agh, Mom. Not more talking. Can't you put on music?" Will interrupted.

"Trying, hon." I had forgotten my CDs and the adapter for plugging in my MP3 player was broken.

I listened for another minute, hoping to hear about recovery efforts for those displaced or injured, but Governor Benitez moved on to relief for roads and airports. She concluded that it may be at least a few weeks before roads were passable and a month before airlines in the northwestern region of the country were operational. Airlines across the country were shutting down, freezing travel. Search and rescue efforts were the highest priority for the National Guard and army right now.

"Mom…"

"Dammit!" I snapped, immediately regretting it. He was right. We'd heard enough.

"I love you, Mom," Will said. "It will be all right."

I chewed my lip. "I'm sorry, honey. I love you, too. And it *will* be all right."

"What if they close more highways? The radio announcer said no traveling in Colorado," Will observed.

"I don't know."

I dug into my handbag again. I found the bottle, twisted the cap, and looked inside. Only six pills remained. Six? My daily dose was two, and that meant I'd need eight to get me to Colorado, and another dozen for the return trip. Perhaps I could refill it nearby at a pharmacy.

I turned the bottle in my hand. *Zero refills.* "Shit!" I'd forgotten to take care of it when we'd returned home. For being so organized, I forgot a lot of things these days.

"Mom!"

"Sorry, hon."

"Mom, I have to pee."

I drove a few more miles on the quiet stretch of highway before locating a rest stop.

"One sec, okay?"

I pulled out my phone.

"Mom, you're always longer than a second."

I grimaced. "Count to a hundred, okay? Please?"

Where would Dr. Martin send the order? Prescription renewals always took forty-eight to seventy-two hours. There was no way I was going to sit around in New York for three days. Heck, we were nearly to Pennsylvania. More highways could be closed. Where would I be in three days? I pulled out the atlas we always carried in our car. Faded by use and time, it was one of the few possessions of Harrison's I'd kept in the car. Father and son alike had always loved maps. I couldn't toss it. I projected the distance.

I hadn't driven this much since Harrison's accident. In fact, in the past year I'd avoided most driving. Brandon had driven on our trip. As for local driving, I placed the kids in carpools and limited my driving as much as possible. Gone were the road-trip days before kids.

My hands began to shake, and a familiar thump permeated my chest. What if I couldn't make it? What if I clammed up and had no pills to help me through it? God dammit, they'd been my crutch for the past year. I couldn't do it without them.

In three days, I'd hopefully be in Kansas. I drew my finger across the Kansas map and located Wichita. Okay, there. Hell, I didn't know which pharmacies would be there. But it was a sizeable city. They'd have plenty of chain pharmacies. I didn't have a damn smart phone and even if I did, reception was spotty. I groaned and refrained from letting tears get the best of me. *AJ, you dinosaur. You idiot!* Harrison with his maps, and me with my dislike of technology and now driving phobia. What a pair we had been.

I dialed the doctor's office anyway. An automated answering service picked up, and I disconnected. I closed my eyes and rubbed my palms against them. It was Sunday. The office wasn't open. I redialed. This time I left a detailed voice message. "Hi, Dr. Martin. It's AJ Sinclair. I'm out of my anti-anxiety prescription. I'm traveling to Wichita, Kansas. I have no refills. Could you please send in a refill to a pharmacy in town? I don't know which pharmacies are there. Perhaps there's a..." My mind went blank. I rattled off a few chain stores, took a breath, and continued, "I know this sounds crazy. Yeah, I'm driving. My son is missing...he's somewhere in Colorado, near the eruption zone. Please, please help. You can reach me at my cell number. I'll try again later. Thanks."

I hung up, the wind knocked from me, my heart hammering. Just to be safe, I'd wean myself to one pill a day, half my usual dose. I had to make them last. If I couldn't fill the prescription in Kansas, perhaps Denver would have a pharmacy that was prescribing. I knew I'd have withdrawal effects, but at least a pill a day was a gradual wean instead of cold turkey.

"Mom...I have to pee...I'm already over a hundred."

"Let's make it quick, okay?" We entered the gas station store, grabbed the bathroom keys, and turned the corner.

"Come in with me?"

"Of course."

After we returned the key, my mind was a muddle of more thoughts than I could manage. I reeled with possible navigation ideas to get to Kansas and locate my prescription.

"Mom, why's the tailgate open?"

I ran to the car. Nobody was in sight. A black sedan sped out of the parking lot. I squinted to note the license plate numbers, but it was too late.

"Shit!" I hadn't locked the car. I peeked in. The trunk space had been ransacked. Bins open, blankets strewn about. "Oh my God, oh my God!"

"What happened?" Will scratched his head. "Were we robbed?"

A quick glance in the meager, unattended parking lot: not a soul around to even inquire if they saw anything. I summoned my strength. "Yes. I need to see what was taken." My teeth chattered as I fought the inner demon.

Upon cursory inspection, some of the food and a gas container had been stolen, the bins rummaged through, sleeping bags unrolled, and my laptop was nowhere to be found. Also gone: jumper cables, my secret money stash, and..."Shit!"

"Mom?"

"It's okay. It's okay." My pulse plummeted, and I grabbed the side of the car, combating the dizziness as blobs of white, purple, and yellow surrounded by jet black danced before me. I blinked through it.

"Three breaths, right, Mom?" Will said, his voice shaky. He wiggled from foot to foot.

"Yup." I did as told, following the advice I repeated to him daily. He slipped his hand in mine for comfort. I squeezed back.

Harrison's handgun, which he had purchased for home protection and would use at the shooting range with his buddies...was gone, too. Not that I even knew how to use it. I gritted my teeth. My aversion to carrying it in my handbag now resulted in its absence. He'd always asked me to come with him to the gun range. I never had.

I renounced my rainbow of swearwords as I

slammed the tailgate closed. "Let's go." My laptop, too. So much for my plan to email Brandon. I thought of everything personal and cherished that had been on my laptop. I hoped most of it was backed up at home. And my extra money…gone. Jesus Christ, and the gun. I tallied my assets: I still had a tire iron, kitchen knife, pocket knife, food, water, the tent. So much for the unrest having not reached the East Coast. I was already in it. Bad luck had a way of following me.

Endless road lay ahead as I cataloged in my mind what remained.

I eyed Finn's empty spare booster seat, then said a few affirmations that I didn't believe and focused on the quiet landscape, the memory of some of my hikes with Harrison infusing my mind like a sweet-scented candle. I tried to not cry.

Golden rolling hills flanked us, and a long cargo train traveled east. I drove faster, futilely seeking out the black sedan. They were long gone. "Look, Will. How many cars do you think it has?"

"Mom, Finn likes trains, not me."

"You did."

"Trains are for babies. I'm a big kid now, Mom."

Well, I tried. I noted the number of engines—two in front and one in rear—and the storybook red caboose. Finn would like to hear about it.

Will didn't ask about the robbery. I didn't bring it up either.

I came upon a lone hitchhiker, my first on the journey, a man with short dark hair. He wore a red and gray plaid long-sleeved shirt despite the August heat, with an overstocked backpack. I drew my glance away from the road and studied him. I'm not sure why this particular person should have caught my interest. It was an odd place to be hitching. We weren't close to the Appalachian Trail, where through-hikers would be trekking north. Perhaps he was local. I locked the doors. My shred of trust had been stolen with the assholes who had taken my stuff.

As I crossed the center line a few feet, I maintained a steady speed and kept my distance. He lowered his hitching thumb, slowly. Then gave the subtlest of nods. He understood. My gaze remained transfixed on him in the rearview mirror as he shrank to the size of an ant. Harrison would never have stopped. He had been cynical about everyone, always assuming the worst. Perhaps during the year since his death I had begun to develop that same disparagement. The naivety and hopeful optimism I felt for all human beings, even the darkest, had waned with my spirit this year. Was there hope for humanity anymore?

I looked back, but the man was long gone.

My thoughts returned to Finn, and that was that.

\*\*\*\*

The colors passed by in a blur as Mom drove through the countryside of New York. Grays, different shades of green, brown. The leaves on the trees looked like they were moving, like a fast train. Will missed Finn, despite his brother's constant talking, touching, and noise. Mom was usually chatty, too, but she also liked the quietness. Today, she was more quiet than usual. Maybe she was still mad about the people who had stolen their stuff.

Although it was August, some of the trees in this area were already beginning to lose leaves. Autumn wasn't for another…

"Mom, what day is it?"

She sighed.

"The date, Mom," he added.

"End of August something…"

He did the math himself. "Mom, there are leaves off the trees, but it's not autumn yet. Look over there, all the leaves blowing around."

"Yes, Will."

"It's not autumn," he repeated.

"Sometimes leaves can fall before then, remember?"

He tapped a finger on his knee. "It's summer."

"Will, I don't want to talk about this now."

"It's warm. It's summer." He tapped his knee again. "Leaves fall in autumn, not summer."

"Remember that year when we got a foot of snow before Halloween?" she said.

Of course he remembered that. "We didn't get to trick-or-treat until two days later." The snow had piled high around their house, and he loved to squish it through his fingers as he shoveled it higher and higher, packing, squeezing, and making a huge volcano, while Finn ran around and made snow angels and dug caves.

"Yes, Will, and it wasn't winter yet. Weather can be like that. Fickle. You know this stuff."

*Fickle*. That was a funny word. He said it a few times to himself and stowed it away in his memory bank for another day. He returned his attention to his drawing on the clipboard. "I'm making you a map for our trip, Mom. I'm almost done with New England. Where are we going after New York?" The hook on Cape Cod was not right. He erased it and redrew it, erased it, and drew the hook just right.

"Will…"

"Mom, I need to get the map right. Ohio or Pennsylvania? Oh, yeah, Pennsylvania, unless we go through Canada. We can't do that though." He ripped off a new page of blank white paper from his notepad, its grain smooth on his fingertips. He loved that feeling. It had a fresh smell to it, like a tree. He'd make a new map for the mid-Atlantic region. He thumbed through his pencil box. Too bad he hadn't packed his scented markers. What color for those states?

Mom drove in silence. She had been crying last night. She cried a lot since Dad died last year. More now with Finn gone. Whenever he mentioned the volcano, she would cry. But the volcano was exciting. It had erupted! Not like the VEI 8 super-eruptions that had occurred 2.1 million, 1.3 million, and 640,000 years ago. It *was* big though. The news had said so. Bigger than Mount St. Helens. The newscasts had shown ash falling as far as Kansas and Nebraska. He wondered if the jet stream and air currents would push it farther east toward them. Maybe they would drive through it. Mom wouldn't let him talk about it, though she knew how much he loved it.

He'd tucked away a few of his books in his backpack. Cool volcano ones. The book with the Yellowstone caldera on the cover was his favorite. The pictures were bright and detailed, and it had many maps. He paused with his mid-Atlantic map and reached into the backpack in Finn's empty booster seat. He flipped through his supervolcano book.

Although he enjoyed the words and the numbers, he liked the maps and pictures best. He turned to page 103, which outlined the ash-fall patterns of the three largest eruptions. The drawing showed three overlapping ovals. Well, they weren't ovals. "Mom, what's a crooked oval called?"

"A crooked oval, Will?"

He put the book down and used his hands to make the shape in the air. "Like this." She didn't look at him.

"I don't know, honey."

The ash-fall "crooked ovals" covered two-thirds of the United States, mostly the western region. He read. "The patterns of ash fall depend on the winds in the atmosphere at the time of the eruption. Most wind goes from west to east. So it went that way. Maybe there will be ash as far as Missouri." He searched his memory to try to recall if the meteorologists had mentioned if it was an El Niño year. That could greatly impact the ash cloud. Volcanoes in the Pacific tropics could cause an El Niño year due to the millions of tons of sulfur dioxide pumped into the stratosphere. But could the current Pacific conditions shift the cloud's projection? He'd check for a weather station when they got to a hotel.

Flashes of images danced in front of his eyes. Gray, fluffy snow-like ash falling on the ground, piling deeper and deeper. The boxes at the Mount St. Helens exhibit had showed the different volumes of ash. Maybe they would see ash rain!

"Will! You brought those books!" Mom said in her screechy voice.

He winced but didn't look up.

"Will…," she said, controlling the screech, to his relief. It always caused his heart to do an extra thump when she spoke like that. She shook her head. She was upset again. He knew that.

He turned to another chapter. "Mom, the rangers said there were no recent earthquakes in Yellowstone, but here it says that there should have been seismic activity to indicate an eruption was coming. Why weren't there any earthquakes reported?"

"What do you mean? There were earthquakes. You saw the news."

"I know that. I meant beforehand—before it happened. Like tremors?"

She said quietly, "Maybe there were some we don't know about."

He read for a little longer, all the while thinking about the leaves falling off the trees. "Oh! The leaves are like Halloween, Mom. When it snowed early. Sometimes those things happen, even when they are not supposed to, or there are no clues that they will happen. Although we did see the weather forecast of the snow. However, it was not expected to be so much, and in autumn."

Her eyes widened at him in the rearview mirror. Susie, his special therapist, liked to tell him that his *eyes smiled*. He wasn't sure how they could smile. They were eyes. Mouths smile. Eyes look. The wrinkles around his mom's brown eyes crinkled, and her eyes were all shiny and wet. Not wet from crying. Perhaps that was "eyes smiling?"

"Yes, Will. Just like that."

He smiled, too—with his mouth, for he didn't know how to smile with his eyes. His thoughts then returned to the picture of ash, covering everything, inches deep. It looked like winter. Maybe Finn was making snow angels in it right now.

Chapter Three
Swallowing a Hefty Pill

Autism.

The A-word. The one as a parent you'd never expect to utter in your household except for the occasional discussion.

I tapped my pen on the journal, pausing. I glanced at Will, who made volcanoes with the dirt along the roadside where we'd stopped for a quick rest. I'm not sure why my journal-writing had veered onto the path of my parenting journey, but here I was again, writing about it.

Accepting your child's autism diagnosis is like trying to swallow a large, chalky, rough-edged pill without the water chaser. It can get stuck, go down sideways, or leave you with a bitter aftertaste. You may need to take it with sweetened tea or a bite of food. Then, the pill sits. Finally, slowly, that pill works its alchemy through your bloodstream, into your pumping heart, and across that brain-blood barrier. Eventually, your body, your mind, and your spirit accept the pill's enlightenment: that pill is going nowhere. And that is okay. Or you try to make it okay.

In the beginning, like many parents, I had not fully accepted Will's diagnosis, felt increasingly dejected, comparing myself and him to other "normal" children and families. A part of me refused to believe I'd swallowed that monster-sized pill.

I'd given in to my negative spirals early on. Will's potential now, though, awakened me more each day. He was a boy with such fervor for life and learning that if we did it "just right" and provided him with the best school, behavior therapies, and tools to succeed, he would. Yet, I wasn't sure I'd attain the acceptance level of that remarkable mom I knew in our school district, Jody, who advocated strongly for her two severely autistic sons. She was the dedicated mom who found enemies on the school board committee and at town meetings. She was a powerhouse who had swallowed that pill with a side of fries. I aspired to be like Jody. Knowing her, she had an arsenal in her basement to handle this catastrophe for whenever it did reach Maine. Hell, she was probably halfway to Florida by now. Shame rose to the forefront of my mind many times for my bemoaning of my higher-functioning child. *Christ, AJ, it's not a competition.*

Meanwhile, I spent too much time worrying if I was correct in saying "autistic child" or "child with autism." I felt like no matter what, I was an imposter and couldn't do it right, couldn't please everyone. Will was Will. Autism was part of him.

I pawed over that one a bit and took a break from my parental ruminations to watch him play.

He finally got bored. I looked at my watch. "Time to go, honey."

Our respite wore off shortly after getting back on the highway.

I braked. Traffic was at a standstill in both directions a half mile ahead. This was too soon for disorder. No police activity. Just a string of traffic…nowhere near a metro area. Most likely some idiot did something stupid. Car accident? *Somebody dropped their coffee?* Harrison's words echoed.

"Look, Mom!" Will said as we drew closer to the stopping point.

I followed his pointing finger. Four people were out of their cars. A man wielded a gun and gestured madly.

"Oh, my God!" My naïve approach to this trip smacked me in the face. Between the robbery and now this ruckus…yes, the chaos *had* reached our side of the country, even if the ash cloud had not. My look darted over the scene. "Holy shit!" Was that the black sedan? Was that Harrison's gun? My palpitating heart told me the answer.

"Mom!"

I nearly growled. "I'm allowed to swear now, okay?" In fact, I had refrained from my favorite juicy swear word that had become habit over the years. I tried, honestly, I tried.

I tapped restless fingers on the steering wheel and made the world's quickest assessment of my situation. Cars leading to the next exit crammed the shoulder. Trees bordered the right side of the road ahead of me while a center rail barrier and the opposing traffic were on my left side. I was the last car in the group and wasn't remotely close to the exit yet.

A man swung a baseball bat and smashed in the black sedan's windows. I flinched. Another man flew out of the car and jumped on the man with the gun. The gun fired into the air, and all I heard were screams.

*Harrison's gun.*

Was this my fault?

I shoved my car into reverse, punched it into drive, and swerved hard to the right. The car jounced through the grassy shoulder as I drove in the direction from which we came. I kept to the shoulder as cars arrived and honked at the crazy woman driving the wrong way.

"Mom…" Will pulled on his trusty black and neon-green bike helmet with a click of the strap under the chin.

"Hon, we're not riding our bikes."

"It's bumpy! Must be prepared!" he countered.

I remembered an exit not too far back. I found it soon enough and made a sharp left turn onto the ramp. I handed the oversized, floppy atlas to Will. "Here, Will. Find this road number. The New York page close-ups are page twenty-something."

He did as told. "Page twenty-four."

I was ever grateful for the atlas we always kept in the car. Harrison used to tease me about not knowing how to use a smartphone's GPS app. Ha, there goes that, Harrison! Cell phones were defunct right now for half of the country. The ash in the atmosphere blocked cell towers from working effectively. I hadn't been able to reach Patsy and George, Harrison's parents in Virginia, since we'd left Massachusetts. I was somewhat glad I'd not followed Sarah's advice to drop Will off with them.

"There, Mom, ahead. Turn on Route 62."

I did and was relieved to find an empty road. I had a feeling that this would be our first of many detours. There went staying on the busier highways like Interstates 86 and 90. This was already taking longer than I anticipated. I exhaled, encouraging my mind to think of placating thoughts. I tapped my finger on the wheel. Known for my back-up plans, I was coming up short on this trip.

A few minutes later, the car released a screech and pulled fiercely. I bit my tongue.

"What was that?" Will asked, his voice tinged with more curiosity than fear.

"Tire, dammit!"

I clamped my teeth as I managed to control my flailing vehicle and pulled it onto the grassy shoulder.

I sat for a moment, head resting against the steering wheel.

"It's okay, Mom," Will said. "Say that special prayer?"

I blew an exaggerated breath. "Trying."

I stepped out of the car and inspected it. Busted tire. "Great."

Will hopped out. "You're using that tone."

"Yup, I am." I waved my hands in the air. "I give up."

"Can you fix it?" He approached the tire and poked at the torn rubber, his helmet still on. Due to his latest fascination with his scooter, he seemed to wear it all the time.

"No. We need to put on the spare." Hands on my hips, I willed the flat tire to magically turn into a new one. Where was a fairy godmother when a woman needed her?

The plus: we had a full-sized spare. The not-so-plus: I'd never put a tire on before. The car had been Harrison's area of expertise. I'd never even put air in the tires. I was a skilled gardener, mower, and snow-blower, wound-kisser and spirit-rebuilder, but cars were not my forte. Yes, that was my excuse, and I was sticking to it. I squatted beside the tire and blew a lock of sweaty hair from my forehead.

My realm was my children and household, and my career had been pushed to the back burner. I dealt with Individual Education Plans and academic meetings at school, behavior therapies, and phone calls and emails with teachers about Will. And my Finn. Both were square pegs the teachers tried to put in round holes. Finn was creative and exuberant, but he didn't fit the typical profiles for ADHD or autism. Sometimes, he was more draining than Will. He was my emotional child. God, how was he now? He could go either way—this was an amazing adventure or he was terrified and wanted Mommy.

Oddly, a smile came to mind as I thought about him chatting Brandon's ear off. The silence with Will was all-consuming and made me restive. I yearned for Finn's ceaseless questions. They always say you miss what you complain most about. Or something like that.

I made my way to the rear of the car and pulled out our now-ransacked and not so plentiful supplies: bins with food, water, camping gear, first-aid kit, one kitchen knife, blankets, toiletries. The other gas container, more water, and an ax—I had watched far too many zombie movies to not have that—were stowed away in the recessed storage area that the thieves had not managed to find. Thank God, I still had that stuff.

Between my worrying and Will's obsession with weather and natural disasters, we usually were prepared for it all. Our car must have looked like Fort Knox to those assholes.

I yawned, wishing I had packed coffee. The gas

station stuff was crap and, now with less money, a luxury. An unexpected wry chuckle escaped my lips.

"It's funny now?" Will asked, approaching from the tire.

He looked at me with full, brown eyes, snapping me from my melancholy. "I was laughing about not packing coffee. Of all things for me to forget, huh?"

"Oh!" Will wiggled past me and climbed onto the edge of the trunk. I put a guiding hand on his back as he leaned in, opened a large bin, and removed a green canister. He handed it to me. "Here!"

I twisted open the lid, humoring him. It's not like I was going to get that tire on soon, not until I could find the tire iron, car jack, and instructions. That meant lugging all this heavy crap out and digging through the recessed storage area. The aroma caught me, and I smiled, heartily. "Coffee!" I stared at the scoops of coffee grounds Will must have packed for me. "Oh, honey, thank you!" I hadn't the heart to tell him I lacked a coffee maker or an old-fashioned steeper. I squeezed him.

"Didn't you look at my list?" He grabbed his clipboard from the back seat. He removed his helmet and tossed it in his booster seat. "I made a list just like you. I showed you."

"Oh, yes, you're right. I must've not seen it on there," I said, feigning ignorance. In fact, I didn't need to pretend these days. Over the past year, my organization and memory had faded alongside my energy. My calendar on the fridge used to be filled with the boys' busy schedules, my work and volunteer activities, and family outings. I had four babysitters on call. Then this year, I'd said to hell with it. I'd tossed the damn calendar and took it day by day. I'd quit my part-time job. I couldn't take the pitying faces anymore. The life insurance would suffice for a few years. Lists had become a distant memory.

Or I'd thought. He shoved the list at me. "Impressive," I said, not lying. He had cataloged the copious amount of supplies I'd haphazardly packed in the stowaway bins, down to the number of red, yellow, blue, and gray Lego bricks he'd brought. Forty-one red, thirty-three yellow, sixty blue, and twenty-five gray…and four sets of wheels.

He returned to inspecting the tire, apparently done with the conversation.

I dialed the number on my membership card for roadside assistance. It went directly to a recorded message about their circuits being busy. Well, it had been worth a try. I could try a tow-truck, but I didn't know of any towing companies to call, and my reception flickered between one bar and none.

My stomach growled. "Come, let's have lunch before we figure this thing out." Defeat stabbed at me. I wasn't even out of New York and had already been robbed, forgotten my pills, and now had a flat tire. What the hell lay ahead for me?

Will grabbed my hand, as he always did, and we went to sit beneath a large tree for a quick meal.

A half hour later, inability overcame me. I cursed and allowed the L-shaped tire iron to slip from my slick hands to the grass. It fell with a thud. The only fruits of my effort were pink burning palms and beads of perspiration on my forehead. I read through the car owner's manual, again. It could have been in Greek. Harrison's delightful voice danced in my head, teasing me about not having a smartphone to discern how to do it.

*God, give me any other task!* Damn cars.

I quelled my frustration, not allowing Will to see as he sat by our picnic, building a tower with broken twigs. I missed Harrison's candor. He might have been cynical, but he was a guy you'd take at face value, easy to read. He'd been a soul-warming spirit in my life, my cheerleader. Then one day…my best friend was gone, and I was left to man all the battle stations myself.

I stood, wiped my raw, dirty hands on my jeans, and leaned against a tree. I was spent. The twenty stress-pounds I had put on after Will's diagnosis nearly three years before had quickly withered away in the year since Harrison's death. However, the pounds lost were not replaced with muscle tone. I was out of shape. Like many things in the past year, exercise lost its higher position on the priority list. I threaded my fingers through my knotty hair, pulling a few loose grays out with the brown. Yup, hair appointments, too. I drew the hair off my neck and wiped the sweat. I then let it fall. I lacked a hair tie, and it wasn't quite long enough to pull back, so I tucked it behind my ears.

Will approached and put his arm around my waist. "Let me help, Mom."

I smiled at him. He was great at puzzles, but neither he nor I had the physical strength to turn that damn tire iron. It wasn't the larger X-shaped iron. No, this was truly an emergency-only tire iron, L-shaped and harder to use. "Let's try again," I said anyway. I had successfully, with Will's guess, put the jack in the correct place and had lifted the car at least. I managed to take the spare off the rear gate after removing our bikes and rack. Brought also for emergencies. Yes, I was a notorious over-packer always ready with the what-ifs.

He put his hands beside mine on the tire iron, and we tried. And tried. I heaved an exasperated sigh. "It's no use, honey. We need more strength to turn this thing. The mechanic has an air-wrench to tighten the bolts." Determination didn't outweigh my lack of physical strength in this case. I tipped my head back and closed my eyes, letting the release of three days' stress buildup leave my body. A part of me was relieved for this momentary setback. A part of me was terrified.

Harrison's grumblings echoed in the depths of my mind. "Knock it off!" I mumbled.

"Mom?"

I swatted my hand in the air. "Nothing."

I returned to sit under the tree next to Will. Even with the shade that protected us from the blazing sun, I rested my arm across my face. Will hummed as he continued playing with whatever it was beside me—rocks, sticks, dirt—his youthful self-soothing a calming mechanism for me as well. I closed my eyes for just a moment.

"Mom, Mom!" Will's voice came through.

I sat up, groggy. "Goodness, did I fall asleep?"

"Yeah. Mom, there's somebody coming!" Will pointed down the road.

Even from far away, I recognized the man's plaid long-sleeved shirt and the large backpack, but now he was walking alongside a bike on his approach.

"Hey, look! It's that guy you drove past this morning!"

I shuddered inwardly. Well, karma just bit me in

the butt.

"How did he catch up with us?" Motherly instinct took over as I rose, my legs wobbly. "Will, stay there. Here, take this," I said, handing him the tire iron.

"We already tried that, Mom."

"Not for that, Will."

He scratched his brown hair, which was overdue for a cut, and looked at me, confusion wrinkling his brow.

"Be my wizard, Will. It's your sword."

"Wizards have wands."

"Will…"

The circuit connected. "Oh…yes, Mom, I'll protect you!"

I smiled faintly. "Thank you, honey." I didn't want to explain further that it was me protecting him. I didn't want to say that if something happened, to run and hide in the woods. Because he *would* run and hide. Then what? Who would come help?

I shoved my hand into my front jeans pocket to nestle my fingertips around the pocket knife I had given Harrison for our wedding anniversary. The man slowed his bicycle as he drew nearer. He gave me an understated, yet significant, nod. The nod of understanding, of kindness. I didn't buy it.

"Hello, again," he said.

*Ouch.* "You're resourceful. Found a bike, have you?"

A nervous chuckle escaped his lips. "Yeah. I passed a bicycle shop in…" He paused and rubbed his chin. "Outside of Olean. The owner was kind enough to give it to me for forty bucks. It was an old one he found at a yard sale. A bit rusty. He said there'd be no use for

49

them soon." He added in an eerie nonchalant way, "Ash, and all that."

"That's a bit dreary. We're not talking an apocalypse, here. I doubt it will come to that." *Really? Zombies and apocalypses...gosh, AJ.* I covered my unease with a smile. Who was I kidding? Was I still floating in denial? I'd been robbed already and my gun had been involved in some altercation out on the main highway. And I was still in New York. My stomach churned with my own mental tally marks, much like Will's charts. Jesus, I wanted to get out of this state.

"You've got a few bikes there, too." He gestured with his chin toward our two bikes beside the now removed bike rack. It had been a last-minute decision. Given what I'd read with Will through the years, we could hit a point where the car would no longer get us through the ash. Will wasn't proficient on his bike yet, though. He still used training wheels. Who knew if the bikes would even work? For once, maybe my over-packing would pay off. Even Patsy frequently remarked that I packed too many clothes for the kids when they stayed with her for grandparent-bonding weekends.

My fingers quivered on the knife's handle in my pocket. "Are you local? Can you point me in the direction of a mechanic or roadside assistance?"

"No, sorry." The man dropped his pack, leaned the bike on the ground, and lifted his water bottle. He chugged it in two gulps, wiped the sweat from his deeply tanned forehead, and then passed his look between the flat tire and me. "I can help you with that. Just need the tire replaced? You have a full-sized spare there I see."

Will swung the tire iron around in wizardlyfashion, humming one of his mishmashes of made-up tunes. *Lovely.* I grabbed the tire-iron-turned-wand from Will. "Not the best choice, honey."

"You said to be your wizard. I said a protection spell, Mom." He put on a slight pout but found himself easily distracted by a stick pile. He sifted through them. He picked a short, knobby one and stacked a few of the sticks. He flicked his wrist and said, "Ignite-o!" to the pile.

I couldn't help but smile at his spell.

"I'm a decent hand with tires and cars," the man repeated. He tapped the flat tire.

"I'm okay, thanks," I said, to no believable effect.

His face broadened into a smile. Days of black stubble speckled his chin and upper lip. "I can help. You're the first person I've seen on this stretch of road. It may be a while."

The genuine warmth of his look caught me off guard. It'd been ages since I'd seen such a pleasant countenance on anyone who spoke with me. "I, earlier..." I stumbled over my words. His gaze was piercing and unnerving to tell the truth. He had that ruggedly handsome look, with slightly longer, smooth, nearly-black hair on the top, cropped closer on the sides, and a prominent forehead with thick, sharply angled eyebrows. I fought labeling him with a typical stereotype; he had a mild accent. Mexican, maybe? Puerto Rican? I was always evaluating people. *Knock it off, AJ!*

The man deliberately looked at Will and then turned to me. He said, belatedly, "I understand." A wayward strand fell over his coffee-colored eyes, and he brushed it back.

Geesh, I had gone too long without a delicious cup of java...or a person's kindness. Now this guy's eyes reminded me of coffee. Harrison had been my coffee barista. Sure, I could brew it, but there was magic in his bringing me a cup after a long day, rubbing my feet, and...

"Thanks." I stared at the tire iron in my hand, wary. "We can't get the lug nuts off."

I didn't let on to my frustration with the task.

"I used to work in a mechanic's garage and had to deal with these tough ones without an air-wrench. They can be difficult." He unbuttoned his sleeves and rolled them to his elbows, revealing a string of tattoos on his muscular right arm. A mixture of twirling dark black lines in a tribal design danced across his skin.

I must have hesitated. He put out his hand, palm side up. "I'll need that." I stared at a second tattoo across the inside of his lighter, more golden-colored wrist: *Ne obliviscaris*. Latin. Not sure what it meant though even with my two years of Latin studies. I handed him the iron.

My inner radar went off, not that I held any prejudice against a man with a tattoo or two. My father had his own badges of memory from Vietnam inked on his body. He now lived the life of a hermit, I reminded myself. Even my stepmom couldn't handle his delusions anymore, and she spent most of her time with the church ladies.

This man traveled alone, and he wasn't local. Everything in my gut said to get moving...but how? My car was going nowhere.

I shoved my fingers in my pocket and refused to peel them from around the closed pocket knife. What good would that do against this clearly fit man? "Hey, Will, why don't you wait over here? Gather your things, please." Not waiting for him to help, I stooped and picked up Will's picnic of cheese crackers and peanut butter.

"I want to play," he moaned as he built a structure with the scattered sticks and then waved his stick-wand and said "Illuminate!" with associated sound effects.

I was in no mood for this, even if it was hotter in the car. "Will, now, please. You can take the sticks with us." My breath grew short, and I paused in my gathering. My anxiety couldn't already be flaring because of my pill shortage. It would take a few days before I felt that effect. Or I hoped. I was proud of how well I'd done so far with driving and keeping my cool. Maybe I didn't need the pills after all...

Will persisted with his moans and mumbles, but I shot him a "listen to me, now" glare. He understood those looks well enough. Nonetheless, he moved like molasses. Harrison used to say he behaved like a floppy rag doll or wet noodle. Either way, I had to light a fire under his butt.

I limited my pacing as the man finished with the tire. He got the nuts off easily enough, pulled off the flat, and was now working on the spare.

Will approached with his group of sticks. "Where's your car, mister?"

The man paused in his work. "It broke down near Newburgh."

"Why didn't you get another car or fix yours?"

Sometimes I loved Will's questions, for I'd been thinking the same thing. Questions from the mouths of babes come off as less intrusive. The man turned to me when he answered. He paused in his work. "I like bikes."

Will gave him an incredulous glance.

The man muffled a chuckle. "My car was beyond repair. No rental agency was nearby. Here I am with old Rusty." He pointed to the blue, and aptly named, rusty bike. "He's got potential, though. Might give him the royal treatment at the shop back home."

"Bikes don't have names," Will observed. "And bikes aren't boys."

"Hmm," I said, unconvinced, but it was a logical explanation. I wondered where "home" was if it wasn't here.

"So, you're biking all the way to…where are you going, mister?"

"Will, please take your sticks to the car."

He slowly gathered the sticks but didn't move toward the car yet. More humming.

I was grateful for the man's good sense to not discuss hitchhiking to my impressionable child. He lowered the jack, easing the car down with its new tire.

The man rose, wiped his hands on his jeans, and looked at me. Silence. I stared at the grease on his jeans and felt guilty for being the cause of that.

"Do you have a tire pressure gauge?"

"Oh. Yeah."

He mounted the bike rack on the now busted tire while I dug through the glove compartment. "Here," I said, returning to him and assisting with the rack and bikes. "Let me check the manufacturer recommendations," I added after handing him the gauge, and then I returned to the driver side. I looked inside the door, then at the man. "Thirty-two PSI."

He measured it. "It looks okay, but you may want to check it at your next gas station."

He drew his hands through his hair and then reached into his backpack.

I retrieved the tire iron, hesitating to return it to the trunk.

He pulled out a lollipop, removed the orange wrapper, and then paused. "Oh, hey, would you like one, buddy?" He glanced at Will, who was already getting in the SUV, then turned to me. "If Mom says it's okay?"

Will said, "Nope, I can't have them. Those have the chewy chocolate centers. I have these expander things on my teeth. See?" He opened his mouth to show off the metal spacers arched on his upper palate and the floor of his mouth, the orthodontic work the insurance company had initially balked at covering. But I had weaved through that red tape.

"Bummer," the man said.

"Thanks for helping," was all I could muster. I didn't want to ask his name. I wanted to be gone. My courage was withering.

He didn't ask. I didn't offer.

I turned on the car, my heart pounding. Stories of women or children abducted, tortured, and murdered flashed before my eyes. Harrison's gun was now in the hands of some thugs. I needed to go. Now. *Breathe, AJ. Breathe.*

The man righted his bike. "Have a safe journey, wherever it takes you."

Will leaned out his open window. He'd already put his helmet back on. "Where are you going?"

*Thank goodness for Will.*

"West," the man said.

"On a bike?" Will probed. "That's going to take weeks or months. By car, it's only about four or five days. An airplane is three to six hours, depending on where you're going. Of course, airplanes aren't flying west now. You need to find another car, mister."

I couldn't chide Will for being chatty. In fact, I'd grown tired of my incessant and negative thoughts as company during the past few days. A bag of pretzels and two apples sat in the passenger-less seat beside me. I grabbed an apple and the bag and rolled the window down.

"Well, it will take a while," the man said. "Maybe I can find a cheaper car somewhere along the way." In the afternoon sun, his eyes glistened pleasantly as he squinted, and he grinned again. Will always had a way of affecting people with his sweetness.

"We're going to Denver to get my brother, Finn. Well, that's if his plane from Salt Lake City landed there and he's okay. The blast zone didn't reach that far, but the ash did and there was a 7.4 magnitude earthquake. Mom says he'll be okay. My uncle will take care of him."

"I hope you find them, buddy," he said to Will. The man then gave a tactful nod.

"Can I at least offer you something to eat?" I stretched and handed the apple and pretzels through the window.

He stared blankly at my offering.

I spoke in a rush. "I have more. In my trunk…"

He took them, his fingertips grazing my mine for a few seconds. "No need. This is great, thanks. Be safe," he said as he hopped on his bike.

I called a humble thank-you and drove away before Will would offer him a ride.

"He should have come with us," Will said belatedly.

I always found Will's observations interesting. He didn't ask me why I hadn't offered the man a ride, though a slew of explanations hovered on the tip of my tongue to appease that potential question. No, that would've been Finn asking me those questions. As we drove, Will returned to spouting off facts about the supervolcano.

I blinked away my own self-reproach and refused to look in the rearview mirror.

\*\*\*\*

That evening, after my detour around Pittsburgh, I pulled over in a big-box-store parking lot off Route 70 in Ohio. An RV with an elderly couple was set up on the far end. Seemed safe enough. Visible, but not a target. I eyed our route in the atlas. "Hello, Peregrine," I said to the aptly named book.

Once, when Harrison and I had gotten lost on a detour to his parents' house in Virginia and I cursed at his smartphone's inaccuracy, the reliable atlas had been our saving grace.

"The phone doesn't like me," I'd said, dropping it into the cup holder like it was a venomous snake.

"Nope," Harrison had teased. He squeezed my knee but didn't take his focus off the road.

I knew that he hankered to be the one looking at the atlas and not me. He loved maps. The apple didn't fall far from the tree with our cartographer son.

"Doesn't Peregrine mean something like 'traveler'?" Harrison asked.

I replied, "You may be thinking of the falcon. From one of those shows the boys watch."

"Here, check." He handed me his phone while he navigated the beltway around DC. The phone was an alien rock in my hands.

"Just type it into the search engine box," Harrison said patiently.

I did, and I laughed, showing him the image. "A falcon, see!"

"Keep reading," he urged.

Dammit, he was right. "How do you remember these things?"

His lips curled into his signature smile. The sun sparkled on blond stubble above his lip. I loved how the sunshine and warmer weather accentuated the golden hues in his now-earthy-brown hair. I'd seen the adorable photos of him as a kid. He'd been a blondie during his childhood years in California, but then his family had moved to the Midwest and his hair had grown darker. Goodbye Cali sunshine, hello winters. The glimmer of ego danced in his blue irises. I poked his arm. "Okay, you're right, Mr. Encyclopedia."

Now, I flipped through *Peregrine's Atlas* as the last tendril of memory dissipated. Harrison's long cursive notes were scribbled on a few of the pages. I traced a finger over them, evoking his spirit.

Will and I had begun our turn south today, which required us to travel on slower roads, but it would allow us to avoid metro areas like Chicago. Not that Route 70 was less busy, but it would take us west. Tomorrow, we'd hit Columbus, followed by Indianapolis, and then St. Louis. Avoiding cities was hard. I had to try to stick to the easiest routes until I couldn't anymore. I highlighted the route and then put Peregrine away.

I pulled out my journal and reread my last entry and pondered the man we'd met today.

Chapter Four
Coexisting

After a restless night thanks to Will's protests about sleeping in the car, the uncomfortable seats, and my despondent mind, we left the parking lot at dawn.

"Mom, can we please find a hotel soon? Or camp again? My neck feels funny."

I swallowed the dryness in my throat. "Yes, honey, I will try." I calculated the money I had still hidden in my handbag and under my car seat. A hotel would be divine. "Soon."

We drove for a few hours, each lost in our cogitations. The farther I distanced myself from New York, the better I felt. Even if it was false optimism, I clung to it as I contemplated plan B and plan C if more shit happened.

I found myself daydreaming. Or rather, swirling back into old times, even if they were laced with melancholy. Harrison's final birthday last year, only a month before his death, came to the forefront of my musings.

**\*\*\*\***

*June, Last Year*

"Stop fighting with your brother!" I yelled at Finn, who poked Will with a piece of his train track.

"Mooooom!" Will screeched. "Stop being a brat, Finn!"

They ran circles around me, and I stepped on the cat. He hissed and darted to safety. *Run and hide, Snow! I'd be there with you if I could.*

I tried my mild, rational mom voice. "Finn, please stop poking Will."

"See?" Will said, sticking his tongue out at Finn.

"No fair! You always take his side!" Finn whined.

"Please play nicely," I growled through gritted teeth. They ignored me and took their brotherly battle upstairs. Thank God. I rubbed my forehead.

I rushed through the dishes, a leaning Tower of Pisa in the sink from last night. I'd worked yesterday, so of course they hadn't been touched. My mind raced through the to-do list. Susie would arrive soon. The grass needed to be finished, and our mower was on the fritz—it had truly become a labor of love. I dripped with sweat. Harrison was on his way home from work hopefully, and I wanted to make his birthday night special. I hadn't begun working on his favorite dinner. The cake had finger holes in it from the kids, and I fought the urge to cut a slice of buttery heaven right then and there for myself. In the humidity, the cream cheese frosting caused the carrot cake to lean like my tower of dishes. I lifted the platter, carefully balancing the sugary mess, and placed it in the fridge.

I wiped the sweat from my brow and returned to the dishes. We had been blessed with a hot June day. Blessed. Ha. I panted. One of the dishes slipped from my hand and fell in a loud crack against a few others, spraying broken pieces of stoneware in the sink.

Shrieks and thumps echoed from the boys' bedrooms.

I cursed, tears welling. I couldn't cry on his

birthday! Oh, but I did. Another screech emanated from upstairs. Instead of fuming and yelling at them, again, I bawled into the sink. I dried my hands on a dish towel and picked up the phone and texted Harrison.

*ETA? Kids horrible. Bring coffee home.*

*Okay.*

I immediately regretted my terse text. *Love you. Good day?*

*No. More drama with client and a tech.*

I sighed. They worked him too hard. He was awake past midnight many nights catching up on the workload. He had missed Finn's final soccer game and trophy presentation the past weekend, too.

*Love you*, I typed. *Made your favorite cake!*

A grinding belt announced Susie's car pulling into the driveway. I blotted my face with a dish towel and hoped she couldn't see the redness.

We exchanged brief hellos and updates on Will's behavioral plan. "He has a lot of homework to complete after being sick."

"Too much work for such a little guy and at the end of the school year, too," Susie said in her melodic twenty-something voice that worked wonders on Will. And me. God bless her patience and enthusiasm.

"He also lost recess yesterday. It dysregulated him. We had to skip karate class because he was off kilter."

I was about to apologize for the mess of paper, masking tape, uncapped markers, and scissors that lay strewn on my kitchen floor and living room sofa. I glanced at the chaos in the playroom, which abutted our open kitchen. Upturned marble-run blocks, train-track pieces, marbles, wooden planks of every shape and size, and creative paper mess winked at me, tempting my inner neat freak. I turned away from it and stepped over the kitchen floor mess. I grabbed his homework binder off the counter and handed it to Susie. Kids were messy. Kids like mine were excessive with their creativity.

Regardless, a thump of anxiety reverberated in my chest.

"Perhaps I can talk with him about the upcoming trip you're all taking to Yellowstone this summer?"

I nodded. "Yeah, good idea. He's excited about that." The trip was only two months away. Harrison was stoked, as was Will. Harrison, in fact, had every detail nailed down. He'd purchased the tickets, booked hotels, and mapped the route. Everything was scheduled. We were nervous taking the boys on their first cross-country flying trip, but God, we needed a break. To get away. It would be wonderful.

Susie and I slogged upstairs. "Come on, Finn. We need to leave Susie with Will. Help me make dinner for Daddy."

Finn was wrapped in his favorite fleece robot blanket, rolling around. "I can't. I have no legs yet. I'm in a chrysalis!"

Will kicked at him. "Go! Stop being so stupid!"

"Will, we don't use that word." Brotherly love, my ass. They did love each other. Fifty percent of the time. "Come, Finn. I need your help."

As I lifted my cocooned child, he giggled. "Wow, this is going to be a big butterfly!" God, I tried. I refused to let the beast emerge from me today even if it was clawing at the edges.

"No!" Will moaned from behind me. "I don't want to do homework! It's stupid. My teacher's stupid. She doesn't listen to me."

"It's your choice to get it done now, with me, Will," Susie began, tucking a long dark lock behind her double-pierced ear, "and then we'll have time to play later. Or we can take two hours to do this and have no playtime. I brought my chess board..." She stood, unwavering.

Will was still resisting five minutes later, demonstrated by loud thumps and groans emerging from his bedroom. I ignored it and shifted gears in the kitchen. "Please set the table, Finn."

"No."

I heaved a sigh. "Set the table."

"Why doesn't Will have to?"

"He's doing homework. Go do it. You can get a star on your chart," I said with my last sanity-inducing breath as I maneuvered around the kitchen and collected the potatoes, veal, eggs, and flour for making Harrison's favorite dish of Wiener schnitzel that I made approximately once a year.

"Okay!" He ran and did as told, wrapped in his robot blanket.

A loud crash erupted from the dining room a moment later.

I moaned instead of using the colorful language I'd wanted to say.

Finn was on the floor, bawling hysterically. I swooped in and assessed. One chair was knocked over, and all the silverware was on the floor next to a second broken plate.

"Ouch!" Finn cried, hugging his elbow. I felt it. Not broken and not bleeding. No ER visit this time.

"What were you doing?"

"The butterfly wanted to fly!" He looked at me with tear-streaked cheeks.

I sighed and sat on the floor next to him. "How about pizza for dinner tonight?"

\*\*\*\*

*Present Day*

"Those clouds are really dark!"

"Uh-huh."

She wasn't looking. Will drew a frustrated breath. "Look how gray those clouds are."

Mom didn't answer.

He continued anyway. "They're gray on the bottoms, but dark blue on top there. Maybe they're filled with ash!" Large, puffy cumulonimbus clouds. Tall, towering, gray, and dark blue. They made his head spin with excitement. One of his weather books said those types of clouds were the result of atmospheric instability, formed by water vapor carried upward by strong air flow—because that's what clouds were. He remembered Dad coming into his class and talking about the water cycle. "They're usually on cold fronts, Mom. Do you think the eruption cooled it down? A cold front is coming?" He chewed on his lip. "Will it affect the climate? I read about volcanic winters in my books, where it gets too cold and then crops and plants don't grow."

She mumbled something he couldn't understand.

He added, "I'm not sure if I'd rather be a meteorologist or volcanologist when I grow up. What do you want me to be?"

"Whichever one you want, dear."

Mom was different this week. She was quieter. Usually, every morning on their rides to school, she would mention the pretty sunrise, or the green—or golden in autumn—farm fields. She loved green hills, and she especially loved flowers. During autumn, they would talk about the rainbow of leaves. Orange and red were her favorite. Finn liked the yellow. Of course, Finn would say poopy words and spit on the window and try to get him to do it as well. Finn could be annoying.

"Love you, Mom," he said, hoping to cheer her up. He wanted her to be happy.

"Love you, too, sweetie." She reached her hand back, palm up in her usual gesture, while keeping her gaze on the road. Except Finn's wasn't there to squeeze, too. It was always the three of them. Mom did it every day after she picked them up from the bus stop. But that was before Dad's accident. She didn't drive much anymore.

Will used two hands to squeeze instead.

He then pulled out his map and drew a line from New York to Pennsylvania, through Ohio, then Indiana. "What's the capital of Indiana, Mom?"

"Indianapolis."

He drew a circle and star and then carefully finished outlining the Midwest states. So far he created regional maps of New England, the mid-Atlantic, and now the Midwest. Indiana had lots of tall cornfields. If he stared straight out the side window, they would pass by in a cool cloud of green and brown. It made him dizzy.

He drew heaps of gray clouds on Indiana to represent what they saw. He had to keep a precise record of their trip to show Finn.

\*\*\*\*

My annoyance mounted after another long day. The plan to travel Route 70 west was thwarted by construction, traffic, and accidents near Indianapolis. It took most of the day to get through Columbus and around Indianapolis. I contemplated how much of the traffic was due to the disaster. Thankfully, I found a gas station west of Indianapolis. I got gas and bought and filled another spare gas container. The car reeked of fuel. I did my best to mask it with air freshener, tight gas container lids, and open windows. Mom and pop shops lined the main street of the town—a hardware store, a bank, a pizza shop...Will begged for pizza, so we grabbed some from the convenience store.

"Need anything else, ma'am?" the shop clerk asked as I approached the counter to pay. He was a balding, burly guy, with a wide toothy smile and ruddy cheeks.

"Mom? Can I get a candy bar?" Will interjected.

"Sure."

He placed it on the counter, and I paid. Unease drew my gaze to two men near an old red pickup at the pump. The younger of the two gaped at me while the older, heavyset man pumped gas. The younger man's sneer gave me the creeps. He was grubby, dressed in hunting clothes, and licked his fingers suggestively while finishing whatever it was he ate. I grabbed Will's hand. "Let's go."

I had to walk around the truck to get to my car on the other side of the pump. The pungent stench of maleness and alcohol floated off the men. I escorted Will to his door and slammed it behind him, then I hurried to my door, locking the car as I got in.

"It's hot, Mom. Roll down the windows."

My intuition flared. I ignored him, started the car,

and left the lot. Grinning creepy man's stare remained on us, glossy and disturbing, as I kept an eye on the rearview mirror. His upper lip curled.

"Mom...," Will said.

I rolled the windows down once we were on the road.

Night was upon us before long, and a drizzle turned into a heavy rain. Like clockwork, as it always did in the last year, my pulse increased with the rain. I gripped the steering wheel, white knuckled. Rain is good for trees. My flowers loved it. It created drinking water and nourished our farms.

It also made roads slippery.

It contributed to car accidents.

And...

Oh, how I wished I hadn't chosen now of all times to forget to have my prescription filled. My head was foggy, my palms slick.

I shoved those thoughts away. Look how far I'd made it already! I'd put in more miles in the past few days than I had in the entire previous year. A mother's adrenaline could get me far. That made me think of Finn. A wave of palpitations hit me.

"Hrmmph," I said, breathless, hands tighter on the wheel.

"You okay, Mom?"

"Yup." I breathed through them. My chest lifted and fell like a galloping horse.

Breathe.

Focus.

Breathe.

"Sad?"

"No, it's my heart. It's flip-flopping," I said, as the

68

final wave hit…then settled.

Calm rushed through me. I picked up my cell phone and tried dialing Dr. Martin again. Busy signal. I dialed again a few minutes later. Nothing. No answer. My phone showed one bar of reception.

As night drew on and Will grew tired, I found a safe place to pull off the highway in an area near an overpass that appeared to be a commuter's parking lot.

"Awww, Mom, you said we can camp or find a hotel!"

"I'm sorry, honey. There's nothing for miles, and it's getting late. I don't want to be on the road at night." Night and rain, my least favorite combo. "Hopefully tomorrow."

"Promise?"

I sighed. "I can't promise, but I will try, okay?"

My guard was up. Perhaps I should've driven farther, but it was late and I worried Will might have trouble falling asleep. I parked the car closer to the trees to keep it shielded from unaware highway drivers.

The sound of the rain was both nerve-wracking and soothing. I kept the windows cracked, the tire iron resting on my lap, insomnia joining me. Thankfully, the heat of the day had simmered with the rainstorm and the interior of the car was bearable. Restless, Will finally succumbed to sleep after eleven p.m.

I heard a truck in the predawn hours.

Instant alarm bells went off. It was like I had known. I truly had tried to keep driving until I found a safe motel. I'd distanced myself from those goons in the pickup. Had I messed up yet again? "Jesus," I mumbled, as to not wake Will.

My keys sat in the ignition. Will was reclined in

the front passenger seat and not buckled in. I would drive off if need be. My fingers tingled, and I held my breath. Maybe they wouldn't see us. Our dark blue SUV blended in with the shadows of the trees in the cloudy, moonless night.

Fishermen? I hadn't seen any lakes or streams.

Very early commuters? Not *this* early.

Lost travelers? Nope.

Harrison's gun would've come in handy now. I clasped my hand around the iron. It was all I had.

This was damn ridiculous. *Did* bad luck travel with me? Was I a naïve fool?

The truck paused at the edge of the lot, about two hundred yards away, and idled, its older engine gurgling and almost groaning with effort. Thick, dark, residual storm clouds hung over us like the gloom that lived within me. I hadn't wanted to admit to Will when he was rambling about the clouds earlier, but I had indeed seen it. The ash-laden clouds were moving east. It was coming. Was this rain already contaminated with ash? Were both our asthmatic lungs breathing it in?

I couldn't see far from my spot. I dared not turn on a light. I squinted. The driver turned off the truck's lights but not its engine.

Call it instinct or having already learned my lesson back in New York…they were trouble. I refused to be caught unaware again.

Clammy fingers returned to the keys, ready. I couldn't close my cracked-open windows without clicking the car on. I quickly checked the locks for the fourth time. Hypervigilant ears were on, detecting my wheeze, Will's soft snore, and the beating of my quickening heartbeat that had not quite reached palpitation potential yet.

A few moments passed. Nobody approached. The truck's high beams went on. I flinched and muffled a curse. Jackasses. They drove off, peeling in a flurry of gravel. I dropped my head to the wheel as my pulse raced. I reclined, pressing palms to eyes. My head roared with a sinus-induced headache from the barometric pressure change in the air.

Suddenly, there was a loud jiggle of the passenger door handle.

What the hell?

Peering through the door was that same repulsive grin I had seen at the gas station. The man rapped on the window. "Come on, pretty gal, need warmth tonight?"

Shit! No, I did not. I started the car faster than I ever had before. Will rolled over.

"Mom?" he said, his voice groggy.

"Sit up, Will, and buckle your seatbelt, now!" I shifted into drive. Lights turned on, I got the hell out of there.

Will was slow to respond, slurring his words. "Mommmm, it's dark."

"Will, your belt! NOW!"

He buckled, but protested, "I'm not supposed to ride in the front seat."

I scrambled to get mine buckled. Last thing I needed was to go headlong through the windshield. I turned onto the highway and accelerated. A moment later, high beams and a row of hood lights probably used for illegal hunting greeted me like the smile of demonic cat—gosh, I must have had cats on the mind with all of Will's wizard-cat books. The red truck drove straight at me. "Shit!" The asshole's buddy had been waiting on the road in the truck. They had gone the strategic route of separating.

Briefly blinded by the bright string of lights, I swerved to the other lane to avoid hitting the truck. My driver's side rumbled through the grassy shoulder. I overcompensated, and the car fishtailed. *No, no, no, don't flip*, I silently prayed for our now unwieldy SUV, but I managed to get around the truck and on the right side of the road. The man in the truck sped to the commuter lot to grab his companion. The screech of worn brakes sliced through the night.

"Shit!"

"Mom! I need my helmet!"

I got the car under control and slammed my foot on the accelerator. "Come on, car. Come on!" I kept one eye on the road ahead, one on the truck in the rearview mirror. I quickly gained distance from it. Belatedly, I reached behind and got his helmet. The speedometer read eighty miles per hour. I was glad for the straight highway. I maintained that speed for ten minutes, until I was certain I could no longer see the truck behind me.

Will was quiet, not outwardly frightened. "Bad guys?" he asked, holding Douglas to his chest.

"Yes."

I grabbed my pill bottle in the cup holder and took one with a swallow of water. Four pills left now.

I then slowed to a reasonable seventy miles per hour and drove until I saw daylight.

Chapter Five
A Gale of Change

*May, Last Year*

"Mom's in the garden, Dad," Will hollered down the steps as he entered the house from the basement and looked through the front windows. "She has her ear things in," he added with a thumb point.

Dad closed the garage door and strode up the basement steps behind Will. Dad's forehead wrinkled in that weird way it did when he was thinking about something and was worried, but when he didn't want to talk about it. Will turned away; he knew that look. Susie was a marvel with helping him understand cues and facial expressions. They would sit there on his bedroom carpet swiping through the tablet program on "funny faces" as Susie called it. Or she would use her index cards with different faces or scenarios and he had to talk about how the person might feel. It was difficult, but Susie always said, "Fantastic!" Sometimes he'd get distracted and count all the birth marks on Susie's face. She had a grouping of them on her left cheek in the shape of the Big Dipper! He giggled about it. She giggled with him.

Still, many times, he didn't understand all the face things. He tried. Mom and Dad wanted him to try.

Dad mumbled something and went outside to talk

with Mom.

Finn bounced into the living room as soon as Will came in. "How was Explorers Club? Did you have fun? Did you see the fire engines? Wanna play with me? I already set the board up."

"Not now," Will said, shrugging off his light jacket and tossing it on the floor. He kicked off his shoes. He looked through the open front window and tapped his hands together. Two, two, one, two, he counted with each tap. Two, two, one, two.

A cool spring breeze floated in, like a kiss on his cheeks. He loved the wind. Except when it was super icy cold. Then it was no fun. He went out in the snow and cold anyway. Winter was his favorite season…he could build snow volcanoes. Summer was nice, too. Sand volcanoes.

He listened as Dad approached Mom. He stopped tapping, his heart feeling less thumpy, and he traced the metal screen with his pointer finger, drawing concentric squares.

"Hey, hon," Dad said with a wave. Mom glanced up from her digging—she was removing another dead grouping of lupine that didn't make it through winter. Those were her favorite flowers. Except, for some reason, they didn't like to grow in her gardens, and it made her sad. She explained to him once that the soil was likely not acidic and sandy enough. Even though their neighbors had loads of lupine, Mom's just never survived. It was a mystery. A few dead flowers lay strewn about the oval-shaped garden. Mom had four gardens filled with lupine, lilies, daisies, phlox, and cat mint, which attracted bees. He didn't like bees. And nothing was blooming much yet since it was still May.

Flowers made Mom happy. Dad liked to bring her flowers.

Mom removed the earbuds from her ears. "How was it?"

Dad whispered, his back to Will's vantage point. Mom's face didn't look happy now. Dad was probably telling her about the field trip. It didn't go well.

He began tapping on the window frame. Two, two, one, two.

They'd visited the fire and police stations, which were joined into one community building. He *was* doing okay even though it was huge, bright, and there were many things to look at. Then one of the boys laid on the horn in the fire engine. Loud and sudden, it scared him so much that he almost peed his pants. He didn't. Only babies did that. It hurt his ears, and he ran out of the garage. Dad chased him, but he ran into the hallway and found an open room and hid under a table. He cried and growled. It was blaring! His fingers danced thinking about it.

He tapped. Two, two, one, two.

A nice lady police officer convinced him to come out five minutes later.

That's why it hadn't been good.

He ran a finger over the window screen. There was a spot where it was torn. He wondered if a bee could squeeze through the hole.

Dad kept talking to Mom, a quiet mumble lost on the wind. He strained to hear.

Finn came over beside Will. "Come on, Will! Let's play. I'll let you have Yellowstone."

Will loved Yellowstone on the National Parks Property game. It was the best one. It usually helped him win the game if somebody landed on it.

"Okay," Will conceded, but not without another look at Mom. Her face was the "sad" face card from Susie's pack. He wished she wasn't always sad.

A few minutes later, there was commotion as Mom and Dad came in.

"You're being unreasonable," Dad said.

"No, I'm not! It's not suited for him. We need to pull him," Mom said.

Will always heard their arguments when they thought he couldn't.

Mom rattled things in the kitchen, opening and closing cabinet doors and slamming the fridge shut.

"I think we should try a little longer," Dad said.

Mom's voice got shrill when she was angry or sad. Dad's was blunt, but also angry. "I think it's time."

Dad thumped a hand on the island. "Fine. Fine." He then left the room to sit by Will and Finn. "How's the game?" he asked evenly.

"Good!" Finn said. He rolled a pair of twos and landed on Yellowstone. "I'm buying Yellowstone."

Will screeched, "No! That's mine. You promised. You cheated on that roll. Dad, he cheated!" He stood and kicked at the game board.

"Now, Will, he landed there fairly," Dad began.

"No! He always cheats! He *said* he'd let me have Yellowstone! You always take his side. You and Mom always take his side!" His head buzzed. He always got Yellowstone. It was his. Finn said he could have it! If he didn't get it, then he couldn't put the four houses and the one station on it. Then he couldn't win. He didn't buy the Acadia or the Glacier or the Everglades properties because he had enough money to buy

Yellowstone. He kicked at the neatly lined money in front of him and it flew into Finn's messy pile of money. "That's not fair!"

"Hey!" Finn shrieked in response.

Will's pulse whirred as he bolted from the room. He didn't run outside anymore when this happened. Mom used to tell him to go to his room to "calm down." In his room, there was no buzzing, or annoying brothers, or moms and dads arguing. His plushy bed helped him drown all that rubbish.

This was Finn being unfair! Will had planned it all—why did Finn lie? This is how they played the game. This is how it always happened. He always set his money aside to buy that property and his station.

He slammed his door and stomped around his room. After a few minutes, he went to his desk and opened his crayon box. He dumped the crayons on the floor, sat, and began lining them up. Each crayon, sharp and brand new because he never used them to color, was aligned perfectly straight on the bottom. It looked like a fence. He shuffled them around to put them in rainbow order, starting with shades of red and pink. He finished with black, except that was not a rainbow color, technically. In fact, brown and white and pink weren't either, so he removed all of those, too.

"Hard day, huh?" Mom said, opening the door and poking her head in.

Will growled through clenched teeth and walked to his tall dresser where he kept all his prized items. He had his gold—well, not real gold, but all the yellow toys he could find. He put them in a box—Lego bricks, marbles, scraps of yellow paper, fake gold coins, gold pipe cleaners, and a few of Finn's yellow cars. He shoved the box aside and thumbed through his karate belts. Mom kept all his old ones in a dresser drawer as he earned each new belt. He had white, yellow, orange, and he was now on purple, and next would be blue.

"Look who's here."

Snow, their black cat, came into the room and jumped on Will's bed. Yeah, real snow was white, but Finn helped name the shelter cat they had taken in and he knew Will liked snow and weather and stuff, so they'd named him that. Will thought it was funny. A black cat named Snow. He would think Midnight would be a better name, but Mom said to *humor* Finn.

Will sat next to Snow and patted him. Snow purred louder with each stroke. Snow was a friendly cat, always sleeping in his bed. Mom got grumpy with Snow in the mornings when he'd howl for food or barf. He always bugged her. Mom was always tired in the morning and wanted her coffee. Once, she tripped over him and hurt her ankle.

He scratched Snow behind his ears.

"He doesn't like to see you sad," Mom said, with a slow approach.

Will kept his gaze away. "Finn always cheats."

Mom didn't say anything.

"You and Dad always take his side. You baby him and don't treat me the same way."

Mom sat beside him and wiggled her feet. She wore Dad's oversized slippers. "It's hard when things don't go the way we plan," she said in her oh-so-soft voice that he liked. Mom always understood. Even though Will knew his brain was different from hers.

"Today was horrible. I mess up at everything. I'm a rubbish pile. I should go live on Mars," Will said, sniffling. His head buzzed. Snow's purrs vibrated in his hand.

"Some days have a lot of hard stuff. But there's always some good."

"No, there isn't." He stroked Snow. "Mom, what were you fighting with Dad about?"

She didn't answer.

After a minute, well, sixty-five seconds to be exact, she said, "What are the three things that are always free, Will? No matter how hard our days get, we have them?"

"Sunshine, oxygen, and love," he said, repeating the words she always told him when he was sad.

She rubbed his back. He leaned into her arm and let a few tears fall. "Every day is bad."

"Not every day, honey. Not all day. We have the sun. We never have to ask for it. It always greets us each day, and granted, sometimes there are clouds, but it's there. Each day dawns anew. The sun rises."

"The sun doesn't rise. The Earth revolves around it."

Mom chuckled lightly. "Yes, that's true. And oxygen. We have air to breathe. Every single day. There's no breathable air on Mars, is there?"

"Nope."

"And we have love. You have my love, Daddy's love, God's love, Grandma and Grandpa's love, and Finn's love."

"I don't like Finn."

"Finn loves you and you love him even when he doesn't behave the way you like."

Will cried harder, the buzzing returning. "I always get Yellowstone!"

Mom rubbed his cheek. "I know, Will."

He rested his head in her lap as he continued to stroke Snow, knowing that in a few minutes the buzzing would cease, and he would feel better. Mom and Snow always made him feel better.

****

*Present Day*

We put in a long day of driving, stopping, detouring. Will's resilience continued to amaze me. I found myself looking over my shoulder at the road behind me, although nobody followed. Soon, I'd create my own tally sheets like Will did for foghorn blares and snow days, except mine would be about how many asshole encounters or mishaps I'd have on this trip. Colorado felt so far away.

Well, there was that nice man who had helped with the tire. I wondered where he was now.

We continued south on Route 57 in southern Illinois. There was no way in hell I was going north to Chicago or St. Louis. South it was. Cities tensed my nerves before the eruption. I couldn't imagine the disorder now.

"How much longer, Mom?" Will shifted in his seat.

"Soon. How are you hanging in there, my love bug?" I was about to say "little buddy," Harrison's own name for him, but I stopped myself.

"Okay."

"Do you have questions?"

He looked out the window, thoughts clearly beleaguering him.

"Those guys wanted to hurt us. Why? Did they want to steal our car?" He tapped a finger on his knee.

"Maybe." *Or more.*

"Why?"

"Some people do bad things, especially during scary times like this."

"Like those people who stole our stuff?"

"Yeah."

"What do you think it all looks like? How wide do you think the caldera is now?"

I bit my lip. Not exactly the questions I sought, but it was my own fault for asking. At least we were done talking about the scum of the world. "I'm not sure, Will. It'll be a while before they clean the destruction and help all the people." It may be a decade, I thought. "Then the scientists will study it."

"In nine years, I'll be old enough to go to college or maybe I can work there, too, and study it. The eruption wasn't gigantic enough to destroy the planet, but it could cause a volcanic winter like the eruption in 1816," he said. "Maybe that's why the leaves were already changing color in New York."

I refrained from stating it was too soon for the climate to be affected. Regardless, it was not the end of the world, as long as society didn't become unhinged.

A silent rhythm dominated our drive. Will's ability to keep himself quietly entertained was a respite from the boisterousness when the boys were together.

My phone buzzed in my cup holder. I nearly swerved off the road. Fumbling, I lifted the phone. My first thought was of Finn and Brandon. My soul danced with hope when I saw it was Sarah. I still hadn't gotten through to Dr. Martin. "Hello?" I said, the word croaking from disuse of my voice for the better part of the day.

"AJ! Thank goodness, honey! Where are you now?" Sarah breathed into the phone.

"We're in Illinois now, I think."

"You think?"

I stifled a strained laugh, but then said seriously, "Brandon?"

"No, hon. I'm sorry."

Hope fizzled.

She said, "It'll be okay. Finn's got him."

"Shouldn't that be the other way around?"

"Nah. Finn's your protector. He'll take care of Brandon."

There was a pause. My mind churned.

"You didn't gather your wits and turn around yet?" she asked.

"Nope."

Sarah sighed and said calmly, "AJ, if anyone is capable of handling this, Brandon can. He's Mr. Fix-it, right? Give him a straw and duct tape, and he'll build you a bridge."

I nodded, though she couldn't see me. Brandon was former Special Ops, but what if he was hurt, too? Or worse? Special Ops doesn't give you an invisible shield from raining cement in an earthquake. "Yeah, something like that," I offered half-heartedly.

"You two and your crazy shenanigans, right?" She laughed quietly.

"Yeah." I recalled the times Brandon and I would play in the yard, reenacting moments from a TV show to get us out of some pretend jam with a villain.

"How are you hanging in there? Is Will keeping you straight?"

"Mom, I have to pee. Can we stop soon?" Will

interrupted.

My gaze passed to the rearview mirror. "Yes, honey," I said to him. If he had to pee, he meant it. If it had been Finn, we'd be stopping every hour. Will fidgeted with the top of his collared polo shirt. It was fastened to the highest button, and for probably the fiftieth time today, he tucked it closer to his chin, making sure his neck was covered. At least I had convinced him to wear a short-sleeved shirt instead of his favorite quarter-zippered fleece. It was too damn hot! I'd compromised on that sensory battle.

"Yeah, he is. How…are things in California? How are Briar and Amelia?" It was a stupid distracting question, but I needed to talk about anything else other than *that*. And there was no way in hell I was going to tell her about all that had transpired in the past few days.

Sarah's singsong voice came through. "Same crazies, different day; dry and warm. Things are okay, except for the travel bans. No ash here, though. Forecasts project it moving eastward, I think. I'm no weather expert like Will. Our television reception and the wireless connection have been on the fritz."

"Sarah, I'm—" I stopped myself. I didn't want to talk about my own difficulties in front of Will.

"It will be okay." Her voice was a soothing blanket. She was surprisingly composed, despite not knowing where her husband was, but as an air force wife, she was already conditioned for these types of situations.

"Uh-huh."

"Girl, a volcano just blew up. It's gonna be hard. Hang in there, honey. Your boy knows that you're coming. You *will* get to him. Brandon has him. You have the best lucky charm of all with you, too. You have the master cartographer and mini-scientist with you! He will get you there."

"Yup, he will."

"You can do this, AJ. You're a fighter. As are your boys."

I nodded. "I can do this."

"I can't convince you to turn around though, can I?"

My conscience tugged at me. "No. I have to do it, Sarah."

"You've got this. Love you, girl."

"Love you, too." The earpiece crackled, followed by silence. Again, my phone showed half a bar of reception. "Thank you," I said to the blinking time on the screen. Her sweet words were a power drink. Hope bubbled in my chest, even if only momentary.

A few minutes later, I found a campground. A shower tonight would be divine. I weaved my hand through my oily, haphazardly wavy hair. Campgrounds had people. Safety in numbers. The sign advertised it as family-friendly.

"There! They have a pool!"

"We're not swimming, Will. I didn't bring your bathing suit. We can shower and eat a hot meal."

I pulled into the campground entrance and called today a wash. A family—a woman, man, and two young children—exited the office. The children laughed. The adults exchanged a shared look of concern but got in their fully packed car and drove to their campsite. Their license plate was from New York. In fact, I recognized their red sedan. It was strange how when on the road, that you'd see the same few cars cross paths with you more than once.

Minivans, sport wagons, standard cars, and the occasional camper or RV all filled the other campsites. Nothing appeared sketchy. Nowadays, what the hell qualified as sketchy?

I released an audible groan as I emerged from the car. I rubbed my neck and did quick hamstring stretches. Soreness radiated throughout my legs and back. The lack of workouts and being cramped in a car were already fatiguing my muscles. I tugged on my sweaty T-shirt and wished I had worn lighter pants instead of jeans.

Will strolled to the welcome office.

A weathered, older gentleman with striking white hair and dark skin greeted us inside. "Good day, ma'am. You in need of a campsite?" His face gleamed with kindness, and he spoke with an old-fashioned gallantry and slightly southern twang.

"Yes, please."

"Many folks are checking in today…traveling west. Are you from out of state?"

"Maine."

He nodded and pulled a paper from a folder beside the register. "Need you to fill out this form. The pool is open until eight p.m., and bathroom is open all night."

"Thanks."

"Hey there, sonny, would you like a pop?" he asked, smiling at Will. Will was already in recon mode. He moseyed around the modest gift shop, touching all the knick-knacks for sale. The man's gaze returned to me. "That is, if your mother allows it."

I nodded. "Just can't bite it, Will."

"I know," Will said.

The man leaned over the counter, offering the canister of lollipops. Will mused indecisively, but ultimately picked the green one. "Fine choice!" the man said. "Many delicious flavors in there."

Will beamed at him but said nothing to the man. "Mom, can we go swimming?" he asked again.

"Thank you," I said for him.

Will parroted, "Thank you."

"You're welcome, ma'am. My name's Frank if you need anything. Tillie serves a breakfast in our kitchen here at seven a.m.," he said, pointing. "Biscuits, eggs, and bacon. Coffee. Three dollars a person. Checkout is at eleven a.m."

I fought the urge to ask if he had heard any updates on the situation in the West, but I saw no TV or radio. With a nod, I said thank you again.

Just then a gray cat jumped on the counter. I gasped.

"Awww!" Will leaned in to pet the cat.

Thick eyebrows lifted over Frank's eyes. "Oh, Lucky's a good ol' boy. He'd love a nice pet or scratch," he said in response to my questioning look.

Will was already stroking him. The lanky, long-haired cat pushed its black nose into Will's hand, purring loudly.

"You got a cat, too?" the man asked.

"Yes! His name is Snow. But he isn't white. He's all black! Like the color of your skin, mister," Will said, nuzzling the cat.

I repressed a moan. The man smiled, wrinkles creasing around his eyes. "Fabulous name for a cat. Lucky here was named after a few of his early mischievous years."

Will perked up. "Did he make a lot of poor choices?"

"You could say that." The man's smile widened, displaying coffee-stained teeth. "He got chased by a coyote once. Then got himself stuck in a fence. Another time, he wandered off and got too close to a porcupine. Tillie was pulling quills out of him for two weeks!"

Will continued to rub the cat. "Sounds like my brother Finn. He gets into trouble a lot."

That was my cue. "Come, Will."

"Enjoy your stay," the man said with a wave as we left the office.

After replenishing supplies in the camp store, setting up our tent campsite, and triple-checking my car locks, I brought Will—and a large kitchen knife, which I hid in my towel—with me to the showers.

"Mom, I hate showers! I'm not that dirty," he protested, turning to leave.

I spun him gently by his shoulders. "Let me see your nails." I reached. He showed them to me.

"Were you *eating* dirt?"

"Mom…," he said, his face dimpling the way it did whenever I teased him lightly.

"Joking," I said with a kiss on his cheek. "You first."

"This is the girl's bathroom."

I gave him a look not to be reckoned with. I pulled out the soap and shampoo. "Do you need help?"

"No." He undressed and wrapped a towel around himself, then stepped into the stall. He handed me the towel, then turned on the shower. I sat on the counter, listening to him hum as he washed. I stole a look inside after a few minutes. His body, though wet and cleaned from water hitting it, was not scrubbed. The shampoo had remained untouched, and his hair was bone dry. I took the shampoo and squirted it in my hand and massaged it into his hair.

"Yuck! Mom, that stinks!"

More tersely than I liked, I responded, "Well, it was the only one we had because you and Finn dumped the other bottle in the sink."

He mumbled grievances, but he didn't press it. "Under the water, rinse, all of it," I ordered robotically. "Scrub your neck, Will. Right there." I pointed to the spot on his neck and behind his ears where the dirt and dead skin accumulated.

A few minutes later, he was dressed, hair patted flat, and sitting in my place. I stepped into the shower. "I remember when you were a baby and would keep me company in the bathroom while I showered." I pulled off my towel, tossed it over the shower curtain, and turned on the water.

"Yeah?" His voice lifted with interest.

I poked my head out to be gifted with a wide smile, short a few teeth, grinning at me. He loved to hear his baby stories. "Yup! You'd sit on the floor, content to play with your toys while Mama showered." A twinge of sad nostalgia infiltrated that sweet memory. My yet-to-be diagnosed son exhibited such joy in keeping himself quietly entertained even at six months old. Lord, he had been an easy baby. Finn had never done that. I was lucky to get a daily shower with an investigative toddler tottering around and a screaming newborn that was only appeased in his swing. They couldn't have been more opposite in that regard.

I shifted gears. "Will, tell me about your favorite parts from our Yellowstone trip." Talking about the volcano was the last thing I wanted, but I needed to hear his voice. I needed to make sure he was okay and right beside me. He was an affectionate, tender, and inquisitive child. His personality reminded me so much of his father.

I inhaled the tangy mint of Harrison's tea-tree shampoo, the only one I'd had on hand in my frantic haste. This shampoo, like many of Harrison's things, had remained untouched in the past year. I couldn't bring myself to use it or toss it. Now here I was, scrubbing my fingers raw as I massaged it into my scalp. It tingled. It burned.

Will rattled off about Grand Prismatic Spring's rainbow of colors and steam percolating the sulfur-infused air. Then he talked about the shape of the lower Yellowstone Falls, how the water cascaded straight along one side but curved on the left side, due to the geology beneath it. He talked about how much fun he had with the infrared thermometer gun, detecting the high temperatures of the hot springs in Upper Geyser Basin. How Finn dropped the gun and Brandon had to squeeze through the railing and hop down to the delicate crust to get it from the edge of Morning Glory Pool. Thankfully, neither it nor Brandon had fallen in!

His enthusiasm was a comforting melody on my ears, and the warm shower a hug to my soul. God, I missed hugs. I missed Harrison's lithe arms around me. I missed his kisses on my neck. I missed my sweet Finn's exuberance and back-scratch requests.

As I scrubbed away the dirt, I scrubbed away the painful recollections. Salty, quiet tears fell down my cheeks. I'd truly not let myself cry much on this journey. I couldn't. Even in the past year, I hid the tears from the boys. I had to. I had to be strong for my sons. I'd gotten through Harrison's death; I could get through this journey, too. Finn would be with us soon.

Like Will, Harrison had been quirky. He and I had both suspected that he hung on the very high end of the autism spectrum, too. Harrison had prospered in life, partly due to Patsy's diligence. He'd acquired the coping skills, attended the best schools, and worked hard. Albeit, he may have been socially awkward at times, but oh, I loved him. I loved his eccentricities. Only recently had Patsy admitted that the words autism and ADHD were thrown at her by doctors when Harrison was a child in the early years of diagnosis. Her revelation explained a lot about Harrison and gave me renewed hope for Will's future. When a person dies, all that remain are the good memories…the bad ones seem to disappear like vapors, and longing and regret dwell in your spirit.

I stood under the water, done with my cleaning, but needing the massage against my tired heart. Will spoke about a geyser, asking me questions about eruption frequency. I mumbled some "uh-hmms" and "yeahs."

Finn had loved the Upper Geyser Basin as much as Will. A tightness filled my chest. I had to find him. I had to find Finn. *Oh, Harrison, be his guardian angel. Watch over my brother and our son.*

The water transformed to pins barraging my skin, my muscles unusually sensitive. I swallowed, triggering a scratchy throat. I vainly willed the cold away. Or was I already reeling from withdrawal symptoms? I had felt subpar ever since we'd left Maine. No amount of orange juice or elderberry would deflect this attack on my stressed body. I eventually turned off the water, dried, and got dressed. I slipped on Harrison's oversized slippers, my daily companion since his death. He'd teased me for always stealing them from him. I'd told him that I liked to walk in his footsteps.

"Ready?" I asked Will, who had shaped his wet towel into a volcano.

A few hours later, after enjoying fire-roasted hotdogs, I tucked Will in with a kiss. I laid my trusty hiker's whistle, more for my sake than his, next to his pillow.

"Why do I need that?"

"To scare off bears." *And creepy strangers*, I wanted to add. I was taking no chances after those truck goons.

"Mom, can you sing the states song?"

"Sure," I said and reluctantly sang his favorite song that I had taught him years ago—all the states of the U.S.A. in alphabetical order. I found myself stumbling on the last lines of it when it got to "north, south, east, west," but I finished it with a smile and a stroke of Will's hair.

"Will you stay with me until I fall asleep?"

I did, and he fell asleep quickly. Pain prickled my spirit. I'd never consulted Will on his feelings about leaving on this trip. Or how he felt about Finn being missing. We had to be strong together. We could do this.

We could do this. We had to. There was no other option.

I was about to rise and dampen the fire, when I heard the shushing of rubber tires kicking dirt. I grabbed my kitchen knife and popped out of the tent as I heard a voice say, "Hello?"

Across from the low-burning fire, about ten feet away, stood the man who had helped with my flat tire.

I released a startled gasp, followed by an audible sigh. "Jesus!" I said, for lack of better words.

"Hey there," he said again, his hands raised.

"You shouldn't sneak up on people like that!"

"Sorry, I didn't mean to scare you. You won't need that." His wary gaze fell upon the knife.

I probably looked like a crazed person from a horror flick. I didn't release it, and I stepped back a foot.

Strange shadows played across his face. I hated that eerie look firelight cast upon faces. It made everyone appear possessed. "I'm Reid. Reid Gregory," he offered.

"Are you following me?" Quivers scaled my throat. "H-How did you get here?"

"Same way as you."

"You're on a bike," I observed, unconvinced.

"I got a ride in a truck."

I tightened my grip on the knife and stepped closer to the tent, keeping a watchful eye on it, as well as on the campsites around. The noise of the evening had quieted to murmurs as people found their way to their beds or sleeping bags, but there were a few people awake, talking around fires. I could scream and they would come running. "What color truck?"

Now it was his turn to look baffled. He shrugged off his heavy pack, which fell to the ground with a thud, a hiker's metal cup clinking and a water bottle sloshing. "A silver beater. Nice old couple." He stepped no closer but lowered his voice. "Why?" His gaze darted around the various campsites.

"Why are you following us? My tolerance has room for only so many coincidences."

"We travel the same roads, that's all. There aren't many primary interstates leading to Colorado. I saw your car and wanted to check and see how the tire's doing. Mind if we share a fire? No other sites available, but they told me to buddy up at somebody's site."

I stared at his bag for a long moment, shifting my weight between feet.

"How's the tire?" he repeated.

Same roads? I had taken more detours and bypasses than I would have preferred in the last two days. We were no longer on the straightaway west. "How did you know we were going to Colorado?"

He looked at the tent and rubbed his chin while covering a yawn. "Your son said Denver, didn't he?"

Oh, yeah. I blinked away fatigue.

"I got a ride from New York on Route 80 all the way to Chicago, then diverted south on 57," he explained, his eyes on the knife. "You guys okay? You seem…on edge?"

I lowered the knife as my heartbeat slowed a fraction. "Yeah. The tire's okay."

"I parted ways with my ride in Champaign. Legs are beat." He tapped his thighs and moaned. "And my back." He guided his bike to a nearby tree and propped it there.

I turned away briefly and zipped the tent closed. I settled on the log Will had laid for me in front of the tent entrance. My legs could also use a stretch. I blew a breath.

"Can I rest a few?" he asked.

"Sure. Just a few though."

He sat on the ground across from me and the fire. He thumbed in his bag and withdrew a hiker's meal, his water bottle, and a metal cup. Putting it all together, he then nestled the quick meal into the low fire.

I released my grip on the knife and set it beside me.

Thoughtful eyes assessed me, and he stepped closer. He thrust his hand in full greeting. "I'm Reid," he repeated.

I stared at his hand.

"I…" He waited, then retracted his hand.

I found my senses, shoved mine out, and shook his hand, his grip warm and full around mine. "I'm AJ."

Attentive to my moves, he gave me space, outwardly releasing a breath and running a hand through the thick hair at the crown of his head. He looked like he'd not showered in days. The fire glinted off his stubble-covered chin. He reminded me of a damn Hollywood actor I'd seen in a recent movie—a guy who played a cop. Or was the character the criminal in a drug lord's ring? I couldn't remember. I coughed to cover my unease. With it, my headache mounted.

"Did you bypass Chicago?" he asked as he returned to his cooking meal.

"Yeah, we took Route 70 across Ohio and Indiana, but that wasn't any better."

"Smart. The East Coast might still be okay, but the Midwest is an entirely different animal." He looked around the campground and added, "Folks here seem okay, though. Many appear to be passing through, on their way to find family."

"No luck on car rentals?"

He pressed his lips together. "Nope."

"How was Chicago?"

"Not great. The mayor has already instituted strict curfews, and there were a lot of National Guard soldiers present."

"Oh, wow." I heaved a sigh and repeated, quieter, to myself, "Oh, wow."

"Yeah. Curfews, military patrols, limited access to gas and food. No air or train travel. All airlines on the East Coast will be grounded soon. I was fortunate to find this nice couple heading south. No ash fall in Chicago yet, but your typical societal disorder after a natural disaster." He shook his head as if erasing some thought, then stirred his meal as it cooked. "It wasn't good," he said solemnly. "I think the shit is going to hit the fan soon."

"Yeah."

"No apocalypse though," he said with a hesitant smile, mimicking my remark from our previous encounter.

"Ha, yeah." My lack of much meaningful adult conversation in the past year left me at a loss for words.

He wrapped a handkerchief around his hand, then removed his cup from the fire and stirred its contents. "So, you're going to Denver?"

"We are. My brother and son are there."

"I'm heading there, too. Well, south of Denver, closer to Colorado Springs and Pueblo area."

"Oh?" My pulse fluttered. Uncertainty slithered into my mind. My fingers moved slowly toward the knife, but I stopped them. That was purely coincidence, that's all. Or was it?

"My sister's there."

"Have you heard from her?"

He shook his head. "No. I need to get to her. Our parents have both passed away, and well…older brother syndrome. Gotta check on her."

So communication was already impaired. That would explain why I couldn't reach anything in Colorado via phone or email. My optimism faded as I pictured what lay ahead for us there. I nibbled on my lip.

"What about your brother and son? Have you heard from them?"

"No." *And now my laptop is gone, so I can't even try email.* "Have you been in touch with anyone else there? Any idea what to expect?"

He shook his head and took a few bites of his meal.

I mulled over the information.

"AJ? Is that short for something?" His eyes, now black in the dimness, danced with interest in the firelight.

"Yeah," I said with a light smile of my own.

He swallowed and drew curious eyes slowly up and down. Assessing? Flirting? Deducing?

I shifted and poked at the fire with a stick.

"Alexis Joan?"

"Nope."

Now he smirked. Not only did he look spooky in the firelight, but he looked…mischievous?

"Alice Jennifer?"

I smiled deeper, to my surprise. "Nope."

"Angelina Jean?"

I snorted.

He ate in silence. I watched in silence.

"Thank you for sharing the fire." He put his backpack on with a wince. "All my years of hiking and biking haven't taught me to pack a light load."

"Good night, Reid."

"Good night, AJ," he said, rising. Seemingly more weighed down by thoughts than the heavy pack, he left, his bike swishing slowly in the night. He paused and turned over his shoulder. "I'll be just over there," he said with a flick of his chin.

"Okay."

Soon, it was me and the sounds of katydids and crickets of late summer night. Their ch-ch-ch humming was melodic, seductive, and soothing. My eyes grew heavy.

I waited until Reid was out of sight and sound before I retreated to my tent. My sleeping bag awaited me. I went to untie my bootlaces but stopped myself. Deciding to keep them on, I crawled into my bag. I laid the kitchen knife beside me, on the opposite side from Will, and then picked up the tire iron, hugging the cold steel against my chest as I struggled to go to sleep, allowing the insects' evening music to lull me. I inhaled the scent of Will's fresh, clean hair and then closed my eyes.

In the early morning hours of daybreak, while Will slept peacefully beside me, I opened my journal. To my delight, I found a map neatly drawn on the inner flap. *Will*, I thought, shaking my head in fondness. He had drawn an approximate blast zone around Wyoming, complete with labeled cities, a volcano in the middle of Yellowstone spewing ash into the air, and a tiny airplane near Denver.

Beside it was our black cat. Snow had a frown.

Will's cute drawing of Snow, even if he did have a frown, spurred me to write about the good I'd experienced since his diagnosis and since Harrison's death. There was hope and humanity out there. I needed to know how to find it and move past my anxiety. My mind briefly darted to my pill supply, but I nixed that. I needed to learn to reset my thinking.

After writing, I tiptoed outside. A thick haze hung in dawn's bright orange glow. Pink hues outlined a sky filled with earth's viscera, the clouds burdened with secrets. They were changing, no longer buoyant and feathery. I could almost taste the metallic rock and glass in the air.

Birds chirped by a nearby stream.

I wasn't the only one awake. I heard the whirring shush of a bike and clank of a metal cup.

*There are good people in this world*, I encouraged myself.

*There are.*

I found myself gravitating toward the sound and taking a deep plunge of trust.

Chapter Six
Reset

"Do you like volcanoes?" Will asked, flipping through his book.

"I suppose it depends on what kind," Reid responded from the seat beside me.

"Why should that matter? Oh, you mean like a stratovolcano, cinder cone, shield, or a fissure? I like the stratovolcano...no wait, the cinder cone. They're not as massive though. We climbed one in Craters of the Moon in Idaho. Finn ran ahead of us all the way. Uncle Brandon chased after him. Mom and I took longer. So which kind?"

With an indirect glance, I saw a smile crack Reid's face.

"He won't stop until you answer. Once you humor him, there's no going back." As I said it, I was surprised to find the trace of a smile part my own lips and work underused muscles. I coughed and flinched at the pain in my throat as I fought the truth that a cold was upon me. With a jittery hand, I grabbed the water bottle and took a few sips to abate that thought.

"Well, I like cinder cones, too. Interesting that we both like the same kind."

Will pulled out a fresh piece of paper and clipped it to his clipboard. "What are you going to call it?"

Reid searched my face for help. "All volcanoes

have names," I clarified, lifting an eyebrow.

"What do you name yours?" Reid asked.

"Mine have all different names. Mantumbo, Punoko...," Will said. "Finn makes up funnier names."

Reid glanced at the *Peregrine's Atlas* I had wedged between the seats. "Peregrine Cone. How's that sound?"

"I'm not sure if there are falcons there."

"Huh?" Reid asked.

"You need to watch animal documentaries, Mr. Gregory," I said lightly. "Peregrine falcons."

"I suppose I do. And it's Reid. Don't need to feel my age."

"Okay, we'll use it anyway and pretend there are falcons there. Mom doesn't like volcanoes anymore." Will lapsed into silent drawing mode.

I tried to not pass too many inquiring glances to our new travel companion. What were the appropriate conversation topics for this type of journey? A guy I'd just met was riding in my passenger seat.

A stranger was in my car as passenger and copilot.

A gosh-darn stranger.

And here I'd thought I'd wised up after the robbery, gun altercation, and the thugs in the red pickup. Yet...this guy seemed different. Perhaps I was being a hopeful romantic, or I believed in goodness in humanity. My radar beep just didn't go off with this man. *God, let me be right. Let me trust again.* What was a world without humanity and trust? I had to start somewhere. I had to believe.

Waves of wheat and cornstalks lined the highway as I drove, lost in a pool of thoughts.

Reid speaking shook me to the present a short

while later. "I think we should stay south on Route 57, then go west on 60." The *Peregrine's Atlas* lay open across his lap.

"Isn't that out of the way?" I tapped my fingers on the steering wheel. More detours?

He cleared his throat and lowered his voice. "Chicago was *bad*. St. Louis may be the same or worse. We're getting closer." He cast a look upon the fields that surrounded us. "We should avoid populated cities until we can't, even if it seems like it'll take longer. If that sounds like a good plan with you? Your car, your decision."

"Yeah. Sounds like a good plan."

"I'll tell you more about Chicago later," he added in a whisper.

Well, if that didn't make me shiver, I wasn't sure what would.

"I heard you!" Will said.

I shared a resigned look with Reid. "The cities aren't the only places with unrest, though," I added, my stomach coiling in remembrance.

"Yeah!" Will said. "We got robbed at a gas station, and some guys tried to break into our car while we were sleeping."

I focused ahead of us, feeling a flush of shame cross the bridge of my nose and flood my cheeks.

Reid's voice lowered. "I'm sorry that happened. You guys okay?"

"Yeah, we're fine."

"Mom drove really fast!" Will said.

I grimaced at Reid.

His eyes said it all. "And a popped tire. Bad luck."

"Yeah, you can say that."

Grayness hung in the air, and it quickly suffocated my spirit like a smothering cloud. We now drove through what might as well have been a soggy and foreboding charcoal wall. Even with the closed windows, it engulfed me. Rain slowly splattered the windshield, and I turned on the wipers. My blood pressure escalated. I'd hated rain before Harrison's car accident. Now…

I tightened my grip on the wheel in hopes to alleviate the tingles in my fingertips. I turned on the headlights.

Only two pills left now. As sorely as I wanted one, I couldn't take it now, and not in front of this stranger.

Because I had listening ears in the back seat, I ventured a neutral conversation with Reid. "Where are you from originally, Mr. Greg—Reid? Did you grow up in Colorado?"

He rubbed his chin and cleared his throat. "I was born near West Point, New York, but my parents moved around a lot and settled in Colorado. Army brat who became an army grad."

"Have you served overseas?"

"Two tours."

"My brother was in the air force. He does security work now and lives in California with his wife and daughters. They're near San Diego."

"Ah, nice. Never been, though we moved a lot." Reid closed the atlas and sipped his water. "My father was originally from Pueblo, Colorado. My mom was from Poza Rica, Mexico. She came here when she was twenty. Met my dad while in college in Colorado," he said casually. "They moved to New York, where my sister and I were born, and then they lived in Texas near

Fort Hood. They eventually retired in Denver."

"Lots of moving for you guys."

He shook his head. "Yeah. The army shuffle. Sorry, you didn't need to hear the entire Gregory family history there. I got carried away."

"Nah, that's okay. So, you know the Denver area well?"

"Pretty well."

"Then I'm lucky you needed a ride, huh?" I said lightly though my pulse quickened with his affirmation.

"Perfect timing or amazing coincidence," he added.

*And hopefully not more crummy luck.* "I'm not one to put much stock in coincidence. I'm more of a fate gal." *Did I really just say that?* More importantly, did I really believe that?

Reid scratched at the coarse stubble on his chin. "Your son is there? Your brother is with him?"

"That's the ironic thing. We just returned from a family trip, yeah. Our flight had been overbooked and delayed, so my brother stayed behind with my other son, Finn. They were supposed to have boarded a plane in Salt Lake City, and the first layover was in Denver. I think they made it as far as Denver at least before it all went to shit."

No reprimand came from Will, although I knew without a doubt he'd heard me swear.

I continued, "Perhaps they'd likely be in one of FEMA's shelters or a mobile hospital or maybe an air force base?" I sighed. I couldn't remember any of the bases in Colorado. Perhaps a few were listed in the atlas. All of Brandon's talks in his heyday of the air force, and I couldn't remember a damn thing. I swear all the information inputted into my brain before kids had been emptied into abyssal trashcans somewhere, unable to be retrieved.

"Yeah, my thinking, too. It depends on how fast FEMA sets up the shelters and where the mobile hospitals are located. I know a few of the shelters based in the area, too. How old's Finn?" Reid asked.

I swallowed. "Seven."

"Man…a little guy," Reid said. "Where'd you last hear from them?"

My grip tightened on the wheel. "Salt Lake. Brandon texted that he and Finn were boarding. It was several hours before the eruption." I traced a thumb on my throat and coughed, my memory sluggish, yet I knew the details all too well. "The flight—mine and Will's—was at eleven a.m., but that's Mountain Time. Brandon and Finn's flight was two hours later, at one o'clock. It took them to Denver, with an arrival around three and then a departure at four to a second layover in Dulles, and then on to Portland, Maine." Saying it aloud made my head spin. That was a lot of layovers for my Finn. "I should've heard from Brandon by seven or eight that night, Eastern Time, when they got into Portland on that day. But…"

Reid finished for me. "The eruption began around three thirty, Mountain Time. Right when they were at the Denver Airport?"

"Yeah," I said, miserably. "A substantial quake hit the Denver area. The news showed the airport…" I stopped, not wanting to go into the gory details around Will.

He was immune to it anyway. "It got wrecked!" Will chimed in with sound effects of explosions and wild hand gestures. "Now that I think of it, Mom, I don't think Finn would've seen the eruptive column from there. It was too far away. Ash fall though for sure. Lots of damage from the quake!"

I tuned out Will's enthusiasm and calculated again what time Brandon should have returned to Portland. "I've never been to Denver. I'm not sure where to start." For a planner, I was still working on that plan.

"Then it's definitely convenient you found me, huh?"

I turned to him. Friendliness glimmered in his face. I lifted an eyebrow. "Indeed."

Reid's voice was gentle. "I'm sorry about your son. Denver's airport is solid. I saw the news, too, though." He paused for a moment. "I have a few ideas. We can check churches and schools that are designated to be disaster relief stations, as well as military bases and hospitals in the region. You think your brother and son are definitely there? In Denver, I mean? You don't know if they caught their connecting flight to Dulles?"

I shrugged. "I'm not certain. That's the kicker. Maybe his plane took off from Denver and landed elsewhere? They would've been grounded in a safer area if they'd taken off. He would've been able to get through to me though. My last message from him was when he boarded the flight to Denver...if he even got on that flight. They could still be in Salt Lake City." I tightened my grip on the steering wheel with that verbal admittance.

"Perhaps there will be information on the radio as we get closer. We can start with Colorado Springs and work our way north to Denver if—" he said, but cut himself off.

I nodded. "Yeah. If it is all still there."

"It is. Denver was in the outer blast zone. It sustained damage from the quake, but not from the eruption. It'll be okay. Communication may be disabled, but the city is not."

*Salt Lake City is*, I wanted to say but didn't. Not a word from Brandon in the past five days. I nodded nonetheless. "You really don't have to help us once we get there. I can drop you off and you can point me in the right direction…"

"Nah, consider it payment for the ride. My legs will be eternally grateful. Besides, I'm a savvy tour guide."

I cleared my throat and mind. "So, your sister. She lives there, too?"

"Yup. The Gregorys have a soft spot for the Rockies. It's a pretty area year-round. Lily lives near Pueblo. I live in Colorado Springs. I had to travel east for business last week, and then, well, then it all went to shit." He gave me a light smile as he mimicked my words.

I released a "hrmmmph" of acquiescence. "I'm sure she's okay, too. Like you said, that area, south of Denver, seems to be okay." I didn't fully believe the words myself. I'd read one too many chapters in Will's volcano books about the aftereffects of eruptions: telecommunication disruptions, blown power transformers, halted transportation, clogged drainage and sewer systems, soiled water supplies, downed cell towers, collapsed roofs, destroyed crops, and horrible health concerns especially for those with lung or asthmatic issues…and death. So many dead.

I wheezed as if on prompt. Then I coughed. Ouch, pain. I hyper-focused on the lozenges in my first aid kit…that was buried in the car somewhere.

I looked at Will. Not a hint of lung distress in him. Yet.

"Where's a woman named Anna June from?"

"Not even close," I said with a grin. "Pennsylvania Amish country originally."

He raised a thick eyebrow. "Like horses and buggies? Didn't know the Amish could drive SUVs."

A lightness and ease danced in my arms at his airy humor. "New amendment to the rules," I teased.

"I visited Hershey Park once as a kid. Smells like chocolate."

"It does. And manure."

He laughed. I suppressed a chuckle.

Did I just laugh?

"Eww!" Will interjected.

"I now live in Maine."

"Sweet. Never traveled there yet. On the bucket list."

"Oh, you should. They don't call it Vacationland for nothing. Lobsters, lupine, and endless shoreline. Our mountains may not rival the Rockies, but Katahdin can give you a run for the money."

"Sounds lovely. I like a challenging hike. The Appalachian Trail finishes there, right?" He shifted, rubbed his knees.

"Yup."

"Someday, then. I always wanted to do the Pacific Crest Trail but never found a buddy to take it on. Never been sailing either. Colorado's a bit landlocked."

"That it is. We live south of Portland, in Cape Elizabeth, near the coast. Closer to civilization. The area is an outdoors hub." I blinked. The cold must have been screwing with my vision. I blinked again. Nope, it was still there. I nodded toward the windshield. "This rain is gray."

"Yeah, it's dark," Reid said, craning his neck to see the looming clouds above us.

I flipped the wipers to a faster setting. Thunder rolled as distant lightning flashed. I jumped but loosened my grip on the wheel.

"No, I mean it's gray." I pointed toward the windshield. The drizzle smeared across it, and instead of being clear droplets, the ones bubbling on the surface were tinged with gray. I turned off the wipers and stared at the windshield briefly.

"Ash!" Will said what my mind thought. I heard the click of his helmet going on. "Need to be prepared for lava bombs!"

"Will! This is not—" My voice broke. I wheezed, paused, and put on my best supportive, understanding mom hat. "Yes, this is exciting, but we're not close enough for lava bombs. You know that. *And* the volcano has stopped erupting."

"Here." Reid offered me my water bottle from the cup holder. I tossed a glance in the rearview mirror.

Will traced a finger on the window, following the path of droplets that rolled backward. "A new vent could open! That supervolcano hot spot is gigantic. You never know. There could be another eruption!"

I downed a substantial gulp of water.

"We're in the ash-fall zone now," Will continued. "No, wait, it's probably air currents and a cold front bringing it this way. They said ash only fell into Kansas with the initial blast, right? Well, the fatter particles fell first in this zone and then the smaller ones will drift eastward," he said, lifting a drawing on his clipboard and tapping it. "See?"

I half looked to see three concentric color-coded circles over half of the country on his drawing. Ash-fall zones, of course. They were like a drawing I had seen in one of Will's many Yellowstone volcano books and amazingly accurate in comparison to the hypothesized drawings that had been broadcasted on the news stations. I wouldn't expect less from Will.

He scratched his head and looked out the window in awe. "Ash! And if it's an El Niño year, the track can change."

I turned the wipers back on. Screw the ash. I didn't want to see it. Tiny particles of jagged rock and volcanic glass that the earth had spewed in its wrath now fell on my car and would eventually work their way into both my and Will's asthmatic lungs. A cough seized me.

Reid whispered, "Are you okay?"

"I'll be fine." I simmered as I took another gulp of water, my dry mouth not abated.

Will asked, "Can we stop? I need to collect ash."

I clenched my teeth. It didn't help the headache building in the right side of a sinus cavity. I sighed. The volcano had erupted. It was his *moment*. I couldn't fault him for that. Some kids dreamed of amusement parks; he wanted a cool eruption.

"There will be enough ash for us when we reach Colorado."

"Good. I brought a few containers," he said.

I kept my gaze forward, wondering what Reid thought of this interchange. He was quiet and, thankfully, distracted by looking outside. I had stopped apologizing aloud for Will a while ago. Still. That hefty pill was lodged halfway down my throat. *Let it go*, Harrison whispered to me. Or as my girlfriend Siobhan always said, *Let that shit go*. I repressed the urge to spiral into the list of never-gonna-happens. That list was omnipresent and long. I had moved past the verbal apologizing, but I clung to the feeling that sat like an obstinate mule within me. He was still Will. He was that unique boy who loved volcanoes and thought and felt differently than others. He was the boy who brought brightness to my days.

"You're sad, Mom. We'll find Finn. Don't be sad. Maybe he already collected some ash."

"Maybe," I said, turning my lips into a half smile for his sake.

****

We didn't get far.

"I'm sorry," I said. The headache raged in my skull.

"Really, no need to say that," Reid repeated for the third time.

I longed for a hotel bed, but I needed to stay thrifty so camping it was. It was a step up from sleeping in the car again. I watched, bleary, as Reid set to work on the tent. Although I'd become a pro at assembling the two-person tent quickly, it was a welcome to have assistance instead of having Will "help" by playing with the stakes and poles.

I blinked and took in the surroundings. This campground was not as crowded as the previous one. My feminist instinct deplored allowing Reid to take the lead on setting up camp, but I was grateful to have a guy with me. Sure, I had worked my way through a field dominated by men, seen other females pave the path for our generation, but when it came to it, with the current state of our country and where it was likely heading…and especially after the last few days, I felt safer having another person with me. Regardless of gender. I had to be more guarded. Yet, here I was giving a lift to a stranger.

Reid worked, unfazed by the muddy ground.

He knew the area. He was an asset, my mind reasoned. And he was friendly…

"Will, please gather a few branches. Stay where I can see you," I said.

"Okay, Mom."

I found myself amused. He fought me tooth and nail on homework, baths, chores, and a laundry-list of responsibilities, but nature, *that* he loved. He was a true naturalist like his mom and dad. Perhaps this new chaotic world would be better for him. The eruption certainly did open his wishful career path as volcanologist, I thought wryly.

Will hummed as he paused in his collecting to create some sort of structure. "Will, those are for the fire."

He didn't acknowledge me, aware yet oblivious. So much for his help. "No worries. There's more," Reid offered, gathering a few decent-sized logs on the forest fringe.

"I should have brought my cooking stove and canisters. Fires are so old school," I apologized. I hadn't been able to locate Harrison's cooking gear stash in my packing.

"Nah, it's classic and versatile," he countered.

"It certainly limits our food choices," I added.

Soreness rose in my legs. As I paced the campsite, the pinching in the middle of my forehead caused me to stumble, and I grabbed a nearby tree trunk.

Reid stopped in his work and laid a fleeting hand on my back, then dropped it. "You okay?"

"Yeah. Headache. I've got a cold and haven't been sleeping well." *I'm also weaning off an anti-anxiety med*, I wanted to add.

"Why don't you rest? I can handle this. Need to earn my keep."

"Thanks." I breathed through it. It wasn't like my usual migraine. Those took a full day to subside. Something was wrong in the air today, too. Well, something *was* wrong. Ash. The rational scientist in me told me this was not triggered from the ash. My mommy intuition agreed with that deduction because I'd had more illnesses than I could count since having kids. That would explain why Will wasn't affected yet, and I was a stumbling fool. A cold with withdrawal effects made a nasty combo. Toss in asthma-triggering ash, and it wasn't the best recipe.

I sat at the picnic table, sipping tepid water. I rested my head on my arms, pacified by Will's humming and traipsing around with sticks and such.

A short while later, I awoke. I yawned, the painful scratch of a sore throat befalling me as I found the campsite empty. I had fallen asleep?

"Will?"

I looked around. No Will. No Reid.

I hurried to the tent and ducked my head inside. Nope. Dusk loomed, and the scent of cooking dinners and smoky fires filled the air. Too much water in my stomach sloshed. "Will?" I said louder. "Reid?" I pressed a hand to my mouth, willing the nausea away.

My gaze skimmed the area, and on cue, palpitations took hold of me, but oddly my fingers didn't prickle with their usual wary concern. Regardless, my mind's paranoia began its downward spin. No, no, no…

"Here! Here, AJ." Reid approached at a quick gait from a cluster of oaks on the far end of the campsite. Will lollygagged beside him while carrying a muddy cat.

I groaned. I hurried to them and brushed a hand through Will's disheveled hair. "Will…"

He ignored me and stroked the cat, a marbled brown and black furball. "The cat crossed our site, and I followed it. He crawled into a bush over there—" He paused with a flick of his chin to behind him. "—and got stuck! I had to save him. It was a prickly bush!"

I shared my best pissed-off glare with Reid.

He quickly said, "I'm sorry. I tried to wake you. You were passed out. Will's kinda fast though. Didn't want him to wander out of sight. We came right back. Didn't want you to wake up and worry…like you just did. My bad." His wide, cordial smile disarmed me but didn't settle my racing pulse.

"We were gonna check and see if the camp manager knows whose cat this is. See, look? Tags," Will said. "Maybe if we can't find his home, he can come home with us. Snow needs a friend."

"I was going to wake you before we went to the office," Reid added.

I tried my best thank-you look with Reid. A short while later, after depositing the cat with the clerk, we enjoyed, if one could refer to it as such, a shared can of chili with bread we purchased at the camp store.

"I need it warmed with butter," Will moaned as I handed him a piece.

"Don't have any. Plain bread will do."

Will wrinkled his nose. "I never eat bread without butter. That chili smells gross! I like yours better, Mom. You're making that slurping sound when you eat it." He pouted, dimples appearing high on his cheeks.

Now was not the time for me to push on the eating front. "Have a banana and pepperoni instead."

Will dug through our bin of food and found what he needed. An evening breeze blew past me, and I shivered despite wearing a thick hoodie. Will stoked the fire with a branch, and I shifted closer to it.

My diamond wedding band twinkled back at me as I twirled it around using the tip of my thumb. The light of the fire cast shimmers of blue and yellow in the simple princess-cut facets. Reid's glance fell upon me. "Is your husband in Denver, too, with your brother?"

"No." Bread caught in my throat, as I swallowed another bite of the awful truth. I never pretended it didn't happen. I blocked it the best a widow with two spirited, challenging sons could.

Instead of eating, Will moved on to collecting stones to create miniature cairns. "Dad's in heaven." He paused in his collecting, handing me one of the rocks. "For Finn, Mom."

Heat flooded my cheeks, and an ache clutched my heart at his indifference. Will had come a long way in the past year with accepting Harrison's passing.

"I'm sorry," Reid said, his expression pensive, his words sedate.

I waved a glib hand but said, "Thanks."

"Were you visiting your brother in Salt Lake City, then, for vacation?"

I realized belatedly that I'd never elaborated upon that part. "Oh, yeah, my brother met us there. He flew from San Diego, and we met him for a family vacation." I sipped my water, the feel of the bread, although long since swallowed, lingering in my throat.

"Ah."

"We went to Yellowstone!" Will added.

Reid swiped a hand through his hair. "No way?"

I nodded. "Way."

Will interjected, "Yeah! We were there *right* before it went kablooey!" He tipped one of his cairn piles for effect.

"Wow," Reid said. He shuffled a few logs around to encourage the fire, which had trouble keeping a strong flame.

Will restacked the rocks. "We also visited a bunch of other parks—the Tetons, Craters of the Moon, Mount St. Helens, and Crater Lake. It was a volcano vacation!"

Reid's gaze passed between an excited Will and my certainly dour expression.

Will rattled on, "I guess some of those aren't there anymore, huh? Well, the Tetons and Craters of the Moon for sure. Not sure about the others. I don't think Washington or Oregon were impacted as much as Idaho and Wyoming. Yellowstone is not there! Did you see the pictures on the news? Obliterated!"

Reid nodded, his attention now focused solely on Will. "I did."

So had I. A magma chamber of grand proportion that had bubbled beneath Yellowstone had unleashed a fiery storm in the blink of an eye. "Will, how big was the magma chamber?"

"Twenty-five by fifty miles, Mom. The chamber can fill ten Grand Canyons."

Tremendous ground drop and collapse. All those magnificent mountains—gone, swallowed into the belly of the earth. Several vents had erupted lava and ash into the air. Lahars had rushed down the larger mountains and destroyed thousands of acres of woodland. Rivers, lakes, wildlife—gone. All those entrancing rainbow hot springs—gone. People. So many people—dead. All of it wiped away within minutes and hours. It had not been a slow eruption. Violent and quick. The world caught unaware. Not supervolcanic level, but...

I rubbed my forehead. The smoke from the fires in the campground was especially permeating, and my head wasn't any better after eating. My throat throbbed. The facts were daunting. I felt like shit.

Will came over. He sat beside me on the log and lifted my hand. He then kissed it with tender affection. I smiled. "Thanks, honey." Just as quickly, he ambled to his cairns. He began to construct a bridge with sticks between two cairn piles.

Reid quietly watched us but said nothing. I caressed a thumb on the back of my hand where Will's wet lips had been. When he was younger, he used to go up to strangers and kiss their hands or rub their bellies as he spoke to them. I'd chalked it to his curiosity and the way he communicated with people—he loved to touch. Perhaps it was his way of connecting with them when he couldn't on the same neurological level. When he'd kissed a random stranger's hand while we were at the dry cleaners one day, it had finally signaled a trigger of unease in my mind. It wasn't usual for kids to do that. He'd been four years old then.

He had quirks I'd disregarded for years.

My head grew foggier, and I coughed.

"How are you doing?" Reid asked.

"Not so hot. A cold. Migraine." *Medication withdrawal,* I didn't add again.

I glanced at my watch. It was only seven p.m., but I was spent. "Will, let's get you ready for bed."

"Aww, Mom. You said I can stay up later in the summer."

"I'm tired today, Will. We can have an early start tomorrow."

I gave Reid a questioning glance. He nodded. "I'll stay awake and wait for the fire to die. I've got a sleeping bag here."

"Thank you."

I then tucked Will in, curled next to him, tire iron in my hand, my head roaring. Will wiggled and insisted that I sing. After, he spoke in a happy whisper.

"I like this guy, Mom. He doesn't seem like a bad guy."

"No, he doesn't," I mumbled, but tightened my grip on both Will and the iron nonetheless. "No wandering off after more cats, okay?"

"But—"

"William..."

"Okay. Night, Mom."

\*\*\*\*

My body may have been tired, but my mind certainly hadn't gotten the memo. I awoke sometime in the middle of the night for fresh air. The rain had not abated the muggy Midwest August heat. I stepped out of the stifling tent, swimming through the dark, damp air and into more mugginess.

I gasped. Reid was leaning against a tree with a headlamp on and was thumbing through a thin paperback.

"Sorry. Trouble sleeping?" he said.

"Yeah," I said, a hand pressed to my startled heart. I closed the tent flap while I recovered myself. "I never sleep well while camping." I turned to face him. "You've been lugging around books in that thing?" I pointed toward his large pack.

He laughed quietly. "Ah, yeah, a few. Going across the country can be a lonely process. Too much time with my own thoughts."

"You're telling me."

He added, "Why not read someone else's instead?" The fire had long since extinguished, and he had the look of a spelunker with the headlamp on.

I shielded my eyes from its glare.

"Oops. Sorry." He removed it and placed it beside him, the light's beam angled away from my face. He reached into his pack, withdrew a lollipop, and unwrapped it. "Want one?"

He stood, shuffled over, and clicked on my lantern that I'd left on the picnic table.

"No, thanks. Sweet tooth?"

A full smile parted his lips. "You bet. A man's gotta have his vices, right?"

I pointed to the book. "Learn anything profound?"

"Nothing I didn't already know." He raised the flappy paperback, and I squinted to read the title.

"*The Great Divorce*? Heavy reading," I commented, recalling the other C. S. Lewis works I'd read in college. I scratched my head, grasping for the theme of this one.

My unconvinced look must've reflected my questions as I sat across from him.

"It's about a man's journey between heaven and hell." His mouth curved with a weighted sadness. "My sister always liked Lewis. I decided it was time I read his work and find out why. I'm a late bloomer with books. I can see the allure now."

"Deep philosophical reads are your way of diving in? Why not start with some thrillers or suspense?"

He shook the thinner, flimsy book, and said, "It's lightweight for travel and keeps my gears turning. Good book-club material. Besides, we have suspense around us right now."

Except it was not fiction. Both of us knew his attempt at lighthearted banter wasn't working.

Instead, we sat, adrift with our thoughts.

I coughed, wishing I'd brought my water bottle out of the tent with me. A yawn reminded me I needed to sleep, but then Reid spoke. "Your son, Will, he…" He scratched his chin as if he didn't know how to raise the subject.

"He's autistic. Well, technically it's Asperger's syndrome, but that label's obsolete now since his diagnosis," I said matter-of-factly, too tired to tiptoe around the subject.

Reid nodded. "Ah. I see."

More introspective silence came from my companion. At least he didn't give me the pity look or the "I'm sorry" or the "It's a blessing" bullshit. My headache inched up the base of my neck toward my skull. A wave of dizziness assaulted me. I breathed through it and grappled with what to say next. Small talk with adults felt alien. The usual parent-to-parent conversations with carpool moms had become stilted these days.

"Do you ever ask why things happen?"

*All the time.* I brushed a hand over my face. "Why *what* things happen?"

"Why the eruption? Why autism?" he said bluntly.

Well, if seeing him reading a classic C. S. Lewis book in the night had surprised me, this nearly floored me. My brain wasn't on prime functioning mode right now. "We've all had times when we've asked why. Just spare me the pity."

"I didn't mean it that way. I'm not one to pity another. Life throws a lot of shit at us."

My hands grew clammy, and I licked my lips. Fatigued and intrigued, I leaned forward. "Okay, I bite. Why?"

"What if the eruption was God's way of resetting man? And—" He paused, looking at the tent for the briefest of moments. "—autism is God's way of resetting humanity. Time for a redo."

I must've looked skeptical and if I had my water bottle, I would've snorted the water. "You've been taking your Lewis to heart. The volcano is science. Period."

He continued, "You're not a woman of faith?"

"I take it you're a man of such beliefs?" I pointed to his book. I was no stranger to C. S. Lewis's theological bent. I remembered that much.

He shrugged. "I'm the product of your typical Catholic upbringing. No shortage of icons in our house, weekly CCD classes, and routine confessions. My mom did a lot of charity work for church, tried hard to mold

Lily and me into well-balanced, compassionate, caring people...," he said, his voice fading. He cleared his throat. "I've traveled some long roads. Have had a lot of time to think...about stuff. Yeah, I guess I am a man of faith...of some sort."

I swallowed, my mouth cottony. I still questioned life's ultimate purpose, but my faith had always remained steadfast in the darkest of days. At least I thought it had. I was beginning to question that now.

There was a long moment. I shifted my weight, uncomfortable with the scrutiny his face held.

"I hate labels," I finally said.

"Me, too. Sometimes kids need labels to get the help they need through our system."

"They do."

"He's very borderline?" Reid said perceptively.

"Yeah." I shrugged. "We live in the land of gray. People don't know what to think about us."

"I like the fringe," Reid said with a kindhearted smile.

It had an appeasing effect on me. "You're a rebel, huh?"

"Sometimes."

"You're familiar with autism?"

"My sister works with kids on the spectrum. Teaches a special-needs class."

"Ah. So, God created autism to reset humanity? And the eruption..." There, I'd said both words. It wasn't too hard, even if they felt like poison sliding off my tongue. "...was like the Great Flood, to reset man?" There were many parts in the Bible that I had trouble believing.

"Why not?" His sincere smile ruffled the lines

around his mouth. "We—*people*—have become infatuated with technology, busy schedules, social status...all of it. It got to be too much. We've developed new idols. We've lost faith. Look at what's happening. Wars of all kinds are contaminating our world. Then autism arises at an alarming rate. Certainly it's existed for a long time, but the rate increased incredibly. Coincidence? No. And we know you don't believe in that."

I nodded. Reid was an exceptional listener.

"Genetics? Maybe. Vaccines?"

I grunted.

He laughed. "Hell no, right? Pesticides? I doubt it. God?" Long pause.

I shook my head. "God."

"Yeah, God..."

"You're going deeper than my brain can handle tonight, Reid."

"Bear with me a moment...I'm on a roll here."

I shifted, wary, drained. "Okay." Faith. Fate. Coincidence. What *did* I believe?

"...or maybe it's just a power greater than us. Autistic people tend to appreciate the details and view our world differently. The hidden gems that we neurotypicals miss. The beauty in that line of ants making for the anthill, the puddles filling with water, the curvature of rocks, the workings of gears...whatever it is. They're attuned to their environment, their senses...the world. They don't give a shit what other people think. They're loyal, hardworking. Maybe they have deeper access to areas of the brain we can't reach yet. They return us to the simpler things of life. How could that not be God resetting us? Maybe one day we'll all have autism. They don't know of a definitive cause. Maybe we're evolving to a new way of being. I'm not a neuroscientist, so take all my musings with a grain of salt."

For an avid talker, I was without words as I digested his reasoning. I blew a breath but nodded in resignation. "The eruption? It wasn't big enough to…to destroy the world. It wasn't a supervolcanic eruption. Life-altering for years to come, yes. Humankind-ending, no."

"True. But life is going to change for decades to come. Perhaps it was time for another clean slate."

"Another flood?" I concluded for him.

He nodded, pursing his lips. "Another flood. Just on a smaller scale."

\*\*\*\*

Despite my middle of the night rising and way too thought-provoking conversation with Reid, I slept solidly and, for the first time since news of the eruption, without a dream about Finn. A sweet, dark oblivion had detained my overworked brain.

Expecting to hear Will's light snoring beside me, instead I found an empty sleeping bag and whistle beside it. Prickles of pain ran throughout my arm which had apparently become lodged beneath my body and the tire iron. I wiggled my arm and pumped my fist to encourage blood flow.

I had to stop waking like this. "Will?" I said, already reaching to unzip the tent flap. What happened to my rigid rule-follower?

"Here," Reid's voice broke in.

I hurried out of the tent. Panic thankfully didn't

have time to set in, for both Will and Reid strode toward our campsite, each carrying a steaming cup of—

"Coffee, Mom!" Will said, handing me the one he carried as if he were cradling a baby crocodile that might snap at him. His face shone with pride.

I gave Reid a stern look and then turned to Will. Oh my God, this child had to stop walking off! Or else I needed to give up on sleep. I'd become *that* mom, from movies, who didn't keep a close eye on her kid while monsters or aliens tormented the living.

"Thank you, Will. Honey, please, don't go off alone like that, okay?" Frogs, cats, and now off with a stranger. My heart couldn't take more of this.

Will made for the picnic table.

"Will…," I said, raising my voice.

"I wasn't alone. I was with Reid. Look what I found at the sandbox near the playground!" He dug into his pockets and splayed his bounty, a rainbow of plastic Lego bricks. "Can I keep them?"

I gave him an "I love you but don't do that again" hug. "Next time, take your whistle, okay?" I whispered.

"I was with Reid, and I didn't need to worry about bears."

"Will…"

"Okay, Mom. Okay."

"Sorry, AJ. I didn't mean to worry you. He woke up a while ago and popped out. I tried to keep him busy while you slept, but he got fidgety and he mentioned you love coffee." He pointed to the flattened lollipop wrapper that sat under my water bottle near the opening of my tent. "I left you a note."

I picked it up and read the few words scribbled with a permanent marker. A pursed my lips. "A pop wrapper?"

He shrugged. "Yeah. Gotta use what I have." His dark eyes held mine. "We grabbed some coffee from the store at the office. I shouldn't have let him come along without asking, but I didn't want to bother you. My apologies," Reid said.

I waved his apology away. "It's okay. Next time wake me, okay?"

"Promise. Sorry." He sipped his own coffee. "Hey, so I glanced at your arsenal in the car."

I lifted an eyebrow.

"Will showed me."

I muffled a grunt.

"...you left it unlocked. You really are ready for the apocalypse." His lips curled into a devilish grin.

"I left it unlocked?"

"Yeah."

I puckered my lips. I swiped a hand through my hair. I must have been more out of it yesterday than I had thought. "One can never be too prepared. I had more than that before the jerks robbed me in New York."

Will was already playing with the Lego bricks on the table. He dipped into his plastic bag of mini-figures and bricks, pushing them around to find the right one. A dozen yellow pieces were carefully lined up in a row on the weather-worn wooden table.

"I also love coffee. Thanks," I said. I sighed with the first sip.

"Hey, so I'm sorry about last night."

"What do you mean?"

"All that end of the world talk and stuff. Two in the morning is not the best time for deep philosophical questions." He shifted his gaze toward Will.

"It's okay. Really. And two a.m. is the perfect time. This kind of event makes us ponder the big questions." A genuine smile creased my lips, and I momentarily forgot how tired and achy I was. I then called to Will, "Fifteen minutes, Will." I turned to Reid. "Then we go."

Chapter Seven
Without

Southern Illinois moved like molasses.

Even with our detour taking us south of St. Louis, my hopes to make it to Kansas without delay were quickly fading.

Reid sat behind the driver's wheel. *Leaps of faith, AJ.* I yawned. I refused to let myself sleep.

"I didn't mean to upset you this morning," Reid said.

"It's okay," I said, sipping my now cold, but still delicious, coffee. I wanted to savor it. Reid or Will had guessed correctly—more cream than sugar. "No need to keep apologizing. You're sounding like me now."

"You feel better?"

"Not really…"

"You were wheezing last night."

"You heard me?"

He shrugged. "The night is quiet, except for the sounds of people sleeping."

"Don't sleep much, Reid?"

"Not much these days. I can get by on less."

"You spend your time reading the classics and pondering life's grand questions." I meant it as a jab, but it came out harsher than intended.

"Sometimes." He flashed me a sideways frank glance. "Like I said, my sister, Lily, she works with special kids..." He broke off, but his gaze went to the rearview mirror. Will was happily playing with his Lego bricks, apparently having built a ship for his figures to fly around in. He made blaster noises and hummed to himself.

"He knows," I said quietly. I had the talk with Will only recently. He seemed unfazed by it. This admission about a sister working with special-needs children explained Reid's interest in the area.

Reid nodded but said nothing further.

I looked at my phone for the hundredth time. No messages from Brandon, Sarah, or Dr. Martin. It was time to make my daily futile calls to the airline and several others that I'd listed in case Brandon had changed airlines, as well as to Brandon, but I paused. "Do you have a smartphone?"

Reid's eyebrows shot up but quickly settled in place. "Yeah, but it's not working well. You can try." He pulled it from his shirt pocket and handed it to me. "You don't have one?"

"Thanks. Nope. I'm a bit slow on accepting technology. And my laptop was stolen."

"You've had a fun run of it, hey?"

I snorted. "You can say that."

I first dialed Brandon. Nothing. Then the airport. Nothing. Then the airline. I refrained from the phone call to Dr. Martin in Reid's presence. I could try her later. Geesh, this was getting old. I felt like a frustrated child who couldn't accomplish a simple task. Channeling my inner Finn, who notoriously pitched a fit when a contraption of his wouldn't work "just so," I stifled a groan. "Can I try my email?"

"Of course. Don't want to dash your hopes, but

I've had no luck with anyone west of the Mississippi."

I tried anyway. I typed in the email server, waiting while my mailbox loaded. I thought of the smartphone I'd finally purchased six months ago, now sitting in a box on my dresser, collecting dust. Harrison's jesting tone in my constant reminiscing had coaxed me to buy one. Yet, I couldn't bring myself to use it. All I saw was Harrison, hardworking breadwinner, constantly getting pings of emails at godforsaken hours. Harrison, the man who worked tireless hours, stressed about problems with his preclinical studies, all so he could provide for his family and for Will to receive the extra therapies and care he required. *I just want you to be happy, AJ*, he would say. He had worked hard for me. For us.

And that work had killed him.

A late run to the laboratory on a rainy July night last year due to a technician's mistake had ended it all for him. I'd been humbled that day with my own prophecy. I'd said work was going to kill him. Well, it wasn't work entirely. The drunk driver behind the other car's steering wheel was equally responsible.

*Dammit, AJ. Stop this.* I cursed in my mind for Will's sake.

Finally, the page loaded on the smartphone. Dumb phone, I thought. I found my grip clutching Reid's phone, and I released it into my lap. I gave myself a moment, then checked my email. There was nothing from Brandon. I did have a response from Sarah, which appeared to have been sent a few days ago after my first call to her. I tapped my finger impatiently on my knee as it loaded.

*AJ,*

*I hope you get this email. I wish I could be going with you, and I wish I could dissuade you. No word from Brandon.*

*Travel on the highways in CA is now prohibited. I couldn't even try; there are roadblocks everywhere. Some of the ash cloud has drifted west over northern parts of the state but not here. Still always sunny in San Diego despite wave warnings from the tsunami that hit north and west of us. But we were spared.*

*I know how hard this must be for you right now, with Will and everything that's happened in the past year. Brandon will keep Finn safe. Remember that trip to Acadia when Will wandered off the trail to follow a stream and Brandon found him...right back where we had started, at the campsite? Sometimes I laugh when I think about how much your man Will is so much like your brother. My point is this: Brandon will protect Finn with all his heart, and Will is your sidekick; he'll help you through this. Will is your home base, Sis. He's your constant. He grounds you. And Brandon...he's Mr. Fix-it himself.*

*Geesh, now I am rambling. This is me trying to cheer you up. Maybe myself, too. Love you.*

*I will continue to try the airport and airline. It'll be all right. I know they made it to Denver. They had to.*

*Love always, your sis,*

*Sarah*

"Tsunami?" I said aloud.

"Oh yeah, saw that on the news. Tragic," Reid said.

"Like a big wave?"

"You didn't see? Impacted Japan, Oregon, and Washington. They think since the tremors have settled, there is no need for the raised alarm, but yeah, a lot of people…" He drifted off.

"Died," Will finished for him. "It was on the radio, Mom."

I shook my head as I typed a quick response to let her know where I was, but after another five minutes of waiting for the email to send, I gave up. "Thanks." I handed it to Reid.

"Sorry," he said, dropping it into the cup holder.

We drove for a while, all of us quiet as Reid weaved through increasingly congested traffic. I thought about Will. I thought about Finn. I thought about what could be, should be…and what had been.

"What do you want to do about this?" Reid said.

The traffic jam had thickened to a near standstill. I grabbed the atlas. "I don't know this area at all. What do you think?"

"It's your car. It's your decision."

"Mom's not great at making up her mind," Will interjected.

"Thanks, honey." I shrugged and sighed at Reid's dubiously furrowed brow. "It is true."

I flipped through the atlas and ran my finger along a few of the highways on the pages. "If we continue this way, our proposed route would take us through the Mark Twain Wilderness of southern Missouri, then we can cut north to Kansas City. This is a lot of detouring to avoid St. Louis. What if Kansas City is impassable?" I muffled a curse. "From Kansas City, it's a straight shot on I-70 to Denver."

"We need to get around all this," Reid said, flicking his hand to the string of cars before us. "If there's more precipitation…," he implied.

"Like ash!" Will said merrily.

I pressed my two fingers against my aching temple. "We need to get off this road regardless. It's going to eat all of our fuel," I said, eyeing the gauge. Down to a quarter tank. "How about the next exit, and we can review our options and find gas?"

"Sure," Reid agreed.

The line for the gas station was worse than the highway. "Jesus," I mumbled. Thirty minutes later, my fuel gauge reading an eighth of a tank, and my pulse elevated, we made it to the pump. An attendant was controlling it.

"You can only get ten gallons," he said as I popped out of the car. "And cash only."

I grimaced. "That's ridiculous. There are no mandates on gas limits."

Reid exited the car and slid to my side. "The government isn't condoning restrictions. Price mandates, yes, but not quantities. We can report you."

"Right," I said, sticking my chin up, suddenly dizzy. The gas fumes made me want to puke.

"Come on, what's the hold up?" a guy yelled from the next car in line.

The attendant, a middle-aged man of wrestler stature, scoffed. "The government ain't gonna do squat. They have more pressing issues. This is our station. Our gas. The fuel trucks have stopped delivering. Owner's rules. Ten gallons per day, cash. You can come back tomorrow for another ten gallons. Or move on." He crossed his beefy arms and gave Reid, who stood six inches shorter than him, a don't-mess-with-me look. Yeah, I doubted this guy was a regular attendant.

"Okay, fine," I snapped, opening the gas cap. I reached for the pump, but the man grabbed the nozzle and did it himself. When he was done, I slapped the money in his hand.

"Mom," Will said as I opened the passenger door to step in. "I have to pee."

"No bathroom," the guy said.

"Come on," I said, gritting my teeth.

He held up a thick, calloused hand. "Look, I would let your boy use it, but the water is not running anymore. They shut it off. Ash contaminating the sewers or something from that rain storm. There's a wooded spot over yonder," he said with thumb point to a patch of trees beside the station.

"But there is no ash on the ground," Will said, perceptively.

"Will?"

"I'll hold it," he said, returning to his clipboard drawings.

We stopped for lunch in a picnic area, and Will happily consumed fast-food chicken nuggets while I opened my journal. I sat at the picnic table next to him.

"Want me to check on the tires? Maybe talk with somebody at the store, there, about routes? Get more bottled water?" Reid asked. He pointed to the gas station beside the grassy picnic pavilion.

I nodded. "Thanks. Yes to all of the above."

I opened the journal to a new page but made another call to Dr. Martin once Reid was out of hearing range. My call didn't get through to the receptionist. I redialed twice. Nothing. Perhaps in Kansas if I couldn't locate my prescription, a pharmacist could call my doctor.

Depleted and defeated, I turned to my journal, keeping a watchful half eye on Will as he ate and played.

My thoughts fell upon my own mother, who died from cancer when I was twenty-five. It had left a gaping hole in my life. Then Harrison last year. A larger hole. It had widened a wound that I thought was healed…but it had been left festering.

Now…would I lose my Finn, too?

I paused. Oh, God, my Finn.

A youthful giggle emerged from a child playing at the other picnic pavilion. It sent quivers through my stomach. My Finn's laugh was a hug for my ears.

Instead of crying, I allowed the ink to be my tears as I poured my thoughts onto the crisp pages. Reid's conversation about God resetting humanity didn't sit well with me. I was a woman of faith and fate. Or at least I had been. Maybe I had lost that faith long before I'd lost Harrison.

I paused, letting the wind that stirred the nearby trees envelop me. A sudden chill ran down my spine as I coughed.

I drew my hand to the page, but there was no stopping the dizzying spiral in my head. Too many thoughts bounced around in there like tumbleweeds. The pen fell from my shaking fingers, and I stared at the page. I'd never put it on paper. I'd never said it aloud. Painful thoughts had carved their own permanent residence in my brain, burrowed in the corner, obstinate and refusing to be evicted. I'd come a long way since last year, and I knew with each day, I'd heal more.

My head grew light, my fingers tingled. The pages blurred. The irregular panicked beat of my anxious heart climbed my throat, and I lost my breath.

"Mommm…" Will's voice came in, higher-pitched

than normal.

Then all I saw was black.

**** 

I awoke in the passenger seat of my SUV.

My scratchy throat and a rumbling in my head prevented me from speaking.

A heavy hand rested on my forehead. "You're warm. I think you have a fever."

It was Reid. Startled into the present, I bumped my head on the hanging windshield visor. "Gah." I leaned back, blinked, and then looked at Reid.

Concerned dark eyes regarded me. His face came into focus as the two Reids merged into one. I reached forward to touch his round chin to ensure that he was not a figment of my imagination. The prickle of coarse stubble awoke the nerve endings in my fingertips. "I'm okay," I said to him.

"No, you're not. Take these." He shoved a water bottle and cold medicine into my hand. He must have raided my trunk stash. I wanted to tell him what I really needed was the second to last antidepressant, too.

I did as told and searched past him for Will.

"Here, Mom!" Will chimed in from the back seat. "Are we going now?"

I shook my head and instantly regretted it.

Reid's hand had not left my forearm. "I'm okay. It's just a cold," I insisted.

"A cold doesn't make you faint."

I pulled my arm from his grip, as much as the warm touch of a hand on my skin that was not a child's comforted me. "Well, a cold topped with driving all day, not sleeping at night, and hardly eating or drinking will do that," I countered, blinking. *And weaning off a* *powerful medication...*I wasn't sure why I felt shame admitting that part.

He compressed his lips and ran a hand through his hair. His forehead furrowed with a frown.

"Should we stop for the night? Maybe a motel? Let you rest in a real bed. I saw a sign a few miles back," Reid offered.

"No. We need to keep going. I-I can't lose another," I said, my voice hoarse. I battled the darkness. I floated in a murky haze. Disjointed visions entranced me.

"AJ, drink this," Reid said, tipping the water bottle to my mouth. I gagged on it, as thirsty as I was. It tasted like dust. Reid tried again, and I took a reluctant swallow. I looked at the bottle. The water sloshed around like an upset ocean. I swatted the bottle away and spit the salty sea of rocks. Was he giving me saltwater? Drugging me? What was going on? Was I dreaming? No, no. There was Will. In the back seat.

"No..." Stars danced behind my eyelids. I kept blinking, but the more I did, the grayer Reid became. Now he was ghostly pale, not his radiant sun-kissed skin. His mouth moved, but I heard no words. His face blanched and then faded against the white sky. A ruggedly handsome chin grew distorted, and his thick prominent eyebrows disappeared.

"AJ..."

Darkness pulled me in again.

****

"Can I have the swipe key?" Will asked.

He loved hotels. It had been one of his favorite parts of their trip to Yellowstone. Well, other than the volcano stuff.

"Sure," Reid said. "We need to get your mom, first. Can you be my helper, buddy?"

Will nodded. "Yeah." He took the card from Reid and flipped it over in his hand. This card had a picture of a white arch on it and read, "Welcome to Missouri." He traced it with his finger. "What's this arch?" he asked. It looked like a smooth bridge. He loved the shape of it. It curved in such an interesting way. It looked like a parabola!

"That's the Gateway Arch."

"Where is it?"

"North of us, in St. Louis."

"Maybe we can go see it. Finn would like it. We can see it on our way home. I wonder how they built it."

They reached the car to find Mom in the front seat, sleeping. She didn't look well. Her face was not as colorful as usual, and her forehead was beaded with sweat. Reid opened the door.

"Will, I need you to open the doors for me in the hotel, okay?"

Will waved the key card. "Uh-huh! Is Mom going to be okay?"

Reid's smile was wide and honest with nice white teeth. He had a little beard on his face, like the way Dad's used to get if he had not shaved in three days. "Yes."

Sometimes people's faces did one thing and the words they said didn't match. Not this guy. Reid's face and words matched. Will liked him. But Mom was sick, and that worried him.

Reid carried Mom to their room. Will had to swipe two times to get the card to work. The green light flicked on, and he turned the handle, shoving the door open. Many smells were gross, but he liked the scent of hotels. It smelled like the clean laundry from the dryer. The towels were all lined up in the bathroom. He ran around, turning on the switches. He nibbled his lip, struggling with a round one. You could push it in or turn it to adjust the light. Interesting. He remembered Grandma used to let him sit in her minivan, with the doors wide open, and he'd play with all the cool buttons for hours. That was when he was four. He was a big kid now and didn't need to do that anymore. Although that round button was cool. He pushed it again.

"Will, can you help me?" Reid laid Mom on a bed. "Can you watch your mom for a little while? I need to go to the store and get us medicine and supplies."

Reid knelt to his level and looked him straight in the eyes. Will flinched at first, but then drew his gaze away from the switch and stared at Reid. He watched his mouth move as he spoke. "Will, did you hear me?"

Will nodded. "Mom doesn't leave me alone."

"It will be okay. You're not alone. You have your mom here, see?"

Will nodded, hesitant.

"Do not open the door for anyone, okay? I have a key. I'll return soon. Here's your bag and snacks. Only drink the bottle of water in your bag, okay? Not from the sink."

"Okay." Will then returned to the switch.

"Will, buddy?"

"Got it. Water bottle. Wait."

After ten minutes, it grew boring. This hotel room didn't have as many cool switches as the other hotels they'd visited. Besides, he wasn't a baby anymore.

Mom told him he was a big kid now. He had to be a role model for Finn.

Will chewed his lip and tapped his knee. He felt Mom's forehead like she always did for him when he was sick. It was hot. He lifted her hand and kissed the top of it. Maybe kissing her hand would work the way it did for babies. Sometimes when Finn was littler, Will would sneak into his room to check on him and give him kisses on his head. If you kiss toddlers and babies while they were sleeping, they had good dreams. Mom looked like she could use a happy dream now. Maybe it worked on grown-ups.

The clock read 2:04 p.m. It wasn't close to bedtime yet, and he was too old for naps.

He flipped through a stack of magazines on the desk. One had the arch on the cover. He opened it and read about the building of the arch. Apparently, it was not a parabola as he'd originally thought. It was a catenary curve, which was different. He read about that, and then analyzed the pictures. After a few minutes, he closed the magazine.

He located the TV remote. He'd already seen the news about the volcano. Most hotels didn't get the weather station or have cool shows like you could stream online. He turned it on anyway. Video of the eruptive column of the volcano showed on this channel. It was a science show, not like the regular news shows. He sat, observing how the plume billowed and rolled. Much like the Mount St. Helens eruption, the vertical column ascended about fourteen miles into the air, which meant it was not supervolcanic or mega-colossal, but it was a VEI 6 or VEI 7 on the scale, at least a hundred times greater than the eruption of Mount St.

Helens based on the ejecta volume, which scientists were determining. Reports were still coming in. Even though the eruption wasn't a VEI supervolcanic eruption, scientists were concerned that another bigger eruption could follow due to magma chamber instability. A video simulation demonstrated how Mt. Washburn and other notable Yellowstone peaks had crumbled into the magma chamber and how the ground cracked and opened up for many miles.

He clicked to another channel. This one was a news show.

It had been nearly a week since the eruption and the newscasters were showing other videos now: forest fires, helicopters rescuing people, towns covered in a fat blanket of ash and people digging like you did after it snowed, and the fallout zone of trees flattened from the blast. That was cool. He liked when they showed those video clips. But there were also people crying. He scratched his head. He didn't like *that* stuff, and that stuff always made his mom sad. They didn't talk much about what the new crater looked like.

A scientist came on and spoke about his experience with Mount St. Helens. Well, that was interesting, but Will had already seen and read everything about that volcano. He wondered if the supervolcano would have dome regrowth like Mount St. Helens. He loved the time-lapsed video his dad had found on a website that showed the dome's regrowth, with its fumes hissing and spitting and more ash building. Maybe it would erupt again, too.

The scientist was done talking, and they returned to the people crying.

He turned off the television.

He grabbed a mandala coloring book and colored pencils from his backpack.

One mandala captured his eye right away. It had a lot of swirling shapes within the middle circle and angled lines around the edges, like the corners of a roof coming together. He traced the spirals with his finger, following the path over and over. It reminded him of Finn, who loved whirlpools and galaxies and black holes.

Maybe he'd save that page for Finn. He flipped through the book and found another equally fascinating one, and chose the blue pencil. Coloring the spiral shapes always quieted the buzzing in his head.

****

I awoke disoriented. Ouch, and a blinding headache as I sat upright. A carousel of colors whirled around me. I winced and eased back. This habit of waking spellbound had to stop.

Will was at my side, shaking my shoulder. "Mom, I'm hungry. It's way past dinner."

"Get a snack from the kitchen," was my reply.

"This room doesn't have a kitchen, and I can't go to the vending machine alone."

Well, that drew me from my haze.

I sat up, albeit slower, and realized not only was I in a bed, but I was in a hotel room. A freezing hotel room. I tugged at the neck opening of my T-shirt, coughed, and lifted a clammy hand to my hot forehead. I shivered uncontrollably.

"How did we get here?" I managed to ask, pulling the covers to my chin. Despite the fear that threatened to besiege me, a sense of relief dwarfed it. Will was beside me. He was okay. Nothing had happened to him.

But Reid...my gaze darted around the cramped room...he was nowhere in sight.

"You fainted. Twice, Mom. Are you sick? Reid brought us here. He's not back yet. I'm hungry. He said he'd return."

"What time is it?" I answered myself by looking at the bedside clock, which read six thirty p.m. I blinked and focused. Yup, the same. "Shit."

I stood, shaking. A search through my handbag yielded only my spare set of car keys. I always traveled with both sets, paranoid I'd lose one. The other set was gone.

Reid hadn't left us. He couldn't have.

"Grab your bag, Will." I pocketed the key card on the nightstand and was already making for the door. "Where are we?"

Will moaned. "We aren't sleeping here? I'm hungry."

I leaned on the desk and shoved the hotel directory aside. I found a notepad that said Illinois. Okay, we hadn't gone far after I'd fainted.

I pulled Will a tad too roughly by the arm, he winced, and I let go. *Get a grip, AJ.* Hurt flickered in his face with the hint of an impending meltdown. "I'm sorry, Will. Let's get food on the way, okay?"

"Do you have four quarters? I want a snack from the vending machine. I know it's not a dinner, but I want cheese puffs. May I?" he asked, voice hopeful, and he instantly snapped back to normal mode.

"Yes, honey."

After what seemed like forever going through the maze of hallways and Will's indecisive choice-making at the vending machine because there were two types of cheese puffs, we made our way to the parking lot. All the while, I wheezed with each step. I dug in my bag for my inhaler and took a puff. A cold sweat moistened the hair at the nape of my neck, and I licked dehydrated lips.

I searched for my blue SUV among the vehicles in the parking lot. I scanned back and forth twice, refusing to believe the obvious. It was gone.

I cleared my throat and invoked a steady composure for Will's sake. "When did Reid leave?"

He was distracted with eating his cheese puffs, meticulously licking his fingers.

For a child who has been obsessed with clocks since the age of four, and who became crippled with changes in schedule, he was undaunted by our dilemma.

"Where did he go?"

He shrugged and crunched on another cheese puff.

I almost snapped, but I quieted the beast. I took Will gently by the arm and positioned him into direct eye contact with me by kneeling to his level. "Will, think hard, okay? This is important. What time did the clock say when we arrived here? We had lunch at the rest stop, then what?" I coaxed, hoping to jog his perfect memory.

Remembrance lit his eyes. "You blacked out, Mom. Twice. Then we drove twelve miles on the highway here to find a hotel. Reid carried you in. He said he was getting medicine and supplies. The clock read 2:04 p.m." He scratched his head. "That was hours ago! What's taking him so long?"

*He carried me in?* "I don't know."

I stared at the lot entrance, willing my SUV to drive through the gate. The minutes passed. I thought about asking the front desk clerk. What would I ask? What would they know?

Tears of rage crossed my vision, and I needed to sit and drink water. We trudged back to the room. Rational AJ believed Reid would return. He was getting supplies. No need to panic.

Regardless, once again, I was without. And it scared the shit out of me.

Chapter Eight
An Angel's Kiss Upon My Heart

I paced the hotel room.

"I'm still hungry. I don't have a lot of snacks in my backpack, Mom."

Nausea fluttered in my stomach. I riffled through my handbag and found my pill bottle. I shook it, knowing that high-pitched clack was one lone pill. I twisted it open and stared at the white oblong pill. I sighed, popped it in my mouth, and downed it with water from the tap. The water tasted gritty, and I gagged while swallowing. It hadn't looked dirty.

I called the front desk. "Hi, the water—"

"Told you when you checked in. Don't drink from the tap. Safe to shower and flush, but you need to drink your own beverages. There's a store down the road." Click.

"What an asshole," I mumbled. *Told me?* Jerk, I was passed out! More like told the guy I had come with...who left me.

My thoughts propelled me into worse-case scenario mode. The thoughts fell atop each other, dominoes in my muddled mind. No car. No supplies. No way to get to Denver. No Finn. I hung my head low and cried a slow, numbing cry of grief. He hadn't even left the bikes for us, to give us a fighting chance. Bastard. My sadness quickly turned to anger. No note! All he had done was tell Will that he'd be back—that was all I could discern from my son. I had been a fool. The crying didn't help my sore throat and throbbing cranium.

Wait...a note. "Will, did Reid leave a note? Another lollipop wrapper?"

Will approached and hugged me. "I don't know. It'll be all right, Mom. He'll come back. He said he would."

I pulled in my despair when I felt the gravity of my child's hopeful gaze. I nodded and rubbed my nose. "Yup, you're right. He will be back." I wanted to believe it. I had to. There was no need to panic yet. He hadn't played us. He'd return. There was still decency in this world.

Or else I just got screwed. Again.

"Can we rent a car or take a train?" Will offered.

"Maybe." I approached the desk and tossed about items, seeking a lollipop wrapper or any note. Nothing. I dropped to my knees and scanned under the desk, around the dresser, along the beds and other tables. Nothing. There went that theory.

I had a lot of cash and credit cards, if they were being accepted, in my handbag. And a hidden stash in my jacket. The car stash had already been looted. I wasn't going to be screwed. A part of me fought with the idea of leaving now, but my body and my sense told me we had to wait. Give Reid until the morning. If he didn't return, then he was truly gone. I held on to hope.

I highly doubted any trains were traveling west into the prohibited zones. Maybe a car rental agency would show me pity.

"Let's see what's on TV, honey," I said, not

wanting to watch news, but needing some sound to drown the silence. "Mom's going to rest here, try to sleep. Will, listen…"

He turned on the television, and then sat beside me. His trusting face nearly ripped me in two. "You may *not* leave this room. You must stay here with me, okay? Sleep next to me. Be my love bug, right? Just like at home when you sleep in Daddy's spot," I said, with a forced smile.

"I don't have my pajamas."

I shook my head, regretting it as pain curled around my skull. "Remember that one time when you were tired and Grandma put you to bed in your swimsuit?"

He nodded. "Uh-huh."

"It will be like that." I coughed.

I burrowed under the covers and shivered from a searing cold. "Will, promise me. You will stay here beside me."

"I promise, Mom."

As I listened to him flip through miscellaneous programs, I went to bed with only one positive thought. Will always kept his promises. He wouldn't leave me, too. He was honest to a fault, like his mother. For that, I was truly grateful. A core rule-follower. Except when he wandered or daydreamed, I thought with a fatigued snort.

The buzzing sound of news reports filled the room as I drifted off to sleep.

*"The National Guard is now present in record numbers in all the impacted states as shown on this model. They've had difficulty navigating the debris and getting into the devastated areas of Montana and Wyoming, and they encourage anyone in those areas to*

*stay put and wait for evacuation, and for loved ones to not attempt travel to these regions, which are experiencing aftershocks. Military personnel have been using drones to assess the damage, as seen in this footage. They have set up mobile hospitals as far east as Kansas. Travel is strictly prohibited west of Dodge City, in this red zone as indicated."*

I coughed and buried myself deeper under the covers even though I should have watched the report. Will would remember it for me. I'd quiz him later.

*"Meanwhile, in Missouri, we experienced our first rain with ash. A moderate tremor was reported in the western part of the state this morning. Tim, tell us about that rain. How is it out there?"*

*"Thanks, Josie. We're here in Springfield. Yes, reports of outages throughout the metro area have us concerned, and utility companies are busy restoring power to those affected. About 4,500 residents are without power. Look here, a light coat of gray ash on almost every surface. Not measurable. Fascinating. You can see what it does when I rub it between my fingers. Hard to imagine that something this tiny could pollute water supplies, cause hiccups in power transformers, and inhibit travel. See, Josie, it's not like rain or snow or mud. It's a different consistency—it's broken pieces of rock, and it will need to be handled in a specialized manner. The National Guard has been collaborating with the USGS on clean-up and removal. We are waiting on word of the scale of the tremor experienced in western Missouri. All citizens are encouraged to drink only bottled water, as some water systems and septic systems are reporting issues already."*

God, he sounded like Will. Were all meteorologists

eccentric?

Click.

"...*the tsunami that hit the Oregon and Washington coasts, as well as the one in Japan. Over 50,000 people are dead or missing after the monster waves hit last week in the wake of the eruption and powerful earthquakes*..."

Click.

"...*El Niño. The ash traveled with the prevailing winds. Ash is expected to continue east over the next week. Weather predictor models suggest it may reach Europe in another ten to fourteen days, depending on which model you go with. This is truly a global disaster and will take years to clean.*

"*Governor Howell has urged citizens to stay indoors, limit travel, and monitor water usage. Prices have been frozen, per federal declaration. Although Missouri has not been greatly impacted yet, long-term impact is yet to be determined, especially on livestock and crops. The National Guard will be distributing recovery packs and cleaning supplies, including masks, starting with areas most in need, closest to the eruption zone. Shauna is in downtown Jefferson City, where reports of vandalism, car accidents, and riots are on the rise. Shauna, what's happening there?*"

Click.

"*The death toll has risen to over 250,000. Thousands of stranded passengers from the airlines are trying to get home to families.*"

Click.

"...*next, scientific light can be shed on this situation. Matt has an interview with the head of the USGS, Dr. Woodhull*..."

I fell asleep, unable to listen anymore.

\*\*\*\*

The snap of a door lock woke me. I had slept fitfully, mother's ears on high alert, not for a child's waking or a nighttime danger...I listened for a saving grace.

A shaft of light broke into the dark room from the opening door, and another headache hit me as I slipped out of bed in reflex, ready for action. I grabbed air, a clenched fist. My handy tire iron was, well, in the car.

Reid entered the room, worn relief etched across his features. He propped the door open with a case of something.

I unleashed my pent-up fears and anger in loud whispers. "Where the hell were you?"

Never mind he carried several plastic grocery bags looped around his arms and two cases of something. Okay, he got stuff. I looked at the clock. It was now past midnight.

"I got delayed. I'm sorry, AJ."

"Delayed? You were gone for hours. Hours! With my car!"

He plopped the cases, which I now recognized to be electrolyte vitamin beverages and children's protein drinks on the empty bed beside us. He allowed the overflowing plastic bags to slide off his arms. Irritation furrowed his low brow, his thick dark eyebrows knotted. It was then that I noticed the cut on the bridge of his nose, dry with recent blood.

He plodded to the door and grabbed his backpack from the hallway. He stumbled to the second bed, his gait wobbly. He dropped his backpack at the foot of the bed. All we had was the light streaming in from the bathroom, a.k.a. Will's nightlight now.

Winded, he said, "You fainted. I searched your car, but the medicine in your first aid kit was rudimentary. I left to get you better medicine while it was available, talk to a pharmacist, grab water and food, and to fill the gas containers." He dragged his hands through his hair with an exaggerated yawn. He tore open the plastic covering on the electrolyte drinks, pulled one out, and handed it to me. Thirsty, I stubbornly took it but didn't open it.

"That took ten hours? And you didn't leave a note. Thought you were a note guy? Why are you all roughed up?" My raised voice stirred Will. His snoring stopped, and he rolled over.

"Reid!" he said, instantly awake, pushing aside the covers and running toward Reid. To my surprise, he gave Reid a hug around his legs. My stomach churned, and I wasn't sure why. I was certain that part of my ire was from the feelings I still harbored about many things. I dearly wanted to keep it together.

He *had* returned. *Calm down, racing heart.*

"Here, buddy," Reid said in a low voice, handing him a smaller bag, which I presumed was filled with snacks. "I got some apples and bananas, too."

I dug my nails into my palms to keep myself from approaching him in anger.

I turned to Will. "Will, please go back to bed, okay?"

"But—"

"You may have one of those snacks with breakfast."

The glimmer of youthful excitement danced across his face.

Will crawled under his covers. I gave him a kiss on his cheek, stroked his hair, and whispered, "I love you."

Neither Reid nor I spoke for a few minutes. I sat at the desk near the foot of the bed, watching Will work himself back to sleep with tossing and turning, while my mind pitched like a ship in a stormy sea. I opened the electrolyte drink and consumed half of it in seconds. Finally, Will's deep rhythmic breathing told me his body had drifted off to la-la land. The sea in my mind calmed.

Reid sat on the edge of the bed nearest to me.

We spoke at the same time. He said, "How are you feeling?" as I asked, "What happened?"

Fatigue caught up with me, and I conceded to being nice. He did return after all, and I lacked the energy for a fight. "Not great."

"What are your symptoms?"

"Other than fainting?" I said.

"Yeah, besides that." He sifted through a bag and removed a thermometer.

I waved it away. "Probably a cold like I said." Cough, malaise, scratchy throat, achy muscles, I wanted to add, but didn't. Oh, and tingles in my fingers and skull. Whirling nausea. Mild heart palpitations. I thought about the empty pill bottle in my handbag. As if in rebuttal, a coughing fit seized me, and I grabbed my inhaler from my handbag and took a puff. I deliberately focused on my breathing as the wheezes rattled in my lungs. Another puff.

Reid's gaze held mine, dark and sharp. The cut on his nose was noticeable from whatever brawl he'd experienced. "Only a cold? You have asthma. Do you think the ash—"

I nipped that one in the bud immediately. "No."

He didn't believe me. "We *are* getting closer."

I took slow inhalations and exhalations followed by a sip of the electrolyte drink as the rescue inhaler worked its way into my system and my lungs relented their siege. "Will, he has asthma, too. But he's not coughing." Yet.

"Do you faint often?"

"No."

"Any other weird symptoms? Anything, like, neurological?"

As if on cue, a shiver radiated through my skull. "No."

"I asked the pharmacist. Maybe you're dehydrated, too?"

"Maybe."

Pharmacist. Crap. I could have tried them. What would come from it though? I needed my doctor to call in the prescription.

"Well, I got you a few things. You need a decent night's rest. That will help. I'll get another room for myself once you're settled."

I sat next to him while he thumbed through his bag. I swallowed the multi-symptom cold pills he handed me. I lowered my voice to not disturb Will. "What happened?" I asked with a gentle and forgiving tone. "And why didn't you leave a note?"

He stretched his jaw. "Yeah, I'm sorry…again. I told Will. Then I was halfway to town when I realized I should've left you a note and I didn't have your phone number. Not that phones are reliable."

I sighed.

"It wasn't good. This place," he said, waving

around the room, "seems okay for now, but I went into town ten miles down the road. It was a mess, disorderly. People vandalizing. Disputes at stores. Looting. The pharmacy was locking their gates when I arrived. The pharmacist said St. Louis was worse than Chicago."

I realized belatedly that I had never asked him more about Chicago. "We're not in the fallout zone, or whatever you call it. We're in God-Knows-Where, Missouri! How can this be happening?"

"Apparently, the ash rain has people freaked. The tremors, too."

"The rain stopped though."

"Many of the water sources are already contaminated."

A muscle twitched behind my eye, and my skin prickled with gooseflesh as our conversation moved to the reality of what was going on around us. I supposed I wasn't as prepared for all this as I had thought. "That doesn't explain the ten hours, Reid."

He rubbed his nose. "I got in a scuffle with a few guys outside the liquor store."

I immediately tensed and fisted my hands on the edge of the bedspread to fight the inner rage. "You went to a liquor store?" The coil within me threatened to unwind at any moment.

"No. I passed it on the way to the car. When I saw the town in shambles, people vandalizing and fighting, I decided to park the car somewhere else. I parked about a half mile out of town, off the highway, and then walked into town." There was a clear pause in his explanation. I read his face in the dim light, seeking the truth.

"Anyway, this altercation. Two jerks approached me, started demanding money, wanted to pilfer my stuff. We had it out. The police were already in the streets, damn riot gear on. I got hauled to the station along with the two assholes. They kept me for hours, but once they determined I wasn't a threat and the two drunks were the ones who needed to be there, they released me. Sorry, AJ. I didn't think to get your cell number until it was too late. Not that phones are working well." He brushed both hands, with swollen and scuffed knuckles, back through his hair and blew another breath. "You fainted. Twice. I had to do something. You sure it's nothing else?"

I gleaned what energy I could. "I'm sorry for overreacting. I feel like shit."

"It's okay."

I sat for a moment. "The car? It's okay?"

"Yeah, it's fine."

He laid a hand on top of one of my clenched ones, releasing my tight grip on the bedspread. He squeezed lightly. "It'll be all right. We'll get to your son," he said, his voice purposely soft-spoken.

I gulped and nodded as he read me too well for somebody I'd just met. Then I fell onto his shoulder, allowing myself to break. The knot in my stomach unwound. He slipped a warm arm around me. It'd been too long since I'd been held by anyone. He felt damn fine.

Wheezing rattled my chest, and Reid pulled back, took my electrolyte drink from the desk, and handed it to me. He brushed aside the moist hair on my forehead. "I didn't mean to worry you."

I nodded. "It's all this shit, you know."

"Yeah, I know."

I rested on him for a few minutes, listening to the even rhythm of his heartbeat and breathing. He cleared his throat. That was my cue. I moved away from him…though I didn't want to.

Finally, he spoke. "You need to sleep. I'll get another room."

"Okay."

I grabbed a tissue from the nightstand, blew, and then inhaled to clear my sinuses momentarily. A different scent struck me. At first it was Reid. He smelled like sweat and spicy deodorant. Familiar already.

Then, it was overpowering, woodsy hops. My head spun.

The burning imprint of that venomous scent summoned the raw memory of Harrison's death from the depths…from a day that had shattered my life the way his windshield had been shattered when the drunk driver slammed into his car.

My stomach lurched, and I gripped my head, unsure why these old memories and sensations assaulted me now. I pulled away from Reid, but not without inhaling as if I was clearing my nose more, and I hovered closer to his mouth than I would have liked.

He reached for me, but I recoiled. "You okay?" he asked, eyebrows lifted in alarm.

"No." I couldn't conjure a compelling lie. I sniffed intentionally, but with another tissue over my nose, exaggerating my drip.

God, the smell stung my nostrils. I couldn't tell if it was on his breath or his clothes. Yet…wait. Was it on his breath?

Oh, my God, was it? "My husband, he was—Reid, you—" I stammered. "You left us. Now you reek of alcohol."

I caught his stare. His usual agreeable countenance was now somber. *Had* he been drinking? I sought evidence of intoxication in his eyes, as illogical as that sounded.

"I didn't drink anything," he said.

Did I know this man who was alone in a hotel room with us? I shifted farther away. "I shouldn't be...you..." The words wouldn't string together. I couldn't tell him why I had this aversion to alcohol. I began again, "My husband. He was..."

My brain spun madly in a direction I loathed. My tongue was tied. Why couldn't I say it?

I put a damper on my racing thoughts while distancing myself from Reid with a few backsteps.

"What's the matter?" He rose, a hand outstretched. "What happened?"

A muted sadness crossed his face. I'd only uncovered the tip of his story, but I could barely keep my eyes open, let alone look at him and expose the entire iceberg. A wave of irrational thoughts ran wild in my mind.

"I..." I couldn't say it all. "Us, this, I'm not sure. Thanks for all you've done, but I think you should..." I rubbed my achy head. "I..."

"Listen, AJ, I get it. I left. It messed with your head. Now I'm back smelling like booze. It wasn't me though. I swear."

I hugged myself, finding it in no way soothing. I nodded but couldn't speak.

Reid opened his mouth but closed it. He

157

approached the desk and laid down his set of car keys. "I'll go. I'm sorry I scared you by leaving like that."

A long, splintered pause hovered between us as he stood near the door.

"Yeah, maybe you should go," I said, my conscience and words not aligning on that agreement.

"I didn't mean to…" He furrowed his brow, pressed thinned lips together, and heaved a sigh.

"Me, too."

His shoulders slumped as he picked up his backpack with a grunt. He then straightened his back, settled the pack, and left without a look back.

The click of the door lock reverberated in the hotel room and sent shudders through me.

My mouth was dry, and tension released from me.

I sat at the desk for what seemed minutes. What had I done? I ran to the door. Maybe he was pacing, waiting for me to get my muddled mind in order.

The hallway was empty. I stood there for a moment, looking, waiting. Maybe he got another room like he'd said? We'd touch base again in the morning when my brain's functioning returned. I slowly closed the door and locked it.

I then crawled under the covers beside Will and wrapped my arms tightly around my baby.

I slept hard.

\*\*\*\*

Giggles woke me.

The bed creaked.

I cracked open an eye to find Finn bouncing on the bed. He laughed hysterically. He was in his red and white snowman footie pajamas. His blue eyes shone with tears of mirth.

"Mommy, this bed is noisy!"

He jumped in slow motion, and my focus fell on each detail: his blond hair, a smidge too long as it curled around his ears like Harrison's did when it was due for a trim, his round cheeks pink from exertion, his toes poking through the holes in the feet of his pajamas because he stubbornly refused to give them up, and his long lean body.

The door to the hotel room opened. The delightful rich aroma of coffee infiltrated the room. I eyed the coffees in Harrison's hands. Will ran to the bed, threw off his shoes, and jumped with Finn. They laughed and bopped each other with pillows. Will made blaster noises, and Finn went, "Beep beep!"

"Looks like a fabulous day, today, hon," Harrison said, handing me the coffee cup, and then opening the curtains. A perky, blue-sky day greeted us outside the Snow Lodge in Yellowstone National Park. I recognized the view of the visitor center and beyond that was Old Faithful Geyser. To my left, by the vanity, were quaint bear-shaped soaps.

"Hey, careful, little buddy," Harrison said to Will, who nearly knocked the coffee from my hand with his excitement. I switched to the other bed to protect my drink.

"Dad! My name is Will!"

Harrison and I exchanged a look. "Okay, little buddy," Harrison said, employing the pet name he had for Will, although Will insisted that he had only one name, Will (or William, depending on his mood).

I sipped the coffee, the dark blend heaven on my palate.

Harrison bent and kissed me. His lips were

honeyed from his over-sweetened coffee. His kiss lingered, and I pulled him closer. I drew a hand through his hair. Stubble on his chin tickled my face. He smelled like fresh tea-tree shampoo and the biting scent of spice deodorant. He shared a smile with me. "I'm happy you did this. It means a lot to me."

His eyes, which had the same rounded shape as Finn's, sparkled. I lay a hand on his chin, enjoying the prickles of stubble under my fingertips. "Of course. Why wouldn't I have?"

"Well, you know why. I didn't want you to be sad."

"Sad? Why? What's sad about coming here? The kids are having a blast. So are you. Why, yesterday you—" I stopped myself. A fuzzy cloud hung over my memory.

Wait, what had we done yesterday? Oh, yes, the Upper Geyser Basin walk. The ranger at the visitor center had loaned the boys a backpack filled with two workbooks, one a Junior Ranger investigation and one a Young Scientist pamphlet, along with colored pencils and an infrared thermometer gun to measure the heat coming off the geysers, rainbow-colored springs, and mud pots. Both boys had loved the boardwalk trail that took us through three miles of bubbling, bursting, egg-smelling steam and glory of the thermal beauty that was Yellowstone's heart. "Remember? When Finn dropped the radar gun near Morning Glory Pool? That was a close call. Gosh, it almost fell into a bubbling one-hundred-sixty-five-degree pool. You retrieved it."

"That wasn't me. It was Brandon with you," Harrison said.

I scratched my head, my mind strangely full but

empty. "That makes no sense. He's in California." I sipped the coffee, but now it tasted like water, no longer fragrant and sweet. The mug had disappeared from my hand, replaced by a water bottle.

The lights in the hotel room flickered.

"I'm glad you went," Harrison said, his voice drifting away, nearly muted as if he were under water.

The bed stopped shaking. Finn leaned over and gave a now-sleeping-under-the-covers Will a kiss on his cheek. "So he can have happy dreams," Finn cooed. I nodded but found that odd. That had been something Will used to say when Finn was a baby. He would kiss his forehead and say that a kiss while he was sleeping would grant him good dreams. Wait, wasn't Will just bouncing a second ago, too?

I blinked. My head was so heavy, I had to support it with a hand.

Then Finn was gone. Like that. Poof. Will was under the blankets, lightly snoring. The pillows were in their place. Fearful clarity took hold of me. The view out the window was overcast, and all I saw was a cluster of trees beside a brown dumpster, and not lodgepole pines, a Yellowstone signature. I turned to Harrison, who sat beside me on the bed. I reached for him, drew him in close, and clung to him like glue.

"Hush, Audrey Jane, my HBA, my honey baby angel. It'll be okay." His embrace encircled me. I rested my cheek against his chest, his heartbeat slow and steady and my compass north.

"How can it be?" The realization caught in my throat. Maybe if I didn't say it, it wouldn't be real. "Y-You're gone. You're dead."

"I will always be with you."

"H-How?"

"In your heart."

I shook my head and sniffled into his chest. I inhaled deeply but could no longer smell him. I no longer heard his heartbeat.

"Find our son. Find Finn. Brandon's got him. He's okay. I will always be with you, my love. Always, my honey baby angel."

My sweet Finn.

My dear Harrison.

The solid chest that I had been leaning against vaporized. I had to catch myself from falling onto the bed. I reached, but my hand went through him. He was no longer opaque. The hotel desk showed through his body. I reached for his chin for one last touch, but my fingers met air. I sobbed uncontrollably. "No, no, no. Don't go!"

He smiled and mouthed, "I love you," but I no longer heard him.

Then he was gone.

I blinked, and the gloomy room returned to me. I was in the hotel in Missouri.

My skin was cool and coated with the sticky residue of a night of sweating. The throbbing in my head had subsided. My eyes burned. I swallowed, thirsty. Will snored beside me, snuggled closely into the crook of my arm, the drab gray and blue hotel blanket to his chin. I readjusted his weighted blanket. He was my early bird, too, but he snoozed away. Maybe he had also needed a solid sleep not on the ground. I slid from beneath him, my arm numb and tingling from his heavy head having rested upon it.

I rose. In the bathroom, I gulped water and then

spit it out belatedly, remembering it was contaminated. I scrubbed my face, hoping to erase the memory of the dream. It had been so real. God, what the hell was I doing? I was in the middle of Missouri, heading to Denver to canvas an ash-covered area on the long shot that my son and brother would be there. What if they had gotten on the Denver flight, but their flight had been detoured...where? They could've ended up in a hundred other possible cities in the entire country. What if they were in Salt Lake City? *Dear God, no.* What if? What if? What if?

All I *did* know was I wasn't going to sit on my ass in Maine and wait for news. Brandon had yet to call. He was not anywhere else. He was in Denver.

I looked through the bathroom doorway at the keys on the desk, regret a heavy weight on my soul. I'd reacted poorly with Reid. Fatigue, illness, and my damn anxiety. I recalled far too many arguments with Harrison because we had both been burned out.

I'd check in the morning to see if he'd gotten a room. Yes, I would apologize and all would be fine.

****

A few hours later, Will and I were off. After no success with the front desk, I passed a hopeful look around the parking lot for Reid, but his bike, which had been hooked on my car, was now gone. If he *had* slept in a room, he was gone now.

I'd screwed up.

I drove onto the main highway and continued the preset course, *Peregrine's Atlas* in the empty passenger seat. Then I looked at Finn's empty booster. I was alone again. Alone. I glanced at Will. No, I was not *that* alone. I had my bright, cheerful, thirsty-for-life son

163

with me. I had Harrison in my soul. And Finnie's kisses upon my heart.

A brief ripple of expectation passed through me when I saw a man on a bike ahead. It was quickly snuffed when I realized it wasn't Reid. I kept driving.

When we reached a stopping point, as I had done many times on the journey, I pulled out my phone to look at a few photos while Will explored and stretched his legs. Even though technology and I didn't jibe well, I did have a camera on the phone. Of course I had grabbed a few printed photos of Finn to bring along, unsure why, perhaps to keep my spirit positive, to keep me motivated on the long haul. My phone was filled with many candid snapshots.

I flipped through them, and it brought an overdue smile to my face. Finn with raspberries on the tips of his fingers, smiling goofily at the camera. Finn next to his Lego tower he had proudly built and had insisted I photograph it "to remember it." A sweet scribbled note he'd written me and tucked under my pillow. A few photos of the geology show we visited this past spring. Harrison would've enjoyed that, but I'd taken them alone. I had to. We either wallowed at home or I sucked it up and took the baby steps of healing. In the photo, Finn stood next to his line of amethyst, quartz, lava rock, "diamond," and geodes.

The next photo was of our refrigerator, plastered with sight words for Finn, the conversation wheel Susie had made for Will, family rules, chore chart, school schedule, photographs, the scribbled note from Finn beside a pressed four-leaf clover he'd picked for me, important phone numbers, a list of "empowering words for children," artwork, a reward chart, and numerous magnets from all of Harrison's and my worldly adventures. One picture summarized my cluttered, demanding life. I'd snapped that photo one day in frustration, texted Siobhan, and she had responded with a "beautiful!"

My life had been, and still was, full. Tears, sweat, blood, emotional roller-coaster rides. I remember wanting to rip everything off that fridge. It'd looked that way the day Harrison died, save for a few extra add-ons. A part of me clung to the past and refused to strip the life from the fridge. To the outsider, it gave a messy impression, a disorganized mother. To me, it was my family. My life. In fact, many other areas of the house had been left untouched. The office bookshelves exploded with piles of books: diagonal leaning books, books laid on their side, papers and scraps from newspapers and magazines. Those shelves had been Harrison's cave. He lost himself in historical, travel, and science tomes. I hadn't touched the shelves since his death, except to dust them, and that was rarely.

Harrison's side of the garage lay empty, his car long since impounded and destroyed after the accident. Christmas ornaments sat in a corner of the children's playroom, waiting to be put away, after my lame attempt at the first Christmas after Harrison's death. It'd been a dark, silent night indeed. All the firsts in the past year were painful. Since that fateful July evening, we've had to celebrate all those "special holidays" without him. I had a hard time with holidays already missing my mom, but now, my dear husband...they were unbearable reminders.

An old familiar sense of determination took hold of me. I was going to get through this. I was going to find my son. Life's cruelties would not take me. Our normal wasn't your typical normal to begin with. Autism and quirks composed our days. Then Harrison had died, and we'd entered a new normal. There would be a whole new normal for many others now, not just us. Change was inevitable.

I closed the photo screen on the phone and plopped it on the seat beside me. Anyone could give up. I'd never been just anyone. I had to keep it together. I'd gotten us through this past year.

I could do this.

Chapter Nine
Heart-Hurting Moments

Will didn't understand why Reid left. Mom didn't explain why. Reid wasn't a bad guy. Will had seen bad guys in movies and in real life. Reid wasn't a crook or bully or meanie. In fact, he was mad at her for letting Reid go. Reid was nice. He tried to not feel sad about it. Now it was just him and Mom. He didn't like too many noisy people, but Reid spoke in a quiet-y voice. He liked that. Finn was noisy, but he was also his best friend, so he made an exception for him.

He tapped a finger on his knee. Mom was talking with the guy working near the gas pump. Will was now up to two hundred and was getting tired of waiting. He poked his head through the open window. "Mom, why are you doing all this grown-up talk? Let's go!" He hated all the adult talk. Every time Mom met another person, it was talk, talk, talk. Too much talking. Like at Thanksgiving and Christmas, when his aunts and uncles and Grandma and Grandpa and cousins would come over. They spent too much time talking. When there were a lot of people all in the house at once, he heard it all—every conversation—it was like a swarm of buzzing bees around him. Yeah, like a beehive. Once Mom had asked him about it, and he told her that it was like that. Some stuff was hard to explain to her, but that was easier.

And he didn't like bees.

It got so loud, the humming and buzzing in his head, that he wanted to bang his head against a wall. Susie and Mom had taught him to go to a quiet place when things like that bothered him. Usually he went to his room, and he could play with his Lego bricks. When they were at Grandma and Grandpa's house, he couldn't hide in his room so he would go to a corner, or once, he sat on the front stoop. He liked it there. He could watch the leaves on the trees move, the blades of grass swish as the wind blew past, or best—the puddles! Grandma's house had lots of amazing puddles! He'd watch the water move when he swirled a stick in it, or he could make it muddy. Lately, Susie was teaching him to explain to others when things bothered him, but that was hard to do. They didn't understand.

Sometimes closets or under chairs were the best places to escape. Nobody bothered him when he was there.

Mom explained to him this year why things like that troubled him, but it didn't make it all better. Mom said that everybody has challenges, and he was special and had his own challenges and that his brain was wired a different way. He was sure brains didn't have wires, though. His science encyclopedia said they had neurons and synapses. Mom always asked him about the kids at school. He went to Lunch Bunch at school once a week with Mr. Hansen and a few other kids. They sat at a separate table, and Mr. Hansen encouraged him to have "social skills" like talking to others, looking them in the eyes, taking turns, and all that other stuff, but he didn't like any of those kids. They didn't like cats or volcanoes or wizard stuff. His friend Oliver did, and although Oliver moved to a different school this year, Mom scheduled play dates once a month. Besides, Finn was his best friend, even if he was a baby sometimes.

He tapped his fingers on his leg. Mom was still talking, and she always talked using her hands. That was another thing Susie explained to him. "Mom!" he hollered.

She looked at him and made that face she always made. "Coming, Will."

She finally got in the car. "Mom, that took more than three minutes. In fact it took three hundred twenty seconds."

\*\*\*\*

For a relatively unpopulated area of Missouri, the road we traveled was terribly congested. My head spun with the residual effect of the cold and the inept drivers. Reid had snagged me stronger cold medicine loaded with pseudoephedrine and a cough suppressant, and thankfully they didn't make me drowsy, too. I was revved. We were in the middle of nowhere, far enough from the cities. Why was there a traffic jam? "This is such a mess!" I snapped as I peered ahead to see what was going on around a bend in the highway. Thick woodland bordered us.

"It doesn't look untidy to me, Mom," Will said.

I couldn't help but laugh. "No, not a *mess* like that." I pondered how to explain it to him. "There are a lot of cars, slow traffic, lots of people and excitement going on. Busy. Construction. Rush hour or an accident. We say that's a mess. Or at least I do."

"Oh."

The speedometer needle trembled lower and lower. With each dip, I tightened my hands on the wheel.

Thirty-five...twenty-five...twenty...

Well, at least it wasn't raining.

Eventually, we came to a standstill, the red needle quaking at the zero. "Wonderful."

"Huh?" Will asked.

I shook my head.

After a few minutes of going nowhere, I turned off the engine and opened the windows all the way. Many people were exiting their cars, gaping, swearing, and gesturing. Red and blue emergency lights blinked far ahead, always a jarring sight. I stepped out of the car and with a crane of my neck confirmed it to be police cars and an ambulance.

"What's going on?" I asked the short, thickset woman in front of me.

She shrugged and removed her baseball hat, revealing spindly unwashed gray hair. "I think they're diverting us. Accident maybe?"

"F—" I began but caught myself. I had been diverted enough. I was already *on* a detour. Now I was being detoured from my detour? We were getting closer. Shit was happening.

Will popped out of the car and came to my side. "Mess?" He chewed on his lip, his gaze already falling on the grassy shoulder and the gathering of lofty trees beyond it. He kicked at a few pieces of crumbled old pavement.

I put my arm around his shoulder to keep him beside me. "Yup."

"Deep breaths, Mom," he said, mimicking Susie's words. *Three deep breaths. Pause. Let it go. Do something positive.*

Sometimes I felt like Will...I could only handle so

much on my invisible plate for the day, and once that extra morsel, that tiny crumb, was plopped on the mounting pile of crap, I imploded. Then I recovered. My heart was covered with bandages, some tightly attached, some hanging on by a paltry piece of adhesive.

I tapped a hand on my thigh and continued to peer ahead, while evaluating the situation and considering the next move.

A tremulous voice interrupted my contemplations. "May need to wait this one out. We're heading north to Greer Spring campground, a few miles off this exit here, and up Route 19. I think there was an accident ahead," the woman near us said, pointing in the direction of the detour and past her old, dirt-splattered and jangling station wagon. A grandmotherly smile creased her weathered skin. A man, in his sixties by my guess, sat in the driver seat, his pit-stained white shirt doing nothing to hide the rotund belly that touched the steering wheel. He cursed and slammed his hands on the wheel. The woman jumped, as did I. "Dennis," she chided in her scratchy, submissive voice.

He grumbled incoherently beneath a grizzled beard and popped open a soda can. He slurped it and burped. "Goddamn traffic," he mumbled.

She whispered, "Our son's in Kansas."

"Ah." I tightened my embrace around Will, who remained silent.

"You going west, too?" She eyed Will and then our fully loaded car with curiosity, her hands on her round hips. Her gaze paused too long for my liking. My intuition blipped.

Ping, ping, ping. As nice as she appeared,

something smelled fishy. I'm not sure why I thought so. Perhaps it was just paranoia. Perhaps it was this entire trip filled with one shitty thing after another.

I nodded and mumbled a "yeah" and turned toward Will. His glassy eyes stared ahead. At first, I thought he was taking in the horde of cars and people, assessing. No. He stared at nothing, a faraway look in his face. "Honey, why don't you hop in the car?" I urged him.

He didn't respond, his body rigid. I tried again. "Will. Will?" I raised my voice and shook his shoulder gently. I waved my hand before him. He didn't blink. "Will?" I said a third time with an urgent shake and my pulse quickening. Finally, he snapped out of it.

"In the car, honey."

He nodded and hopped in, not asking a single question about the commotion outside. That was double-weird. He stared off like that sometimes, but to not ask questions?

I turned around to see the woman standing closer to me.

"Where's your man?" Her squinting look fell on the wedding ring which encircled my left ring finger.

"Meeting us," I vaguely lied. Thankfully Will didn't hear me as he shut the door behind him. He dug out his paper and pencil box. Okay, well, he seemed in check now.

"Clara, get your ass in here. The traffic's moving now!" her husband said.

"Comin', Denny." The woman lowered her head like a chicken caught out of the coop, muttered a "good day" to me, and returned to her car. The old wagon rumbled, a belt screeching, as he accelerated. It clunked sickly as they continued on their way. I wasn't sure their car would make it that far.

I got back in my SUV.

I glanced at the clock on the dash. It was fast approaching dinner. I yawned and swallowed the bland, gritty taste on my tongue, the kind associated with colds. I grabbed two cold medicine tablets and took them with a chug of water. As I reached for a bag of hard candies, my heart did a flop.

Shit, no.

I needed to move!

The transient scent of sulfur infiltrated my nostrils.

Flop. Thump.

Wait, that *was* ash. I couldn't see it—yet—it lingered in the air, minute particles slowly making their way east. I coughed and urged Will to buckle his seatbelt. "Detour, honey. Camp tonight."

My mind spiraled down the dark path as I shifted the car into drive.

Ash. Driving. Slick roads. Those guys who robbed us. The guys who tried to hurt me. Contaminated water. Gas restrictions.

Finn.

Will.

Reid.

Flop. Thump.

Palpitations seized me.

A horse barreled within my chest. I knew I didn't need to look to see my heart pounding and chest heaving. The traffic stopped again. I closed my eyes and eased my head back against the headrest.

Breathe, peaceful thoughts. Breathe. Shit, not now. Not now!

Somebody honked for us to go. I ignored them.

"Can we make a fire?" Will asked.

My fingertips tingled again.

The only way to get my body under control was to sit perfectly still, breathe, or better, and it was not an option, lie down.

"Mom?" he asked again, higher-pitched.

"Sure," I said, too tersely, fighting for control.

The person honked again. I accelerated.

As I breathed through the anxiety attack, gulping air, we followed the line of cars north on Route 19 to the Greer Spring campground.

As suddenly as they had begun, the palpitations ceased with a soothing rush of blood pressure and heartrate returning to normal. It was a wave of immediate relief much like when medicine kicks in or a cramp goes away. My body responded like it had just run a marathon.

We arrived to a swarm of others like us with fully stocked vehicles. We couldn't get an adequate campsite, but the managers told us to park wherever we could locate a spot. My claustrophobia kicked in. This part of Missouri wasn't exactly a metropolis according to the brochure the manager handed me. *Mark Twain Forest*, it read. *Where plains meet forests and streams, and where folks lose themselves in its quiet woods to hike, fish, and explore.*

Mark Twain made me think of Reid. I wondered if he had some Twain packed in his backpack with the Lewis.

We found a spot along the edge beside another family. A mother clucked at her two young daughters to stay nearby while she carted items out of her minivan. "Samantha, don't ya go too far!" she said with a thick southern twang. "Get over here and help your pa, please."

This part of the park gave the impression of intending to be a private, secluded campground, surrounded by a jungle-like forest of oaks, hickories, and maples. Now it was tent city. I was tempted to sleep in the car again. I had a feeling that I wouldn't get much rest tonight.

The near whisper of a river echoed among the trees and thick branches as we emerged from the car. I blinked and took purposeful breaths, still recovering from the anxiety attack. My stomach twisted. Perhaps food, water, and rest would help. A nice campfire with Will.

I checked the locks, the bikes, and mounted tire, although I wasn't sure who'd want a blown-out tire. Regrettably, I had forgotten to pack my cable lock for the bikes. The rack was secure though, bolted near the middle of the tire. On Will's insistence, I set up the tent.

He paced in front of the car, his range slowly getting farther away from me. "Not too far," I compromised. He needed his mental break as much as I desired mine.

He threw a few sticks into our meager log pile that wasn't lit yet. He then poked around the front of the car and briefly disappeared.

"Will..."

No response.

"Will..." I stood from my campfire prep, my muscles throbbing. "Want to explore?"

"Yes!" He was already moving.

After checking our locks, we made our way to the visitor's information sign at the nearby trailhead.

Apparently, we picked an ideal spot for my young explorer.

"Greer Spring," he read. "The second largest spring in Missouri, dumping two hundred million gallons of water daily into the Eleven Point National Scenic River." He traced the map. "Only a mile, Mom. Let's go!" He hopped from foot to foot.

The river beckoned us, its urgent whooshing reverberating throughout the campground. I envisioned a nerve-wracking night's sleep. Will's obsession with water dwarfed any serenity that came with listening to a river while sleeping. He might get it in his head to wander off to explore. That kid and water. Be it puddles, ponds, frozen patches along a roadside, rivers...it didn't matter. Finn would be the one running off the school bus to embrace me in a hug or offer a grimace and tell me how he didn't get "green" on his behavior chart, while Will was the one who made a beeline for the nearest puddle or the pile of hardened sand and ice in winter that had been cleared to the roadside by a plow. Every day. Every single day.

Being this far from our campsite sent my pulse soaring again. "No, Will, it's late. We need to get—"

"Finn. Yeah, I know," he said with a kick of his shoe in the dirt. "I'm tired of this trip, Mom. This is taking way too long. We're not *seeing* anything." He started for the trail.

"Will, we have to go back. I can't leave our stuff unattended." *Dammit, AJ.* Why had I offered him an excursion if I couldn't follow through?

He began down the trail.

"Will..." I grabbed his shirt sleeve. "No."

His face broke. "You said we could explore!" The

dimples on his high cheekbones deepened the way they did when he got upset.

"I'm sorry. Another time."

"Will we be back here?"

"I don't know."

He tried again to go on the path, blatantly ignoring me.

Lord, his mind was already set. I'd screwed up. I grabbed him firmly. "No. We have to go back. Now."

"Urghhh!" His face flushed red, and he shoved me as he bolted for the campsite.

I tripped.

"Jesus!" I said. "Will!" I righted myself and chased after him. He was faster, nimbly weaving between campsites, around a rock, and past tents and cars. I ran around one such car and collided with a guy carrying a heavy duffel bag.

"Harrumph!" the man said.

I echoed his sentiment. "Sorry!"

I lost sight of Will and reached our campsite a moment later. He was nowhere. This was not the place for this to happen. I could handle the meltdowns almost anywhere, but not in a sea of tents, cars, people, and trees. Eyes, so many eyes. "Will!" I hollered, disregarding the stares from onlookers. Worry warmed my cheeks and my breath caught, as my lack of energy took its toll. I pulled open the tent flap. Not there.

"Over there," a sweet, twangy voice said.

It was the mom at the campsite beside us. "Huh?"

She pointed toward our car.

I hurried to the front bumper.

"Thank God!" I said, rushing to him as he crouched by the tire.

I scooped him into my arms. I bit my tongue for chiding him, but did say, "I'm sorry, Will. I'm sorry."

"The car was locked," he said through tears.

I rubbed his cheek and let serenity override his unease. I didn't need to say much. I knew it would pass. Crisis averted for now.

He tapped his hands against the car's frame. "I want to go home."

I nodded my agreement, feeling one of the bandages on my heart peel away. I took his hands and curled them within mine so he could safely tap as we sat for a few silent minutes.

We returned to our spot and started the fire in mundane ritual, quietly.

Then he asked, "What's for dinner?"

I rummaged through the storage container. Will climbed into the SUV. I withdrew a can of highly processed spaghetti.

"Yum!" He grabbed it from me, found the can opener, and set to work. Bam, back to normal. It was like it hadn't happened.

For him.

My pulse was still fitful.

He was a roller-coaster ride for my sanity. As was my own damn anxiety.

He fastened the can opener onto the top of the can with great care, working his fingers around the handle, clicking it shut, and then twisting the crank. He didn't whine or grow frustrated. He concentrated on it like he would on anything else, like building the proper Lego structure, lining all his crayons in rainbow order, or constructing a long bridge using his marble-run pieces and blocks. It struck a chord in me watching him. I pulled out my journal.

Will had dinner covered. "Oh, Harrison, you'd be proud," I whispered. Despite the meltdown only moments before, I had to admit that he had come far from years past.

I sat beside Will as he dumped the can of spaghetti into a pot, then delicately, like the pot was a breakable glass filled to the brim with water, laid it on the grill atop the fire. His flip-flopping between cautious scrutiny and assertiveness baffled me. Which way he shifted on those scales depended on the task or project, and just as I thought I had him figured, he'd shift on me.

He grinned at me. My soul quivered. It wasn't his usual "Am I doing this right?" or "I know I am different, Mom, please don't be sad" or "I'm confused" or "They don't understand me" look.

I returned the smile. *Yes, honey, you are different. Oh, but, you are such a wonderful different.*

Seeing as he had dinner covered, I turned to the next clean journal page.

I found myself writing about him.

I'd kept a long list in my head of all his "quirks" that in the early years I'd pushed under the rug and attributed to his unique personality: screaming when the blender or vacuum was on, being afraid to sit on grass until he was three years old, keeping to himself, forming fond attachments to his teachers, flipping over and spinning the wheels on anything, even doll strollers...the list had become so long, I truly stopped keeping it.

The dots finally connected once he approached grade school. He'd have horrible panic-attack meltdowns when he couldn't find us, and he was overwhelmed by busy, loud places. He struggled with flexible, gray thinking. He loved routines. He kept his kindergarten teacher on track with the time and schedule. He obsessed on topics too mature for a preschooler and kindergartner. He drew the same things *repeatedly*. My friends doted on that marvel. Admittedly, yeah, his maps were spot on.

When his first-grade teacher called about behavior concerns, the nagging voice in my mind had grown to siren-level.

Then came all the testing at school and with physicians. That December, right before school break, the schedule had been changed due to a holiday program. Trigger. He ran the entire loop of the school hallways, and ended in his classroom, recoiling, growling, and crying in a corner of books while the school psychologist tried to coax him out.

Bittersweet sentiment pervaded my memory. He'd come such a long way since then.

He removed his dinner from the grill and scooped it into his bowl.

I paused with my pen. What about me? Was I getting closer to acceptance?

Did I push conformity upon him? Questions bounced around in my head daily. Usually, I could quiet them, but some days they raged, they roared, they crushed my spirit.

"Here, Mom." Will handed me a bowl filled with the meal and a spoon.

I laid the journal aside. "Thank you, honey."

No more introspection tonight. I was doing damn fine with him. And he was doing damn fine with himself.

"It's going to be a gibbous moon tonight, Mom. Finn would be excited," he said, chewing happily. He loved to eat with his fingers, and I didn't nag him to use his spoon. The world was going to pot; he could eat any way he pleased.

"It was a full moon when you born."

"And gibbous for Finn, right?" he asked.

"Yup."

He pulled out some of the alphabet spaghetti and lined them on his paper towel that lay across his thigh.

"What are you spelling?"

"Finn."

"Pardon me," a voice said from nearby. It was our camp neighbor, the mom who pointed out Will's hiding place.

"Hi," I said.

One of her daughters approached, too, her matching short fair-haired bob bouncing with each light step. The girl, roughly Will's height and probably close to his age, toted a bag of marshmallows and a gray plush animal.

"Would you and your son like a s'more? Well, not really a s'more, but we do have marshmallows and chocolate bars," the petite woman said, stepping closer. "I'm Geena." She wiped a hand on her cut-off jeans and offered it. Sweat beaded at her temple, and bangs fell across her forehead. She blew a breath to toss the wisps aside. "Geesh, it's hot tonight."

I shook her hand. "AJ."

"Hi! I'm Sam," her daughter said to Will. "Want a marshmallow?" She showed him the bag.

"I can't have them unless I roast them," he said,

181

returning his gaze to his dinner bowl and scooping the last bite.

"We have chocolate, too," she said, stepping closer. "Who's that?" She pointed to his plush dog.

"That's Douglas," he said matter-of-factly. "Sam is a boy's name."

She plopped next to him on the ground. "It's a girl's name, too. It's short for Samantha. This is Winnie, my gray cat. Do you have a cat? We have one at home. We'll be home in a few days."

Will perked up. "I have a cat. His name is Snow. He's black though, not white like real snow. Do you like volcanoes?"

"Not really," Sam said. She reached into her bag and pulled out a marshmallow. "I need a stick."

Will stood, his face alight. "There are nice ones here," he said, leading her to our extra pile of wood. "But not those, there. Those are wands."

Geena smiled at the two of them. I sighed. "Where have my manners gone? Would you like to sit?" I asked.

"Aww, thanks. Y'all heading home, too?"

"Not exactly. You?" I stretched my legs with a moan. I sipped my water, wishing it were coffee. Iced or hot, I didn't care. I was wary of venturing to the office, feeling a need to stay close to our site this time.

"We're heading home to Atlanta. We were on a trip to see family in Kansas when well, you know...," she said with a hand flourish. "Need to get home before it gets worse."

Her breezy demeanor broke through my guard. "I'm driving west to meet with family...well...my brother and my other son." There. I said it.

She clasped a hand across her chest. "Your son?"

I nodded.

She exhaled, breathy. "You're going west...into this stuff?" Dark green eyes lit with intrigue. Or was that dismay?

"Sort of?" I said meekly. "They're missing. I've not heard from them."

She released a throaty sigh. "Sorry to hear that. There's no sort of about it, love." She fanned her face, the campfire's heat adding to her perspiration. "Well, you've got some gumption. But hey, it's y'all's family. You do what you gotta do, love. Nothing gets between a momma and her cubs. I'd do the same." When she said that, her regard drifted to Will and then returned to me. "Sweet kid," she added in a whisper.

She shared a look with me that only mothers who understood did. No judgment. No derision. Clear, unadulterated understanding.

Will and Sam already located sticks and were roasting a few marshmallows. They laughed and talked about cats.

Boldly, I said, "Kansas...where did you come from? How was it?"

"Not good, love. Not good. We drove south from Topeka. Things ain't good there already. No ash there yet, but I heard about some in the western parts, near Dodge City. Power is down in half the place. Contaminated water from the rain, too."

I fidgeted with the edge of my T-shirt. She didn't ask for details on where we were heading and a part of me didn't want to verbalize it. Instead, we both watched the kids in silence as they roasted marshmallows and ate chocolate. She gave off a pleasant vibe; for once, I didn't feel the need to make idle conversation.

Will brought me a roasted marshmallow on a stick. "Here, Mom," he said. I took it off and let the gooey inside and the crispy outside dissolve on my tongue.

"Thanks, honey." I wiped my mouth with the back of my hand.

Melted chocolate accented his dimpled cheek when he smiled.

"Mom!" Geena's other daughter hollered from their camp. "I need help with my braid."

Geena rose with a muffled groan. "Coming." She turned to me. "Was nice chattin' with ya, AJ. We're yonder here if you need anything. Anything at all. Maybe come join us for breakfast? Come, Sam."

"Bye, Will," Sam said, skipping to her mother.

"Best of luck," Geena added to me, her eyes somber and true. "You'll get your cub, momma bear."

****

"Three more pages, Mom?"

"You said that twelve pages ago, honey."

Endearing eyes held mine over the flicker of the lantern. "I know I can read it, but I love listening to you read it. You read better than Dad."

Ouch. "Okay, three, but that's all," I said through a yawn. I continued reading the book to him in my best lyrical and expressive voice. Harrison had bought this book about a boy's adventure in Alaska for him. Will had enjoyed reading with his father each night. They'd already read the first book of Will's wizard-cat series together, and I toted along the second one.

Will yawned, too. "Time for bed," I said after finishing the pages.

"Aww…Mom, a few more," he said as he wriggled

himself inside his sleeping bag and rested his head on his pillow. "But…"

I gave him my no-nonsense look. "I'll sing the states song. Here's your whistle."

He nodded, laid the whistle beside his pillow, and closed his eyes.

After singing, I made my way to the tent flap. "Love you, honey."

"Love you, Mom."

I was outside the tent when he said, his voice halfway to sleepyville, "I miss Dad."

That was the first time he'd said it in the year since Harrison's death. Of course, he'd said it in the early weeks, but he'd stopped. I poked my head in. "I do, too. You're my main man now, Will."

His eyes remained closed, but a smile curved his lips. "I'll take care of you, like Daddy did. Finn will, too, when we find him."

"Here." I cracked and shook a glow stick. "Illuminate!" It glowed neon yellow.

"Impressive, Mom, but you're not a wizard," Will said, taking the glow stick from me.

I zipped the tent flap most of the way closed, leaving the lantern near the opening. I stoked the fire aimlessly. I popped my earbuds in.

A few minutes later, my phone vibrated in my pocket, scaring the hell out of me. I fumbled with eager hands to see if it was Brandon. It was a text message from Sarah. *Checking in. Be safe, honey. Thinking about you.* I tried calling her, but it didn't work. I had no idea when she'd sent it. I texted a response, but that didn't send either. I was officially in the blackout-zone now. I was surprised her text came through at all. At least she hadn't tried to dissuade me from going again. Heck, I was halfway there.

I took her message as a sign. I was going to get through this. I emptied my mind as dusk's shadows lengthened and the fire dwindled to black remains. Geena had long since disappeared with her daughters into their pop-up camper. All my neighbors had settled in for the night.

I was going to find my son.

Despite my upbeat tunes, exhaustion wrapped itself around me as the last orange flames disappeared. It was only eight p.m., but driving all day had taken its toll, my cold lingered, and I was pretty sure the blackouts and anxiety attack were from my antidepressant withdrawal.

Emotional and physical fatigue had set in for sure.

I was about to turn in when the familiar whoosh of bike chains froze my step. Even with the chatter and rustlings among the overflowing campground, I recognized that sound instantly. I hadn't noticed any other bikes in the campground. With my senses alerted, I searched the obscurities of late evening, surprised with the hope that filled me. I had messed up with Reid.

I squinted. The whoosh drew farther away, and I found myself stepping from my perimeter of safety—the ten paces I had allowed between me and Will and our stuff.

Whoosh. Clink, clink, clink. Whirr.

There it was, but it receded as the bike distanced itself from our site. Had he seen me? I wanted to holler, "Reid!" but I didn't. He screwed up, too, but I was the bigger ass. Why would he come back? It probably wasn't him anyway. I returned to the edge of my perimeter.

I stood for several minutes, ear outstretched, ignoring the clamor of the camps. Nothing. He was gone…somewhere in that dark vastness of people, tents, cars, and trees.

I returned to the now dead fire. I cupped dirt and plopped it on the remaining embers and cozied myself beside Will in the tent, tire iron in hand.

Chapter Ten
Missing

*September, Two Years Ago*

"Come on, slow poke!" I hollered as I reached another impassable granite boulder. By boulder, I meant car-sized obstruction on our trail. Good grief, Katahdin was a relentless mountain. Most challenging one yet. Especially on our mid-thirty-something bodies.

Harrison huffed as he caught up to me on the trail. "I'm not the spry guy you traipsed all over New Zealand and Australia with, am I?"

I wiped sweat from my brow and then did the same to his high forehead as we both caught our breath. "Slow and steady wins the race." He removed his ballcap and ran a hand through his thinning, ash-blond hair.

He managed a tight-lipped smile, but a lively twinkle sparkled at me. He planted a peck on my lips. "If we ever get there." He slid his hat on his head.

I sipped from the water pouch tucked in my daypack and examined the large granite glacial rock before me. "The books said this trail was the easiest way. Ha. Longest. Definitely strenuous. Easiest? I beg to differ."

Harrison equally surveyed the mounds of rocks before us. He rubbed his arthritic knee. "Yeah, hardly."

the squawk of birds by the stream. What was
n and tents? Perhaps it was the intimacy. We
compact, two-person tent that lacked standing
fering plenty of opportunity to get close.
smirked back. "Never."

were pushing noon. I was going to hurt for
erhaps the hotel we'd presciently booked for
had a soaking tub. Daylight was going to be at
k by the time we completed the eleven-hour,
e hike.

wever, a sun-drenched September with a
t sky and ideal temperature gifted us. Pleasant
y, too, although he continued to grumble.
rrison stood and looked skyward. "We need to
he summit soon."
e scrambled, huffed, moaned, and stopped
.
rrison cursed as he slipped and scraped a knee.
wrinkled his high forehead.
top it," I said.
e glared at me. "Stop what?"
Thinking about work."
e compressed his lips in his usual passive-
ssive avoidance.
They're okay. They won't die without you."
*could use you*, I wanted to say. I wasn't going to
another argument today. I'd let the resentment
the laundry list of tedious tasks I did daily
se my husband worked long hours continue to
le and hiss. Another time. It's not like he didn't
dy know about my grievances. He wasn't going
here. We'd get through this phase like we did with
e others.

"Okay, strong guy. I need help. No grips or
ladders. Push me."

He did. He gave my bottom a firm push. His hands
purposely rested longer on my rear than was necessary.
I chuckled and then heaved myself over the boulder.
"How do short girls, with no knights at their side, do
this? You can't exactly push a strange woman up by her
backside."

Harrison laughed as he hoisted himself effortlessly,
although with a painful wince, after me. I stuck my
tongue out at him. "You suck."

We scrambled over granite boulders the size of
refrigerators and sofas. I shielded my eyes from the
nearly midday-sun glare. An endless azure sky and
craggy mountain dominated the scenery.

We drew closer to the peak. "Maybe this is it?"

"Two false peaks already."

Nope, it wasn't. Damn, this mountain was hard.
Katahdin provoked us as we continued our trek over a
third false peak. "I think we're getting close," I said.

"Well, the Gateway is the toughest stretch,"
Harrison said.

"I'll be doing the ouch-shuffle for days," I added,
rubbing my quads, allowing my heartrate to recover. I
puffed my inhaler and paused. "Let's rest," I offered as
Harrison caught his breath and grimaced,
unsuccessfully hiding his knee pain. The doctor had
said no more hikes. Did he listen? Well, part of it was
me. You only had so much time in life to enjoy your
passions.

Several other hikers found our cluster of carefully
stacked rocks to be a worthy resting spot. We
exchanged exhausted smiles with them.

Harrison opened his trusty old compass, which had joined us on our trips to New Zealand, Australia, Utah, California, and Scotland. Bulky, it'd triggered a frisk and closer examination by the TSA staff at an airport on our way to Utah. I smirked. "Why do you carry that clunky thing around? Doesn't your smartphone have GPS?"

"It's fun," he said.

Old atlases and compasses...my husband who worked in a high-tech science career still loved the classic tools of explorers. He worked the compass, and then he pulled the map from his backpack. Well, even *I* thought trail maps were cool.

"You're my North," he said.

I smiled and leaned in for a kiss. "And you're mine."

I handed him a clementine and captured a few photos of the green valley carved by glaciers. Far below us, streams meandered and trickled through the tree line and waterfalls cascaded down the rocks we'd traversed hours before. A sudden wind gusted, and I clung to our precarious outcrop. Harrison embraced me, and I let my body rest into his, not bothered by his sweat.

"We've got this," I said to him.

"Always the optimist, my darling," Harrison said, rubbing and stretching his knees. I was impressed though. He was hanging in there.

"It's how we roll. I'm your cheerleader, honey. I'll get you there. Just don't lose me on the way down."

"Never, my HBA."

Honey baby angel—my nickname he had given me in grad school. HBA. Not sure how we'd created that one.

---

We laughed. On all our mounta[...] one who cheered us up, up, up. He [...] and heaved. He was the one who [...] around on many hikes. Not me. [...] descent was a different story though[...] knees buckled, and feet ached as w[...] He'd always lose me in the scree s[...] maze of rocky boulders. We made [...] our climbs though: Mt. Washingt[...] Ridge in New Hampshire, Mt. Mar[...] and next, Mt. Marcy in New York. [...] all the highest peaks in New England[...] bagged our fair share of mountains i[...] like Beinn Eighe in Scotland, parts o[...] Mt. Cook in New Zealand, and a f[...] Sierra Nevada range. I was his yin an[...]

Now Katahdin. The beast. Or at [...] liked to call it.

I searched my pack for a choco[...] bar.

"Katahdin means 'greatest mou[...] the Penobscot Indians," he said matter[...]

I tore open the granola bar and b[...] the calories. I'd burn five thousand [...] mentioned that before."

He scratched his chin. "Ah."

He had a habit of repeating the sa[...] and statistics as if it were the first time[...] son. I loved that about him though.

I poked his shoulder. "You too [...] morning?" We'd camped in Ka[...] campground the night before and had [...] start after an early morning tent dallia[...]

The sulky quietness continued as we huffed along through car-sized sections of boulders stacked, wedged, and nestled in such a way that made climbing hard without the few handholds and simple metal rungs for gripping. I was sure I'd be seeing gray-speckled granite slabs in my sleep.

Harrison said, "Allen is such an ass. He was harping on me about delegating work. Delegate to whom? He won't hire me any replacements for Rob or Chandra. The clients won't let up. Allen says work harder. Harder? Yet also delegate? How do I do both? I can only put in so many hours a week."

*Try seventy.* Yeah, I'd counted. "They're okay. You can check your email when we get to the hotel tonight."

*Could we enjoy one day without them?* I fumed internally, attacking the rocks.

Finally, the false peaks and miles of boulder scrambles were behind us, and we reached the alpine tablelands. I adjusted my backpack, chugged water, and turned to enjoy the 360-degree view. We had another mile to the actual summit, but I absorbed the eerie beauty. "It's like another planet."

"Ha, like Mars. I bet Will would say that, huh?" Harrison echoed my sentiments.

"Wow, yes." Rusty red-brown vegetation and short alpine grasses carpeted the rocky and mostly flat mile of tableland. My feet, knees, hands, butt, and abs all sighed. I squinted at Katahdin's summit, Baxter Peak, in the distance. One final five-hundred-foot ascent after the next mile and we'd be there. I paused to look around, and of all places, on the flat tableland, took a wrong step and nearly twisted my ankle.

"Damn!"

"Close one. You okay?" Harrison said, approaching.

Frazzled, I inhaled but breathed a sigh. "Yeah." Ever since my tumble down the steps to feed our cat Snow, and the sickening cracks associated with that fall, my right ankle liked to give me a hard time.

"And to think the kids want another cat!" Harrison said too gleefully for my liking.

I shot him my best evil glare. He laughed. I rubbed my ankle.

I was grateful we'd taken this way instead of the Chimney Pond route. We'd hiked to the pond on a previous trip, and one glance up that steep side had me reconsidering the Knife's Edge. Hell, no.

Quite opposite from the placid, gravelly, and peculiar tableland, party central welcomed us at the summit. Harrison pointed to a couple of twenty-somethings sharing beers, yes, beers at the top. One guy stood by the Katahdin signpost and held his tattered backpack over his head. He was definitely a through-hiker who had conquered the entire two thousand miles of the Appalachian Trail. People laughed, snapped photos, drank, and—

"God, is that champagne?" I asked.

Harrison sniggered. "Naturally!"

I snapped dozens of photos. I gawked over the other edge, and by edge I meant sheer drop, to Chimney Pond and the three trails leading to the summit from that side. Below seemingly tiny deep blue lakes winked at us. To our east teased the jagged Knife's Edge. My fear of heights—okay, my fear of falling—would've halted me there. However, it was a breathtaking sight!

"Look at that!"

"You wouldn't have made it," Harrison said.

"Nope. Glad we took the Hunt Trail."

We ate in silence, taking it all in. "Maybe one day, the boys would want to do this," Harrison said.

I bit into my turkey sandwich. "Maybe."

We were both aware that Will didn't have it in him. Finn, maybe. "Let's try smaller ones first. They do like camping."

"Is he going to be okay, AJ?" Harrison said, his voice low as he tipped his head back to look at a cluster of puffy clouds.

I rested my hand on his knee. He interlaced his fingers with mine.

When Harrison's melancholy about Will kicked in, my hopeful optimism evaporated.

A perfect metaphor straddled us. Rough-edged granite boulders. I was my family's rock. Even rocks cracked and eroded, though. Doubts wormed their way in and joined the turkey sandwich in my stomach. And here I'd thought I had adjusted well to Will's diagnosis. Maybe not so much. "Yeah. He will be."

"It's my fault," Harrison said.

"Nonsense. He's both of us."

"Yeah, but…"

"Nonsense," I said firmly. "You've done well in life. Look, you've got me!"

My attempt at humor didn't work on him. He hunched forward, a frown creasing his face.

I thought about all the childhood tales that Patsy had regaled us with through the years. Harrison had been a tough kid. He'd been labeled with ADHD and autism, but Patsy scoffed at labels, and I never got a real answer from her about the "label." The 1980s had been a nebulous decade…they had pushed the limited meds available at the time on her as a solution. Not for her son. Instead, she shuffled him to different schools, quit her job, and worked hard to see him and his younger brother, who now lived and worked in London, succeed.

Beside me sat a PhD scientist—with an awesome and understanding wife—who had prevailed. Sure, he was quirky, socially awkward, and not the best at reading me…but God, he was loyal, loving, smart, and we shared a great fondness for learning and nature. All couples had their flawed communication skills and longing to be understood by their partner. We tried. We tried damn hard. He was a doting father to the boys. We shared a lot of similar interests and sitting on this weathered granite intrusion was one of them.

And I loved him dearly.

Okay, Will *was* a lot like him. So what? Harrison turned out well. "He'll be fine," I repeated.

Despite my hiker's appetite, I couldn't finish my sandwich. "I think I should quit my job."

"What? You love writing for the magazine."

I tucked my sandwich away, turning from Harrison, because the real reason I needed to quit couldn't be said. I didn't want to stir up an argument of who did more. Nobody ever won that debate. Frankly, I couldn't juggle it all anymore between Will's needs, the household, my part-time work, and dreams to write. The list was long. I was the one who stayed home and rearranged around the quandary of snow or vacation days, summers, appointments, illnesses. Work at home with our two kids was impossible. Novels took a lot of time, too. It wasn't a nooks and crannies kind of career. I was tired thinking about it all. All I said though was, "I need time to work on my novels."

Harrison saw through my vagueness, but he didn't say anything. He knew. I knew. Something had to go. Although I identified with and enjoyed my journalism job at the magazine, where I interviewed locals along the Maine coast and into the Massachusetts and New Hampshire regions, and highlighted the cultural and socio-economic hallmarks of New England, it wasn't my passion. I loved writing fiction.

"Maybe in a year?" I offered in my usual indecisive fashion.

"Yeah, give it time, honey baby angel. You'll get there," he said. He took my hand in his and kissed it. I smiled at his baby blues.

We hiked quieter, Harrison grumbling less, both of us reflective. That's the thing with hikes. Your brain pondered, daydreamed, worried, zoned out. You snapped at your spouse from exhaustion. It brought out the best and worst in you.

"Wouldn't it be great to take the boys to see Yellowstone?" Harrison said on the descent.

"It would be."

"Then let's do it."

I heaved a resigned sigh as I gauged the hike down. Well, it *had* been worth it. "Can you swing the time off?"

"Allen can suck it. Yes. I have so many vacation hours, and I get that bonus in January. Next summer?"

Elation eased my achy knees, shins, feet, and hands as we daydreamed about our first family trip via airplane to Yellowstone and the grand Northwest circle of a volcanic wonderland. Harrison mused, excited to explore an opportunity that the boys would adore.

We laughed about the boys' latest escapades at home. We gloried in Will's abilities to remember facts and draw kick-ass maps and charts. We fantasized about all the parks we'd visit on our trip. Harrison teased me about my fear of bears. I poked his slightly bulging gut, pointing out how many calories and pounds he'd shed today.

We held hands through the flatter tableland until we reached the drop off to start the steep descent into the rocky boulders and tree line. I slid on my hands and bottom more times than I could count, and my scraped palms would surely remember it come morning. Harrison soon lost me in the maze of boulders that were the Gateway.

We fell into our comfortable hiking rhythm as we let the day settle into our souls, as it warmed our hearts, and reconnected us in the way it always did.

****

*Present Day*

Usually a light sleeper, and probably half expecting our former travel companion to reappear, I was roused around five a.m. by heated whispers in our campsite.

"Clara, check the doors," a voice growled.

I lay perfectly still and listened, stupefied with sleep and still clinging to the dream—well, a vivid memory, actually—I had about Harrison. I blinked as wakefulness shrouded the last threads of my dream.

I held my breath.

"They're all locked, Denny."

Heavy footsteps trotted toward my car. Somebody jiggled the door handles louder and cursed. "Come here. We'll take the bikes at least."

I felt around for the tire iron and realized it was still in my numb hand. Will stirred beside me. He had my morning alertness. *Don't wake*, I willed him. No use. He spoke. "Mom?"

*For f's sake.* Okay, there, I didn't say *that* word as much as I wanted to. Perhaps Will's reminders were working on me. But my God. Another robbery or attempt? This made three on my trip, and I was only in Missouri. What the hell was wrong with people? Did I wear a target on my shirt?

"Mom, what's that noise?" his voice squeaked, not frightened, but curious.

I put my fingers on his lips to shush him.

"Bad people?" he whispered, getting the hint as I slowly removed my fingers. He hugged Douglas closer to his chest.

I nodded. I needed to pay better heed to my intuition. Should have slept in the car.

"Stay here, Will. Do *not* leave," I ordered. I grabbed the whistle and put it around his neck. "Okay?"

"They're not bears," he said.

"Quiet, honey. Blow the whistle if-if-if...just stay, okay?"

"Mom...," he said, his voice breaking.

"Shush," I said. I gave him a brief squeeze. "Brave wizard, it'll be okay. Stay. I *will not* leave you. I need to make these bullies go away, okay? Give them a stern talking-to."

I then crept to the tent flap, the sleeping bag crinkling noisily. I had to surprise them. I opted for the tire iron instead of the kitchen knife. It seemed less dangerous, less lethal. Less...permanent. This was not a time to kill. It was a time to kick someone's ass. Although I wished I had Harrison's gun to wave in threat.

"Get away from my car!" I shouted, raising the tire iron with shaking arms as I emerged from the tent. My elbow gave with the quick, heavy movement. I fumbled, cursed, and regained my stance, hoping to look like the devil.

It was the old man from the beater station wagon. He jumped. He had one bike halfway off the rack. He turned and glared at me. "We need this more than you do, darlin'. We were gonna leave your bikes."

I remembered their wheezing station wagon, and the truth clicked in my mind.

Clara retreated from her fiddling with a door lock and raised her hands. "Come on, sweet gal. You won't be hurtin' if we take a few things. We need to get to our son."

"So do I, and I'm not getting there by bike," I said, louder. I surprised myself by drawing closer. "Step away from my car, and leave my bikes the hell alone."

"Look, darlin', we don't mean you no harm. You look like you'll be okay. I'm sure you got money to get there," Dennis said in a cool voice, but his face said otherwise as he evaluated me in the way a panhandler eyed a person in a designer coat. He approached me, hands outstretched. Seeing that Dennis had me under control, Clara returned to her lock picking. Could people actually pick car locks? What the hell?

I maintained strong eye contact and straightened my posture.

Dawn's murky shadows stole across the campground. It all happened at once. I shifted my stance, clamped both hands around the tire iron and swung as Dennis lunged at me, a scowl twisting his unkempt bearded face. Clara unlocked my door and muttered a "sweet Jesus." The heaviness of the tire iron as I wielded it surprised me, but I made like a baseball player aiming to hit one out of the park. The iron thudded into Dennis's pudgy belly, the equivalent of a heavy gym bag. The impact recoiled in my arms. I dropped the iron.

I groaned.

"Oof!" he wheezed and staggered, but then continued toward me, shaking his head.

I cursed like a sailor and stumbled backward, my only weapon gone. I didn't have the pocket knife. Where the hell had I left that? Oh, yeah, in the cup holder in the car. The kitchen knife was in the tent. I groped for my car key in my back pocket and hit the alarm button, sending a piercing shriek through the campground. Drawing attention and help was all I had now.

Clara stumbled back from the car like she'd been scalded. "Shit!" she cried.

Dennis was upon me, beefy hands pinching my upper arms. I shoved my key into my jeans pocket, thanking the stars that I hadn't changed into pajamas last night. I would be damned if he got my car. He smacked the side of my face, not once, but twice.

I lost my footing and fell.

"Mom!" Will cried, emerging from the tent.

Blood trickled from my mouth. My teeth rattled. Oh, my God, they felt loose. No, his punch hadn't been that hard. Pain radiated from my cheek to my temple. My ears rang. Instinct took precedence. "Run, baby, run!" I instantly regretted it, but the momma bear, echoing Geena's words, couldn't let them hurt him. Geena…did she and her family hear my car? Where was my help? Somebody? Anybody…

All the moves I'd learned in the women's self-defense class I took at Will's karate studio…emptied from my brain. *Claw the face. Bite his ears. Make noise. Knee moves.* Oh my God, what were those leg moves? *Up, get up!*

Will whimpered above me, near my head. "Mom!"

I felt Dennis's hovering presence over me as he kicked me in my side. "Bitch!"

Will was there. He kicked Dennis in the shin. "Leave my mom alone, you bully!" He did one of his karate moves, I think his front jab, and got Dennis in the groin. Three years of tiring lessons had paid off, momentarily at least.

"You shit!" Dennis cried, reaching for Will.

I swiped my foot, caught his knee. Yes, that's where. The burly man fell right beside me. "Will! Run, honey! Hide!" I screamed it now.

A crowd formed around us.

"Leave her alone!" a man said. Geena's husband?

"Somebody stop him!" Geena's voice shouted.

"Dennis, you ass! Get over here. Forget them. I got the door open!" Clara's voice shrilled. "Find the keys! Or else I gotta hotwire it. Hurry!"

I blinked away darkness. No, no, no. I wouldn't pass out!

His hands were on me again, searching for the keys. He grunted like a wild pig. A man grabbed him. He shrugged the guy off with a growl and punch.

"You bastard!" Geena cried.

My weaker fingers fought against his as he dug into my pockets. He slapped me around, muttering curses through heavy nasal breathing.

Clara moaned as somebody restrained her. "Let go of me, you ass!"

Jesus, he got the keys.

"No…," I said weakly. "My keys…" I struggled to rise as a dark shape emerged from the crowd and moved past me, stealthy and crouching low. The tire iron scraped the dry ground as he picked it up. The heavy thud of iron met muscle. Dennis grunted in surprise.

"Wha—" Dennis barked.

Painful tears burned my vision. Oh, but I was able to hear, despite the ringing in my ears.

My rescuer didn't hold back.

Crack. The tire iron hit bone.

Crack.

Splatter. Nauseating thuds.

"Oof!"

More screeching. "Denny!"

Crack.

I threw my hand in the air. "Please! Stop!" I breathed, teeth aching.

"Leave her the hell alone!" Reid said to my attackers. His booming voice rippled through me. Then I heard nothing. Muffled ear ringing replaced the car alarm blaring, Clara's shrieking, and the nauseating cracks. Reid's mouth moved with questions.

Soon, the others closed in the space. Geena knelt and helped steady me. Her husband was beside her with a bloody nose.

The ringing in my head lessened, but everything

spun. I blinked and darkness lured me. No. *No*! I swallowed the blood that had pooled in my mouth.

Suddenly, I snapped back to the chaos around us. My hearing returned, sharpened.

"I've got you, love," Geena said.

"I called the police," an older man's rough, croaky voice said. I caught a whiff of stale cigarettes as he hurried past me. "Sonny, get over there. Don't let them leave!"

"Y'all get me some ice, okay?" Geena said to somebody.

I doubted Dennis was going anywhere, his gurgling gasps sickening. Top that with Clara's howling and my car alarm, and I felt I might puke. Somebody grabbed the keys and silenced the alarm.

"Will," I said hoarsely.

My knees swayed.

"Sit, AJ," Geena soothed. "We'll tend to ya."

"No! Will…" I scanned the area. He was nowhere to be found. "Oh, my God. I told him to run. Oh, my God!" Hyperventilation gripped me.

Reid approached. "Breathe, AJ, breathe. We'll find him. Put your head between your knees."

I swatted him and Geena away but did as told. Still unsteady, I turned my head.

Geena said, "We'll help find him. Jared?" She gestured to her husband. Sam approached, clutching her gray cat stuffed animal.

I collected myself. "He's in blue and green jammies," I began with an unsteady voice. "Oh, God." I frantically ripped open the tent flap, futile as it was. Empty. "Will? Will!" I cried. He was nowhere. "Maybe he's in the campground somewhere?"

"We'll search around here," Geena offered. "He couldn't have gotten far."

*Yes, he could.*

I nodded and clung to Geena's empathetic eyes. "H-He likes water...lakes and rivers. He also likes to hide when he's scared. He could be hiding anywhere. He's quiet, skilled at blending in. He likes closets, corners, and tight spaces."

"We'll check tents," she said. "Come, Sam. Jared, you check over there." She waved to her husband and other daughter.

"My brother likes to hide, too," another teen girl said, but it didn't abate my racing fears.

"Yes, tents. Or-or-or, yeah, check behind cars. Under cars. Behind trees. Anywhere a kid could tuck away." My heart almost broke. I'd become accustomed to his coping methods of hiding, but seeing him curled in a closet or under a chair never got easier. I almost added, "He has autism," but I was tired of explaining him that way. Other kids ran and hid, too. Maybe not exactly the way Will did, or for the reasons he did, but all kids got scared. He wasn't a growling lion an adult couldn't approach for risk of him biting their fingers off.

"It'll be okay, AJ," Geena cooed, clasping my hand. She squeezed. "Want me to stay with you?"

"Th-Thank you, but no. I need to look, too," I said through chattering teeth. Worried adrenaline coursed through me. I shook my head, hoping to dislodge my stupor, but instead it pitched me into another dizzy spell. Will was either hiding in a tent, taking flight to God knows where, or...

Visceral emotion told me exactly where he had

gone—to that spring. "The woods, Reid. The woods! That damn spring."

"Thank you, please, go," Reid said to the helpers. "We'll check the surrounding woods."

I stared into Reid's piercing dark expression, hypnotically drawn to the dirt and blood splattered across his cheek and brow. It wasn't mine or his. Retching swelled in my throat. I bit it back.

The woods.

"Wait, AJ, wait!"

I was fast. Reid was faster. He grabbed my arm and stopped me in my tracks, my heels skidding across a patch of gravel on the edge of my campsite. I nearly tripped over an exposed tree root. "We need to approach this sensibly."

He had just beaten Dennis to a bloody pulp and he was telling me to be sensible?

Reid continued in a cool even tone, "He may be close. He may be far. We need to bring stuff."

"Stuff? What kind of stuff? I don't need another checklist! My son's out there because of those assholes, and I need get to him. If he's not hiding in the campground, then he went to the spring. Geena and the others have the campground covered."

I passed a look on the forest before us. Sweeping oaks and ancient evergreens encircled the campground like protective guards to a secret castle. The heyday of summer—dense shrubs, fanning ferns, leaf-covered trees, and burgeoning flowers—thickened the forest. Early dawn's light had begun to penetrate the canopy as long shadows blanketed the campsite. I shivered.

"The longer we wait, the farther he gets," I pleaded.

"We need to be prepared," Reid countered, guiding me toward my car.

Although it wasn't nearly as pine-dominated as the forests in New England, there was no lack of green. I recalled the trailhead post had mentioned this area was sparsely used and the land beyond the campground was privately owned. Normally, such an area would seduce me with its beauty and solitude. Now it was a vise grip. My baby was out there in a damn jungle. Day had barely broken. He didn't even have a glow stick.

I hesitated only for a moment, waiting for the neurons to fire, and it was enough time for Reid to coerce me back to the car. "AJ."

I shrugged from his grip. "Yes. Okay. Can we be quick about it? What the hell do we need?"

Reid already had my keys and handed them to me. I unlocked the car doors. I shifted on my feet, my pulse quickening as he opened the rear hatch door and riffled through bins. I inhaled, and a rasp gripped my lungs with its familiar rattling. Reid located our backpacks; one was Will's backpack from school, covered in weather badges and logos Harrison had sewn on for him, and the other was mine. Well, Harrison's. He'd loved that pack. It was made from recycled plastic water bottles or something silly. Reid tossed in a few waters, snacks, a rope, and the first aid kit.

"We won't need all that," I said.

He held up old bolt cutters, giving me a quizzical glance.

I took them from him and shoved them into a crevice between two totes. "Don't ask."

"Jeez, AJ, you've thought of everything." Reid lifted the case that held the walkie-talkies Finn and Will had gotten for Christmas. They loved to play with them in our backyard and they had a long range. I even had a handheld emergency radio with crank flashlight. We had yet to use that on our trip. With any luck my usual over-packing was just that—I hoped to not need half of this stuff. And this was an already diminished supply thanks to the people who had robbed me in New York.

"Resourceful," I mumbled.

Reid zipped the pack and handed me a flashlight.

"Please…we need to go." I was already inching away as he grabbed my arm and shoved a walkie-talkie into my hand. He took the other. "We're not going together?"

"We may need to split up at some point."

"It won't come to that."

I unzipped the backpack and tossed the walkie-talkie in.

The campground manager and his wife approached. She handed me a wet towel. "I don't have any ice. Sorry," she said. I glanced quickly for Geena. Her family must've already been off in the farther areas of the campground canvasing.

"Huh?" I asked.

She pointed to my face.

"Oh."

I dabbed my cheek with the damp towel, wincing with the touch. She handed me a water bottle, and I took a sip, sloshed, and spat. I repeated it a few times until my spit was no longer bloody. I returned the towel with a muffled thank-you.

"We'll wait here for him if he returns. I've put a call into the police. We'll keep an eye on your car and these sons of bitches. You can give a statement to the police later. There are enough witnesses to take care of this for now," the manager said with a flick of his chin to a hunched Dennis and whimpering Clara. I restrained myself from punching them. Violence would do me no good now.

"Perhaps we should wait for the others who are searching the campground," Reid said.

"No. He's not here."

I shifted away from Reid's dubious look. He spoke to the manager in an unruffled whisper, shook his hand—why did men always do that?—and then we ran to the trailhead. I shouted Will's name, my voice growing hoarse with each call. "Will, come back! It's safe! Will!"

My head pounded from Dennis's assault, but I did my best to ignore it. My son needed me. He couldn't have gotten too far yet. I hoped.

Chapter Eleven
Search and Rescue

Will ran.

He ran like somebody was chasing him. That old meanie coming after him made his legs move faster.

Mom said run. So he did. He ran faster than he did in gym class (which wasn't fast compared to the other kids). Faster than when he played with Finn in blaster and wizard battles. Faster than playing zombie tag in karate class. He was adept at ducking behind the weighted dummy so nobody ever caught him. Faster than the time when he was worried that he couldn't find Mom outside. He was a sneaky hider. He'd find a place to hide until it was safe. One time he was watching the weather forecast and there had been a tornado watch, so he hid under the basement steps. Dad was mad. Well, only a little.

A scream rang behind him like a fire engine's blaring horn. It was that old lady. Her screech bounced off all the trees and boulders. The tiny hairs on his neck rose, and a rush of cold fear ran through him. That old man moaned and growled like a bear. He ran faster. Were they chasing him now?

They were mean bullies. They had tried to steal from them, and they'd hurt Mom. He stopped for the briefest second. Maybe he should go back to check on her. He clutched Douglas tighter to his chest. No, she'd said run.

His heartbeat pounded so loudly in his head, his hearing grew fuzzy. He hated it when that happened. The campground hummed with noises. The buzzes took over. People talking, shouting, moving. Clanging, scraping, chatter. All the noises and movements around him blurred like he was on a merry-go-round. He covered his ears and ran on.

He made it to the Greer Spring trailhead in forty-three seconds. He had already memorized the trail map, so he turned onto the trail, following the faded blazes. It was almost a mile to the spring, and the path descended fast. He would hide there. That was far enough away. The bullies wouldn't follow him there.

He went into stealth mode, humming to himself. If he hummed, he couldn't hear all the other noises. He slowed his pace as the trail sloped toward the river and it grew darker under the thick canopy of trees. It wasn't as steep as the hike they had taken to Crater Lake on their vacation. Now *that* had been a steep trail! It had been fun. He and Finn had run all the way, zigzagging on the switchbacks, kicking up dry dust. Mom had kept shouting to slow down, but it was too fun. When they'd reached the bottom, they climbed over all the large boulders that lined the lake. Mom had brought extra clothes and towels and a lunch, so he and Finn swam in the cold bright blue water. The caldera water was a deep darkish blue like a sapphire. Finn had scaled the larger boulders, spread his arms, and made silly noises. Will had preferred rolling his shorts up and allowing the cold water to tickle his ankles.

The swooshing sound of rushing water floated to him as he got closer to the stream. He loved the sound of it. Finn liked whirlpools and galaxies, anything that spun around and around. Will liked that, too, and he loved to set up solar systems in the yard with dozens of different sized balls. What he liked was the movement of the water as it glided past rocks, lapped against the shoreline, trickled over a rock face, or rushed in a ferocious roar of a waterfall. Mom understood. He was "curious," as she liked to say. He loved the water. Tides at the beach were even more fascinating.

The smooth, slimy, moss-covered wet rocks slicked his palms as he slid on the steeper parts. Even though the sun was rising, the trail was shadowy. If Finn had been with him, he'd have been running ahead, nearly killing himself on the granite and dolomite slabs of rock (according to the trailhead sign), while Mom screamed for him to be careful. Mom always worried like that. Sometimes her worry made him worry. If she freaked out, then he freaked out. It made his heart do that thumping thing. She didn't understand that part.

Maybe if he found an interesting rock specimen, he'd grab it for Finn. But he had to get safe first.

The morning sun finally broke through the trees, lighting his way. Pretty five-petal blue flowers—he thought they were phlox; Mom loved flowers and she taught him a lot about them—green ferns, and mosses covered the smaller cliff that he edged down. He no longer heard the sounds of the campground above. Maybe it was safe now?

The water lured him with its gentle swishing. Mom had told Susie once that water calmed him. He wasn't sure what that meant. It did make the buzzing go away. He heard everything all around him, including his mom when she thought he wasn't listening. She always asked what was going on in that "big, beautiful brain" of his. Lots, he told her.

He reached the water, placed Douglas on a nearby rock, and crouched, dipping his fingers in to test it. The water was an icy cold hug around his fingers. Not too hard, not too soft. Just right. Like Goldilocks! Earth was in the Goldilocks zone. Just the right amount of oxygen and stuff in the air for humans.

Long stringy green pondweeds filled the lagoon-like area on the stream's edge. He dipped his hand farther in and twirled the weeds around.

He then found four sticks and stuck them in the stream upright, wedging them between a few baseball-sized rocks. The water swirled and diverted around the sticks. Nearby, water gurgled in a mini-waterfall over a pointy rock that jutted into the stream. Foam bubbled where the water rushed around rocks and logs. He didn't see the spring. That was probably farther. This part was nice though.

He allowed the mist to tickle his face. His shoes squished into the mud. He stepped in deeper, the water seeping into his shoes. He wiggled his wet toes. The wet didn't bother him.

After a few minutes, he heard feet crunching and muffled voices on the trail above him. His heart began to do that thumping thing, and he ran.

\*\*\*\*

"This is taking far too long. This is taking *too* long!" I said. *Don't spiral, AJ*, Harrison's voice chided. His face flashed before me, tight-lipped, head shaking. I hated that look. He had always been the cool, rational one in our relationship.

"We'll find him."

I didn't acknowledge Reid's comment. My fears had me falling into the depths. I had to find him. There was no alternative. I wouldn't allow room in my mind for the other option. I tripped on a tree root, and Reid caught me by the arm.

Belatedly, I said, "Yeah, this journey though. It's taken so long. And now this!" My baby Finn had been without us for a week now. A goddamn week!

My legs were leaden. What was wrong with them? Like the heaviness I had felt with my epidural after Will's birth.

"You're sure he went this way? What about—" Reid said.

"Yes!"

We reached the trailhead, and Reid paused at the sign.

"Come on!" I said.

He scrutinized it like Will. "Just one sec…let me assess our situation."

"Assess our situation? He went on the trail. There's a spring and stream. That's where he went! It's this way. It's like a mile down, Reid! And he has time on us."

"Are you…"

I glared at him.

"Okay, okay."

"On the long shot he hid in the campground, others are looking for him," I added. He wasn't in the campground.

We scurried down the trail. "Will!" Long, arching ferns brushed against my shins, their serrated leaves like fingers fighting me. I tripped on the overgrowth across the path and dropped my flashlight. The beam cut out. I picked it up, shook it, and it went back on.

Reid practically ran down the sloped trail, distancing us in a matter of moments as he glided over the terrain with an enviable agility. He surely moved like a tactical soldier. His lithe form grew smaller, his black T-shirt blending in with the shadows of the canopy.

He paused, deftly balancing on an outcrop. Once I caught up, he continued.

Before long, the rushing of the stream beckoned me as we approached the bottom of the ravine.

A sudden memory of a dream I'd had several times in the past few weeks caused me to stumble. I hit a rock, twisted my weak ankle, and took a fall. "Jesus!"

Why, now, of all times were all these memories surfacing? My brain had more important things to do. My ankle pinched with a radiating pain. I had stepped wrong, throwing the sole up and ankle twisting to its side. I stopped to gather my wits.

Reid came to me. "You okay?"

"I think so. Bad ankle. It's never quite healed from an injury before."

I rubbed it, thankful I hadn't heard the sickening cracks from the first time I hurt it. That was close.

The damn dream about the kids lured me in. Each time I experienced it, it was slightly altered. Horrified, I would wake drenched with sweat, pulse racing. A hybrid of both Will and Finn played the role in the dream. There was one central theme though: the boys were drowning—in a pool, a lake, or the ocean—and each time I had to save them. And I did.

What about now? What if I was too late?

Would I find Will?

Would I be too late to save Finn?

A trench of blackness, of both mind and heart, ensnared me. *Stay alert. Stay strong*, I ordered. Sweaty fatigue and nausea dominated. Now was not a great time for a wave of withdrawal effects or panic attack. I exhaled. Doubts lurched in my mind, and anxiety reared its ugly head. "Maybe he didn't come this way. Maybe he's in the campground. Maybe I was wrong." Tears were on the edges of my eyes, waiting to fall in a torrent.

Reid looped his hand through my arm to assist me. The ankle was okay. It just stung. Thank God.

"Then we have others searching there like you said," he said almost too coolly. His demeanor had done a full reversal from what he'd displayed with that creep Dennis. I shuddered at how quickly a trained soldier could do what was needed in the moment and then transition to "being."

"Right…," I said, voice quaking.

I found my answer once we reached the ravine floor. There was Will's Douglas, sitting on a large rock next to the stream, which resembled a river here…but my son was nowhere to be seen.

I grabbed the stuffed dog and scanned the whirring stream before me. "Will! Will!" I cried, looking in both directions. I sloshed into the part that lapped against the shore, disregarding the water that got into my shoes. I didn't believe in premonitions, but…my scan jumped from tree to tree beside and behind us. "Will! It's Mom!"

No response.

Languid legs brought me to the ground in a crumpled heap.

Reid rested a hand on my shoulder. "It'll be okay. He probably went to the spring. It's this way. Come, let's go."

What ifs and worst-case scenarios bounced around in my mind. I grew light-headed.

Reid knelt to my level. "AJ...," he began, his voice competing with the roar of the river. "We *will* find your son. You can't give up."

"Oh, but Finn! My Finn is gone, too! I have nothing. Nobody. Th-They..."

I quashed my fears and tightened my hands into fists, not allowing the claws of defeat to pull me into the emotional abyss.

Perhaps I was the one who was drowning. I'd worked hard during the past year to pull through it all. To be strong for everyone. Now, I was a pile of mush again.

"AJ, you can do it," Harrison's voice said to me. He held me, rubbing my shoulders, soothing me in that special way. I lifted a hand to his cheek, feeling the scruff of a beard on my palm. "Harrison, you need to shave," I said, perplexed. Harrison was always clean-shaven. I blinked, and the hazy form of my sandy-haired husband transitioned to one of a man with smooth, dark hair on top and a peppered sun-kissed chin. Brown eyes bore into mine beneath thick turned-down eyebrows.

Reid took my hand from his cheek and squeezed it. "AJ, let's go. Look! Small, recent footprints," he said, righting me and pointing to the trail that continued to the spring.

The crisp cry of a whistle pierced the air and ripped me from my spiral. "Did you hear that?"

Reid also stopped. "Yes."

There it was again, an unmistakable shrill call of a whistle.

My knees gave way from sudden deliverance. "Will!" I stumbled but steadied myself and ran faster to the spring.

That was the whistle; I was sure of it. I purchased it out of my incredible fear of bears. It was top-notch.

The whistle blew again, its high-pitched cry heard over the rushing water as we drew upon it a few minutes later. The spring was wider here as the water emerged from beneath a high smooth granite slab overhanging a cave. The stream shuttled around moss-covered rocks in a loud whir like the drone of a crowded football stadium. It was deafening. Not too far from the cave, the water twirled into a whirlpool. Oh, heavens, Finn would have loved it. Then I saw the depth of the water. The morning sun-speckled blue laughed at me as white caps spun, entrancing, terrifying. I couldn't see the bottom.

"He can't swim well!" Had he fallen in and whistled for help before the water engulfed him? "Will?" The noisy water swallowed my cry.

I kicked off my shoes, the incessant nightmares of the boys drowning washing over me in violent remembrance. Statistics flew through my brain. Over ninety percent of autistic children's deaths were due to drowning…after wandering.

Reid grabbed my arm. "He's not in there."

The swirling water taunted me. "He is!"

"We just heard the whistle," he said sensibly. "And it's hard to whistle while struggling in water."

Just as I tore my arm from his grip, a quiet voice

from behind froze me. "Mom?"

I spun around to see my son, muddy to his knees, half smiling his awkward "should I be upset or scared or happy?" smile. I scooped all fifty pounds of him into a bear hug. "Will!"

"I used the whistle, Mom, like you told me. Did you hear me? This water is loud!"

I tried to not sob into his neck as I nuzzled him, squeezing tight enough that he released a squeak. "Yes, yes, yes! You're such a smart boy, honey."

A wave of relief rushed through me. The feel of his thin body wrapped within my embrace was a balm to my wounds. Screw it; I cried. The thought of Finn came forth in my mind as well. I had to find him. I needed our family whole.

****

Reid shifted gears from task-driven soldier to conversationalist as we hiked up the trail. Will's steps ahead of me squished and squashed as he took his time in sloshy shoes, seeming to stop for every log, odd looking branch, or puddle.

"I enlisted in the army when I was twenty-five, older than the usual recruit. Did two tours, Bahrain and Afghanistan," Reid said.

I couldn't remember how Reid had begun his story.

"Uh-huh." I hugged my arms around my middle. Adrenaline shook me. My lungs rattled; my inhaler had been left at the campsite. I kept my legs moving. Even if my mind had not fully returned, the lower half of my body worked now.

"You're in shock, AJ."

"Uh-huh."

"Was Harrison your husband?"

"Uh-huh."

"On one of my tours, I experienced..." He puffed a breath, tossing a glance at Will.

Will stopped to investigate a puddle on the side of the trail.

Reid continued in a lower voice, leaning closer to me. "It was supposed to be an easy op. Insurgents caught us by surprise. Our team got trapped in a burning building. Three of us survived out of eight. One guy, a great man with two young kids and a wife, took his own life when we got stateside. My other buddy, he couldn't handle it either. He's in a rehab facility in Texas."

I awoke from my stupor enough to recognize what he was saying. "They all suffered from PTSD."

"Yeah." He moved a low-lying branch out of our way and motioned for me to go first.

"Come, Will," I said.

Will actually did as told and ambled ahead.

"What about you?" I asked.

"I struggled for a long time, but I've found my ways to cope," Reid said vaguely.

"Like hitching and biking across the country, reading C.S. Lewis, and habitually eating lollipops?"

A sliver of a smile creased his lips as he pulled a lollipop from his pants pocket. "Why not? Want one?"

"No. How many do you have in that pack of yours?"

"Plenty. Never know when I'll need one."

I stifled a laugh. I didn't press, but I thought about what his real coping mechanism could be. I distinctly remembered the earthy scent of alcohol on him in that hotel room. I passed a cursory glance over him. He

"I'll help, Mom!" Will chirped, taking my hand.

For the length of this entire journey, as short as it seemed in the scheme of things, I had felt like a ghost of myself. I was floating along, robotic. Doing what needed to be done. I had never truly let it sink in. I wasn't a superhero.

Was it time I allowed help in?

**** 

Flashing blue and red lights greeted our return to the campsite.

My chest tightened at the sight of three police officers collecting statements despite seeing Dennis and Clara slumped in the back seat of a police car. The officers approached us. I don't know why, but I instinctively grabbed Reid's hand. His palm was sweaty, his hand warm.

One officer locked eyes with me while two others pulled Reid aside, disconnecting our transiently joined hands.

"Please don't arrest him," I said, clasping my hands together and speaking quickly as I was taken away from Reid and the two other officers. "He helped me. This guy," I began, pointing toward Dennis in the car, "attacked me. His wife tried to steal my car. He tried to hurt my son. Reid was just protecting us. They hurt others, too," I added, reminded of Geena's husband who had tried to help.

The lanky, gray-haired officer beside me rubbed his chin and jotted notes on his pad. He smelled of strong aftershave and breath mints. He reminded me of an actor I'd seen on a crime drama on TV. "Sit, Mrs. Sinclair, here," he said, pointing a pencil toward the picnic table.

wasn't wearing his usual red and gray plaid button-down shirt. Instead, he wore a simple black shirt, jeans, and boots. The shirt hugged his torso and upper arms, highlighting his fit stature. His sparse beard had filled in an even carpet of black hair, with a trace of gray, covering his chin, jaw line, and upper lip. I suspected the scruff was only a result of his journey and he was usually a well-groomed guy.

Knowing some of his history and having experienced firsthand the dangers on this trip, I wasn't put off when my scrutinizing gaze fell upon the knife in a holster on his belt. It must have been hidden beneath his long-sleeved shirt the other days. If I had to guess, I presumed he was in his mid- to later-thirties like me, although he was a hell of lot more fit.

"Have you talked to anyone about your..." He exhaled and chewed on his lip. "...issues, AJ?"

"Now you sound like a therapist."

"Sorry." He brushed another wayward branch aside. He stopped with his prodding.

I awoke from my blankness. "I don't have PTSD."

He nodded, slowly.

"I don't!"

He shifted his gaze from the path for a moment and held mine. I swallowed but didn't speak.

"What's PTSD?" Will chimed in.

Never one to skirt the truth, I said to him, "Post-traumatic stress disorder. When something bad happened to you and it still bothers you. Like nightmares and stuff."

"Ah. Like Grampy?"

"Yeah, honey, like that, like my dad."

Will scurried ahead, apparently appeased by that

explanation.

"My dad was in Vietnam," I added to Reid.

He nodded with an "ah."

"I told you that my sister…works with children like Will. Parents sometimes exhibit signs of PTSD or trauma reactive disorder, whatever you want to call it, and—" Reid began.

I wrung my hands together. "Look, I don't need…I…"

"Sorry, I didn't mean to say…" He heaved a sigh. "I've been there before. That's all I wanted to say."

Instead of snipping, I said, "Thanks. Sorry." I detained the rest of my thoughts behind gritted teeth. I understood it—PTSD from war, yeah, that was one thing. Losing your spouse and having a child diagnosed with a disability were different things. I did *not* have PTSD.

Or did I?

I fell silent, and he did as well. I rubbed my cheek, as the pain seeped to the surface. I could still taste the blood in my mouth. My skin was sensitive to the touch and already swelling. It was going to leave an awful bruise.

"No need to poke it. It's already puffy," Reid said.

I gave him the "Are you trying to be funny?" look.

He shrugged. His face grew solemn. "I'm sorry I didn't get to you guys sooner."

*We're not yours to protect*, I thought, but said nothing. Another minute of quietness passed as we both pondered. "Did you follow us here?" I blurted.

"No. But I do want to help."

"I'm not a charity case."

"I know that. And I'm no therapist."

I shot a look to him. He smirked.

"Why do you want to help us?"

"You seem a nice woman, and you're traveli[ng] alone with your son…I dunno. I just wanted to he[lp] And catch a ride, too."

His explanation couldn't have been more elusi[ve] but I didn't press.

Help. It had poured in after Harrison's death for [a] short time, but before then…when I was spinnin[g] plates, the help had been minimal. Life had forced m[e] to be the do-all-er in our family.

It'd been a long time since I'd had help…rea[l] intentional help. I carried the burden in my ow[n] backpack. Had I become bitter? I resented all the worl[d] I'd done, unacknowledged by my tender but obliviou[s] husband, who thought he was doing his part by being the provider.

I missed Harrison. I missed *him*. I also missed the help. A lot of the turbulent emotions I'd experienced this past year with Will were actually about Harrison dying and me running the ship solo.

I had already been missing him before he died.

I plodded ahead of Reid, slapping at tree limbs that dared to get in my path, warmth flooding my head, and my muscles quivering. I passed Will, who had stopped, once again, this time to inspect a log.

Reid closed our distance and said undemandingly, "I will help you if you let me."

"You don't know me. I don't know you."

"So?"

"Nobody's ever helped me," I said, feeling small.

"I will," he repeated.

I shrugged.

I did as told while Will darted around the campsite. He was muddy but appeared to be in neutral spirits. I elaborated, my explanation a hurried jumble, as the officer, an Officer Browson, nodded and transcribed. My wary gaze danced between Reid as he was questioned by the other two officers and Will, who settled by a puddle. He dropped a few leaves and twigs in it. A paramedic approached and tended to my face.

A quick search for Geena found her sitting at her own picnic table. Sam was beside her, wiggling foot to foot. I gave Geena a shared maternal nod, and she released her grip on Sam, whispered in her ear, and then Sam scurried over to play with Will.

"You won't need stitches," the paramedic said, blotting my face with clean gauze and antiseptic. I winced with the touch.

The officer closed his notebook when I finished explaining. He cleared his throat. "Dennis and Clara Katzmann have a long criminal record. They're wanted in two states on various charges. Mrs. Sinclair, do you want to press charges?"

I shook my head. I wanted to put these two creeps behind me. "Not really. Do I need to?"

"We've got them on other accounts of larceny, assault, and manslaughter. They're both looking at time behind bars. Your charges aren't necessary, but I do need to ask."

"Manslaughter?" I said, shivering. "No, no. You have more pressing things to handle right now." *Did those two even have a son in Kansas or was that part of their ploy, too?*

Officer Browson's countenance remained stalwart. One of the other officers, a woman, approached. She stood by while Officer Browson asked, "What about Mr. Gregory? Did he hurt you? You can speak with Officer Carella here alone if needed."

I shook my head adamantly. "No. He helped us."

*He helped us.*

"You said you met Mr. Gregory on this trip?"

I nodded. "We're both heading west to find family."

Officer Browson's lips thinned. "Travel is banned beyond Kansas."

"I understand."

"We need your information, ma'am, in case we need to contact you further."

I gave it to them.

The third officer had already escorted Reid, who was not cuffed, to the police car. The officer frisked him before placing him in the back seat. He pulled the pocket knife from Reid's jeans.

"Please, don't take him," I pleaded, running to them.

"It'll be okay," Reid said. "I'll go with them and clear it all up."

"Ma'am, we need to question him further at the station. He's coming voluntarily."

I stared, helpless. After all this, and now they were taking him away?

Reid shared a composed look with me. Yeah, the bloody brow and scuffed cheek didn't give him the look of complete innocence.

I said, "I—"

The door closed. Reid nodded behind it.

Chapter Twelve
Two Truths and a Lie

"Y'all keep in touch, okay?" Geena said, sweeping me into a hug as late afternoon shadows lengthened across the campground. For her petite stature, she had a firm embrace.

The whiff of campfire smoke that resided in her short hair tickled my nose. I wasn't surprised by the heaviness that filled my stomach at her departure. We'd spent the better part of the day hanging out and waiting. I learned about her family in Georgia and Kansas, and I'd told her more about ours, even Harrison. Her nonjudging, nonpitying vibe was truly freeing. Something I'd not felt in ages from another mom.

"Thanks for keeping me distracted today," I managed.

"He'll return. They do have more important matters to deal with," Geena assured.

I wrote my phone number and e-mail address and slipped the page into her hand. "I will. Thanks, Geena."

Sam ran to Will. "Wanna hang on to my cat?"

"Nah, I've got Douglas."

She said sweetly, "Yeah, Snow might get jealous." Sam kicked at the dirt. "Okay. Have a good trip, Will." She climbed into her family's minivan.

"Well, I suck at goodbyes. You sure y'all will be okay?" Geena asked again.

"We will."

"Good luck, AJ. You're a momma bear. You'll find your cub." She waved a finger at Will. "And don't you give your momma too many more gray hairs, okay?"

Will nodded.

Geena stepped into her minivan toting their pop-up camper, gave me a final wave, and her family drove out of the campground. For somebody I'd just met, she had left a special place in my heart.

I spent the evening thinking and writing.

News trickled into the campground. There was a huge car pile-up on the westbound highway complete with a fire and oil spill. The campground was abuzz. First, it was talk about Clara and Dennis's assault on me. Then, it was about the accident. People grumbled about needing to leave, but roads would not be open until nighttime at least. I was stuck. Only the folks traveling eastbound had been able to depart.

Factors compounded, I decided to rest one more night at the campground, as much as the idea made me queasy. Will was tired, although not nearly as rattled as I thought he would be. Tomorrow, I would make up for lost time, I promised myself.

Hell, I needed to rest, too.

And I needed to wait for Reid.

After tucking Will into his sleeping bag, I returned to the fire. I stared at Reid's bike and pack, which I had brought over after locating them.

"Now don't you think of taking them," a voice said.

I startled from my stupor, ran to Reid, and hugged him without hesitation. "They let you go?"

"Yeah," he said.

"Really?" I didn't want to say it aloud, but Dennis had been mangled.

"They had bigger fish to fry and a massive accident to deal with. The station was swamped. They barely had room for Dennis and Clara, and the Feds are coming to take them away."

"I don't understand. They're not charging you?"

"Nope," Reid assured.

"Luck seems to follow you," I said with a smile. The first one I think I cracked all day. Ouch, it hurt. I yawned. That hurt more. God, and unluck followed me.

"Want to learn a trick?"

"Sure." I sat by the fire, drawing my hooded sweatshirt closed and zipping it, despite the warmth in the air.

He clicked open his pocket knife and cut a coffee filter into two pieces. "I got a filter from a fella yonder," he said, angling his chin toward the site beside us. "Got your coffee canister?"

I raised an eyebrow. "You stopped to get a filter before coming to make sure your bike and gear were here?"

"It was on the way. And I knew you'd find them. You're resourceful, aren't you?"

I muffled a chuckle. "Okay...yup. So are you." I pulled my coffee canister from a bin and handed it to him.

He settled beside me on the log. He leaned close, spreading the filter.

"First you take a filter, cut it in half, and then put grounds in it. Just a tablespoon. Then you tie it, like a pouch." He continued to demonstrate as he spoke.

"Here," he said, handing a twine-wrapped pouch like a teabag to me. I plopped it in my empty cup.

I still had hot water cradled in a metal pitcher in the fire from making Will's instant mac and cheese. Reid wrapped a handkerchief around his hand and poured water over our pouches. "Steep it for two to three minutes. Presto!"

It was bitter, slightly weak, and could use cream. I dumped in a sugar packet and powdered creamer packet Reid handed me, stirred, and sipped it. "Not the same as an aromatic slow-drip, but it will do." It was about the same as the coffee in the manager's office. I pretended it was a delicious pumpkin spice latte. As the sun set, a cool shiver ran down my spine. The fire crackled before us, and I heaved a sigh, feeling somewhat lightened. I tossed a quick glance at my companion. The man with the dark-roast eyes had become my new coffee bearer. An acrid taste filled my throat with that sudden comparison to Harrison.

"Wanna talk about it?" Reid said out of the blue.

"The psychoanalysis continues?" I replied, sipping.

"Don't mean to prod. Just trying to—"

"Help. Yeah, I know." I had no desire to talk about what had transpired with the assault if that was the "it" he referenced. Or perhaps it was my meltdown in the woods? Either way, I said instead, "I'm worried. About Finn." *And Will. And my life.* I didn't add those obvious sentiments.

"That's understandable."

"Do you have kids?"

"No."

I nibbled on my lip. "Despite Will's challenges, Finn has always been my difficult child. Lord, he ages me. He's had a hard time finding his place in our family." *He needs me*, I wanted to say. "He inherited the brooding, melodramatic, fireball attitude from me, and the inquisitive, engineering brain from my husband."

"Interesting combo. Sounds like a great kid," Reid said, sipping his coffee.

"Aside from his emotional side, he loves to tinker with things. He's always considering what he can do or make with anything. Wicked smart. He exhausts me. Yet...I miss his chattiness." My fingers prickled, wanting to scratch his back the way he liked it. It was one of his coping mechanisms when his emotions gripped him.

"A tinkering chatterbox! He's my kind of dude." Reid moved a few logs around in the fire, encouraging the flames to take the bait. He leaned back. "Finn's the misunderstood misfit."

"You could say that. I'm still figuring him out. He copycats Will in many ways, but he has his own unique set of challenges and gifts." I paused and lowered my voice. "I miss him. I worry about him. I feel like..." I couldn't say it.

"Will gets more attention because of his needs?"

"Yeah. You're quite perceptive, Reid." That admission never sat well with me. Even on this expedition, the purpose exclusively to get my youngest child, my thoughts had been consumed with Will, Harrison, and myself. I could hardly think about my misfit without crying. I recalled my torrential breakdown at Easter this year when Finn accidentally hurt a neighbor's grandson, who had been teasing him. "Am I going to jail?" Finn asked between whimpers while he sat on his bed and I explained the ramifications for his impulsive reaction. Misunderstood misfit. Yup. God, I wanted to hug him right now. It'd been our first Easter without Harrison. My worst Easter by far. I'd spiraled quickly with Finn's behavior that day.

"Finn knows you love him."

I rubbed my nose. "I suppose."

"Everyone needs you, don't they?"

"Yeah. I'm tired of being so needed." My hands shook, and I set my coffee down. "I'm broken. And I just want my family to be whole again."

"We're all broken or bent a bit. But we're not irreparable. Even me."

I eyed him dubiously.

"I've my own complicated past," he said with a dashing look, but there was truth behind the joker's mask.

"Don't we all. Wanna tell me?"

He rubbed a thumb over his tattoo, his gaze downtrodden. "Maybe later, okay?"

I cleared my throat, suppressing the pugnacious pain that wrestled to claim me. "What does it mean? Your tattoo. It's Latin." I moved closer to him on the log, our thighs touching. Feeling foolish, but not giving a damn, I lifted his hand into mine, the irrational need to touch somebody driving my actions. I wanted to trace my finger over the cursive words "*Ne obliviscaris*" but resisted the urge.

"Forget not," he said quietly.

His hand was cold within mine. His reservation caught me off guard. Maybe the tattoo was from his army days…a haunting reminder from his deployment.

An intricate tribal tattoo meandered over the rest of his lower forearm. I was surprised he didn't have an army tattoo. Even Brandon had branded himself in the ritual of a tattoo from his air force days. Yet, I saw only the two. Of course, there could be more…and for the first time in a year, I wondered what lay beneath the shirt of the man beside me. *Lord, AJ. Knock it off.* Had Dennis knocked my wits, too?

He continued, speaking as if from a sad, far off place, "Perhaps it was part of my own grieving process."

"You're enlightened on the process? Like the five stages of grief or whatever it's called? After your deployment?" I asked as I released his hand with a tender squeeze and wiggled a few inches away.

"Not enlightened. Educated, maybe."

I stared into the dancing flames. I'd had enough camping to last me my entire life. The smell of fire, although usually an alluring scent, now reminded me of what I was doing. Camping. On my way to save my son. After nearly losing my other son.

We sat quietly, lost in thoughts. I could tell that Reid was avoiding going deeper with our talk, and I was okay with that.

"Ever play campfire games?" he asked.

"A hundred years ago…" I glanced at the tent to make sure that Will was indeed asleep. I cast Reid an uncertain sideways look but welcomed the change in subject. It appeared Reid felt the same, for the intimate vulnerability hovered as thick as the fire's smoke, consuming us both.

He rubbed his chin. "I'll keep it clean."

"Sure, why not?" I shifted on the log.

He sipped his coffee. "Truth or dare?"

I shook my head. "What, are we twelve?"

"I spy?"

I gave him another look. "Finn loves that one."

"Okay...spin the bottle?"

I laughed now, nearly snorting my coffee. "You don't know any campfire games, do you?"

He smirked. "No clean ones."

A strange sense of déjà vu lingered around the edge of my mind, and it caressed my spirit as I smiled involuntarily. The movement of those underused muscles around my mouth was foreign, and I winced, but that was from the soreness in my cheek. Reid had made me smile more in this past week than I had smiled in a year. Our indecisiveness reminded me of a Saturday night when Harrison and I were flipping through the lame offerings on TV to find a movie we both agreed upon. Sometimes we'd spend more time looking for something to watch than actually watching it.

I saw where Reid was going with this. I had my own assessing to do. "What do you miss while you're on walkabout?"

He ran a hand through his thicker hair. "Walkabout?"

I grinned, subtly weaving a few fingers through my own tousled locks. I missed my hairdryer. "Aging myself from outdated movies." I lifted an eyebrow.

"Well, I'm old then, too. Dated but entertaining movies about Australian walkabouts and large knives. Remember that?" He flashed a smile.

I nodded. "You're not getting out of this question, Mr. Gregory."

"Diversions don't work on you, do they?"

"Nope," I said.

"Okay, I miss reading the newspaper comics."

"The comics, huh? No crossword puzzles or, or…"

"Deep thought-provoking articles at breakfast? Nah. I do love to read those types of books, but a guy's gotta have fun or he goes mad with all that philosophizing and prophesizing."

I rubbed my chin in feigned examination, pulling my best detective voice as the caffeine from the coffee kicked in. "The classics or new comics with twisted political bents?"

"Classics of course. The goofier the better."

We shared an understanding smile. Lord, a smile felt damn fine. I sighed. "Newspapers age us, too."

"Yeah, but who cares? Okay, your turn."

"Me? Oh." I licked my lips. "What I miss?"

"Yeah."

"I miss coffee in the morning. Well, rich, creamy, dark-roast coffee." *Brought to me by Harrison*, I wanted to add. "I miss tucking the boys in bed each night with a story. Writing. Going on daily walks along the shore near Portland Head Light and in Fort Williams Park and, oddly, the sound of the foghorn. Will keeps a daily tally of its blares. The few days it was under repair and didn't sound—oh, that was quite eventful in our house!" What else did I miss? Most were disenchanting. I missed Harrison. I missed my Finnie. I missed the daily calls with Patsy before the accident when we'd talk about gardening or Will's latest achievement. I missed my former life.

I changed the subject quickly before I traveled down that path. "Tell me about your sister. She works with special-needs kids?"

"Yeah. She's the younger of us two. She was always set on a path to teach. We have a cousin with Down Syndrome, and she was fondly attached to him when they were kids. I think that led her on that career path. I took a few education courses myself and helped in her class a bit before and after my tours. She's the one who got me reading the philosophical texts of Lewis and his gang."

"She sounds like an amazing woman. I'd love to meet her. I hope you can find her when we get to Colorado."

"Me, too," he said.

"You're the older one, huh?"

"Yup, and I'm also a Junior. Named after my dad."

"Interesting. How about we play two truths and a lie?" I suggested. "You need to pick the lie."

He smirked. "Okay."

"I used to play it during my girls' nights. Those were the good days. When four of us moms needed a break from the kids and husbands, we got together at one of our houses to eat, laugh, and unwind." I sighed, twirled my hair, and said to my surprise, "Those nights seem so distant now."

Silence had crept back into our conversation, and I worried I had overshared when he said, "That sounds clean enough to me. I'll go first." He pondered for a moment, clearly taking the game suggestion seriously. "Okay…"

He looked me straight on, his proximity unnerving. He was so close I could smell him. And he smelled enticing. I liked his mixed scent of spice and sweat.

"My uncle was a Mexican senator. I have four

tattoos. I can knit a darn nice scarf."

I belly laughed, and my ribs ached from Dennis's kicks. "Jesus," I said with a grip of my side.

"What?" His mouth twisted wryly with jesting astonishment.

I waved a hand. "I never took you as a knitter."

"My mom taught me."

"I'll say the tattoos."

He leaned forward and splayed his arm as he rolled up his sleeve. "Just the two tats. I guess the uncle was a given?"

"That was too easy. Ah, well. The Senate?"

The final shafts of sunlight got lost in the trees around us and shadows danced upon Reid's face. "Yeah. He saw the corruption in the Mexican government, and he urged my mom to move to the United States. Your turn."

I tapped a finger on my thigh. I had forgotten how hard this game was. How personal it could get. I sipped the last drops of my coffee, which was now cold but was still better than electrolyte drinks. "Okay, me…I've gone bungee jumping. I've toilet-papered a car. I've taken belly dancing classes."

He pretended to deliberate. "Toilet paper?"

"Nope."

"Really? A woman named Allison Jessica couldn't possibly have—"

I laughed. "College. Peer-pressure. And it's Audrey Jane," I relented, finally giving him my full name.

"Shoot, never would've guessed that."

We shared a smile.

"Audrey Jane," he repeated, my name falling off

237

his tongue, smooth and melodious. "Belly dancing?" he asked.

"Yup."

Sleep enticed me, but the desire to continue our conversation kept me firmly planted on the log. Besides, I was having fun. God, how I'd missed conversations that didn't revolve around IEPs, behaviors, demanding jobs, or…other things.

"You like to jump off bridges?"

"Hell, no. It was terrifying. Honeymoon in New Zealand. Queenstown is the adventure capital of the world, after all. Harrison wanted to do it."

Reid poked at the fire. "Okay, me again…let's see…I've read all of Shakespeare's plays." He paused and licked his lips, then drew them in thoughtfully. "I was married once. I think you have the prettiest eyes."

I swallowed, tucking a strand of hair behind my ear. Oh, gosh, now I missed my hairdryer *and* flat iron. "That's a lot of plays."

He gave me a charming look. "I read all the greats, don't I? Thirty-seven plays to be exact. Lily sent me a bunch while I was overseas. Had to start with the classics, right?"

Heat flushed my cheeks, and it wasn't from the fire. "Such serious reading."

"Hey, I've got my comics to prevent me from becoming too dour."

An awkward giggle escaped my lips. "No wife, huh?"

"Nope."

I chewed my bottom lip. "A shame. You seem a good catch."

"You do have soulful eyes," he said, sharing a look

with me longer than was casually comfortable.

I shifted my weight but didn't move away. I muffled a tight laugh and swatted his thought away. "You've got a knack for changing the subject."

"Eyes tell a lot about a person's journey." He moved closer to me. Only an intimate inch remained between our hips.

"I knew this man, Aubert. He was French-Algerian, a coworker of mine when I worked full time before the kids. He flirted with me like mad. He was older than my father," I said, not looking at Reid. I traced a finger over the subtle woven pattern in my faded jeans. "He loved my eyes."

Lord. I edged away from him. I distracted myself with stoking the fire. "He was still with the company although he didn't do much research anymore. He was long past retirement. Anyway, he would roam the halls all day long. He'd visit me daily, poking his head into the lab. He told me I had that classic look about me. Mostly my eyes. Silly, I know." I drew my gaze to Reid and stuck my chin out, swallowed the dryness in my mouth, and said, "What do my eyes say?"

I expected more flirtation. I was giddy with fatigue and the bottoming out that came after the adrenaline rush. I was spent. The coffee had done little to revive me. My cheek ached.

He slid closer and placed a hand on mine and squeezed. "I see a strong woman who has been hurt deeply. I see a resilient mother who would journey through hell for her children. I see somebody who has become jaded and has trouble trusting, unable to sort through friend and enemy. I see a woman with hope." He held my gaze. "And I'd like to be your friend,

Audrey Jane."

My jaw may have dropped. I wasn't sure. I recovered quickly. Or at least I tried. "You've been talking with my therapist, haven't you?" God, I was teasing him. I was joking. I was like Will. Will always got goofy with his peers in social situations when he didn't know the expectations, or how to behave.

Either way, Reid didn't laugh. Thin lips pressed into a frown that I couldn't decipher.

I didn't prod any further. I broke the gaze and released my hand from his, then stoked the fire for the tenth time, sleep luring me with sweet abandon. I tossed the stick into the fire. "I should turn in."

"I'll stay awake," he offered. "Until the fire goes."

"Okay." I nodded, though the fire could have been quickly snuffed.

I paused in my opening of the tent flap, turned around, and peered at him. My arms dropped to my side, my hands still. "I'm sorry about the hotel. I was sick and wasn't thinking straight. Thank you for your help today." A part of me couldn't disclose the unvarnished truth. Part of it had been crazy withdrawal-symptoms AJ. The other part—I'd been paranoid he'd been drinking. Harrison's death remained a ghostly echo in my mind, perhaps clouding my judgment. The scent had been on his clothes though. I was sure of it. The more I pondered, I believed his story. Perhaps I *had* been triggered. Perhaps I really did have trauma or PTSD. I shook my head. I didn't know.

Firelight glistened off the growing beard hairs on Reid's chin and spots of amber danced in his dark, round eyes. Speaking of soulful eyes…

"You were looking out for Will. I understand. I had

been gone far too long."

"You had a legitimate reason. Shit happens," I countered.

His lips curved into a resigned smile. "Yeah. Rest, Audrey Jane."

"You, too, Reid," I whispered. I added in a deep exhalation, "And yes, yes, I'd like to be your friend."

As I stepped into my tent, I observed Reid's normally straight shoulders slouch a hair. Perhaps he, like all of us, was on his own road of atonement. Searching for meaning, searching for answers…searching for absolution.

I had treated him poorly.

I didn't know what the hell had just happened between us, but I tucked it away into a corner of my brain to contemplate upon another time when I was lucid. My remorse had lifted somewhat.

Ignoring my exhaustion for at least a few minutes, I clicked on my headlamp and pulled out my journal. It was time to unburden my heart.

Chapter Thirteen
The Road to Nowhere

I slept restfully. And awoke rejuvenated, albeit sore as hell. I rolled over, encouraging the dream to remain just a moment more. It had been heavenly. But it hadn't been a real dream...for it was a memory from one of our weekends without the kids. I shifted, pulling the sleeping bag up higher. Well, rather, it was a dream-memory hybrid. My eyes closed, I clung to the vapors and sensation of it as my body roused, my mind sharpened...

Harrison and I were enjoying a blissful morning in bed with no kids. Will and Finn had gone to Patsy and George's cabin in New Hampshire for the weekend.

Harrison's touch on my bare arm sent shivers over my skin. I shifted to the side to face him, his body solid, secure against mine beneath our green and blue patchwork bedspread. The sheets had that freshly laundered smell, yet our bubble beneath the covers held the scent of exertion and sex. I nestled in closer to him and ran my fingers through his short hair and I drew it into sweaty spikey tips. My gaze drifted lazily beyond him to the nightstand beside our bed. The collection of dusty travel books and magazines that usually adorned his nightstand had been replaced with a bursting bouquet of petite flowers that protruded from a squat clear glass vase. The clusters of periwinkle flowers winked at me with their vibrant yellow eyes. Forget-me-nots he'd picked from my garden.

Harrison didn't speak. He held my gaze for a long moment. He kissed my neck, his light beard like sandpaper. It tickled, triggering a gooseflesh response on one side of my body from my neck all the way to my toes. I moaned.

I leaned in to kiss him. He reciprocated it with fervor and whispered, "I love you, Audrey Jane."

"I love you, too, hon." I weaved my fingers with his.

"Pancakes?" he asked.

"French toast?"

"Oh, you rebel."

I chuckled. The boys always wanted pancakes. When was the last time we'd had our own favorite breakfast dish, and not a meal catered to the kids? "Oh, and bacon!" I curled my cold toes around his warm calf, knowing how much he loved bacon.

"Sounds good! Rest, my HBA," he said, pushing the sheets aside and pulling on his boxers. I admired his strong, lean, muscled legs as he left the room.

"Your coffee awaits!" he called over his shoulder.

I blinked as the last bits of the dream faded. I touched my lips, summoning his kiss.

Unhurriedly, I opened my eyes, saw my sleeping Will in my arms.

With an aching body and a longing of the heart, I rose to attack another day on the road.

**\*\*\*\***

I was thrilled to say farewell to the Mark Twain Wilderness area of Missouri. Bring on Kansas, I thought with a sliver of buoyancy. Will moved like a

243

snail around the campsite. "Move it, mister!" I commanded, collecting the remains of our camp and tossing them in the car. In unspoken agreement, Reid had once again attached his bike to the rack last night.

"You're less furry," Will said, running to Reid as he returned from the bathrooms.

Reid's wet dark hair was brushed back. He grinned at me, his notable black stubble cleanly shaven. Morning sun shone in his eyes. I mumbled a "good morning" and turned, trying to appear busy. He looked kind of hot, and that thought troubled me. What was I thinking?

Will patted Reid on the belly, talking quickly and incoherently. "My star base, here, it has the ballistic cannons and..." He took Reid by the hand and chattered, leading him to his Lego structure beside our extinguished fire.

"Will...," I said. After yesterday's hellish delay, I wanted to get going. Now.

He ignored me, continuing to do whatever he was doing with a pile of rocks and his Lego bricks. I began to dismantle it. "We need to go."

"No!" he cried.

"I told you five times already. We need to clean and go."

He kept playing. "You told me three times."

I stood my ground. "You may take your cannon and ship in the car. We need to go, Will. Your brother—"

"My stupid brother. It's always about Finn!" he snapped, his face puckering.

"I'll finish the tent, AJ," Reid said quietly, pausing and squeezing my shoulder.

"Will…" My patience vanished. I braced myself and approached him. I had to get the meltdown under control before—

"I feel like Mars!" Pink blotches formed on Will's forehead and cheeks. He kicked at his structure, the rocks and Lego bricks scattering. He made to run, but I was quicker and caught him by the elbow. I knelt to his level.

"What do you mean?" I said, my tolerance thinning as my mind said, *Not this again.*

"Mars is dead, lifeless, and gets pelted with asteroids!" Tears streamed down his face as the splotches grew.

The vise squeezed tighter around my heart. Will used to say he felt like a rubbish pile. Where the hell had he learned that phrase? He'd said it a few times when he was misunderstood or wrongly called out or when he had a difficult time with another kid. My child was great with metaphors. It was a shame they held a negative connotation.

"Will, honey, you *are* loved. You exude life. You have a wonderful spirit. Why do you say such things?" Insufficient energy remained for this battle. Ugh the dreaded "why" question. Had I not learned anything from all my parental reading?

He rolled his eyes and turned, but his tension released as he allowed me to embrace him. "Never mind." His face was still splotchy and red from his outburst. Finn got that way when he was upset, too. Both of them, ever since they were babies.

"Will…"

He kicked at the ground. "Never mind!" he repeated, his lip trembling.

At least today, he wasn't giving me the excuse of "nobody understands me" or "you don't understand my brain." Sure, those had pulled on my heartstrings the first few times he'd said them. Experience told me that he made excuses to get out of things he didn't want to do, like all kids did. It was a delicate balance of what was autism and what was developmentally expected.

I caressed a hand across his brow and cheek. "I remember when you were a baby you loved me to rub the side of your face, like this," I began, as I contemplated what the trigger might have been. It wasn't the Lego bricks. Was it jealousy about us looking for Finn? The encounter with that awful couple yesterday? His running into the woods? Or all of the above? I continued stroking his face as I knelt, the feel of his baby-soft skin gratifying under my fingertips. "I would do this, and rock you, and then you'd love it when I put a blanket here, over the side of your face, and you'd fall asleep in my arms."

"I still like it," he murmured, nuzzling into my embrace. "Your face is red and purple, Mom." He stroked my cheek in same manner I stroked his, but I winced with his touch.

"It will heal." *As will your hurt*, I wanted to say. "We always heal. Sometimes it takes longer."

A stubborn smile cracked through his grimace. "Mars is a dead planet," he repeated.

"But you're not."

"Mars has volcanoes."

"It does. So does Earth."

He glowered at me, but with the meltdown momentarily diffused, he rose and went on his way toward the car.

"Will, your Lego bricks…"

"Okay, okay. I know, Mom."

He picked up his toys and tucked them in a bag, and then drifted toward the car. Reid, thankfully, ignored the situation to let me handle it and had loaded the rest of our supplies in the car.

We drove away without another look. *Goodbye, Missouri.* I hoped to never see you again.

****

"Mind if I put on the radio?" Reid asked as he drove.

"Go ahead." Not that I wanted to hear more news of the devastation, but the silence was maddening.

Reid flipped through a few channels that were broadcasting news. We shared a look of resignation. He scanned through a few more channels. Most were static. No music. Nothing but news.

"So much for that," he said, clicking the radio off.

"I have my MP3 player, but the adapter here is broken," I said, pointing to my center console. I passed a glance at a road sign. "Do you think the best way is Route 70 toward Kansas City?"

He scrunched his brow. "Seems like all the cities have had detours."

"Yeah, we may need to improvise." I closed the atlas and tucked it away. Best laid plans were that—and on this road trip, those plans got changed a lot.

I opened my journal to distract myself from doomsday talk. I scribbled along the edges, writing HBA. I crossed it out and drew a few flowers instead. I remembered reading that people doodled when their brains were thinking, that it was part of the creative process. So far, my journal included Will's maps, numerous entries about my life and family, and pages of information about the eruption. Now I added flower and cube doodles to the mix.

Even though writing and reading in a car usually gave me a wicked case of vertigo and nausea, the pull to write made a stronger case. I skimmed my previous entries. Writing about Finn the evening before had been hard but cathartic. After a few doodles, I turned to a new page and began today's entry. I wrote the date. My God, I should have been preparing the kids for their first day of school, not journeying across the country.

I processed that bleak thought for a moment, and then continued writing.

The car bumped a pothole, and my fancy pen skittered a swirly blob that almost looked deliberate.

"Sorry," Reid said.

"Is the tire okay?"

"Yeah, was just a pothole. It's a full-sized spare. It's okay, but we can check it at the next stop if you want," he said.

"Yeah, that's a good idea."

I turned a look over my shoulder at Will. He was contently gazing outside.

"What are you writing?" Reid took his attention off the road briefly to glance at my journal.

I closed it, no longer really feeling the urge to write…not like my writing today was anything short of scattered. "I suppose it's a journal." I flipped down the visor. I poked the bruise. Purple and red had been an understatement. I didn't care what Reid thought as I pulled out my compact and dabbed concealer on it. I swiped through my hair that needed a clarifying wash and a cut as it now grew past my shoulder.

"About your life?"

"Well, it began as a telling of the current events, but it's evolved into a story about my family. So, yeah."

"Am I in it?" Will asked, always attentive.

"You betcha," I responded.

"Do you write other things, too?"

"I had a part-time job working at a local New England magazine, but I recently resigned. Life got lifey. I've wanted to focus on novels. Haven't had much success in that arena yet. I've also dabbled with short stories."

"Fiction is fun. I love a thought-provoking story, as you know. What kind of stories?"

I shrugged. "Historical fiction, with romantic or fantastical elements, and I have a few ideas for high-concept mainstream stuff. Not the same as the philosophical greats, but yeah. I love to immerse myself in fictional worlds, but lately I've been drawn to writing about families like us. Perhaps something non-fiction to help other parents."

"Write what you know—isn't that the motto?" Reid said astutely.

"It sure is."

"I'd love to read your work."

I surprised myself by saying, "Sure. Maybe. This one is for me though. What about you? Do you write?"

He cast me a lopsided grin. "Nah. I just read and philosophize. Leave the writing to those with a knack for it."

Will asked, "What does philosophize mean?"

"You like big words?" Reid asked.

"I like to know what they mean."

Reid scratched his bare chin. "Well, it means to

talk about logic, ethics, and values as they relate to human beings. And also to understand the beliefs of groups."

"Like understanding what people care about and why they do things?" Will asked.

"Pretty much, buddy."

"Are you from Puerto Rico?" Will blurted.

"Will!" I apologized for Will's bluntness with a pleading look.

Reid squeezed my arm. "It's okay." He looked in the rearview mirror at Will's reflection.

Will looked back.

"Close, buddy. My mother was from Mexico, but my dad was born here. What gave it away?"

"You look like a kid in my class, Javier. His parents moved here from Puerto Rico. He speaks Spanish. Do you know Spanish?"

"*Sí!*"

"That means yes. I know a few words. Javier taught me at recess. Wanna know what volcano is in Spanish? Javier told me."

"*Sí.*"

"*El vulcán!*" Will said. "There are a lot of volcanoes in Mexico—a whole range traverses through Mexico to Central and South America. The ring of fire!" He smiled to himself and returned to daydreaming.

"What do you do, Reid?" I realized I'd never asked. "Now that you've retired from the army, I mean. You'd mentioned traveling east for business."

"I've done the odd job here and there. Five years in the army, following the footsteps of my father I suppose. Since then, I've been doing this and that.

Worked at a mechanic's shop for a short time, but I don't find cars interesting. I can fix tires though, right?"

"That you can."

"I took a few college classes after my tours, while helping my sister in her class like I mentioned. I like to see how things work and fix problems. I wasn't sure what direction to take—education, law, philosophy, or engineering. Lily really got me interested in special kids. My mom encouraged me to be a surgeon. That's a mom for you." He shrugged. "My uncle, the senator, well, he opened my mind to government policy. Lots of choices. Ultimately, I never finished school."

He didn't mask the distance in his voice. "Anyway, I've also tinkered at a clock shop—yes, yes, they exist!" he said in response to my surprised look, his demeanor quickly changing.

"Clocks!" Will said, always listening. "We have one on our living room mantel with Roman numerals. I learned how to read it when I was four, right, Mom?"

"That's right," I said, fondly remembering how he'd kept his kindergarten teacher on track with the schedule.

"Clocks are neat, aren't they? All those gears and such," Reid said delightfully.

"Not another one," I said in jest.

Reid laughed. "I'm a tinkerer! What can I say?"

"Finn loves gears and stuff, too. Daddy…well, he did, too," Will said.

I heard Will dig through his backpack. He thrust his hand between us, Harrison's old metal compass on his palm.

"It doesn't work well anymore. Maybe you can help me fix it?"

251

I pressed my lips together. Reid raised an inquisitive eyebrow and I responded, "That's a great idea, Will."

"Finn loves this. He used to sneak it into his backpack and bring it to school and play with it on the bus."

Now *that* I didn't know. In fact, I'd not seen it since my last hike with Harrison. Like many of his belongings, it had been tucked away in bins in our basement. Or so I had thought.

"I take it there's not much business in clock shops?" I asked.

"Nope. Now I work in a bike shop. Marshall, the owner, sells cycles for the diehards who love to mountain bike the trails of the Rockies, and he also runs a tour business, taking people in bike groups on the southeast slopes, or to Pikes Peak. I've done my share of work with the tour groups in the Southern Front Range area. Marshall isn't able to travel as much as he needs to. He sent me to upstate New York to follow up on some online leads. He collects old cars and classic cycles and needed parts and what not. That's why I was where you found me."

"Sounds interesting," I said. That certainly explained riding a bike cross-country and with a heavy pack.

"What about all these books you read?" I said, upbeat, and with a thumb pointing toward his backpack that was buried somewhere. "Did Lily get you into other authors besides Lewis and Shakespeare?"

"A few. It definitely keeps my brain busy."

"It certainly must. Ever consider re-enrolling in college now?"

He scratched his head. "I'm too old."

"Never too old."

"Never too old to give up on your writing dream either," he said.

I nodded. "Touché, Mr.—what's your army rank?"

"Corporal."

"Well, then, Corporal Gregory, well played, sir," I quipped.

He laughed. I laughed. He stuck out his hand to shake mine. "I will go back to school for education and philosophy if you continue writing what you love. Deal?"

"Deal. Finn always does that," I said.

"Does what?"

"Makes deals."

"My kind of kid, like I said." Reid flashed a smile.

"I'm hungry." Will's voice broke into our discussion. "It's lunchtime."

The clock on the console read 12:15 p.m. "We'll stop soon."

He moaned but was thankfully distracted. "Look, Mom! They're like a thousand suns!"

I hadn't paid much heed to our surroundings in Kansas. I'd been happily distracted by the conversation with Reid, while we drove long stretches of highway flanked by ripening cornfields. The vast open fields rustled in a strong breeze, and I rolled down my window for air.

Then I noticed the milky grayish smog obscuring the sun. I coughed in reflex and rolled it up. Will coughed once, too.

The wide cerulean sky that I'd remembered from a childhood road trip was lacking. My scalp prickled, and the hairs lifted on the back of my neck. The foreboding real-life villain hovered above. This was no fictional villain from my novels. Ash-filled clouds threatened to unleash upon us. I swallowed, parched, despite having had a gulp of water.

"What do you mean, Will?" I asked belatedly. "I see just one sun, honey." And even that was hazy and dismal.

He pointed ahead of us. I squinted. Then I saw them…an expansive field of golden yellow sunflowers, tall, robust, and swaying.

"Wow, they're stunning." I'd never been one to dote upon sunflowers, even with my love for gardening, always considering them to be out of place…tall and awkward in clusters of three or four along someone's garden fence. However, when I saw them in the hundreds—thousands—wow.

"I've never seen so many flowers, Mom. Except for when we went to see the lupine."

"Lupine?" Reid perked up.

"Yeah, they're one of my favorites. We used to go to this place nearby where there were fields of them, wild. Used to go every Father's Day weekend, because they peak in June," I said. I blinked back sudden tears. "In some places, they're considered invasive weeds, but I just could not manage them to grow in my gardens. So to the wild I went each summer to enjoy them."

Reid was soft-spoken. "Ah, I see."

"Mom, I think we need to turn south."

I bounced a curled knuckle against my mouth. "I want to go through Wichita, honey." It's where I'd asked Dr. Martin to send my prescription. God, that was days ago…

Reid crinkled his brows and looked up through the windshield. "It does look awfully gray over that way, west. And given the disorder in the other cities in the Midwest, I am wary traveling through Wichita."

I pulled open the atlas. "We can't be certain it's lousy there, too. The news had shown the plume more north than this."

"El Niño, Mom."

"Huh?" I flipped the pages. There were only a few roads in southern Kansas that looped down and then through Dodge City. I followed with my finger. The best route dipped into Oklahoma.

"How far are we from Wichita?" I glanced for road signs.

"Not sure. Not close yet, though," Reid said.

"I was watching the news and was reading in my books. Volcanic eruptions in the Pacific have triggered El Niño years," Will said.

I tapped my temple, a dull headache returning. "But El Niño is in the winter, honey. It's not even September yet."

"Yes, they usually start in the winter, but an eruption of this size could greatly shift the weather patterns. The winds could be all mixed up. We already know the blast sent a plume east and northeast, but it's going to be pushed south because the news said the trade winds in the Pacific died as a result of the eruption. And the earthquakes. Plus that tsunami."

I scratched my head as he continued. Was my head actually spinning? Sarah had also mentioned road closures in northern California…but that was west of the eruption, not south. "Okay, slow down a bit, Will. The newscasters said the ash cloud is traveling north

255

and east, not south," I countered.

"I know, Mom. But look at those clouds! I think it's shifting because of the jet stream, too. El Niño can affect a lot of things. The eruption and earthquakes triggered the tsunamis. The tsunamis disrupted the Pacific Ocean's balance, and there is a lot of rain in southern California now already...El Niño is coming."

"How do you know all this?" Seriously, were we driving into a goddamn disaster movie? "Shouldn't the ash have settled by now?"

"There was a lot on the TV. Plus, my books, like I told you. And that ash rain we drove though? Probably moved faster and east because of the El Niño shift. Ash can remain in the atmosphere for a while, get picked up by the winds and stuff, Mom."

Reid said, "We'd drive right into it if we stay on a northern route."

"Yeah," Will said.

A brick wall hit me.

I couldn't get to my medication.

"Yeah, but I don't understand...," I said, grasping. "I'm not driving south into Oklahoma! We may never get to Colorado."

"Maybe just go a little more south, Mom. Then we loop back up?"

"Okay," I mumbled, staring at the atlas spread open on my lap.

We drove for a few hours, looping south of Wichita and dipping into Oklahoma. My blood pressure rose as I considered other places to try to get my prescription filled.

"Look, pizza! Can we stop, please?" Will asked as we passed a cluster of billboard signs.

"Sure," I said.

"Sounds good to me." Reid massaged his neck with a slight groan.

"Yum, pizza!" Will said.

Chapter Fourteen
Salty and Sweet

The smells. Spices and tomato sauce. Baking crust. My, oh, my, Will loved pizza. The colors! He'd never seen a restaurant like this before.

"Hey, what's this?" he asked, making his way to the brightly colored gizmo in the corner of the shop.

"Oh, that's a jukebox," Reid said.

"A what box? It's not a square or a cube. It's round on the top. See." In fact, the top part was like a rainbow, made of three colors—well, it wasn't a rainbow then—bowing stripes, that's what they were. It was fascinating.

Mom moved toward the counter. "Cheese, please!" he said, his interest fixed on the jukebox.

Reid knelt beside him. "It plays records."

"You can't play records."

Reid laughed. "Not that kind of record. A record is also an early type of a CD, but bigger. It plays music."

"Oh, like Mom's CD player in the car? Not like a radio, which transmits via radio waves."

"Exactly. This one doesn't have records anymore. Just digital recordings…probably on a computer, much like an MP3 player. The old jukeboxes used to play records. The records would be lined up inside the box, and a special mechanical arm would grab the record and move it, then play the music."

Will ran a finger along the polished wood. It was carved. This jukebox was colorful, too. Neon pink and blue and orange, with shiny silver along the edges. He skimmed the rectangular buttons. Each had words on them. "Are these songs?"

"Yeah. Want to pick? A quarter gets you three songs."

"I don't know any songs."

"What type of music do you like?"

Will shrugged. He counted the rectangular buttons. There were thirty-six. The carvings weaved along the edges and ended with circles. That reminded him of Finn's favorite things—black holes and whirlpools!

"Will, answer him, please," Mom said from the counter.

"I make up my own songs, from movies and TV."

"What about your mom?"

"I don't know. Sleepy music? Lovey music? She also likes to listen to annoying people reading stories on CDs. Audio books, she calls them. Yuck!" He stuck his tongue out.

"Okay, well, let's pick three that look interesting by their names. Here is a quarter. Put it in there."

Will plopped the quarter in the thin slot. It was like the games at the bowling alley. He didn't know what any of the songs meant. They all sounded like lovey songs. He of course could read them all—Mom said he was a reading champ and that he was all set for fourth grade—but they were all silly phrases. He picked one that had unusual words.

" 'Bohemian Rhapsody.' Good choice," Reid said, patting him on the back.

Will selected two more songs. One for Mom. One

weather one. He hoped the one he chose for Mom would make her smile. She hardly smiled anymore. He missed her happy faces and goofy stories and tight squeezes. Reid made her smile though.

After memorizing all the control buttons on the jukebox, he wandered around the pizza shop. His stomach growled from the yumminess. There was a map of Italy on one wall, surrounded by lots of framed black and white photos of people. The photos seemed old, like from many years ago.

Checkered black and white tiles also covered the floor. He counted the black ones.

He paused at fifty-six and returned to the jukebox.

Tiny gears spun in a six-inch by three-inch window, his guess without a ruler. He presumed that's where the records used to be. He watched each one twirl as the song—that had begun quietly and then got noisy—bad choice!—continued. It was a bad rhapsody.

He returned to counting the tiles. He finished at one hundred twelve because he couldn't count all the tiles under the tables and booths, and behind the counter. He ran a finger along the textured wall and stopped at the counter. There was a four-inch figurine of a fat guy in an apron wearing a chef's hat. A cactus shaped like a pickle sat in a flat round pot next to the fat guy. He dug a finger in the pebbles of the cactus pot.

"Will!" Mom said from a booth behind him. "Stop that, please."

He continued touching the pebbles.

"Like rocks, do you?" the man behind the counter said.

"Some. Only the cool ones. My brother Finn loves all rocks. He likes to dig holes in our yard looking for gemstones like topaz or ruby. These aren't rocks. They're pebbles."

The man smelled like garlic. It was stinky but not as gross as mom's coffee breath. "Ruby?"

Will shrugged and took seven of the pebbles out, lining them up from largest to smallest. "Well, he thinks they're rubies. I know they're not. Mom tells me to agree because it makes him happy."

He moved the pebbles around to equally space them. The largest one was the most interesting. It was marbled brown and white, while the others were all solid black or brown.

"Those look nice all lined up. That big one there came from a quarry nearby. Do you want to take it with you?"

Will shrugged and looked at the fat guy. "This guy is funny." He tapped the figurine. "He has a fat belly!"

"Hey, that's my Grandpa Vito!"

Will glanced fleetingly at the man, his gaze passing from the man's wide nose to the large brown hairy mole on his upper cheek. He passed a quicker glance at the man's dark brown eyes, which had green flecks in them, and then focused again on the pebbles.

The man said, "Just kidding."

"I know. This guy is pretend. Aren't you scared, mister?"

The man's eyebrows knitted together, making them look like a long caterpillar. "Scared?"

"About the eruption. We already saw ash-rain! Have you had any yet?"

"Not yet."

"You will. It's coming. We saw the clouds."

The man cleared his throat.

Will continued, "I saw lots of people packing their cars, like ours. All the shops here—their lights are off and *Closed* signs are on doors. We had to wait thirty-two minutes again today to get gas, and nobody lets you use their bathrooms...sewers and pipes are all messed up from the ash rainstorms. Why are you open? Aren't you scared?"

"Nope. Plus people need to eat, so I'll keep making pizza until I can't. And I've got an outhouse out back if you need one. Our bathrooms and water aren't working well either. I might have to close up tomorrow."

"You should be worried. It was a supervolcano. They don't think the entire magma chamber erupted—that would be catastrophic—but enough did. Haven't you been watching the news, mister? A lot of the ash cloud went west, though. You should watch the news."

"I try not to."

"Will!" his mom called from the booth.

He kept going. "There've been eleven VEI 8 eruptions...those are the largest...so far. Three of them in the Yellowstone hotspot. This one would be the fourth, but it wasn't a super-eruption, so I guess not. Scientists are still figuring it out. My guess is VEI 7, way bigger than Mount St. Helens. Crater Lake—we visited it on vacation—was a VEI 7."

"Then that's good news," the man said, smiling, his teeth large, crooked, and pale yellow.

"Well, not really. Lots of dead people, mister. And dead animals and crops and ash everywhere. It's going to take them a long time to clean it all. The climate is going to change, and El Niño is coming."

"You know a lot about all this."

He nodded. "My brother would like that rock."

"You can have it."

Will then returned to the map of Italy on the wall. Italy had a lot of volcanoes which this map didn't show. It only showed Etna and Vesuvius. He recalled that Italy had like nine or ten. He needed to confirm that in his book in the car. He stood in the booth beside the wall to enable him to trace Italy's border, which was shaped like a boot. He drew his finger halfway up the coastline of Italy, making volcano sounds.

When Vesuvius had erupted in 79 A.D., eleven thousand people in Pompeii were buried alive under ten feet of ash. That one wasn't a supervolcano, only a VEI 6.

****

"He likes to do recon?" Reid said to me as Will fluttered around the room.

"Yeah, that's exactly what I call it," I said, sipping a grape soda while "Bohemian Rhapsody" played on the juke. The soda was sweet and bubbly and divine. I hardly ever drank it now, but whenever I did, I thought of Harrison's addiction to soda. I had always told him the aspartame or saccharin in the diet cola would kill him. I said a lot of stupid things back then.

"Assessing his situation. Smart kid."

"Overloaded kid," I responded, with a peek out the window to my parked and locked car. "He does it to feel safe and familiarize himself with an area. Kids on the spectrum are more sensory than us. They need to take it all in, memorize it, and feel safe for the next time." I paused, sipped. "Here I go explaining him again. Sorry. It's a habit I need to break. You know that stuff already, from working with your sister, right?"

"Yeah. Will's an exceptional kid."

"It's just Will being himself."

Even as the words came, I felt burning stares of reproach. Two older women sat a few booths away from us, and one was giving me the most disapproving look. I scowled at them and returned to sipping the sugary heaven of my soda.

Without turning around, Reid said, "Don't let those fuddy-duddies bother you. They have their own issues. He's not bothering anyone."

"Yeah."

As much as I wanted to prevent it, the twang of embarrassment and hurt slivered my heart while the women continued with their critical looks. *Let it slide off like butter*, Siobhan used to tell me. She did say that her shit-tolerance factor had changed greatly once she reached her fourth decade. Perhaps when I turned forty, I wouldn't give a shit anymore. I found my thoughts falling on her. She lived in South Carolina now. I hardly ever saw or spoke with her these days. Or any friends for that matter. I really missed them. Mental note: call her when we get home. *If we get home?*

Reid sipped his root beer. "Ah, delish, right?"

"Yup. When the world goes to hell, we drink soda."

I looked outside at the car.

It wasn't my fear of the car being stolen that had me nervously looking outside. Locked, barred, and shuttered windows lined Main Street. Stacks of luggage covered car roofs and spilled from the trunks of the remaining cars. Most people were gone. Or were leaving. Had they been evacuated? I didn't think to ask the pizza shop manager.

The man happily chatted away with Will at the

counter.

"Will!" I called, seeing as another customer was waiting behind him. The owner gave me a friendly smile and wave of nonchalance.

Well, this fella wasn't going anywhere yet. Either he was optimistic that the ash cloud wouldn't fall upon Kansas, or he was like those people who waited out a hurricane with planks covering their windows, ignoring the winds that bellowed around them.

Distant thunder cracked. This pizza needed to hurry.

Reid whispered, "We'll leave soon."

I tapped nervously on the table.

"I'm sorry about Wichita."

"Yeah. Will was right about the clouds moving." I suppressed my dark thoughts. When I'd ordered the pizza, the owner had confirmed Will's suspicions. Reid had also inquired when we stopped for gas. Both said the same thing: Wichita was a no-go zone and that cloud was moving east. Great call on Will's part.

Reid shifted in his seat. "AJ, are you okay? I mean, after…what happened?"

Staring at the ominous overcast sky and the vacating town didn't help me. "You mean with those— those…," I began, unable to say their names. "Those two assholes who tried to take my car?" I finished. I let my gaze fall on the consolation of Reid's brown irises.

"Yeah. My behavior…," he said, but stopped. He rubbed his chin. "I know what you must be thinking."

I sipped soda. "It was justified."

Silence.

"And I needed your help," I admitted.

"What I did, though," he said, quietly, regret-filled.

He released another sigh.

The crunches and thuds and the old man's cries reverberated in my mind. I shivered. "You did what needed to be done."

"I shouldn't have hurt him like that. I could've restrained him. I sort of snapped when I saw him hurting you. He was about to reach for Will, too." Reid's stare shifted to Will, who was at the map of Italy on the wall, tracing the outline.

"Sort of?" I raised an eyebrow.

"Okay, not sort of. I did. Sorry."

I gave him the benefit of the doubt despite my wariness being raised. Perhaps with all his PTSD talk, he had some extent of it, too. "That's twice now you've been taken to the police station. Hoping this isn't a habit of yours?" I attempted mirth, but it didn't come off well.

"It's not. I'm not a bad guy. I'm sorry."

"Isn't that what bad guys always say?" I waved a hand. "Anyway, Will's okay. He's a resilient kid. He'll be all right. You didn't scare him if that's what you're asking me."

Reid stumbled on his words. "I…but you…"

"Really, Reid, you don't need to say any more. It's okay." I slid my hand across the table, squeezed his, and then withdrew it. "Thank you."

Reid rubbed a thumb over his tattoo on his inner wrist. Even though I said the words, the recollection unsettled me. He'd moved in quickly, defensively…and violently. I could've been hurt more, especially given the rap sheet that couple had. Those two had been hell bent on stealing my car. If I'd lost that, then what? If Reid hadn't leapt in, I wasn't sure somebody else would have come to my defense, except maybe Geena, but I was less confident in her punch. And the creep Dennis had already given her husband a bloody nose when he tried to intervene.

Reid looked up from his musings. "Your son *is* resilient."

"He is. I just hope I don't mess up the boys too much." I pulled out a napkin from the holder and began folding it, distracting myself from his penetrating look.

"Don't all parents worry about that?" he asked.

I lined two edges, folded. "Yeah. It's been harder since Harrison died."

"How long ago did he pass away?"

I brushed my throat with two fingers, the bubbles and acid not mixing well. I spoke in a halted voice. "A year ago in July. This trip of ours, the one we finished before this all happened—the one to Yellowstone—had always been Harrison's idea. He knew how much Will would love it, how it would foster his interests." Those calls to the airline and hotels last summer to inform them of my husband's death had been excruciating. There was no way I was going on that trip right after Harrison died. Will hadn't spoken to me for a week afterward. Finn had been equally furious.

"Your brother stepped in this year in his place."

"Yeah. A year belated but appreciated. The boys really wanted the trip, too. So we did it."

"How—" Reid began, but he retracted his question.

I swallowed. I knew what he was asking. It had been ages since I'd spoken with anyone about the details of Harrison's death. Instead of avoiding Reid's look, which I did with everyone to ease the asker's comfort, I blew a breath, lifted my focus, and stared at him directly. He didn't seem to be the uncomfortable sort who avoided the topic of death. God, look at the books he lugged around with him! "It was a late, rainy night. Something happened at work, and he had to go in. A drunk driver hit him. Both my husband and the drunk man, a young guy in his twenties, died on the scene."

A dryness tickled my throat and inside my mouth, like cobwebs had settled in there. I crinkled the napkin, tossed it aside, and sipped the soda. It no longer quenched my thirst. I had never said goodbye. No, instead, we'd had a heated debate about Harrison's overworking. My last words to him were spoken in frustrated anger. I traced a thumb over my lips. I had at least given him a kiss goodbye.

"I'm sorry." He shifted his gaze to his tattoo, rubbing it in a daze.

"Cynthia, the mother of the young man who had died, still reaches out to me every few weeks. After I told her to stop calling, she started sending letters. I'm not ready to talk with her about it." I remembered the most recent letter, unopened, and tossed with the junk mail when Will and I had returned home from Salt Lake City.

Both of our attention fell upon Will, who was still doing recon.

"Reid. I...," I began, moving from one uncomfortable topic to another. *Just spit it out, AJ.* "I need to find a pharmacy in town."

"Do you need more cold medicine? You're looking better. Less green."

I drummed my fingers on the table. "No. The cold's fading. It's..." I heaved a sigh. "I have a prescription I need. I called my doctor earlier—a few days ago—and asked her to send in a refill to Wichita, and well, we're here and not there. I asked the shop owner at the counter about local pharmacies when I ordered the food. He said there are a few, but most are already closed. I need to check around after we eat. If they can find my info in their system…"

"Geez, I didn't know. Yeah, sure thing," Reid said.

Will ambled around the restaurant. He shifted from the mural of Italy on the wall farthest from us to what looked like counting the squares on the floor.

For a chatty fella, Reid had grown gravely quiet with the mention of Harrison's death. Had I been wrong about him? Was he like all the others? I cleared my throat. "I should have brought Will to his grandparents. He shouldn't have to bear this burden with me. This trip. It's been a nightmare."

Reid turned his focus to me, usual countenance resumed, the glow filling his eyes again. "Your parents?"

I shook my head. "No, my father lives in Arizona with my stepmother. We talk when we can, but I don't see them much these days. My mother's deceased. Harrison's parents are the ones my kids know well. They live in Virginia. God, what was I thinking? Why did I bring him?"

"Because you're his mom. You knew he would be safest with you."

If it hadn't been for Reid…

"How many times do you plan on saving me?" I asked, lightheartedly, but inwardly, I cringed with the thought. How many times *had* he saved me? He helped me with the tire. That was one. He helped me after I'd passed out. That was two. He saved me from the attack. Three. He helped me find Will. Well, that was sort of four. Even though he hadn't technically saved me physically there, he'd definitely saved my sanity and helped me find my son. Who, for all we knew, hadn't really been lost. I had told him to run and hide, and that's what he had done. Literal kid. Smart kid.

"You've reached your quota." His face broke into a smile.

I shook my head. "You weren't following me?"

"Nope."

I sighed, allowing myself to defuse. "Right time, right place?"

"You can say that," he agreed. Handsome dark brown eyes held mine. They made me thirsty—for coffee. Or more. I shifted in my seat, feeling my desire grow. God, and it scared me shitless. My stock in fate was outweighing coincidence at this moment. Perhaps everything in life was meant to happen, when it was supposed to happen, and for a reason. That was a hefty truth to swallow.

If that was so, then why did Harrison have to die when he had?

I hated when my mind turned down this path. I grabbed a few napkins, placed one in front of me, and one for Will's spot. "I certainly hope you won't need to be my knight anymore on this trip."

"If I did need to be, would that be awful?"

I stared outside to delay answering. Then sipped. The straw made a slurping sound as I drained the cup.

"Lighten up, Audrey Jane. Such a serious name for a serious gal. It's going to be okay. I'm not on a mission to save. Okay? We're both going to the same place. You're my ride; I'm your map. The stars aligned. Luck. Right time, right place." He smiled.

*Was I fated to find him?*

Just then the young waitress arrived.

"Saved by the pizza," Reid said.

"Thank God," I agreed. "Excuse me, could I get a cup of coffee with cream and sugar?" I asked the waitress.

"Can't do coffee. Our water is really limited. In fact, we may be closing tomorrow. Another soda?"

I grimaced. "Sure."

She nodded and returned to the counter.

"Will!" I called, but he had already swooped in, lured by the sweet aroma of oregano, sauce, and cheese. He slid beside me in the booth.

"That one," he said, pointing to the largest piece. "And that one."

I placed a slice onto his plate. "Start with one."

He adjusted his collar yet again. Tucked it under his chin.

After waiting a moment for the slice to cool, Will proceeded with removing all the cheese first, setting it aside, and eating the bottom layer of crust. He would then eat the cheese last. Many kids did that sort of thing. Even Finn had adopted this habit. At least Will didn't ask me to cut it into "two big pieces and ten little pieces" anymore...those were the fun preschool days of autism. I distinctly remembered Sarah criticizing me for giving in to his quirky demands. "I would never do that for the girls!" she had said. Everything—sandwiches, pizza, cheese slices—had to be cut a certain way for Will.

"Oklahoma may be a boring state, but they do

make delicious pizza," Reid said, devouring his piece.

I bit into mine and moaned. "Heck, yeah."

"Good job, Mom," Will said at my lack of swear word usage.

I patted his head. "You keep me accountable, honey." At least aloud.

"Can I have a soda?"

"Yup. A special treat for today." I handed him a cup and straw. It was lemon-lime.

Reid snatched the straw. "Want to see something cool, Will?"

"Okay," he said, half-interested as he picked the rest of the cheese off his slice.

"Check this out." Reid partly removed the straw wrapper, blew air in the straw, and shot the piece across the table like a rocket.

"Cool! Can I try?" Will took the other straw that lay on the table and did the same. He whooped with joy.

Just then, the second song came on the jukebox. I recognized it immediately.

Delight spread Will's face. "Oh, good! The weather song is on!"

"No Rain" by Blind Melon, a nineties song, played its upbeat tune, with lyrics entrenched with meanings of loneliness, depression, and acceptance-seeking. I'd always thought of Will when I heard this tune, which made it to my playlist a few years ago. It was both bitter and sweet. He was my nontypical sweetheart, who loved puddles and rain—the simple things in life— and he only sought acceptance and love of his unique traits. A weather song. Of course. He was such a sweet child. Lord, he elevated my heart to a new level.

Reid shared a jovial smile with me. "Ah, a classic!"

"A what?" Will asked, his focus on the straws. "It's about rain."

"Shh…classic? Now that *truly* ages us!" I said.

Reid smirked.

We ate in silence as the tune played. Memories tumbled around in my mind.

The next song came on.

"Mom, I picked this one for you." Will licked his fingers as he finished his second slice of pizza.

Van Morrison's "Brown Eyed Girl." "Now *this* is an oldie but a goodie!" I said cheerfully. "Will, you're a fabulous choice-maker with the songs. Something unique, something weather, and something for me." I kissed his cheek, and he smiled. Its buoyant tune belted from the jukebox. I relished the respite even if just for three minutes.

****

Will held my hand on our way to the hotel room. To hell with camping. I didn't care how much it cost me. I was staying in hotels from here on if I could. If they were still available.

"Love you, Mom," he said.

I squeezed his hand. "Love you, too."

He yawned. "Can I play before bed?"

"Sure, honey."

Pain slid up my back from yet another day of long driving. I yearned for a nice stroll to stretch my muscles, followed by a warm bubbly bath. But given the water situation—we were sternly warned at the front desk to only use the toilet and the sink—the bath would have to wait.

"You two go ahead. Left something in the car.

Mind if I use the keys?" Reid asked, pressing a casual hand on my midback. I didn't mind. I liked his nearness. Strangely, wanted more of it.

"I thought you lugged your life around in that." I hitched a thumb toward his heavy pack.

He grinned and brushed a hand through his hair. "Yeah, most of it. One thing I forgot."

I nodded and swapped him a set of car keys for his backpack. After the incident in Missouri, he had insisted I keep both sets of keys to my car. I had one set in my pocket and one set in my handbag. He paused. "Want me to ask at the desk if they know of any other pharmacies?"

"Sure, thanks." There was no need to verbalize my doubt. We'd stopped in all the larger towns on our deviated path south of Wichita, through northern Oklahoma, and now in Dodge City, Kansas, where we were calling it quits for the night. Reid was a determined fella though. It took Will's whining and my aching feet for us to give up our canvasing here in town.

I had inquired with countless pharmacies and grocery stores. Most were closed, with no indication of when they'd reopen. Two refused to refill anything despite my suggestion to call my doctor. Their phone lines had been on the fritz all week. And one pharmacy had been able to reach my prescription via a website server (after several failed attempts, and one pissed off pharmacy tech) and obtained the prescription, but it was out of stock and they had no suitable substitute. They were also closing their doors as well. We'd tried dialing my doctor's office from both our cell phones and the store phones, to no avail.

If I was taking stock in fate, I'd say that fate had other plans for my prescription. On the positive side, at least we'd avoided the traffic and ash, for now…though that cloud and distant thunder had loomed all day.

"Mom, you've been doing well driving. You're not scared anymore?" Will said as I helped him button his pajama top. He clicked through the TV channels.

"…*in an unexpected turn of events, the direction of the plume has shifted south. Wichita was hit with ash rain this afternoon. Many roads are in poor condition, powerlines and trees are down in this neighborhood with what we think could have been an F2 tornado, and sewers are flooded. Citizens have been ordered to stay in their homes until the National Guard reaches them, and it could be a day or more. Public Works has advised all people in this region on the map to not use running water. Gerard, tell us more about this change in the weather and that reported tornado…*"

I ripped my ears from the TV and said belatedly, "No, sweetie, I'm not scared anymore. I'm feeling better now."

"That's good, Mom!"

A part of me wondered if I needed the med anymore. After fainting, which may have been exacerbated by the cold, I'd been feeling less woozy. Still woozy, definitely, but less. The tension from all the searching and worrying suddenly released as I sat beside Will. Perhaps I was going to be okay.

"…*due to the tsunami and earthquakes, we think the El Niño year is upon us far sooner than we'd expected…*"

"Wow, honey, you were right about the clouds," I said, my fingers shaking as I did the last button on his top. Shivers swept through me. That had been too close. Dammit, we were still too close.

Click.

"*Most roads in Colorado are now closed or impassable.*"

"A tornado!" he said with glee.

I took the remote and turned off the TV. "Play time for a little?"

After a few minutes of playing with Lego bricks, I tucked him in like I always did, feeling less weighed down by at least one thing.

He began to cough. "My throat tickles, Mom."

"I don't have any honey. Here, drink some water." I handed him his water bottle. I brought the blanket to his chin, followed by his weighted blanket. I casually felt his forehead; he was tepid, no sign of fever. Feeling the itch in my own throat, I sniffled without thinking.

Having finished the Alaska adventure book, I moved on to book two of the wizard-cat series, albeit reluctantly and with a bittersweet swell forming in my gut as I read. His eyelids fluttered as he fought sleep.

"Do you think Reid plays chess?" he asked, rolling to his side.

"I don't know."

"Maybe I can teach him, like Dad taught me."

"Maybe." I kissed his cheek. "Good night, sweetie. You're a blessing in my life, Will. Do you know that?"

"Yeah. Love you, Mom. You smiled tonight, Mom. That made me happy. We'll find Finn, Mom. No need to cry anymore. And I like Reid."

I swallowed. "I do, too."

I'd not been pleasant company since…God, since when? Will's diagnosis? Since Harrison's death? Did I really cry that much?

I gave Will another kiss and stood upright. The child radiated a serene love. Autism challenges had not hardened him; instead, he had grown into a tough, ever-loving child. No tears tonight. No more perfectionism. My life would never be suburban-soccer-mom perfect or "normal" by societal standards or my own imposed expectations. It was our own perfect. It had to be okay. Or else I would kill myself trying to achieve a preset notion I had for perfection. Finn completed the picture. The three of us would make our home our own again. Screw it all. No more excuses.

I pulled the curtains closed, slipped my feet into the comfort of Harrison's slippers, and turned off the light beside the bed to darken the room. Heavy legs brought me to the bathroom, and I flipped the light on. Shades of amber crossed the worn hotel carpet and illuminated the mediocre pressed-wood desk. All else in the room was enveloped in the blackness of evening.

"Enough night light, hon?" I asked Will.

"I guess so."

"Need any glow sticks?"

"No, thanks."

The scent of dampness and mildew infiltrated my returned sense of smell. We were lucky we had snagged a room. Rain pattered on the locked windows. Tent camping in rain was no fun at all. The car was no better. I was eating my cash, but I had packed plenty, despite the robbery, and we were almost there. Reid had given me some money for this room, too. It was a split room of sorts, with a wall and sliding door dividing the two sleep areas. It even had a mini-kitchen, though we wouldn't need it.

Gosh, we were so close, I could taste it.

I buzzed from the sugary sodas. I stared at myself in the mirror, scrutinizing my wrinkles, the gray strays within the chestnut brown, and the deep circles beneath my eyes. "Ghastly," I murmured, touching the soft flesh where the blood had pooled together on my cheek. Reflexively, I grabbed my meager cosmetic bag to reapply concealer, but I stopped. Who cared? I closed the toilet lid, sat, and beheld the haggard Audrey Jane Sinclair reflection. I thought of nothing. Not Harrison. Not Finn. Not my hurt. I zoned out for a few minutes.

I was tempted to disregard the warning and run a bath.

Reid knocked. I opened the room door. He held a foil-covered plate. "Is he asleep?" he whispered.

My love bug beneath the oversized hotel blanket snored lightly. "Yeah."

"I've got something for you," he said, holding a plate and fork. He motioned to the door. I slipped a key card into my pocket, grabbed my hoodie sweatshirt, and followed him into the hallway. I softly closed the door behind us. My child was nine, and I still tiptoed to avoid waking him. I supposed we could've sat in the other room on the other bed, but I liked the hallway better. It was nostalgic.

"I figured it was too late for another dose of caffeinated soda. But it's never too late for cake." He removed the foil to reveal a slice of carrot cake on a disposable plate.

"It's never too late for caffeine," I corrected. "Or dessert. Got another fork?" I didn't add that I was wondering where he had wandered off to.

He sat on the carpeted hallway and leaned against

the wall. "I'm all set. Here you go," he said, handing me the plate and then pulling a candy bar from his top pocket.

"Not another lollipop?" I teased.

"Nah, tonight calls for a chocolate bar."

"Pizza, soda, and cake. Salty and sweet. What else could a woman ask for?" Carrot cake. Harrison's favorite. "Thanks." I slid beside him and stretched my legs with a sigh. Reid munched on his nutty chocolate bar. I thought of Harrison and wiggled my oversized slippers.

"The front desk was no help on other pharmacies. I'm sorry."

I shrugged. "It'll be okay." I hoped. We would see how I fared with the remaining driving. I had done well, to my surprise. Had it been the medicine? Or had I somehow gotten over my mental block, despite a year of working at it and failing? Reid didn't ask more about it, but this time, I decided transparency would be best. "I have anxiety. I've always had it, but once Harrison died, it hit me full blast. I also struggle with driving because of what happened."

He nodded. "I see. We can keep looking."

I shook my forked hand. "Nah. Really. Maybe all the mumbo jumbo my therapist has tried on me the past year is working."

"Maybe it just took the right motivation," Reid said.

"Yup." I licked the fork. "But who knows, I may still need the medication. And that's okay, too. Head stuff is hard to get over."

"It can be. Your symptoms...do you think—?"

"Yeah, I suspect withdrawal, compounded with a

cold, too."

He slid his body closer to mine and tapped my knee. "I'll help any way I can."

"Thanks, Reid." I inhaled, enjoying his nearness. "I used to love to bake cakes. Gosh, this is tasty. The real deal."

"You have a lot of used to's."

"Don't we all?"

He released a throaty affirmation. "We do."

"What are some of yours?" I took another forkful of deliciousness.

He chewed and swallowed. "I used to call my mom every day, and she insisted we speak in Spanish only, to improve my fluency. I miss her. My Uncle Jorge taught me the flavorful Spanish swear words whenever he'd visit though."

"The same uncle that was a Mexican senator?" I raised an eyebrow.

Reid smiled and nodded. "You bet."

"I used to go on more demanding hikes every year with Harrison." I wiggled my toes in his fuzzy slippers. "We enjoyed the challenge."

"You can still do that...well, with your boys, I mean," Reid offered.

"The boys can't tackle rugged hikes. We stick to kid-friendly, easy trails...ones with streams, ponds, rivers, or towers. Those are their lures. I haven't been out much on our local trails with them this year. Yellowstone was the first time that we'd gone on longer hikes. It was amazing." I thought about the lupine, an annual trip that was no more. Perhaps I'd take them next year. I also thought of Yellowstone, which was no more.

"Pikes Peak is remarkable. Perhaps I can give you a tour if you want to visit?"

"Perhaps. Got kid-friendly trails?"

"Definitely."

We were silent for a moment as I scraped the last morsel of frosting off my plate.

"I used to play board games with my sister every weekend, at least when I was home. I brought a few with me on my tours."

"Well, we know you're not the best at campfire games." I poked his arm.

He gave a "hrmmphm" and laughed.

"What's your favorite board game?" I asked.

He scratched at the teeny hairs that had begun to sprout on his clean, round chin. "Lily always liked games with world domination or buying properties. I prefer trivia games."

"She'd get on well with Will, then. He's obsessed. I've had to ban some board games from our house a few times. The first time, it didn't go well."

He nodded and crinkled his wrapper, tucking it in his pocket.

I eyed him. He laughed. "For future notes."

"You don't plan on leaving again?"

"Nah. You just never know."

"I used to enjoy tending my flower gardens. I have a thing for flowers. Day lilies and lupine are my favorites."

"You don't anymore?"

I shrugged. "I do. It's...I don't know. Truthfully, I don't know why I don't find joy in them as much as I used to. Harrison had helped me dig and get the garden beds started, but that's not why." I turned to him.

"What made you choose the army? All those choices—your mom wanting you to be a doctor, your senator uncle, your sister in education...was it for your dad?"

A smiled parted his lips. "Actually it was for me. I was a rebellious teen. Thought I had to prove myself...well, and yeah, a smidge for my dad." He flicked a thumb to my oversized slippers. "Nice kicks."

"Thanks."

He shared a tender look with me, and I had an acute sense of my own heartbeat in that moment.

"I remember when Will was a baby, and a few times when we traveled, Harrison and I would sit in the hallway like this while Will fell asleep in his travel play yard. Funny, huh?"

The dark sensitivity in his eyes deepened. Lord, it was like a sea that I wanted to explore more.

Harrison's voice popped into my head. *It's okay to miss me, honey baby angel, but it's okay to keep going, too.*

I pointed to the artwork before us. It was a painting entitled *Ghosts of Santa Fe*, a sweeping and peculiar landscape with subtle emphasis on old wagon-wheel ruts and a lone, haggard oak tree. "Interesting stuff."

Reid scratched his chin. "You got a favorite artist?"

"Well, after my mom, I love Monet and the Impressionists. I used to watch my mom work at her easel. She loved to draw Native American portraits and commissioned portraits."

"Fascinating. Maybe that's where you got your creative gene? Writing?"

I nodded. "She was an inspiration. She also favored and incorporated poetry in her art. She died from cancer before I became a mother myself."

"I'm sorry," Reid said.

"Will was born the day before her birthday. I like to think that he is her reincarnated in a way, for he has such an artistic, loving soul."

Reid smiled. "I can see that."

We were quiet for a minute, as I pondered.

"Being a mom without a mom can be tough, huh?"

"Yeah. It's hard when you don't have a mom to call about all the kid stuff…concerts, activities, milestone moments. It really sucks. I thought I was doing okay with it…but then Harrison died, and well, it's been hard."

Reid took my hand in his and squeezed. I loved the feel of it in mine and didn't let go.

"You were young when you lost her?"

"Yeah, in my twenties. Patsy, my mother-in-law, she tries to fill that void, but…" I drifted off, not elaborating. Reid didn't prod.

I sniffed and blew a breath. "She'd read my work though. My mom. She loved it. That early work was total crap, but my mom was my cheerleader while fighting her own battle."

"Moms are amazing."

We sat quietly, musing.

Reid must have sensed the prickly friction that hovered between the inches that separated us, too, for he released our interlocked hands and stood. "I'm going to walk around, stretch my legs. Check out some of this art. Is that okay? Wanna come?"

"No thanks, I need to stay here. I'll enjoy the quiet."

It was hardly quiet. The rain pattered against the exit door at the end of the hallway.

The sugar high from the cake was already fading, as was the soda buzz.

"Is it okay if I sleep in the car?"

Here it was. I'd avoided mentioning the room situation during our conversation. The hotel was booked solid. We'd gotten the last available room; Reid paid for half. I tapped a finger on my leg. "No. You should take the other bed. There's sort of a wall and sliding door. It's cool."

"I can't ask that of you. It's not—"

I shoved a key card into his hand, my fingers pausing on his for the briefest moment. "You're not asking."

"If you're sure?"

"Yes. You've definitely earned your keep, Corporal Gregory."

"Okay. Thanks. I'll be back in a few. Oh, I almost forgot. I found this in the gift shop. A scene from one of his movies was filmed here or something. The teen guy at the counter rambled. I thought you would like it." He pulled a thin copy of *On Writing* by Stephen King from his back pocket.

He flashed his smile before he turned on his heel and strode down the hallway, leaving me gawking at the book in my hand.

Chapter Fifteen
Not in Kansas Anymore

The moans woke me.

"Not again," I mumbled. Will had already awoken a few hours before. With a resigned exhalation, I rolled to check him, but his mouth was agape and he snored.

I brushed back his sweaty hair and admired how he looked like a baby while sleeping. I listened as my vision adjusted to the semi-darkness. The clock beside the bed read 1:04 a.m.; it was too late for a night terror. His always struck earlier between nine and ten p.m. Usually, once was it. Fatigue, new places, weird sleep schedules...they attributed to his night terrors.

I heard it again. It came from Reid's area of the room, beyond the half-opened slider door. I rose and approached the doorway.

Reid tossed and turned. "No...don't...please help!" He writhed and groaned.

He must have been having a nightmare, from his deployment maybe? I knew nothing about that experience, aside from what I had seen in movies and television shows and from the limited knowledge my father shared with me about his own demons. Reid appeared all too familiar with PTSD.

The wretched pain in his voice persuaded me. I slipped closer to his bedside.

"No!" he said, louder. I knew he wouldn't wake

Will at this time of night. Will was a light sleeper around daybreak, but in the middle of the night nothing could rouse him, except for a strong thunderstorm, and the storm had weakened a few hours before. Regardless, I closed the slider door. Instinctively, I sat beside Reid and laid my hand on his cheek. It was damp and warm. I rested my hand there, as it was my modus operandi for calming anyone…Harrison had loved my cheek caresses, as did Finn and Will. Touch soothed. God how I missed it, somebody touching *me* and not in the clinging kid way.

"Hush," I said. "It's all right. I'm here." I didn't think before I stroked and said, "Think happy thoughts." Like I always did for Will's terrors. I wondered what Reid's happy thoughts would be to pull him from whatever nightmare he faced.

"*Lo siento…Es culpa mía…¡Dios mío!*" he said, breathless, locked in sleep. The glow of the light on the nightstand, which he must have left on, fell upon his features. His eyes were tightly closed. It wasn't a terror then. Did adults get terrors? He would remember this. Will never remembered his terrors, only his nightmares. I knew little Spanish, but I deciphered "sorry" in his disjointed words.

Reid's whimpers turned to whispers, and his hand slid over mine. "I…" He grumbled as he squeezed mine hard. He switched to English. "Why didn't you listen to me? Why?" His tears wet my fingertips.

Images of burning bodies and exploding tanks, gunfire, flaming buildings, shells going off, and flying debris raced through my mind.

I inched closer to him. I let his hand rest upon mine, and I moved my other one to his forehead.

"Hush. Happy thoughts. Happy thoughts. You're not there. You're here in Kansas. Lots of cornfields, farmers, quiet." Gosh, was I Dorothy from *The Wizard of Oz*? No sand or insurgents or tanks or bullets. I searched my brain for some theological or philosophical quotation but drummed up nothing. My almanac of words to live by tended to revolve around parenting.

Nada. Nothing. Blank.

"Help...," he slurred in a painful gasp.

What would be his happy thought?

"It's me, Audrey Jane."

I waited another long moment.

My left hand dropped from his forehead and landed on his round, sweaty, and bare shoulder. He must've taken off his shirt when he'd gone to bed, but I couldn't remember. He'd been awake, reading, when I turned in for the night. The feel of his naked skin sent a familiar twang through me, and I removed my hand. My other hand remained on his cheek. I couldn't pull it from his grasp, which tightened around mine.

His eyes shot open.

The pain from the remnants of his nightmare resided in his gaze. I held his stare and smiled the best I could. "It's me. Hush. It's okay." I slid my left hand to his free hand and squeezed. He squeezed back. I released a thumb and rubbed it along his wrist, tracing where I thought his tattoo would be. I fought the desire to stare at his chest.

I felt oddly exhilarated and moved to pull away.

He squeezed my hand again. Not hard. Not soft. It was the squeeze of internal longing, like the one of a lover who could not bear to part ways from their partner. He swallowed.

"Audrey Jane," he said slowly as he drew himself from the nightmare's hold.

I smiled deeper. "Happy thoughts," I murmured.

I shifted on the bed to give him space. He countered with sitting upright and keeping my one hand in his, with both of our hands firmly pressed to his cheek. He placed my other hand—still locked in his— on his chest, naturally drawing me closer. I didn't want to pull away from the intimate connection.

*Dear God.*

I could smell him, he was so close. The maleness and sweat of him. I inhaled. His heart beat into our locked palms.

Perhaps it was my need for soulful resuscitation. Perhaps it was my vulnerability. Or perhaps I liked him. Oh yes, I did like him, very much.

He pulled me toward him, and I allowed it. His kiss was warm, heavy, and slow. It was goddamn heady, and I drank it in like a parched desert cactus. I parted my lips wider and allowed the stubble on his chin to brush my face. Tender lips caressed mine. Our hands remained interlaced, one set on his cheek, one set on his heart. His heart beat quicker under my hand. His breathing deepened. God, oh, how I had forgotten what this was like. His mouth was inviting and stirred my dusty desires. A flicker of guilt danced in my mind, but I shushed it.

He removed his hand from mine on his cheek and drew it to the base of my head, urging me closer for a deeper kiss. His touch tickled the fine hairs on the nape of my neck. He tasted like mint toothpaste and sleep. I reveled in his mouth upon mine. I found myself shifting my position, desire reaching another area of my body. I moaned as my breasts pressed against his chest.

Before it went too far, he pulled away and stared at me, only inches from my face, dark eyes swirling with sentiment, a slight smile upon his lips. I exhaled. He held my gaze for a long moment while all I heard was the clock ticking on the nightstand. Then he fell on his pillow.

"Good night, Audrey Jane." He closed his eyes, a deeper smile upon his face.

"Night," I whispered.

I bit my lips and drew my fingertips to them, wanting to hold on to the feeling of his mouth upon mine, the scratch of his light stubble, and the taste of his mouth.

Instead of sliding away and returning to Will's bed, I stayed beside Reid. Bold, crazy, or needy, I didn't care. The feel of a man's body beside mine in a bed was too consuming, just too…dammit, I needed it.

I lay wide awake—just me and my racing heart.

My thoughts went to Harrison, as I replayed what had just happened, and my chest tightened. I twirled my wedding band, the gold steadfast, infinite. My heart reminded me of my vows, but my mind told me this was okay. It was okay to move on.

I must have fallen asleep but awoke to arms around my waist. Reid coughed from behind me. He murmured incoherent words, then readjusted. I glanced at the nearby clock. It read three o'clock.

I needed to return to Will's bed, though his deep snoring echoed through the thin slider door. He was out like a light. Lifting Reid's arm, I began to wiggle from his grip.

"Don't go," he said sleepily, deeply.

My heart danced with his dreamy tone. His fingers traced my hip. I was wearing just a long T-shirt. It had been hot when we'd gone to bed, and my yoga pants lay beside my spot on the bed for a quick slip on in the morning along with my bra for modesty. So much for that.

I was in a bed with a man, both of us half-naked. My mind fragmented with his caressing fingers as he lifted the hem of my T-shirt and found the edge of my panties. *Lord, lord, lord.*

I missed a man's touch. And Reid was a gentleman. Surely, if I swatted him away, he'd take no offense. But I didn't swat him away. He kissed the back of my neck. "Audrey Jane…," he cooed.

My soul longed for nurturing, for human touch, for that personal connection of lovers. I squeezed his hand with my own instead. Then, partly chiding myself for it, I rolled over to face him.

A racing heartbeat met my aroused nipples as our chests pressed together. His hand remained under my shirt, on my hip.

"It's been so long…," he said to my own thinking.

"Me, too."

"I shouldn't."

As I leaned in to kiss him, I said, "You should."

I moved my wedged hand between us to his cheek, and the other fell upon his own hip. Yeah, he was down to his boxers, too. Hard longing pressed against my belly. I could say no. I could roll out from beneath the heat under the covers…

He returned the kiss, passionately. My mind was a dizzy mess of should or shouldn't, desire and guilt, want or didn't want—oh, I did want. Will was asleep, we were alone, and it had been a year. I had to move on. The world was going to hell around us, and who knew if we had more time. I needed this. An escape from the chaos.

"But...," he said as he came up for air.

I didn't beg and didn't pull away. I answered with my mouth again, against his. We moved slowly, partaking in the touch of each other's skin beneath trembling fingertips. His hand drew north under my shirt, caressing my breast. I gasped with the sensations. Passion and yearning had become a distant memory this year. Reid relit the flame. Even if it was just for this one moment. Maybe this was our end—the end of our country, the end of a journey with a man I might never see again—tears came to my eyes with both thoughts— dammit it all. I needed this. Seemed like Reid needed it just as much.

I held him tighter. I could not get enough of his kisses, which on the kissing scale were oh-my-God amazing. A microsecond of concern passed through my brain—I had no protection, but I did have an IUD in place. Good enough. I doubted Reid carried condoms around in that backpack of his. I nearly snorted with the thought.

He brought his face up for air. "Funny, am I?" he teased. He trickled kisses down my throat. Goosebumps rose on my skin.

I was deliriously aroused and fatigued at the same time. "No. Just was wondering if you carry condoms in your pack, too."

He froze. "No. Sorry, I don't. We can stop. I used to get screened for the army though, and well, I've always used protection since. Not that there's been much since. I'm healthy." Now a frown formed. "I'll stop. It's best."

Oh no, I ruined it! "It's okay, I'm okay, too," I quickly said, kissing his chin.

My heart raced. I had blown it…there I was again, too responsible, too robotic. Why couldn't I just embrace the moment? *Because you have a family to care for, AJ*, my mind hollered.

"You're quite more than okay, Audrey Jane. You're like a taste of the divine." His lips drew down over my T-shirt. He then slipped the shirt up, taking each breast into his mouth. I writhed below him with a silky groan.

Responsively, I parted my legs and allowed him to touch me. He tenderly stroked the essence of me with his fingers, and I muffled my moan at the intimacy. My heart opened to him, bandages and all. *Reid, please don't break my heart*, I wanted to say. Instead, I allowed my craving for physical connection, to be *with* someone, to fuel my moves. Still unsure if I was ready to move on, ready for *this*, I did it anyway. It was time to jump into the deep end.

He rolled over top of me, drew down my panties. I shook with excitement and nerves. He kissed my hips, my belly, and then drew back to my mouth. For a long moment, we took a break from the kissing and held each other's gaze as he stroked my face. Desire, attraction, and sincerity all blazed in his dark eyes as I allowed him inside me. I quivered beneath him.

He slowly made love to me in the wee hours, our bodies rocking, in a nurturing connection. Kisses rolled over my skin as we swayed, and my fingers raked his finely chiseled back, arms, and shoulders. I gasped as he brought me to a new plane of pleasure. He muffled a moan as he reached his own peak. God, he felt so *good*.

His mouth and body breathed life into me.

We were two souls lost at sea for so long, finally finding an island amidst the chaos, for however long we might have.

**\*\*\*\***

I awoke again, early, around five thirty a.m. In a few hours, we'd set out for Colorado. I wriggled free from Reid's arms.

"Don't go," he said, echoing his sentiment from a few hours before.

"I should go lie with Will," I said.

"Yeah. You're right. AJ, I..." He reluctantly removed his arm from around my waist, and I slithered out from beneath the blanket and sheet.

I leaned down and kissed him. "It's okay." It was all I had. I wasn't sure what else *to* say.

After a restless thirty minutes in bed with Will, I sat at the desk, insomnia plaguing me.

Qualms had returned with vivid lucidity after my lovemaking with Reid. I touched my lips, the hum of his mouth still upon mine. His lips had done more than just kiss my mouth. I shivered thinking of it, as if I could still feel him within me.

Would I regret it?

No, dammit, I would not allow guilt or shame to creep in.

This trip, spurred by my fear of losing Finn, had been one filled with copious moments of frustration, mishaps, exhaustion, and dare I think...enlightenment? Through the years since Will's diagnosis, I'd assigned myself my own motto: I try; I survive; I love. Dammit, I tried. I tried so hard. I survived because I loved and because I had to.

The bathroom light flickered, and I waited for the power to stay on. Outages were inevitable. We were getting closer. My lungs told me. I reached into my handbag and pulled out my inhaler for a puff. Thunder drummed again, louder. We'd finally reached the fallout zone, or at least the fringe of it. The man at the front desk had told us we could stay one night. He was closing in the morning, and everyone had to leave.

I itched to be on the road. The lights stopped flickering.

Saturated in my musings, I tuned it all out. The hum of the mini-fridge, the on and off cycling of the awful air conditioning unit, and Will's snoring were filed away into the ambient noise folder. My eyes grew heavy, and I contemplated returning to the comfort of the bed. I already missed Reid's warmth.

I startled when my barely-charged phone pinged in the predawn hour. It pinged again. I grabbed for the phone. In my excitement, I pushed it off the table. It tumbled to the floor as if in slow motion.

I fell to my knees, leaned under the dimly lit desk, and found it. Ping.

Crap, another ping and it would go to voicemail. What the hell? When did its ring switch to a ping?

The voicemail inbox was full. I had to get it—now.

My brain clicked. The screen said, "Caller Unknown." I answered. I half expected Sarah to have gotten through, but it was early for Pacific Standard Time. Early for anyone, actually. I'd given up on Dr. Martin. "Hello?"

The line crackled in my ear, which was weird. I was used to phone calls fading or becoming muffled with quiet patches. Not crackling.

"AJ?"

It was a male voice. My stomach lurched. "Brandon?"

Muffled words.

My voice rose, and Will stirred. "Brandon? Brandon?" I nearly screeched into the phone. I moved and smacked my head on the underside of the desk.

"I'm...," he said.

Crackles.

"Brandon! I can't hear you!" I pushed the phone harder to my ear, as if that could make me hear him better. Within the crackle, I listened for any word or syllable or breath. I righted myself, disregarding my throbbing cranium, and hurried to the window for better coverage. It didn't help. My pulse beat in my head so loudly that I had to cover one ear with my hand to focus on the garbling on the other end.

The phone went dead. Silence.

I frantically dialed his number.

Nothing. No ring, no busy signal. Not a goddamn thing.

****

Will remained asleep as I hurried about the room gathering our stuff. Reid leapt into the room with my commotion.

"What happened? Are you okay?" His voice was spiked with unmasked worry. He tossed a glance to Will, who lightly snored in his bed.

"It was my brother, Brandon. He called! H-He..." I stopped, rubbed my head, which hurt like hell, and continued with my tossing random things into bags. Will's Lego bricks, marbles, and clothes lay strewn about on the carpet. I chucked them all into his backpack, crawling on the floor and feeling with fingers in the dimness.

"Brandon? Your brother? That's great! What did he say?"

I sat against the bed, knees bent. "Nothing. I heard him say my name, and he said 'I'm' and that's it. We got cut off." I faced Reid.

He crouched beside me.

Tingles raced along my arms to my fingertips. I dropped Lego bricks into the backpack. "He's okay," I whispered to myself. "He has to be okay. But why did he call so early?"

I stared at the dead phone on the floor. I quickly plugged it in, and the screen reillumined. I dialed Brandon again. Nothing. Okay, maybe it wasn't my phone that had cut us off.

I locked eyes with Reid. The bitter taste of adrenaline dribbled down my throat. I swallowed. My body shook from lack of sleep, lack of nutritious food, and from whatever virus I may have had on top of the withdrawal symptoms. God, I wanted a white pill right now.

"My Finn, though, Reid. I don't know if—"

Reid clutched my hand. "He's okay. He's going to be okay. Brandon's alive, and so is your Finn. Maybe Brandon was calling you every hour or so, like what you've been doing?"

I pursed my lips, determined, trying to convince myself. "Okay. Yes. He's going to be okay. Brandon is with him. He got through to me. God, I don't know where they are!"

"Stick to the original plan? Colorado?" Reid asked, standing, pulling me with him.

"Yes."

Will woke up. "Mom?" his sleepy voice said from beneath the covers. He yawned and stretched. "Is it seven o'clock yet?"

Close enough.

"Let's get the hell out of Dodge," Reid said with a sideways look and uplifted dark eyebrow.

Despite my angst, a sliver of a smile emerged at Reid's iconic saying. "Yes, let's."

"I've always wanted to say that." He squeezed my hand before letting go. "Let's find your son."

****

When they stepped outside, Will was excited to see the gray ash that covered everything! It was unmistakable. They'd gone to bed with an overcast evening, and then a thunderstorm passed through during the night. He wondered if it was the same dark cloudy front they had been trying to avoid in Wichita. Had it traveled even farther south while they were sleeping?

It woke him up once. He hated the sound of it. It made his body shake.

Now they were on another planet! It was like the gray debris inside Mom's vacuum canister.

"Ash!" he said, running toward the car.

A thin coat covered everything. This was week-old ash, carried by the wind and storm fronts from the fallout zones closer to Yellowstone. Trapped in clouds, then rained down.

Mom muttered a few curses. He heard the "F" one.

He drew a finger along one side of the car, making

a zig zag trail, causing the ash to drip to the ground in its wake. He rubbed the ash between his fingers. "Oh, it feels cool! It's not light and fluffy like I thought! Hmmm." He coughed, feeling a painful scratch in his throat, but he continued exploring.

It was heavier than he'd expected, too. He lifted a wet, gritty fingertip. Upon closer inspection, it was no longer like the vacuum collection chamber innards. Now it was reminiscent of wet dryer lint.

Wow. Pulverized rock, volcanic glass, and minerals: it was the essence of the earth!

"Let's go," Mom said as she wiped off the car with a snow brush. It fell in plops.

"I'll drive," Reid said. He squeezed Mom's hand.

"The winds must have carried it here. It dipped more south than they thought!" Will said as he climbed into his seat. "The volcano only erupted for thirteen hours, so all the ash was already in the air and the fatter particles fell first. That was like…" He counted the days since the beginning of their trip. "Ten days ago…all the ash got stuck in the atmosphere, and now it's traveling around the globe. I wonder how far it will go? With the El Niño effect, it could travel farther. And we'll have more rain!"

He quietly mused over all the statistics he'd heard on the news.

"Mom? Mom? Did you hear me?"

"Yes, honey."

"No, you didn't."

"What is it?"

"Did you pack my goggles and face mask? The protective goggles Daddy got us last year? You know, for all of Finn's digging in the backyard and the geology stuff we do? Did you pack them? They were on my list."

"Yes, Will, I did. And the face masks."

"Good, because we'll need them." He coughed and couldn't stop for a long minute. His ribs hurt from it. Mom then turned around to watch him. She stared at him, frowning. "I'm okay," he said, coughing, and then reaching for his water bottle.

"Just a tickle?" she asked.

"Uh-huh."

"Could he have a pop?" Reid asked.

"You can suck on it, and not bite or chew. It will help soothe your throat," Mom said.

"Okay."

Reid held two pops out. "Orange or cherry?"

"Orange."

Reid handed him the orange one and then smiled at Mom.

Will's coughing subsided as he sucked on the pop, and he returned his gaze to the gray landscape around them. He ran through a list in his mind, a comparison between the supervolcano and Mount St. Helens.

Mom was quiet. Reid was quiet. Instead, he took in the happenings outside. Reid drove slowly through Dodge City, and then got onto the highway. There was ash everywhere. Everywhere!

It flew off cars that drove ahead of them.

An hour passed.

Mom still hadn't said anything. He tried to understand her feelings. Susie was always working on that with him. He looked at faces on cards and talked about what to do in certain situations. He didn't know what was bothering his mom. They were getting close to Finn. She should be happy! She always got quiet when she was upset. Or she swore. A lot.

"I love you," he said, as he always did. It helped cheer her up.

"Love you, too, Will," she responded.

Outside, the cornfields disappeared and were now replaced by grasslands and high plains of rolling hills. The road was long and straight. Brown and green grass covered in gray, grimy ash…rocks…long farms. It was ashy everywhere. No mountains. The Rockies were west. No cool rivers or anything. It was just a long boring stretch. It reminded him of Idaho. A few white and yellow star-shaped flowers poked their noses from the spiky green plants that looked like fans. Well, those were kind of interesting.

His throat was scratchy, and he was tired today. The thunderstorms last night had given him nightmares. His eyelids kept closing. He didn't like to nap in the car, but maybe this one time, he would rest a little because his head also hurt…

\*\*\*\*

I replayed the phone call repeatedly in my head. It became a distortion of whirring sounds and static.

No amount of obsessing could bring me to Finn sooner. Brandon was alive. But where? What about Finn?

Reid drove slowly but not by choice. Bumper-to-bumper cars blew trails of ash and dirt into the windshields of the vehicles behind them, the ash the consistency of mud. It was gray sludge, clogging the wipers and splattering everywhere. As the sun rose and we traveled away from the storms that had beset Dodge City and Wichita, the ash transformed. It was drier, dustier, and scarier. There were a few scratch marks on the windshield from the larger particles that cars kicked up from the road. At least it had stopped raining. Nothing was directly falling out of the overcast sky. I was going to count that as a plus.

Shit, it covered everything. One vast gray blur.

I crossed and uncrossed my legs. Flipped through the glove box. Nibbled on my nails. Drank water. I did everything I could to not think about Finn or the what-ifs. The ash had driven my worry to a new level. Before I'd embarked on this trip, my coping mechanism had been to work myself into a catastrophic tizzy and then relax and let reality settle in. Harrison used to sit and read a magazine, the mail, a scientific paper— anything—and say "uh-huh" and nod through my episodes. He knew I was a tornado with my emotions and that I'd also recover.

But now, now it was real.

"What did you go to college for, AJ?" Reid asked.

"Huh?" I shifted in my seat and readjusted the seatbelt. "Oh, college."

"What's your background? Did you study journalism?"

"Nope."

The traffic ahead slowed to a near stop, and Reid took that moment to survey me.

I supposed talking could distract me, at least for a little while. Surmounting worry wasn't going to help me. I took a sip of water and cleared my mind. Nausea and dizziness gnawed at my frayed edges. So much for feeling better...

"Botany?" he said.

"Close."

"You mentioned working in a lab and doing research. My guess is something else that ends in 'ology'?"

I scratched my head. "I did?"

"Yeah, the campfire game, remember? Aubert and your eyes?"

Embarrassment filled my cheeks. "Yeah." I licked my lips, remembering Reid's touches just hours before. No regret. I felt only affection when I thought of it. I pulled my gaze from him and stared ahead.

Will chimed in, "Her and Daddy both went to college to be scientists!"

"A scientist? Not botany...hmmm," he said rubbing his chin.

"They study germs!" Will interjected. "Well, not anymore. Mom's home, and Dad's gone."

Gone.

The word was a rock falling into my stomach. Maybe one day it would be more like a pebble instead of a rock.

Reid laid a hand on my knee and squeezed.

Feeling my vibe, he withdrew his hand but not without a subtle smile.

"Germs? Like viruses, micro stuff?" Reid continued.

I smiled. "Yup. Microbiology and immunology. Believe it or not, my first love, after writing, was sharks. I get seasick though. Microbes also fascinated me, and I went that route instead. Harrison and I met in grad school."

"Very interesting."

"I worked at a clinical research organization while Harrison finished his post-doctoral research. When Will was born, I switched to part-time with science writing, and when that work stopped, I had Finn, and I took the job at a magazine writing local stories. I dropped that this year. Here I am."

"And here you are, taking care of your family. You also write novels," Reid added.

"Yeah, well, that was a dream of mine since before science."

"*La autora*," he said in Spanish.

Lord, it sounded sexy when he said it that way. I found myself blushing, reminded of our night. "Maybe I'll toss a handsome Latino into one of my books."

He chuckled.

I rubbed my lips subtly.

Silence fell over us. I'd seen too much of this country for my liking. I was done.

We drove several hours without much conversation, the traffic easing here and there, and I snoozed.

When I awoke, a black and orange transportation department sign on the roadside blinked the disheartening words "No road travel beyond Lamar. Seek alternate routes."

Travel ban. We were here. I straightened in my seat.

Chapter Sixteen
Heartbreak

A few minutes later, we reached the city limits of Lamar, Colorado. The amount of ash that covered everything was dumbfounding. This wasn't ash caught in winds and rain. This was it. Ground zero. Well, ground one or two—the outer ring of ash fall.

"Oh, my God," I said.

Reid clicked the door locks as we approached a cluster of cars on the side of the road involved in an accident. People were out of their cars and yelling. Fighting. Pushing. Crying.

Reid weaved around the stranded, bewildered people.

"It's been over a week. Shouldn't they have already left the area? Isn't the Red Cross here? FEMA? National Guard? Clean up crews? Where's the help? The news said..." My wheels were turning too fast. There was no need to finish the sentence. Well, I knew where Finn got it from. Finn was me incarnate.

He shook his head. "I don't know. Maybe they're people like us, either fleeing belatedly or coming to find loved ones?"

Cars lined the shoulders and clogged traffic in both directions. Our car slowed further, nearly to a stop. I flipped through my handy atlas. We were on Route 50 and about halfway to Pueblo from Dodge City.

Theoretically, we'd be in the Colorado Springs and Denver area in a few hours. So close...

Panic seeped in, and I banished it with unspoken curses. At least Will wouldn't scold me.

"There's got to be shelters and emergency FEMA stations. We'll find some info," Reid encouraged.

He squeezed my restless tapping hand. I squeezed back. I didn't know what *this* was, but I would take it.

We made our way through downtown Lamar by way of side roads. Others had the same idea. The going was slow. If the response in Dodge City had been worrisome, then the sights in Lamar were disheartening. Everything was closed, windows covered with wooden planks. Nobody was cleaning off cars. Instead, all the cars idled in the street with impatient drivers and passengers eager to get out of town. Or into town—to travel west like us.

"There, see." Reid pointed ahead. A large stone church had been transformed into an emergency hospital. Bright orange traffic barricades lined the front lawn of a towering old cathedral-style building. Medical workers, patients, family, police, and military buzzed across the grassy lawn in and out of a patchwork of open-sided tents. Humvees, ambulances, and fire trucks lined the front like a valet service.

"They must be taking the injured to mobile hospitals in towns outside the blast zone," Reid said, echoing my unspoken thoughts.

The sight of relief of any kind fostered my dwindling hope. "I want to check here first, okay? I know it's impossible for me to check all emergency mobile stations, or know where they all are, but I must start somewhere. I have to do something."

Jean M. Grant

"Of course. What's your brother's full name?"

"Brandon Monahan. Do you think they have checklists?" I leaned forward and surveyed the mobs of people for any chance of seeing Finn or my brother. Was Finn wearing the same clothes or had he changed? It'd been well over a week. He might not have had access to his luggage.

"Yeah. It's a long shot. There's bound to be dozens of mobile hospitals."

"Let's check. We can at least gather info, right?" My hand danced on the door handle.

Reid made several circles around the block before he found a suitable parking area.

If it weren't for Will's slow pace, I would have run to the church.

"Mom, I'm okay. I'll walk with Reid."

I took his hand. "I really want you with me, honey." I wasn't going to lose him again. As we drew closer, realization hit me. Blood, wounded, and dead awaited us here. Like other natural disasters such as earthquakes and hurricanes, the injured could dribble in days after the initial impact. "Will, listen, you may see yucky things here. Just keep your eyes open for Finn and Uncle Brandon, okay? Can you help me, honey?"

Will did a thumbs-up. "Got it." Gross stuff usually didn't daunt him. He and Finn loved the gore of Halloween. That was fake. This was real. However, Will had been the kid on the sofa also unaffected by the destruction of tornadoes and weather disasters. He always took things at face value.

"What do they look like?" Reid asked.

"Huh?"

"Finn and Brandon."

I shook my head, chastising myself. God, for the briefest of moments, I'd forgotten Reid was there. I'd thought he was Harrison. I clicked through photos of Finn on my phone.

"Adorable kid. Looks like Will."

"Yeah, more than one person has said they look like twins."

"Got it. What about Brandon?"

"He looks like the male version of me, shorter hair. About your height and build. He always wears a ballcap." I scratched my head. "It's orange and blue with a ski logo."

Reid was already scanning the crowd. "Should we locate a registration or information tent?"

Again, I chewed my lip. "Do you think they have one?"

"Probably."

The place whirred with activity. Stretchers, nurses, doctors, National Guard soldiers, police officers…they all moved around like a well-oiled machine, maintaining a careful balance of activity and control. It'd been a week, and the ad hoc hospital appeared to run fluidly. At least it wasn't like an ER, with blood and chaos. Everyone had a job, and they were doing it.

"Excuse me? Where is the registration tent?" I asked a nearby attendant in scrubs.

"Over there," she said, pointing her chin toward another tent. She blew an exasperated breath as she wrapped a bandage around a young woman's arm.

"Do all people go through that tent? The injured, I mean?"

"All people coming in are registered. Name, gender, age, discerning descriptors if needed. Even for the deceased, if we have it," she said.

"My brother's not dead," Will said.

The woman stopped and passed me a painful, pitying glance.

My pulse grew fitful as we approached the registration tent. Reid took my hand and held it.

"Mom, I'm thirsty." Will coughed for effect.

"In a few, honey."

Luckily, I was first in line. "Name and age?" the woman asked.

"Finnegan. Finn Sinclair, age seven, with my brother, his uncle, Brandon Monahan, age thirty-five."

The woman, obviously a volunteer in civilian attire, flipped through the pages quickly. "Not here." Her green and white badge read *ERT, Early Response Team*. I wondered what organization she hailed from. I distinctly remembered an early response team some members of our church belonged to. Quite often they were the second ones in, after the immediate crew.

"You barely looked. Can you check again?"

She scrubbed a hand over her face with an exaggerated sigh. A line had formed behind us.

"Move along, lady!" a man grumbled.

"Please, check again." My voice hinged on a precipice. I stood my ground and admonished my blood pressure to stay in check.

She pursed her lips and looked. "Not here."

"Where are people being brought in from?" Reid asked.

"This isn't an information booth. Move along!" The man behind us growled. Reid ignored him, but I saw his clenched fist.

The woman sighed. "West, north. Cities in the

hardest hit zones."

"Any people from the bases or Denver Airport?" Reid asked.

She scrunched her brow. "Bases? You mean the army and air near the Springs? Yeah, some, the critical ones that need transport to the hospitals in Kansas and Texas. They bring them here first. Not sure about the airport, hon."

"Are there any other mobile hospitals like this nearby?" Reid pressed.

"Nothing else in Lamar, except for the hospital. They all come through here first now before being sent over, if necessary, so if they are in that hospital, check in is through here first. There's one hospital station in Nebraska, a few in New Mexico. Not sure about the western slopes or in eastern Wyoming. Look, I'm tired. I'm a volunteer. The National Guard is overwhelmed...they just got here. Mostly Red Cross and local doctors here," she said with a random gesture and another sigh, "since the first few days after the eruption. The Guard is working on recovery and transport. We're understaffed. I'm filling in for now until more soldiers arrive."

"We came all the way from Maine," Will said to the woman.

She looked at him, fine wrinkles forming around puckered lips.

"Okay, sweetheart, look." She spread a nearby map. Will leaned on it. She pointed to areas circled in different colored ink. "There's a unit north, here. Folks in that blue ring are being sent to a mobile unit in North Platte. People in this green ring are going south to Santa Fe. The red ring is us. Mostly the lower right quadrant of Colorado. That's all I know right now. If you have more questions, you'll need to ask the National Guard. There's an officer over there. He arrived this afternoon." She pointed to the convoy of Humvees and military vehicles in the church parking lot. The rest of the military and emergency vehicles idled in a line on the street, waiting to be directed to other parking areas. She added, "They've also brought the deceased here to be transported elsewhere. Most are going to Texas."

"Please look again," I begged.

She lifted a different clipboard which had the words DOA on top and scanned that much longer list. "Physical description?"

My God. I muffled a gasp.

Reid stepped in, his palm on the small of my back. "A skinny boy, blond hair, blue eyes, seven years old. A man, our age, brown hair, orange and blue ballcap with a ski logo."

I added, "The man, my brother, he has an air force tattoo on his upper right shoulder."

The woman's finger stopped toward the bottom. I craned my neck to read the upside-down writing on the dirt and water-splattered pages. Many of the dead lacked names. Scribbles of descriptions only. She paused and turned her face to mine. I noticed every wrinkle in her aged face now. She was about Patsy's age and stature: fit, with brilliant blue eyes and thinning colored sandy hair. Her scrutiny shone with maternal sadness, her lips turned down. She then waved to a man nearby. "Phil? Can you take these folks to the—" She looked at Will. "To the youth identification area?" A middle-aged man, a medic, stepped closer.

Just then, two National Guard soldiers in full

uniforms approached from the parking area. Relief filled the woman's uncomfortable countenance.

I turned to them, numb, yet flushed with humiliation. Were they all looking at me now?

"What's the holdup?" one asked, a young man, his face hard-edged with matching chiseled short hair. Not waiting on an answer, he turned to the woman at the table, "Ma'am, we're here to relieve you." He then angled toward me. "Ma'am, we need to keep this line moving."

"Ah, okay. Rob said you'd be over," the woman said, her voice weary.

I lifted myself from the fog. "Wait! Wait! My son. Is he on that other list?"

The Guard soldier gave the woman a commanding look. She shrugged vaguely. "We have one that meets that description. You'd need to ID him though."

A gurgled cry escaped my lips, and my knees buckled. I grabbed the table edge to prevent myself from collapsing.

My head spun. My chest tightened.

Reid swooped in. "Her brother? The man? Brown hair, eyes, mid-thirties, my build, baseball cap, the tattoo?" Reid asked, a hand firmly on my back to steady me. "Is he on there, too?"

The woman, whose badge read Barbara, said, "I'm not sure. That's a general description. But nobody with an air force tattoo. We have many that meet that ID. We don't have the resources to do full body checks yet, so I don't even know."

The other National Guard soldier took her clipboard. He skimmed the DOA list for what seemed like way longer than a short minute.

Prickles raced through all ten fingers, up my wrists, and joined the unrest in my chest.

Barbara bent and helped lift me upright. "I'm sorry. Maybe it's not your boy."

The Guard soldier shook his head. "No adult males with that description."

We turned to follow Phil.

Phil, the Grim Reaper. Not that he looked like death's escort. I clenched and unclenched my hands. A wave of dizziness hit me.

"No need. This man will relieve you, sir." The Guard soldier pointed to his companion. Phil offered an apologetic look. Then he was gone before I could say another word.

Barbara gripped my wrist. "Aww, dear, it's probably not your boy. You said he came with an uncle. Well, Uncle is not on either list. He should be on the survivor list if they came together."

Unless something had happened to Brandon. Maybe no body was recovered? No. Brandon was okay. He had just called me! My brain could not tell fact from fiction as languid legs drew me away from the registration tent.

I voiced the rational to Reid as we plodded through the crowd toward the church. "Brandon called me this morning. It's not Finn. It can't be Finn."

"Right. It's not him."

"Unless..."

Brandon was alive. But what about Finn? What about Finn!

Regardless, I shivered with each excruciatingly slow step to the identification area as we followed the soldier around tents. He led us inside the church.

Seconds felt like hours as we passed through the wooden pews. There were at least two dozen people in the large cathedral-ceilinged sanctuary. Many were praying. A priest glided among them, murmuring prayers and condolences. I willed him to not approach me however much I might have needed God right now.

A modest chapel had been transformed to a morgue and sat next to the larger sanctuary. The pews had been removed. This congregation wasn't eager churchgoers awaiting forgiveness for their transgressions, but rather the dead, carefully bagged and lined up in rows. I fought the urge to vomit. I couldn't take my son into a room with dead bodies.

Reid squeezed my hand harder as we stepped through a stone-carved and arched doorway. "I will look. You stay here, AJ."

"No. I need you to watch Will."

Reid gave me a pleading look but then took Will's hand. "Let's wait in the sanctuary, Will. Check out the stained glass there, the tall ceiling."

"Those people are all dead in there?"

"Yes, they are," I said.

"But Finn's okay?" He coughed, deep and raspy.

Reid squeezed my hand one more time. Then he took Will to the pews in the large, vaulted sanctuary, while the soldier led me to a row of smaller corpses. Dead children.

Bile tickled my throat. Thank God I hadn't eaten much today. Dry heaves taunted me.

It couldn't be him. What were the odds? The first mobile unit we come upon...and my Finn? I shook my head, willing it to cling to reason and odds.

The man reviewed his clipboard page and

compared it to the tags on each bag. All the bodies were larger children, except for one, which was Finn's size. He turned to me, eyes glassy, despite his calm disposition and facial expression. "Ma'am."

I nodded for him to unzip the bag.

Shit, I had done this before.

Harrison.

Except he had been under a sheet on a cold metal slab.

*Not Finn, not Finn, not Finn...*

The zipper pierced my heart. The bag crinkled in the silent, incense-infused air like nails on a chalkboard.

*Don't be Finn. Don't be Finn. Please, don't let it be my child.*

I was praying that it was another mother's child. I hugged my arms to my body, shivers erupting.

*Don't you do this to me again! Not again. I can't take anymore!* I yelled at God. Forget praying. I hollered at Him, as the sound of the zipper penetrated my soul. I screamed at my heavenly Father to let me get a pass here. *No more death. No more!*

I drew in a breath and looked.

A frail pale-skinned child lay in the bag. A bony clavicle protruded. Long eyelashes covered his eyelids, forever closed. Ear-length blond hair, streaked with dirt and ash and brushed to the side, adorned the little boy's face. I reached for the boy but stopped myself. My hand hovered for a moment above his face. A hodgepodge of auburn freckles crossed his cheeks. He had a sharp angular face, not the smooth rounded one of Finn's.

It was not Finn. Finn had no freckles. I couldn't pull my stare. I looked at the cheek near the right ear. Finn had a light brown dime-sized birthmark there. This

boy had none. He also had different-shaped ears.

"Sweet angel, rest now," was all I could say, and I silently prayed for the mother he might have left behind.

I looked at the soldier. I shook my head. "No."

When I returned, Reid's face reflected hope. I shook my head and burst into tears. "No, not him. Not him…" I shuddered violently.

"He's okay, Mom?"

I nodded. "It was another child," I mumbled, nearly choking on the words.

Will hugged me. "Look, Mom. The light is shining right through the stained glass. Streaks of red and green and blue, all over the cross."

I swiped salty tears. Jesus and other indistinguishable Biblical figures stood before us on an intricately carved altar. The beauty and glow of light pierced through their designs and splattered the altar with a rainbow of color. Incense perforated the air, performing a holy purpose, but I suspected it also served to cover any stench from the dead next door.

**\*\*\*\***

Our convoy was quiet after checking the hospital in town, too.

I pointed toward the police barricade a quarter of a mile ahead of us on Route 50 as we drove west. "Look."

Reid turned the car into an alley.

I gripped the side handle in reflex as he whipped around the bend. "What are you doing?"

He parked, got out, and pulled his hefty pack from the trunk. "Plan B."

Still spellbound from the church, I was utterly

confused as he first withdrew army fatigues from his pack and then unlaced his boots. With no hesitation, he stripped to his undershirt and boxers in the middle of the alley. He carefully placed his knife into a pocket in his backpack.

"Reid...what is Plan B?"

"Did you actually think we were going to be able to just drive in, AJ?"

Heat flushed my cheeks. I hadn't planned for this. I'd planned for everything but not this. "I don't know."

"Sorry, didn't mean to snap. But there's no way they'll let us just drive in if there are National Guard soldiers present."

He had it all, and he dressed fast: combat camouflage trousers, embroidered coat, nylon belt, and a cap. He tucked his wayward hair under the cap and put his regular boots on.

"Cool! Do you have a gun?" Will interjected. He hopped out of the car and began rummaging through Reid's backpack.

I grabbed his hand. "No, Will. Not our stuff. Boundaries, remember?"

"No, I don't have a gun," Reid said.

I wouldn't bet against a pistol being in there somewhere. Philosophical and theological books, knife, United States Army fatigues, tattoos...

I was lost. "Uh, Reid, I didn't see military at that barricade like there were at the mobile hospital. I saw only police officers. You brought that gear along this entire way?"

"Plan B," was his response as he tied his boot laces.

"Gosh, I am a moron," I said.

"No, you're not. You were thinking with your heart...you had the car, provisions...and everything you needed to get to your son. Heck, you even have bikes in case," Reid countered.

"Wait. You're telling me you travel with your retired uniform all the time? You were in New York on business. You flew to New York before the eruption."

"No, I didn't travel with all of it. I did keep my jacket and ID in my parents' old storage unit in upstate New York. Sentimental maybe," he said wryly.

There had to be more behind his reason.

"I bought the rest of it in an army thrift shop in New York after the eruption."

"You anticipated this?"

"I didn't know what to expect, honestly. I suspected it may come to this." He waved his hand cryptically. "There are also several military bases in Colorado, so I expected a decent military presence. Like I'd said, I need to get to Lily, so the idea came to me in New York."

I sighed, exasperated. "Will this get you past police officers? I highly doubt they'll let Will and me through. You saw the sign as we entered Lamar. Travel ban. They won't let us pass unless we're all military."

"We can try, right?"

"Okay, but I really don't think it will work."

He was about to get in the car when I tapped him. "Your scruff?"

"Yeah. Smart." He returned to his pack, withdrew a razor and water bottle and did the world's fastest shave. "How's this?"

I touched his chin. "Smooth as a baby's butt."

"Ewww," said Will.

"Good." Sweet dark eyes shared a look with me, and I withdrew my hand. Fatigue mangled my mind.

"We're not in uniforms," Will said. "Do they make kid-sized ones?"

"You have a special job, Will." Reid turned to him.

Will said, "Oh?"

"I have a favor to ask, and I'm sure your mom will be okay with it."

I lifted an eyebrow, but I followed his train of thought.

"I need you to hide in the back, and we'll stow your bike in there somewhere…"

"Hide?"

I didn't ask why, as the gears chinked in my brain. "Reid has a plan, honey. Can you do that for us? You can play with one of your glow sticks, and it'll be for only a few minutes."

"I don't know…there's a lot of stuff in there," Will said, his voice hesitant.

"I have the booster seats, too, Reid. Do we need to hide them?"

"Yeah. This may be the only way."

We removed the boosters and shuffled my gray storage totes to the back seat. By a great engineering feat, we got Will's bike tucked in the trunk area as well. Now the totes sat in the back seat and the kid stuff—and the kid—were hidden under blankets in the back space. I was thankful for tinted windows and a large SUV.

I cracked a few glow sticks from Will's supply and handed them to him. I was about to say "think good thoughts," but I opted against it. Instead, I handed him his water bottle. "Don't wiggle and be as quiet as a

318

mouse."

"Mice squeak."

"Okay, be as quiet as…" I combed my mind. "A wizard under an invisibility spell?" I tried, weakly. That stuff worked better on Finn.

"Good one, Mom. I got it." He wedged in, drew the blanket over his head, and was still. "Yuck, it smells like gasoline!"

Reid had moved the spare cans to the back seat. "Sorry, honey. You like hiding though."

"Yeah, but not in stinky places."

Once in the front seat, I asked, "Our bikes won't flag us?"

"Let's hope not."

I double-checked our transformed back seat. "Crap. There are stickers on Finn's window." Finn's mishmash of cartoon character stickers was plastered all over his window. Even Will had a few on his window. "It's tinted, but if they look in the car…"

Reid opened all four windows. "There. The air quality is sort of okay here in town. And it makes for easier inspection."

"It'll have to do. And me? I'm not dressed as military."

"You'll be okay. You can be civilian. Got any colored tape? Red, specifically?"

"Does masking tape work?"

"Probably not. No bother."

We joined the lengthening line of angry drivers waiting to continue on Route 50 through Lamar and westward. Each one was being turned around when they reached the barricade that was manned by two police cars. My stomach fluttered. "What *is* Plan B?

You're killing me here, Reid."

"Working on it," he said. "We're lucky there are only police here and not the National Guard. I saw active army at the mobile hospital, too. I'm sure they will be here soon. We need to get through before they arrive."

We drifted closer. Now we were the fifth car.

"What's your brother's rank?"

"Huh?"

"Rank. In the air force."

"He's retired."

"AJ...," Reid said, his voice resolute, but his patience wearing thin.

"Uh, let me think."

"Was he an enlisted airman or an officer?"

"An officer. First Lieutenant."

"Perfect," Reid said, gripping the wheel tighter as we drew closer to the front of the line. "This will work in our favor," he said to himself.

"I don't understand."

I peeked over my shoulder at the lump that was Will.

"No more of that. Look forward, okay? He's all right."

"Okay."

"The mobile hospital gave me an idea. You're a doctor, okay? I'm your escort."

I nodded. A few minutes later, we reached the front of the line. Reid immediately straightened his posture and put on a serious face, keeping his hands at the ten o'clock and two o'clock positions on the steering wheel while staring straight ahead, his attention fixed on the road.

A police officer with dark sleep-deprived smudges beneath his eyes raised his hand. He didn't look at us or at my out of state license plate as he said, "You need to turn your vehicle around, sir. Go to your home. Wait for your recovery packs to be delivered. No travel beyond this point. Mandatory travel ban."

"Corporal Reid Gregory. I've been ordered to escort Dr. Sinclair to Colorado Springs." Reid flashed his ID.

The police officer squinted with suspicion and fatigue. He gave the ID a cursory glance. "You're not in a military vehicle. Do you have written orders?"

Reid carefully clipped his ID onto his jacket pocket. "No, sir, but you can call Schriever Air Force Base and request to speak with First Lieutenant Brandon Monahan, who put in the order."

The officer pinched the top of his nose and sighed. "One moment." He trod over to his car and spoke with another officer in the driver seat. This man, whom I presumed to be the supervising officer, drew his scrutiny from a clipboard, stared at us a moment, and then spoke with the other officer with apparent irritation.

The tired officer marched over to us. "What is your purpose there? And your specialty, ma'am?"

"Medical assistance. I'm a pulmonologist," I said with confidence.

He raised an eyebrow.

"Lung specialist, Officer," I clarified.

He eyed the totes in the back seat with a few of my carefully folded blankets atop.

"You're civilian?" he asked me.

"Yes."

*Please don't ask which hospital*, I willed him. I'd have to come up with some BS hospital out of state.

Now I understood about the literal need for red tape. A Red Cross doctor. But I lacked a uniform. Damn, of all the things to need. The boys loved tape. All kinds—masking, duct, packing tape—I drew the line with colored tape.

The officer sighed. He returned to his supervisor.

The man in the car held Reid's stoic gaze for a long scrutinizing moment. He nodded and gave inaudible orders to the awaiting officer.

"Reid," I whispered. "How is your ID not expired?"

"It is. Tired police officer and carefully placed finger."

Impersonating a medical worker and an active army corporal were hefty offenses. We weren't exactly smuggling in missiles. A child and supplies were nothing to set off alarms.

The officer spun a hand and directed two other officers to move one of the barricades aside. He returned to Reid's window. "You'll need to check in at the state patrol Pueblo Troop Office, where air force and United States Army regulatory units are working with the state police force. All vehicles going north toward Colorado Springs and Denver will be inspected, prepped, and monitored, including those with military personnel."

Reid nodded. "Yes, sir."

"Are you meeting a convoy to escort you the rest of the way?"

"Yes. National Guard 89th Troop Command in Pueblo," Reid said.

"The air filters, engines, brakes…everything…is affected by the ash. Civilian vehicles won't make it much farther north than Pueblo. You'll need a properly equipped military escort." He tapped the hood, waved at the other officers, and let us through. "Good luck to you, ma'am," he said to me.

"Good Plan B," I said once we were through the barricade and on the road. "You know your stuff."

"I have a few friends in that troop. A tired officer helped," he added. "Not sure if it will get us as far as we like, especially once we draw closer to Colorado Springs, but it's good enough for now. We may need to travel afoot or by bike at some point."

"You're telling me that you had planned to sneak in with your uniform all along?"

He shrugged. "Only if it came to it. Like I'd said, if that had been Guard there, we wouldn't have made it through. Not putting down the police, but the military has different procedures. Tired or not."

I could understand the need for finding family. Lily must have meant a lot to Reid. I fought the urge to check on Will or to look at the officers in the side view mirror. "Just another minute, Will. Okay there, honey?"

"Squeak!" came his muffled voice. He giggled. I snorted. *Love that boy.*

"Got through there by the skin of our teeth, huh?" Reid said.

"You can say that. Do you know much about disaster relief?"

"Some."

"Now that we're here, fill me in, Corporal Gregory," I said as light-hearted as I could. The image of that boy's face still played before my eyes, and if I let it get to me, I would be sick.

"Usually local and state police take care of matters. To federalize the National Guard, it requires written orders from the governors of impacted states. Those orders are sent to the DOD and then to the president. The Guard is the first to be mobilized. The president has released active army to assist as well; that's the next step. The big guns are coming. This is all good. The military has the resources, capacity, and operational ability to take care of those areas in need. There's usually a strict divide between civilian forces and military, but the Guard has been called, so all bets are off. As a country, we've never experienced a disaster of this magnitude."

"I see. What's the deal with Schriever Air Force Base? You think they could be there?"

"Maybe. I was thinking about it. Your brother's retired air force, and that's the closest base around that he may be familiar with. Bases will take on refugees if something happened."

"Like if his plane was downed?"

"Yeah, or diverted. Or if it didn't take off. It's only a couple hours' drive or quick flight from Denver. Your brother could know about that base. If he is as resourceful as you," he said with an admiring smile.

I nodded. "He is."

He added, "There are the other bases—Peterson has tight security though. Cheyenne is also an option. And any other mobile hospitals."

I nodded, digesting all this knowledge. "Still many options."

"Yeah. We'll do our best, AJ. We need to check, cross it off, and move on to the next place. The bases have strong infrastructures, medical facilities. It's quite possible he's at a base. Or a hospital. Or another place secure enough to house the injured…a stadium, large churches…"

"Can Will come out now?" I asked with another look in the side view mirror.

"Yeah. Come on out, buddy," Reid said. Will popped up from his hiding place. "We'll stop in a few minutes to get your booster back in. Hang tight, little guy."

"Mom, you guys lied to that police officer. Are you gonna go to jail?"

I cringed as I tried dialing Brandon again. Nothing.

"We didn't lie. We are heading to that base," Reid said.

"Mom's not a doctor."

"She's a scientist though. Some scientists are called doctor."

"But Mom isn't. Dad was a doctor scientist," Will said.

"No, you're right. We had to stretch the truth a little," Reid admitted.

I added, "Sometimes you need to do that. It doesn't hurt anyone, so it's okay."

"Are you a soldier? You protect our country from bad guys and stuff, like Uncle Brandon?" Will wiggled around, playing with his glow sticks like wands. In Will fashion, he had already moved on from the subject. Finn would have hounded me on the lying thing. Asking why, why, why. Then filing that information away for another time.

"Yes, I am, or I was," Reid said. "I'm retired."

"Will, sit still, honey, until we're safe enough to

get you in your seat."

He did but smashed the glow sticks together and hummed.

I shared a look with Reid. One hurdle down. On to the next one.

Chapter Seventeen
Survival of the Fittest

I turned on the radio to find channels of static. No news. As we made the arduous drive along a desolate Route 50 to Pueblo and central Colorado, I found my mind on Finn again. The relief of getting through the first hurdle at Lamar had worn off. I tapped a finger on my teeth and stared.

I silently apologized for cursing God. Perhaps I still needed those damn white pills.

The air conditioning whirred, unlike its usual robust hum. I looked in the side-view mirror. The ash was deeper here, and our tires stirred a trail behind us like a storm cloud. Crosswinds blew the ash across the surrounding hilly grasslands and onto our path. Drifts piled and curled around the occasional boulders, ramshackle buildings, homes, and signs along the road. Prairies comprised our landscape, but sagebrush and a few yucca plants dotted the edges. If there had been any flora like coneflowers or asters, they were gone, torn to bits by the power of the wind.

The car shook with each wind burst.

Reid focused on the road, white-knuckled and, well, bruise-knuckled. Shadows of dusk snaked along the highway. I yawned, stretched, and clasped my hands together. "We check Pueblo first, and then head north for Schriever?" I asked like an impatient child on

Jean M. Grant

a road trip.

"It depends on the roads. I don't know, AJ, but that's my plan."

Will was quiet. We had quickly switched his booster seat and a tote. In fact, I looked back to find him snoozing with his helmet on. How was that comfortable? He never napped in the car. His breathing was heavier and hoarser than normal, and it drew my concern. I wanted to pull over and check him, but with the way the ash settled here, stopping could potentially strand us.

Another wary look at the fuel indicator—yeah, we had enough.

As if he sensed my look upon him, Will sneezed, rubbed his nose, and briefly opened his eyes. He cracked a smile and said, "Love you, Mom." Then he returned to his catnap with wheezy snores.

"Love you, honey."

The wind released its scratchy claws upon the car in short-tempered bursts. With the impending night, I was grateful that Will was sleeping. I didn't need my anxiety to rub off on him more than it already had. Fewer and fewer tire tracks paved the way for us. Reid was careful, deliberately driving within the two thin lines of our predecessors. Those lines were quickly disappearing.

Neither of us needed to verbalize that fear. Reid had stopped asking if I was okay.

Each time a vehicle, usually a military Humvee, passed us traveling in the opposite direction, I counted my blessings. They had bigger things to contend with. Reid didn't show an ounce of trepidation, except for his board-straight posture and tightened hand grip on the steering wheel. He stared forward, resolute in his task—his mission? I could only assume that the military passerby saw his uniform and didn't care or dusk's shadows helped. Luck remained with us as each vehicle continued on its way.

"Hey, Reid?" I whispered.

"Yeah?"

"Last night in the hotel..." Much had transpired since last night. I was quick to add, "Were you having a nightmare?" I didn't mention the *other* thing, though it was still vivid in my memory.

He cracked his wrists and tightened his knuckle-grip on the wheel. "Yeah..."

"Do you remember...you said some things..." I fought all the sensations that begged my lips to be touched. His taste had long since left them. I shivered thinking of his hands upon me. *No regrets.*

"I didn't mean to wake you. I sometimes get them when I'm stressed." He cleared his throat. "And us...I shouldn't have—"

A spindly stray branch scraped the windshield.

"Wha—?" My heartbeat quickened momentarily.

"It's getting gusty."

The moment was lost. "I'm not sorry," I said anyway. "No regrets."

He gave me a look that made my insides quiver again. "Me neither."

When he spoke again a few minutes later, I almost jumped. "In the woods, when we were looking for Will, I didn't mean to imply you had PTSD. It's not my place to diagnose. I didn't know about your husband..."

"No, it's really okay. I get where you are coming from. Maybe I did, or do, have a form of it."

"Maybe."

Soon, we saw no vehicles. An hour passed. Nobody. Sleep lured me, and the sun, or what resembled it behind all the gloom, dipped lower in a brown-gray sky. I allowed sleep to take me. I needed it, even if just a few minutes.

**\*\*\*\***

Sudden movement jolted me awake.

"Shit," I said, startled from a dream…where Reid had been kissing me.

Reid fought against the car, which was fish-tailing and wheezing like it, too, had inhaled too much ash. I whacked my shoulder against the window. The engine rumbled and struggled.

I clung to the handhold on my door. "What's happening?"

Reid shut off the sputtering air conditioning. The lights on the dashboard blinked off, then on. "Dammit," he growled.

The tailpipe roared as he worked the accelerator. "Dammit," he repeated. Slowing, the car rolled into a grooved area beside the shoulder. The dashboard lights flickered a few times, all the freak-out lights coming on. The car shuddered and then came to a halting stop, rasping its last breath as it succumbed to its ashy battle.

Reid tried the ignition and pumped the pedal. Nothing.

Again. Nothing.

He stopped and took the keys out. "Don't want to flood the engine."

"Glad I had my helmet on!" Will, now awake, said from the back seat.

I rubbed my aching shoulder. Ash obscured the

road signs. "Where are we, anyway?" My gut twisted. I thought we'd make it farther before this would happen. Or maybe I'd been hopefully optimistic that it wouldn't happen at all.

"Just east of Pueblo."

"How much east?"

"I think a few miles based on the last signpost we passed."

High undulating hills of plains surrounded us. I already disliked Colorado. Add that to Missouri on the never-to-visit-again list. And New York.

"I pushed the car too much."

"No, you didn't." I flipped to the Colorado page in the atlas. "We're not near Colorado Springs yet."

"We've got a few options."

I closed the atlas and looked around the dark car. I exhaled and listed them for him. "Wait for help. Call somebody...," I began, pulling my phone out of the cup holder. One bar. I dropped it in the holder.

Reid stated the third option. "Or we bike into Pueblo and get a ride from there."

I swallowed. "If we can get somebody to give us a ride."

Reid shrugged. "We can try. At least first check Pueblo, right? Then work our way up to the Springs and Denver."

"Yeah." We'd be stuck here if we waited.

"Want me to check under the hood? See what's going on?"

"Yeah. Maybe you can fix it?"

"I can try but don't want to get your hopes up. We might be able to get the replacement parts in Pueblo. However, it may need a tow," Reid added.

Jean M. Grant

"Okay."

My phone pinged at nothing short of a fateful moment. I jumped. Reid stopped in his opening of the door. I grabbed the phone from the cup holder. It only read one bar of reception, but I saw that it showed "caller unknown," and I hit talk. "Hello?" I said, sharing a look with Reid.

"AJ. It's me."

"Brandon!"

"I'm in...Springs..." His voice faded and was drowned by a buzzing crackle, but I recognized that voice anywhere.

"Brandon! I can't hear you! Colorado Springs?"

His mangled voice returned. "At...the base..."

Crackling.

"Finn...he..."

More damn crackles.

"Brandon, repeat that."

"AJ..."

"Is Finn okay? Brandon?"

Silence.

"I'm coming, Brandon! I'm coming! I'm on my way. Stay there!"

Muffled words.

Click.

Shit. Had he heard me? Did he know I was coming?

I turned to Reid. "It was Brandon! He's in Colorado Springs. At a base, I think."

"Which?"

"I don't know. He said something about a base and springs, but it was hard to understand."

"Finn?"

"I don't know. It was garbled."

Reid clasped my hand. "He's okay. He's going to be okay. Let's check Schriever first. That's my bet."

I tucked the phone in my pocket, determined, trying to convince myself. "Okay. Yes. He's going to be okay."

"I'll check the engine, then we can decide what to do, okay?"

"Okay. Please be quick."

\*\*\*\*

"Put on your jacket, Will."

I put mine on, too, and pulled out a baseball cap. I grabbed my sunglasses, even though a thick gray haze obscured the sunset.

Reid buttoned his jacket. He put on sunglasses. I handed him a surgical mask.

I put on a mask as well and handed one to Will.

"Can't we fix the car?" Will asked again.

"We can't. Not with what we have here. We need to take the bikes, Will," I said.

"I don't understand." His fingers danced on his legs, and he looked outside.

"It's the only way, honey. Here, put this mask on. You need to wear your goggles. There," I said, pointing to the goggles in the seat beside him.

He protested.

"Will!"

He began to sob, dimples appearing on his pink cheeks.

"I'm sorry, honey. But we must. You understand?"

He nodded. "Yeah." He finally put them all on.

We each had a backpack. Reid tucked Will's in his own oversized pack. We had the essentials: water, food, equipment, clothes, the last of my money, walkie-talkies, flashlights, and headlamp. Not essential, but unwilling to leave it behind, I tossed my journal in mine as well.

"Wait! We need the compass." Will dug through his messy back seat, grabbed it, and plopped it in Reid's pack. "What about my books?"

I shook my head. "Too heavy. We'll be back for them. I promise."

"Just two small ones?"

"Okay," I relented as he grabbed the Alaska adventure book and his wizard-cat book. Reid didn't object to the added weight.

Reid and I both pocketed a set of keys. The wind whipped around us as we emerged from the suffocating cocoon of the car. Sulfur burned my nostrils even with the mask. Reid lowered the bikes off the rack, and I instantly missed the smell of leather and crayons and stale air conditioning. My refuge, guiding compass, conveyance, and home for the past ten days—eleven?—had been the confines of a vehicle the size of a bathroom. I wanted to crawl in there, smashed crackers and all. I set my bike aside and then held Will's upright for him.

"You've got this, Will. Volcanologist adventure, right? Here." I double-checked his goggles, mask, and helmet. "See? All ready."

"I want to drive there." He fidgeted with the mask straps.

I gave his arm a tender squeeze. "We can do this, Will. I know you can."

"Show time, buddy," Reid assured. He glanced at me, his voice muffled behind the mask. "We'll bike into Pueblo. It's only a few miles from here. Then, we'll find a hospital or mobile unit and go from there."

"Okay," I said, doubtful. If the ash had besieged my car, what would it do when we tried to bike through it?

****

Will didn't mind the helmet, but he wanted to take off the goggles. They dug into his head, and that stupid face mask pinched behind his ears. Ash blew all around them, and he had to focus on his pedaling. His training wheels kept getting stuck in the ash and dry dirt on the road, and Mom or Reid gave him nudges. He focused harder. He wished he could ride a bike without the trainers, the way Finn was learning now. Finn rode laps around him. He wasn't as good at that kind of stuff as Finn.

The ash was cool. It was also scary. He was glad it wasn't dark yet. As the sunlight dwindled, it looked like another planet. Like Mars, but Mars had dry red dirt. Not gray. He couldn't see the sun anymore; there was a hazy yellow glow to their west, sinking to the horizon.

He got stuck again. The goggles dug. The mask pinched. He hopped off his bike and removed the helmet, goggles, and mask, tossing them to the ground. "I can't do it!"

His heart thumped. More buzzing. He coughed and cried. The ash scratched his hands and his face.

"Oh, Will!" Mom picked up his helmet. "Please, sweetie. You'll get hurt. Please wear it."

He cried into her chest, and she wrapped her arms around him to protect him from the biting, smothering ash wind.

"You two should return and wait at the car. I could

go ahead and get help," Reid said.

"No. That will take longer. What if they relocate? What if you can't make it back?" Her voice competed with the growling wind, and it rumbled into Will's face as he cried into her chest. "Our phones won't work, and who knows if the walkie-talkies will."

"Mom, I want to help find Finn. I do," he said.

"I'm sorry, Will. I'm sorry. Do you want to go back with me?" Dirty gray tears ran down her cheeks like a little trickle between her oversized sunglasses and facemask. "I shouldn't have asked you to do this."

He grabbed his goggles and put them on. "I'm your brave wizard." He coughed. It hurt his chest. Mom gave him a sip of her water. It tasted like dirt.

She clicked on his helmet and wiped off his face mask, assisting him with putting that tight fuzzy annoying thing back on.

"Reid, I think we need to walk," Mom said. "His training wheels keep getting stuck and even our bikes are struggling. It can't be any slower than riding. We can leave the bikes here and come back for them."

"Can you manage, buddy?" Reid asked. "Just a few miles left."

Will nodded. He would try his best. "A few? Do you think one, or two, or more?"

"I'm not sure, buddy."

"We hiked for three miles at Yellowstone, on the geyser trail," Mom reminded him.

"But there was no ash," he said. His head ached again. He rubbed it.

They walked for ages. Mom held his hand the entire time. Reid assured him it was close. With the wind pelting him, it felt like *forever*. Mom and Susie and his teacher always told him to focus, that he could get through it. He hummed to himself to drown the buzzing. He pretended the scratchy particles of ash were asteroids, and he had to dart and weave to avoid them. He focused like he had the magic within him even though wizards were only pretend.

Finally, they came upon what appeared to be another roadblock or checkpoint. This time, there were two military vehicles and people in camouflage uniforms. They had guns and wore face masks a lot different than their own. The masks covered their eyes, nose, and mouth. He counted four of them outside of the two vehicles.

Will was happy to be done walking. His knees shook. Reid approached one of the guards, his hands up. He began talking with a guard. Mom stood next to Will and put her arm around his shoulder. He coughed and wheezed. "Mom, my throat really hurts. My—"

Then...

\*\*\*\*

Will was on the ground and his helmet was off. Did he fall? Who took off his helmet?

Mom was above him, swimming against the grainy sky. There were other people around.

Her mask and sunglasses were off. The sky was darker.

Her lips moved, but he didn't hear any words. He reached for her, but his arm didn't budge. Up, up! He commanded it. He looked at it and told his fingers to move. They didn't. Slowly, his other hand rose to touch the skin on her cheek. His chest tightened as his heart pounded in his ears.

He said, "Mom," but heard nothing.

Jean M. Grant

Something had happened for him to be on the ground, but it was like he was missing a span of time. Had he time-traveled? No. That wasn't real.

Blinking, fear welled within him. What happened? He wasn't sleeping, but he felt weary like he had just run laps in gym class. He was awake.

Black spots danced in his vision as dizziness erupted in his head. He thought he would go black again, but he didn't. He felt that he might puke.

Her lips continued to move. She was crying. No sound at all, like he was out in the universe, because there was no sound there.

It reminded him of the one time in swim class where he jumped in and went all the way under the water by accident. He never swam beneath the water. Ever. But that one time, with that mean swim instructor who lied when he said he'd catch him, he went under the water.

All the way under…

He remembered.

He sank like a rock to the bottom. It was only four feet deep. He swallowed the gross chlorine water. It burned his nostrils and filled his throat. He thrashed, but his arms moved slowly in the tepid water. He kicked hard on the bottom and surfaced, warm red blood oozing from his nose. Mom ran to him and spoke with her comforting words, wrapping his oversized towel around him.

He never returned to that class.

Then Mom put him in a different class, with two boys. One flapped his arms a lot and bit his fingertips, and the other one always said "No" or "Go home, go home" and ran away from his dad and sometimes

338

screeched.

They didn't go to that class anymore either.

He blinked and focused on Mom. The edges of his vision were dark, like black oil was dumped in his eyes. Mom, Mom, Mom! His brain cried. Tears burned, and his vision grew murky with the black oil.

She touched his face, her palm warm on his cheek. He cried and shook as the dark oil left his vision and it became fuzzy, like when he first woke up in the morning. Slowly, the world with all its buzzing returned to him. He wheezed, "I want Dad."

Mom said, "I'm here. You're okay. We're going to take you to a hospital. Honey, you had a seizure. It will be okay."

Sei-what? Like fissures? The kind of vents that came out of volcanoes?

He felt his head. No, there weren't holes in it, no lava spitting out. A seizure must not be like a fissure.

Then he saw Reid. Strong arms lifted him, cradling him like a baby. He didn't dislike that; tight hugs were a great way to block the ceaseless lights and droning of the world. He heard the doors of a heavy vehicle open and close, people step in, deep voices murmuring, Mom's lovey voice. The ride was bumpy and slow.

Mom offered him his water bottle, and he shook his head. He could still taste the chlorine from the pool memory.

"Wha...my...wha..." The words babbled. His mouth was not working.

She stroked his cheek. "Hush, Will, honey. It's okay. We're going to a hospital now. You'll be all right."

His head roared. Why did it hurt so much? He'd

been wearing his helmet.

Mom was good at making him feel better. She was smart and gave him the best hugs. He felt the pain in her voice. Tear droplets bubbled in her eyes.

"I'm okay, Mom. I'm okayyyy…," he said.

"Rest, Will. Mom's here. Rest. We'll be there soon."

Chapter Eighteen
Atonement

"It was a tonic-clonic seizure, Mrs. Sinclair," the doctor said after we stepped through the door to Will's hospital room and into the hallway.

I stared at her blankly.

"Nomenclature has changed. They used to be called grand mal seizures. Up to thirty percent of children with autism also have epilepsy," she continued. She rattled off statistics, but I tuned them out as I stared into the room at my son. Will lay, exhausted, in the hospital bed with an IV line and monitors hooked to his skinny body. His chest rose and fell, shrouded by a gown too large for him, as he wheezed and slept.

"He's stable, Mrs. Sinclair, but we need to keep him here for a few days to monitor him, especially because of his asthma, and well, if he inhaled any of the ash…" She drifted off.

A long, bustling, pristine corridor in the children's wing of the hospital surrounded us. Nurses, doctors, orderlies, and various staff shuffled in and out of rooms and worked behind the central desk on computers next to stacks of folders and paperwork. The occasional Guard soldier strode past, the camouflage uniform, helmet, and holstered weapon a stark contrast to the clean, fluidly operational hospital with its white walls and colorful signs.

One such soldier brushed past me. "Excuse me, ma'am," she said.

Will had had a seizure.

After I encouraged him to ride his bike then walk through the ash.

After I dragged him across the country.

The doctor pushed her round, black-rimmed glasses up her nose and tucked her clipboard beneath her arm. "Have you noticed any peculiar staring spells?"

"Huh?"

Reid materialized beside me and cupped a hand on my elbow. "AJ," he coaxed.

I blinked. How long had he been standing there? I looked behind me at Will's hospital room. No light broke through the slats between the blinds. Night was upon us.

I returned my focus to the doctor. Through grainy eyes, I read the name badge on the pocket of her white coat. *Dr. Isabel Hwang.* "Well, yeah, he has autism," I snapped. "He daydreams, stares off." I folded my arms across my stomach and cradled myself. The tingles began in my fingers. I remembered his staring spell on the highway near Greer Spring, when we had been stuck in traffic. "Seizure. He had a seizure," I stuttered.

"Yes, he did. Any prolonged staring that you couldn't shake him from?"

I clenched my hands tighter. "No."

"Facial twitches?"

"No."

"Muscles jerking, unexplained confusion, or headaches?"

I suppressed the groan. She was only doing her job.

"No. If he had a headache, he'd tell me." Jesus, would he?

"Sleep disturbances?"

Bingo.

"He has night terrors." Dread settled within me as I averted her gaze. The thought of epilepsy had entered my mind on many occasions. Of course, in those early months I'd read everything I could about autism...its link to gastrointestinal issues, epilepsy, incidence between siblings, nutrition, vaccines (that was total BS), environmental factors, genetic factors...the list never stopped. There was always something to read.

I'd stopped reading.

"Tell me about the night terrors."

I recounted the details. Had I denied it all along? I hugged myself tighter, as shaking erupted from my knotted stomach, quivering out to my extremities like a full-fledged tremor. "He's had them for years, since he was like two or three years old. They're usually triggered by sleep-deprivation, stress. They come in clusters, and then we have long stretches of none. His eyes are open when it happens. He moans, cries..." My explanations broke off. *Keep it together, AJ.* "He never remembers them. And yeah, yeah, sometimes he stares off into space. And lately he is more anxious about falling asleep."

Reid's hand squeezed my elbow. I blew a deep breath and elaborated upon his symptoms.

When I was done, the doctor said, "Well, those are definitely night terrors. They could be seizures, but I wouldn't know unless I monitor him. There is a checklist here. I need you to read through it all. Some symptoms are usual autism behaviors, but some could be a cause for concern. You've been traveling. The drive, sleep disturbances, illness, allergies, diet, stress, dehydration…those things can affect seizure control. I've called in for our neurologist. We'll run an EEG, but we need to catch an event. Some of the neurological abnormalities with autism may contribute to seizures. Chemical imbalances in molecules that send signals…"

Her voice faded as her mouth moved. She was speaking, but my brain wasn't listening. I noticed all the fine hairs at her hairline, the old acne scars across her nose, the fatigue in her dark eyes…Her lips moved in slow motion.

I blinked and snapped from my daze. "I understand," was all I could say.

Her thin, black eyebrows shot up with relief, and she nodded.

"We watch and wait," Reid interjected, taking the clipboard and questionnaire from her.

"Yes," she said. "This could be an isolated event. I'd like to run a few tests if possible, Mrs. Sinclair, but our hospital's overwhelmed with people injured from the eruption. They're still being brought in from other areas. We can't do all the tests immediately. I can monitor him. He needs to rest. More travel right now could trigger another seizure. We will monitor his night vitals particularly right now. You're fortunate your son has a bed, given all the—" She cut herself off. She rubbed under the bridge of her thin glasses. Weariness creased the pale skin of her forehead.

"We wait," I repeated Reid's words. "For how long?"

"Mrs. Sinclair, he needs rest. I can't say how long. A few days. If he's clear, then you're free to go, but I urge you strongly to follow up with a neurologist when you get home. You're welcome to stay in his room. There's a chair that reclines."

"Dr. Hwang." A man in scrubs approached the doctor. "We need you in Room 203."

The doctor gave me an undecided look. "How is your breathing, Mrs. Sinclair?"

"I'm okay. Thank you."

"The neurologist should be here shortly." She adjusted her glasses again and hurried off.

Finn.

A few days. Brandon's words replayed in my mind. I didn't even know if Finn was okay.

I turned to Reid. "Reid, I—"

"I'll inquire about a ride to Schriever and check with local mechanics for car parts," he said, reading my mind. "I'll check at the desk downstairs to see if they have any other info."

"Thank you." I squeezed his hand for a long moment.

I returned to Will's room with the clipboard and sat beside him on the bed. His chest moved in that deep sleep rhythm a mother loves to watch. He lightly snored. I brushed sweaty hair from his forehead and felt a warm, rosy cheek.

I pulled out my phone. Zero bars. No messages. I pulled my charger from the backpack and plugged it in with the phone.

The choices rippled through my brain while I attempted to answer all the questions on the form.

Should I leave Will here to get Finn? This hospital was sound, safe. The nurse had informed me that back-up generators weren't in use yet. This was a solid hospital, and patients from regional health centers and smaller facilities were being brought here. Aftershocks were done, or I'd hoped. The Guard had the hospital under control and monitored entrance and flow. I had yet to see Pueblo in daylight though. It had looked horrific by night.

Will would be okay. He would be okay.

I groaned. What if he had another seizure, and I wasn't here for him? How the hell was I to sleep tonight? How was I to leave him? I couldn't leave him alone in this hospital. I couldn't.

How could I not?

Brandon's call had me rattled. Was Finn even with him?

Maybe he wasn't? What if he was hurt? What if Brandon had been trying to tell me that my son was dead? Based on what I saw in Pueblo on our drive in, I could only imagine the cities north. Harrison's voice poked into my mind's racings. *He's at a base with your brother, AJ.*

What if I sent Reid to get him?

Reid, my army-savior-I-wanted-to-kiss-again friend.

The maybe more than a friend, given our night together.

The guy who beat the shit out of people when he got pissed.

The philosophical heart struggling with PTSD.

I knotted my fingers together and found myself praying.

Will. Finn.

*Don't be irrational and emotional, AJ*, I chided myself. This wasn't some twisted moral choice. Both boys would be okay. There was no lesser of two evils choice with this. I regarded the obvious facts: I didn't know if Finn was alive, and Will could likely have another seizure.

The lights in the hallway flickered twice.

Will's snoring stopped.

"Mom?" his dry voice rasped.

I smiled. "Hi, honey."

"Where am I?"

I rested a hand on his chest, his bony frame thinner than usual beneath my fingers. The wheezes in his chest vibrated into my hand.

"We're in a hospital. You, you—" I couldn't say it.

"My head hurts. My body, it went all funny, Mom. I felt like I was under water."

"You—" I stopped to regain control. I rubbed his cheek, and then squeezed his hand. I said firmly, "You had a seizure. It's like your brain had to shut down for a second and reboot, restart. Like when you turn off a computer."

"Did I do something wrong?"

"No," I said with a fragile voice. "It happens to some people."

"Is it because of my brain thing? That you told me about. The autism?"

He struggled to sit.

"No, honey. This is different. It happens to some people with or without autism," I repeated.

"Is it going to happen again?"

"It could, but you're in the hospital." I threaded my larger fingers with his smaller ones. "They'll keep an eye on you, and if it does happen, you can take medicines and they'll take care of you. You'll be okay."

"How long do we have to stay here?" He coughed.

I got the water from the bedside table and handed it to him. "A few days."

His face crumpled. "But Finn."

"We'll take care of that. Don't worry." I turned and dug through his backpack beside me. "Here, I have Douglas. Dougie's first time to a hospital."

He took him and nestled the plush, golden dog on his pillow. He then laid his head down and blinked a few times. He coughed, hoarse, lungs rattling.

A hospital worker—doctor or nurse, I didn't know, my mind a whirl of people in blue scrubs and white overcoats—entered the room pushing a cart. "We need to do a nebulizer treatment now that you're awake, hon." She passed a glance to me. "These are in high demand right now."

I sat on the chair while she situated the mask on his face. I was not unfamiliar with this treatment, as we'd used it once or twice after a cold and once after pneumonia. Now, it served as treatment for those suffering from the aftermath of inhaling shards of rocks and earth innards...sharp, piercing daggers tumbling down their throat and into their lungs.

The woman looked at me for a moment. Her lips crinkled into a tiny smile. "I'm a respiratory therapist. He's in excellent hands, ma'am. He probably won't need an x-ray. His symptoms appear minor. We'll monitor him and see how this goes, then determine if he needs an x-ray."

"We wore masks," was all I could muster. What about before that? The poisonous gases? Did the masks do anything for those? Seizures and respiratory problems. My mind jumped to the long-term effects of

348

both, fears circling.

This was all my fault.

She nodded, her gray hair bouncing in her loose bun on her nape. "Good, good."

I was thankful she didn't divulge the nitty gritty— ha, no pun intended, I thought, nearly snorting—on ash and the particulates. My geologist lying in the bed was already an expert on all that, and as a result, so was I.

He fidgeted with the mask on his face. She readjusted it.

"We'll do it for about ten minutes, William. Breathe normally, but every four or five breaths, take a deeper breath. Can you do that?"

"Mom calls me Will."

"Okay, Will."

He nodded. "Four *or* five? Which one is better?"

"You choose," she said, cheerful kindness infused in her tone. She shoved a loose strand of hair behind her ear and pushed her glasses up on her head as she leaned in to read the monitor. I wondered how long she'd been awake. Everyone here appeared haggard.

"Okay. I will do five."

"I'll be back in ten minutes," she said. She squeezed Will's hand, then mine with a reassuring look.

I swallowed the dryness in my throat. I then coughed. Perhaps I'd need that nebulizer next.

I pasted on an encouraging smile as Will breathed normally and every fifth inhalation took a deeper breath as the fine mist treatment entered his lungs. I pulled out the two books from his backpack, holding each out until he gave me a thumbs-up. Wizard cats it was.

I read to him for a few minutes as he breathed in, then deeper, the whooshing motor of the pump and vaporized air flow the only sounds other than my voice.

The therapist returned after fifteen minutes. The clock was behind Will's head, saving me from his keen observation that it had been more than ten minutes.

"Rest, honey," I said after she removed the equipment and left the room.

"Sing the states song?" he requested through a yawn.

I sang it and rubbed his cheek.

His eyelids fluttered.

I hummed and then let silence settle upon us as he yielded to sleep.

I yawned, too. I could escape for a few minutes. He'd be okay for a few minutes. I needed to get fresh air. Not something I could do in a hospital or in the current atmosphere that was Colorado. Coffee would have to do. If their cafeteria was even up and running.

I left the room and glanced both ways.

"Looking for Reid?" one nurse said from the desk.

I spaced out momentarily. My wayward companion. How could I have forgotten about him? He was indeed like a ghost...He'd gone to check on a ride, my brain reminded me. "Yeah." I handed her the clipboard with the questionnaire.

"He went to speak with the officer at the main desk, first floor. Coffee is in the cafeteria. You look like you need it. I should warn you they're swamped, and we haven't been able to get food deliveries in a few days. You'll be lucky if you can get a cup. They have to save most for patients."

"Thanks." I halted in my step and licked my lips. When I had checked in, I had only given my name. Had Reid told her his name? That sexy smile was an asset, but...Reid's jacket only said GREGORY on it; he had pocketed his ID. I scratched my head, dog-tired.

Still, something didn't sit well with me. My fingertips prickled, and I shoved them into my pockets. I asked boldly, "You know Reid?" This was his hometown area after all, I told myself. Of course, he might know people, even if he lived in Colorado Springs now. Yet...I fidgeted with the key in my pocket, sensing my radar blip.

"Of course. He used to come to the hospital all the time after the accident. Everyone knows Reid."

My mouth dropped open. I snapped it shut. I wasn't expecting that answer. Hell, my first thought had been maybe she had dated him.

That nagging familiar uneasiness shook me. Despite my lack of sleep, my neurons were firing fast. I removed my hands from my pockets and resumed my cradling, hugging myself tightly. "Why? What accident?"

I glanced down the corridor, half expecting the subject of our conversation to be ambling toward us at any moment.

The nurse barely looked at me and continued with her work. I shifted on my feet. When I hadn't moved yet, she tapped her pen and gave me a penetrating glare of impatience. "Is there something else?"

My pulse grew fitful. "I'm sorry, I don't mean to pry." Okay, yeah, I did. "This is the pediatric wing. Not sure how..."

Nurse Gail Chapman, per her badge, heaved a sigh, and her tone softened. "Everyone knows Mr. Gregory here, Mrs....?"

"Sinclair." Caffeine-deprivation caused me to grit

my teeth. She remembered him but not me?

With a yawn, she weaved a pencil through her hair to pull the long auburn locks into a low bun. "Small towns know all the dirty secrets."

Huh? I blinked. "This is the *pediatric* wing." My jaw hurt, and I forced a polite smile. My look must have reflected my contempt.

"Of a small hospital," Gail added, with uplifted eyebrows.

Did she want me to read her mind? *Lady, I am tired.*

She passed a glance to the coworker—supervisor?—behind her and then leaned closer to me, lowering her voice and finally divulging, "I know Reid from high school, too, right before it all happened," she clarified. "Anyway, they brought his sister over from McMillian Oaks a few days ago."

It? I was certain blankness fell across my face. So much for my neurons firing. "The accident?" I fed her a line, hoping I had heard correctly.

"It's a long-term care facility. They had to transport many of their patients here after their generator lost its juice. He's probably checking on her, too."

I swallowed. Dread loomed in my throat. "What? Why?" I said, tripping on my own words.

The nurse compressed her lips and gave me a look of pity.

Screw pity. I had seen enough of that to last a lifetime.

The supervisor from behind cleared her throat and approached. "Gail," she said sternly.

She wrinkled her brow and shrugged, then returned

to her work.

I mumbled a thank-you. My head spun as I reached the elevator. Reid's sister was here? I mentally thumbed through all our conversations like they were filed neatly in a cabinet. All the times we talked about his sister, albeit it was minimal, he'd always spoken of her in a way that implied she was okay and he was going to check on her, like any loyal sibling would do, especially since she was all the family he had. She was a teacher.

She was here. In a hospital. Moved from a long-term care facility? Why? Had she sustained an injury—a broken leg that needed physical therapy? Chronic pain associated with a disease? Cancer treatment? Autoimmune disease? The nurse said "accident," though.

I passed the coffee vending machine, despite the allure of the brown frothy cup of java on the display. I made for the elevator and pushed the first-floor button. With each ding of a passing floor, my fingers tingled, and my heart thumped louder in my ears. There had to be an explanation.

The elevator chimed, and the doors slid open. As they did, I almost hit the close button to hide inside.

I emerged into a swarm of people in the hospital lobby. I had blocked them out when we arrived a few hours before. Now, they awoke me like an electric zap. Much like the mobile unit in Lamar, mobs of families, uniformed Guard and army soldiers, and hospital employees moved around in a synchronized dance. For a moment, it reminded me of what Will used to say he felt like—a buzzing beehive.

With heavy steps, I treaded to the information

desk, which was also overrun with people making inquiries. The Guard soldiers, one man and one woman, who looked as frazzled as I felt, were fielding questions and concerns. Reid wasn't there in the long line. After another glance around the overrun lobby, and to no avail, I returned to the elevator, my dread not abated. I reached the pediatric floor, ignored the enticing coffee vending machine again, and was back at Gail's desk.

"Look, I know you can't give information on patients, but I need to find my friend." There, I'd said it. Was he my friend? Was he more than a companion on this long hellish journey? Well, I'd slept with him! I sighed. "Reid. His sister. I don't need to know her room. Just the floor."

"I'm sorry I can't," Gail said. However, as her superior shifted and turned the other way, she held up three fingers.

I nodded.

Back to the elevator I went, after a quick check on Will. Fast asleep. Despite all the walking, which was a lovely release on my deprived muscles from days of driving, I couldn't quiet my unease. My knees knocked.

I pushed the button, and the ceiling lights flickered again. Stairs, it was.

The third floor also hummed with activity. Extra stretchers and patients and bottlenecks of people lined the hallways, making it easier for me to slip past the primary reception and nurse station to begin poking in rooms. Most of the doors were open, and disregarding my guilt about being nosy, I went room by room. I turned a corner, down another corridor, checked all the rooms. No Reid. I made it to the end of the wing, indicated by closed automatic doors and a sign that displayed directions to other wings and wards. I turned around to give the rooms another glance.

"This is ridiculous," I mumbled.

I continued my search nonetheless.

There he was, approaching as I'd envisioned him on the other floor, toting two coffees. One for his sister? His face lit up when he saw me.

"Reid."

"AJ, I was on my way to see you." He handed me one of the coffees. "For you."

There went my theory. I took the coffee. "Thanks."

"Coffee in the cafeteria is sludge…instant packs with bottled water. This is from a Joe's Java across the street. They're serving meals and drinks to any and all until their supply runs out. Most of the residents in town have been evacuated to safer places south, but the ones that remain are the mandatory workers, volunteers, and those relocated from the harder hit areas. It's nice to see some generosity among the chaos."

I wrapped both hands around the coffee, its heat a mild comfort to my cold fingertips. The scent of cinnamon wafted to my nostrils. "Reid."

"Yeah?"

"Your sister's here, in this hospital. Why didn't you tell me?"

Despite his deeper tan complexion, color drained from his cheeks. His hand tightened around his coffee. He opened his mouth to speak, and then stopped. He blew a breath. "I…" Another exhalation.

"You can tell me."

"It's better if I show you," he said, nodding toward the direction from which I'd just come. We entered a darkened hospital room that housed two beds and with what seemed like more equipment than I could imagine. A frail woman in a blue polka-dotted gown lay in the first bed. She was connected to a ventilator, eyes closed. She had long dark brown hair and tan skin like Reid, though her complexion lacked the golden luster Reid's usually held.

"I…," I began, wordless.

He placed his coffee on the table. Then he reached for mine, took it, and set it beside his. "She resides at a nearby long-term care facility. They lost power after the eruption. They brought her here this week."

"Is she in a coma?"

"Yes."

To my surprise, tears found their way down my cheeks. I'd thought I shut off the waterworks. "I don't understand. You said she's a teacher."

"She is a teacher." He shook his head. "She *was* a teacher."

I grabbed his hand. "Reid." I steeled myself for whatever he had to say. "Just tell me, okay?"

He straightened upright and drew his look away from me. In fact, it was fixed on his sister. I stared at her, too, unable to look away. Her chest rose and fell as the ventilator worked oxygen into her body. Smooth, freshly washed wavy hair cascaded around her face. She had high cheekbones, thin, angled eyebrows, and pierced ears absent of earrings. Her skin lacked the vigor I imagined she likely had, well, before. Her body was gaunt beneath the gown and blankets. Reid's worn copy of Lewis's *The Great Divorce* lay on the bedside table.

Reid swallowed. "Lily and I had our differences. She is younger, but I think we had the roles reversed. I was the rebel; she was the rule-follower and overachiever. I did a lot of stupid things before and after my military career. I made shitty decisions in the wake of my deployment." He rubbed his chin. A ridge of ripples formed in his forehead as he gathered his thoughts.

I braced myself. I knew already.

"Guys drink and smoke way too much when we're on base or abroad. It passes the time and helps us deal with the crap we'd seen or had to do. It's when I began reading the philosophical greats. A deck of cards loses its appeal after a week or two, and you can't exactly play board games by yourself. I had to escape the demons," he said with a slight snort and dry, sad smile. "I returned home unsure what to do with myself. Books and a few classes weren't enough to dampen the ghosts. They didn't block the memories. I was angry. I drank. A lot."

He stepped closer to me and reached to touch my arm, but then quickly retracted his hand. He hunched his shoulders, chin down. To my surprise, I didn't recoil, despite the emotion that knotted my stomach. Reid had been an angry alcoholic. Was he still?

God, there was more. The evidence lay in the bed before us.

His eyes clung to mine, imploring. Painful memory filled them. "I've been sober for five years now," he said in defense.

He stopped himself, brushed a hand through his hair, and continued.

"One night, shortly after I'd come home, six years ago, having completed my stint with the army, Lily was on a date with a guy I knew from high school—a guy I urged her against dating. He was a jerk. He had a bad rep and got out of a sexual assault charge in high school mostly due to who he knew, parents in the right place and all. She called me…hysterical. He'd hurt her."

I inhaled sharply.

"No, well, he didn't do *that*," he said reading my shocked mind. "He'd come close. She got away from him and ran to the local drugstore and waited for me. She called for me to get her. I had been drinking a lot that night. My parents were in poor health—my dad's dementia and my mom's chronic pain—and they didn't drive anymore. Not too many taxis run in the later hours here." He released a throaty groan. "I wouldn't let her take one even if they had been available. I had to get her myself. Stupid ego, I suppose," he added quietly.

He pumped his fist, looking down at his tattoos.

*Ne obliviscaris.* Never forget. The idea that the tattoo wasn't from his army days had never occurred to me before now.

"Anyway. I picked her up. I was too proud to admit that I'd been drinking, but she saw right through me. I drove to the bastard's apartment. She waited in the car while I beat the shit out of him."

He stopped talking, swallowed, and turned his gaze to his sister. "I'm sorry," he whispered.

I didn't know who it was for, me or Lily.

My heart raced as all the puzzle pieces found their connections, as his story came together. I now saw why he had been riled when that awful guy Dennis assaulted me and Will. It *had* been like something had snapped in him, and I'd attributed it to protective testosterone or PTSD.

"I refused to let her drive. I drove her home. It was my job, as her brother. To protect her, you know? I was an ass." He stared at me, a twisted sad smile emerging as he shook his head. "She yelled at me while I was driving, wanted me to let her drive. She grabbed the wheel. I was snaking all over the place. God, I don't remember much. I was toasted."

He swallowed a heavy sigh. "I do remember her scream when I drove off the road and hit a tree."

Remorse teared in the corners of his usually comforting, but now sorrowful, eyes.

I swallowed the truth, my mouth drier than ever. Even though it was beside me, I didn't touch the coffee. I had enough bitterness swirling in my stomach. "You could've told me," I mustered from the depths of compassion.

He drew his face away and looked at his sister. "No, I couldn't. A pissed-off drunk as your companion across the country? Around your kid?" he said, raising his voice. Then, in one whoosh of a breath, he added ever quietly, "A stupid drunk who...who..."

A flash of remembrance entered my mind...the alcohol I'd smelled on him in the hotel in Missouri. He had said it wasn't him who had been drinking. Had he lied then, too? That seemed like ages ago, yet the rawness returned in a torrent. Had he relapsed?

"Your husband," he said in an aching whisper, refusing to look at me. Instead his stance was directed toward his sister's frame.

"The hotel. The booze...I-I can't," I said, spinning to leave. I couldn't think straight. He lied. *He lied.* He was a damn drunk. Or a has-been drunk. I didn't care. His sister. Dear God, his sister. He had done *this* to her.

And I…and we…

All the pain flooded back to me.

I gasped and hurried through the door into the corridor, my only instinct being to flee, at least while I got my head wrapped around it.

"Wait, AJ. Wait! Please! They're moving the refugees from Schriever. I was coming to tell you."

I froze and turned around so quickly that my right foot caught on a cart of machinery. A grisly series of cracks sounded in my troublesome ankle, sending a shooting pain up my shin. I tripped into Reid's arms with a curse. Reflex pulled me upright, away from him, as I kept my right foot hovering while hopping on the good foot. I whimpered. "What?"

"Here, come, sit."

"Not in there," I said with a look to his sister's room. I reluctantly leaned on him as he led me to a nearby empty wheelchair. Once sitting, I put my foot down to test it, foolishly, like a child told not to touch the hot plate, but who touches it anyway. Pain seared through my foot like a scorching iron.

My mind shifted gears. "What did you say?"

"Let me get a nurse for you. You might need an x-ray."

"Reid, please."

A five o'clock shadow had reappeared on his face. He drew his eyebrows together and cleared his throat. "When I checked downstairs with the officer on duty, he mentioned that they're moving the refugees from Schriever Air Force Base south to various hospitals in New Mexico or west to Nevada. They can't send them here. No more room. Mobile hospitals are also overrun. Anyone in moving shape is going south or west."

"Do they know if Finn or my brother are there?"

He shook his head. "The man I spoke to didn't have names, but he did mention the earthquake in Denver; some of the injured may have gone to the base."

"Will they go through Lamar? Can I head them off there?"

He shook his head. "No. Everyone's being routed south to several hospitals and mobile units."

"When?" I swallowed as tingles in my hands joined the awful sensation radiating from my injured foot. Dammit, my ankle. Why now?

"Tomorrow."

I yelped.

"Let's get your foot checked, okay? Then we can go."

"But Will!" I couldn't leave him alone. He was safe here, but…what if he had another seizure? Or what if the power went out? On cue, the lights flickered yet again. They stayed out for over a minute this time before coming back on.

The minute crept by as pain vibrated in my foot, heart, and soul. I knew what Reid and I had shared was some transient connection during a time of need. That's all. So why did I feel brokenhearted?

Suddenly, a flurry of orderlies, nurses, doctors, and soldiers shuffled in the hallway toward the main desk. Voices hollered.

Reid cut off a scrambling orderly. "What happened?"

"Another earthquake in Denver. Large aftershock." The man dashed down the hallway.

"Maybe somebody can give me a ride to the base?"

I said, sickened, my voice a pathetic whisper. The pain welling in my ankle didn't help.

*Who would watch Will if I left?*

"Your foot first, AJ."

"Okay, quickly." I cooperated marginally. "My Finn, Reid. I must get to him! I must find him. What if he's d-dead? I just can't—" I broke into racking sobs.

Chapter Nineteen
Facing the Past

*July, Last Year*

"I'm sorry, Mrs. Sinclair. There was nothing we could do," the weary police officer said. He removed his hat and placed it across his chest, large distressed eyes staring at me. "I'm sorry."

I fell to the floor in my front foyer, a weeping mess. Will hurried to my side.

"Mom! Mom! I'm here. Don't cry!"

Then he was crying in my arms. Finn came. He wailed and screamed and hit me. We lay in a heap on the floor.

The pine-scented cleaner stung my nose—I had washed those floors that morning.

My children's tears soaked my blouse.

The officer continued with his apologies, his voice muffled by Finn's howls. When my baby lowered his wails to sobs, his face still red and blotchy, the other officer crouched beside us. "Mrs. Sinclair, we have grief counseling. I can get you information from the station. We have a counselor there we can connect you with," she offered.

I nodded, her words falling on deaf ears. I inhaled, then exhaled. I chewed on my lip to stop the trembling. "Do I need to come and…" I couldn't finish it.

"Yes, ma'am. A visual ID helps us confirm. When you're ready. We can send a car for you or you can come with us."

I nodded. "I need to get a sitter. M-Make calls."

Patsy and George. Oh, my God. I had to call people. I had to tell them that Harrison was dead.

"Come on, honey, stand up, okay?" I said to Finn. Will had already risen. Finn got to his feet, but then he pounded his hands into my chest.

"Noooooo!" he howled, crying harder. "I want Daddy!"

I turned to Will. His face was also splotchy and tear-stained. "Come, Finn. Let's go upstairs," he said.

Finn resisted and spat at Will. He then ran upstairs, growling.

My heart could not break any more than it did in that moment.

"I'll watch him, Mom, while you call Grandma." Will took each step painfully slow as he went upstairs, sniffling. He paused. "He's really dead? Gone? Not coming back?"

I gulped. "Yes, honey, he's not coming back."

"Your mom will take care of him in heaven, right?"

I was wrong. My heart broke more.

After an excruciating call with Patsy, the stringently clean morgue identification room awaited me. Nobody tells you about this part of death. I remembered my mother's death as well, but I didn't have to take the lead on all the calls or arrangements. My father had shouldered that burden. Now I was the adult. It was my job to break the awful news. It was my job to identify my husband and arrange a funeral.

It was my job to raise the kids alone.

Before me on a metal slab, lay my husband, mangled and bruised, but recognizable and cleaned. Forever closed were his baby blues. His dirty blond hair was swept away from his forehead. I memorized his face...the curve of his chin, the long slender nose. He didn't have his glasses on, which now he wore for more than reading. His long, wispy eyelashes...the speckled freckles that dotted his arms and across the bridge of his nose...the simple, gold wedding ring that was no longer on his left ring finger, and instead in a plastic bag along with his wallet and cell phone, now tucked in my handbag.

My children would never see their daddy again.

Part of my soul left me that day at the hands of a drunk driver.

I cried for the life I would never have again. Just like that, fate steered me on an alternate path.

I still heard Will and Finn's cries of "Mom" deep within my bones.

Chapter Twenty
Found

*Present Day*

Will's hospital room came into focus. A few red and amber machine lights blinked in the darkness.

"Mom!"

I bolted upright. "What is it, Will?" Disoriented, my scrutiny fell upon each corner of the room. The hospital room. Dammit, I was still here.

"Look at your foot! What did you do?"

He sat up in his bed and began coughing. Instinctively, I reached for the water jug on the wheeled table. He took the cup I offered him and sipped.

Oh, there it was, my wrapped foot. The blanket had fallen off my lap. Well, wrapped was an understatement. It was in a boot. Ah yes, the injury and x-ray. I remembered now. It was a slight hairline fracture. My tricky ankle had done me in again. The doctor had told me to keep it elevated (and it was, resting on another chair in front of me). I shifted in the uncomfortable chair and stretched my neck, an awful kink pinching the base of my skull. God, how long had I slept? I had a heavy pain-reliever hangover.

Light from the hallway filtered into the room. I squinted at the clock on the wall and let out an expletive when I saw the time—2:13 a.m.

Will fumbled around in his bed. "Where's the TV remote?" He found it and pushed a few buttons to find a channel he liked.

I decided against arguing with him that it was the middle of the night and that he should be sleeping. He had slept half the day yesterday, after all, and his body was probably as out of whack as mine.

Yesterday. It was tomorrow already.

Urgency pulled me to standing, and I awkwardly hobbled to the nursing station.

A different team of staff was posted there now. A lanky, young male nurse greeted me. "Ah, Mrs. Sinclair. Too soon to be up. You need to rest with your son. I'm sorry we don't have another bed for you. We need to keep space for others who may be arriving."

Others. My stomach hardened.

Groggy determination brought me to his desk, and I curled a fist, the feel of my wedding band heavy, smooth. "The aftershock? What happened?"

The skin on his forehead wrinkled, and his sandy eyebrows turned up. "News says it was a 6.2. Epicenter was north of Denver. Nobody is going in or out of the city. It's still a wreck from the quake last week."

I swallowed a cry. I had to get a ride north to the base now more than ever. "My friend. Reid. The army corporal I came in with. Corporal Gregory. Please tell me you know where he went?"

"Yeah, he left you a note here. He left when I came on my shift." He handed me a folded candy bar wrapper. It still smelled like nuts and chocolate. The man snorted. "I told him we have paper, but he insisted on the wrapper. Said you'd understand."

I opened it with shaking fingers. *God, Reid, don't*

*you ghost me again.* My heart knew otherwise and was rewarded for its loyalty when I read his words.

It read, in neat print:

*I'll get Finn. Stay with Will. I promise I will take care of this.*

*I took a walkie-talkie. Turn it on when you can, on the top of each hour. I'll try to contact you when I get closer.*

*P.S. I found a mechanic that can help you with your car. His info is at the nurse's station.*

\*\*\*\*

I turned on the walkie-talkie for ten minutes, listened, waited. Turned it off to save the battery as I had for the past few hours, on the hour. These walkie-talkies had a twenty-mile range. All I'd heard were jumbled messages between military personnel.

"Don't worry, Mom. He's got my compass," Will said, spooning another mouthful of applesauce into his mouth.

"Huh?" I pulled my gaze from the window and my view of the hectic morning street below. In such a daze the evening before, I hadn't taken the time to really absorb it all. The hospital seemed orderly enough, albeit overrun. But outside. Lord. With sunlight came illumination. Ash, blaring horns, people running to and fro, a few scuffles, military patrols…

Ambulances unloaded the injured, those covered in gray debris from collapsed buildings, or wrapped in bandages. It had been over ten days since the initial eruption, but the country was still in recovery mode…and with continued tremors to boot.

"Jesus Christ," I mumbled.

It was exactly like what we had seen on TV.

Except, now we were here. Order hinged on disorder. However, there were military personnel everywhere. They would maintain command. The country—the world—would not crumble under this. It couldn't.

I drew my attention to Will. "The compass?"

"While you were sleeping, Reid and I tinkered with it. We fixed it. He then took it with him when he left. Now he can find Finn. Don't worry, he promised he'd bring it back."

"He fixed it?" I scratched my head and yawned. A night on that uncomfortable chair was like camping on the hard ground. Pain slithered up my backside.

"Yeah, he came in to check on you before he left. The noise of the nurses at that desk woke me up. He offered to help me fix the compass. And he did! It wasn't that hard. I asked him to take it to help find Finn and so Uncle Brandon would know he was with us. Like a secret code. Colorado Springs is directly north. He could follow north on the compass!" Will looked pleased with himself. He coughed lightly.

"Ah," I said, jittery from the woozy aftereffects of whatever pain medicine I had been prescribed. Dark spots swam before me.

I stole a look at Will's chart in the plastic holder by the door. He was holding strong, seizure-free, and they had scheduled him to have his IV removed soon.

There wasn't much I could do. I had tried in the early hours, twice, to reason with the Guard soldier at the front desk in the lobby to let me call the base. Reception was sketchy, and he couldn't make an exception for me. He assured me that everyone there was safe. They were doing all they could. They *were* relocating, especially considering the recent aftershock.

I kept calling Brandon on the hour, too, but that was also futile.

All I could do now was look out the window and squint at any military vehicle that arrived, and there were many. My pulse raced.

The hospital clock ticked, its sound deafening. Will turned on the TV, but the channels were hit and miss as well. He slurped the last bit of applesauce and then opted for drawing. "I miss Snow, Mom," he said, as he drew our cat's long black tail.

"Let's put a smile on him," I offered. "We'll see him soon. Marcy's taking care of him. Lots of snuggles and kisses." I silently prayed that our neighbor was sticking to her promise to watch our cat. A cat-lover herself, she wouldn't let any harm befall him, even if she had to leave for some reason.

"Okay."

Will stuck out his tongue in that concentrating way as he shaded in Snow's black and gray marbled fur.

"How do you spell seizure?" he asked a few minutes later.

I grimaced but spelled it for him.

Clarification lit his round face. "It's spelled like seismograph!"

I couldn't help but smile. "Yup. Your brain sort of made its own seismic waves."

"Cool."

I allowed my mind to drift.

When the clock struck the hour, I turned on the walkie-talkie and sat, hopeful for news. I gambled a try. "Hello, Reid?"

Click. Garble. Click.

"Reid?"

Click. More garble. Click.

After the week with Reid, I missed his voice. Drunken stupid mistake aside. Horrific mistake. Gosh, I missed talking with him. Of course, I anxiously awaited word that my son was alive, but I also found myself longing to speak with the man who had become my travel mate and friend—and more—over the past week.

Another hour passed. I clicked the walkie-talkie on to immediately be greeted with Reid's voice. "…close. With the Guard…I have…"

Garbled words.

"Oh my gosh, Reid! Do you have Finn? Repeat!" My hands shook, and I dropped the walkie-talkie. I swiped it and hobbled to the window, my gaze rapt on the vehicles below. An ambulance arrived. The paramedics pushed a child, a girl, on a gurney into the emergency entrance. No other arrivals.

Static and crackles. Muffled words.

I tapped my uninjured foot on the floor.

"Reid?" I said into it.

Nothing.

"Reid?"

I gave up, the crackles and slurs turning into silence. I fell into the seat at the window.

Ten minutes later, I heard the familiar squeaking sound of a young boy in the hallway. I shot to my feet, and just as quickly my blood pressure plummeted. Yellow-black spots danced in my vision. I blinked, took a breath. A soul-deep inhalation, a steadying arm on the chair, and I cleared it.

"Finn!" Will and I said in unison.

"Be right back, honey," I said to Will, who was still hooked to an IV and monitor.

The sounds of the room faded, and I heard only my pounding heart. Tingles raced through all my fingertips, but not in innate warning. Nervous anticipation shook me to my core. My Finn. My Finn! It had to be him. I had become attuned to all the sounds and voices in this wing during the past twenty-four hours. That voice was a new sound to the choir of the pediatric wing.

My heart nearly burst.

And there he was.

I blinked. Yes, it was them. No dream, no nightmare, no memory. Flesh and bone.

He strolled down the corridor, happily sucking on a lollipop. Brandon was by his side, Finn's plush Otter tucked under his arm. Finn's sweet smile deepened when he spotted me, too.

I tottered to him, ignoring the pain that screamed in my ankle.

"Mommy!" he screeched in his happy sing-song way. He waved a casted lower left arm.

My feet couldn't get to him fast enough. I knelt and threw my arms around him, his skinny body foreign but familiar. Twelve days had been twelve days too long. I kissed his cheeks repeatedly. I cried into his flaxen hair as I inhaled his little boy smell. It was like holding my newborn baby for the first time again.

He was alive.

"Oh, my Finn."

"Ick! Mom! You're sliming me!" Finn cooed. He didn't pull from my embrace though.

A deep, guttural cry of relief broke free from the dam as I allowed the tears. I quaked with the insurrection of emotion.

Brandon shone with relief.

"Thank you," I said to him, hoping he understood the gravity behind those words. For all I knew, he'd been through hell, too.

I looked past Brandon as I stood upright. Reid was nowhere to be found. I swallowed and hugged my brother.

"Where's Reid?" I asked, pulling back slowly.

Brandon said, "He went to check on his sister. Wanted to give us some time alone."

"Okay," I said with a nod, turning with him as we returned to Will's room.

****

My usually clean-shaven brother was scruffy from days of travel and sported an almost shaggy hairdo. "Brandon, I don't know how to thank you. What you endured," I said. "Will you tell me?"

"AJ..."

"Brandon...I'm a big girl. I can handle it."

He sat beside me on the bed.

"It was an adventure!" Finn said, whizzing past me, touching all the equipment in the room.

"Finn, honey, please play with your bag of rocks, there," I said to his gift-shop bounty spread out on Will's bedside table.

Brandon drew me over to the window, where we both sat in the chairs. "Like I said, we had made it to Denver. We were in a newer terminal of the airport when the earthquake occurred. We managed to stay under cover."

"That's when Finn broke his arm?"

He nodded.

The need for details gnawed at me. "And?"

"One of the passengers waiting to board the plane

was enlisted air force. I chatted with him before we were supposed to board. After the quake, he helped me pull as many people as we could from the rubble. It was chaos. Anyway, we snagged a ride with a military convoy to Schriever. Some of the injured were sent to local hospitals as well. It took us a few hours to get to the base. We spent the last week and a half hunkered down at the base, eating snacks and playing games. My cell phone hardly worked. I couldn't even get through to Sarah the entire time we were there."

"I had lots of candy, Mom!" Finn added.

"That's it?" I prodded.

"Uh-huh."

Well, that's what he admitted. I could only imagine the pandemonium. I didn't buy all of Brandon's story, which tasted quite sugar-coated. My son was alive and well, and that's all that mattered. I was certain he'd divulge more details of the story to me in time.

Brandon squeezed my hand. "You would've done the same for my girls."

I smiled back.

An hour later, the boys were already back to their normal routine of goofing off in Will's bed with the rest of their gift-shop trinkets. I tapped a finger on my thigh. Reid had not come up to see us yet.

"I'll be back in a few," I said to Brandon. "Can you watch them?"

He nodded.

I left to check on Reid. When I reached his sister's room, he wasn't there. Her ventilator droned. I glanced around the room. His backpack wasn't there either.

My heart sank when I saw the two lollipop wrappers pinned under a cup of now tepid coffee.

"No," I said aloud, tears finding their way to my eyes again. I was tired of crying. I unfolded the wrappers, and this time it had been written with a pen instead of a permanent marker, the words tiny and neat across both wrappers.

*Audrey Jane, the serious woman with a serious name.*

*I'm so sorry. There's not enough space for me to express my regret. If you do find it in your heart, I would value your forgiveness. It's best if I leave now. Say goodbye to Will for me. He's an amazing kid, and you're an incredible mom.*

*My home address and phone number are below. I'll be your friend or more, any way you'll have me, when you're ready. I'm heading to Austin, TX, first to check on a friend.*

*And, Audrey Jane, there is no forgetting that night. It was sweeter than one of my lollipops. I'll cherish it.*

*Affectionate, grateful, and truly sorry,*

*R.*

I tucked the wrappers into my back pocket. I approached Lily and brushed a swath of hair off her forehead. "Be at peace," I said, turning from the room, my heart swelling with a vast sense of loss.

I picked up the coffee and sipped the bitterness of it, sweetened a tad, just how I liked it.

\*\*\*\*

I dialed Reid's number a third time on my trudge back to Will's room. No connection. Nada.

I reached the room to find it empty. Before even asking as I poked my head out, the nurse at the desk responded, "They went to the gift shop."

"Again?"

She shrugged.

"But Will's IV?"

"We removed it."

I dialed again. Gift shop, I thought with a smug smile. I plopped into the seat by the window. As if one trip hadn't been enough. Those kids and their trinkets.

The walkie-talkie lay there still. I picked it up, turned it on, and found an open channel. I swallowed, finger lying on the transmit button. I listened to the static for a few minutes. It was the top of the hour again, ironically, and Reid had never returned the other walkie-talkie.

Reid's voice came through and startled me. In the words of my lovely Finn, I said, "Seriously?" Odds were finally in my favor.

"...not sure you can even hear me now. But somebody's listening. So, consider this my confession. God, I hope it's you, AJ. It's on the hour now, maybe you turned it on..." Crackles.

"Anyway, here goes. I should've been upfront about Lily, but after you told me about the way Harrison died, the guilt I thought I'd worked through crippled me once again. I made the worst kind of mistake, and I live in daily atonement...I had to atone by placing one foot in front of the other for as long as it took—even if it meant hitchhiking across the entire country. Then you came along. I felt tested. You know by now that I'm not a deeply religious man, but I do believe the universe—or God or some powerful being—brings us choices. You came. You and Will trusted me. I felt needed again. I was given a second chance. Fate, maybe?"

Crackles. My finger still hovered. My heart

pounded in my skull. "Oh, Reid," I whispered to myself. "Just do it, just do it," I cajoled myself. My finger danced. I listened with anticipation.

"That night in Missouri…I never took a drop. That was all true. I've stayed sober for five years. I'm sorry I freaked you out." He paused. "But I did lie about one thing. I *was* following you. I was worried about you and Will. Perhaps it was Lily telling me to keep tabs on you. She would've done anything to help you two, especially Will."

Silence. My finger danced. I clicked, but no words came out of my open mouth. I unclicked.

"I don't even know if you can hear me. You're a great woman, AJ. I also know you will do more than survive. You will live. You will…"

Garbled words. Crackles.

His voice grew quieter. I was unsure if it was from distance or something else.

"…I could never replace your Harrison. I'm a guy on his own questionable path. I allowed impetuous addiction to destroy not just my life, but my family. But I am so, so sorry. Please forgive me."

I exhaled. My pulse and breathing raced against each other.

"Thank you, AJ. You brought sunshine to my darkness. I must forgive myself. I've journeyed through purgatory for far too long. Thank you. Be safe. Be whole. Just be. Try not to worry too much about your boys—Will is going to make it. Both of you will rise up from this."

I couldn't wait any longer. I clicked the transmit button. "Reid."

Static. Crackles. Muffled words.

"Reid?"

Radio silence.

**\*\*\*\***

I hesitated in my journal. What day was it? I was tired of counting days. Instead, I wrote:

*The End: The day I was found*

*Gratitude comes in many forms. It smacks you. It trickles in. It's a slow burn.*

I wrote a few examples of those "wow, we were lucky" moments from the past nine years as a parent. Good grief, there were many. I prayed a wholehearted thank-you to God for those moments. They were wake-up moments indeed. And this journey to find Finn. I did it. Albeit, with help, but I'd found my son. Luck had finally found me. Unless it was really God or fate.

I also found faith again. Trust was tested, shattered, but reaffirmed.

I flipped to the next page of the journal, which said "World's Best Mom" across the top in Will's cute scrawl. Geesh, that boy.

My mantra returned to me: I try, I love, I survive.

I live.

*I live.*

I was wrong earlier about questioning that.

I paused and reflected.

*Despite it all, my heart is full.*

Maybe it wasn't Finn who'd been lost after all.

"More coffee?" Brandon asked.

"Huh?" I tore my concentration from my journal to find my brother hovering near me.

"Coffee," he said.

I capped my pen. "Thanks."

Will and Finn darted around me, making blaster

sounds as Finn wielded his casted arm like his own personal wand.

"I'm going to finish here, then go. It's been a few days, and I am eager to get home," I said, tapping my pen to the journal. "We got cleared this morning from the doctor. No more seizures. Our asthma is in check. She told us to take it easy on the drive home and to follow up with Will's doctor."

Brandon handed me a white paper bag. Prescription bottles rattled inside. "Meds for Will, in case, and they refilled your prescription, too. And some inhalers."

I took the bag. "Thanks." I shoved it in my handbag. Even though I had gotten through the journey having depleted my supply, I knew it was okay to still need the pills. Help in friend or pill form was okay. And I was going to be all right. Maybe one day I wouldn't need them.

"I'm happy to see you writing," Brandon said as he sat on the bed.

"Did you finally get through to Sarah?"

"Yeah. They're okay. I'm going to catch a ride with another military convoy to California tomorrow."

"You sure you don't want us to drive you?"

"AJ, you've driven across the country to get to us...I know there's no stopping a determined Audrey Jane Sinclair. You have a long haul home. I can't ask that of you. Unless you want to take me up on the offer to come stay with us for a while?" He raised thick brown eyebrows at me in earnest.

I sipped the coffee. "No, it's okay. I need to go home. I may visit Patsy on the way."

He nodded. "You should. She'd be happy to see

you. I know it's not the same as having Mom, but she does care for you. You sure you're ready for the drive?" He pointed to my bandaged ankle.

"Yup. It's okay to drive on. I've let it rest enough. I'm ready for anything life throws at me."

It was time to begin again. I had a lot more living ahead of me.

The boys' playing turned into an argument about something life-altering, like whose wand hit the other first. I rose to intervene. Brandon stopped me. "Finish what you're writing. I've got this. You get to deal with battles on your two-thousand-mile drive home."

"How's the car?" I asked.

"All set. The mechanic Reid found took care of it. You're damn lucky that a tow truck was able to get it here, and they put your bikes on it, too, but you had three. Two adult ones?"

I nodded. "Yeah, one was Reid's."

"Ah. They've started clearing the main highways, but the mechanic suggested going south. You'll need a Guard escort out of Pueblo, but Route 25 is cleared for traffic heading south because they've been relocating people to New Mexico. Oh, here. Forgot I had this," he said, reaching into his jacket pocket. He placed the compass in my hand.

I stared at it as the needle swept back and forth until it found its bearing. This compass had traveled the world with Harrison and me, and now with us on this journey.

By this point, my thin journal was nearly half full. Admittedly, wary of the drive that lay ahead, I was content in the moment and decided to write another passage. I opened the journal, already bent at the edges from use.

I had my son. I had both my sons.

I had gained the most unlikely of companions in the span of two weeks…a friend along the way. Again, I'd pushed somebody out of my life due to my own battle against inner demons. Maybe that's why Harrison had worked himself weary—to escape me. Had I pushed him away, too? Why else would Reid have left without a formal goodbye?

Maybe Reid had been more than a friend. I may never know. God, I missed him already.

I didn't blame him for leaving.

I adjusted myself in the chair to stretch my bandaged ankle. The journal slipped off my lap and tumbled to the floor. It fell open. I leaned over and picked it up. I was about to turn to the page I had left off on, but paused. There was writing toward the end, about ten pages in from the final page. I flipped to the page, anticipating another map or cat drawing from Will. He already completed his map at the beginning of the journal.

I didn't expect to see the note from Reid. The rush of anticipation filled my cheeks, like a schoolgirl reading a note from a childhood crush, absurd as the comparison might be.

I read it with unsteady hands.

*"There is no other day. All days are present now. This moment contains all moments."*—C.S. Lewis, The Great Divorce

*R.*

*P.S. Don't worry, I didn't read your journal.*

I contemplated. How had he…?

That night when he left to find Finn…had he come

in here and written in the journal, too, when he helped Will fix the compass?

*Reid, I don't hate you*, I said in my mind.

I closed my journal.

I had no more words.

Epilogue
Finding Home Again

After parting ways with Brandon, the boys and I left for home in my fueled, repaired, and restocked SUV. My plan was to travel south first, and then east toward Virginia. I knew why I drove south first, well, other than the regulations by the National Guard.

Perhaps…he was long gone, but I could hope. Austin, Texas, was on the scenic way to Virginia. I didn't think the kids would mind a short detour.

When I saw the sign for New Mexico, I kept driving. Goodbye, Colorado.

Ever observant, Will said, "Don't we need to take a road north to Maine, Mom?"

"You're such an astute navigator, Will. We're going to see Grandma and Grandpa Sinclair in Virginia. Plus we have to go south first."

Finn and Will both released happy shouts. "Yippie!"

"Gram always lets me eat an extra cookie," Finn said, glowing. I watched him in the rearview mirror. God, how I'd missed his enthusiasm.

"Mom, we don't need to go through Texas to get to Virginia," Will observed.

"Scenic route," I said. I released a sigh but fastened a smile on my own face. It was time to see Harrison's parents. Patsy would never be my own mother, and

George, well, he reminded me of Harrison. They were my family now and forever. I loved them. The boys loved them. Patsy would embrace us with her usual courteous hospitality. It was time to move on in the next stage of grief together.

If I happened to drive through Austin, Texas…

I also decided I was going to visit Cynthia, the mother of the young man who killed Harrison—Clayton Attwood—there, I said it. I knew too well the grief Cynthia held for a love lost, for a son lost. I had to forgive and move on.

We drove across the Colorado border, the boys laughing in the back seat. Finn poked Will, Will poked Finn, they giggled, and they shared stories. I stuck my hand back, palm upward, in our familiar gesture. Each boy squeezed my hand. God, how I missed doing that.

A welcoming horizon greeted us, the rising sun fighting its way through the gray obscurity that hung in the air. The round orb poked its nose above the hills ahead and brightened the dark world with life. I no longer drew my gaze to the rearview mirror, except for watching the boys goof off together. No more ash—although it still draped over the countryside in a heavy charcoal blanket—but the roads were cleared enough for safe travel. No more frantic searching.

The journey to find Finn had been my compass's north. I had found my way across the country. The atlas had helped. Reid had helped. My own perseverance had helped. Hope had led me to my Finn, like the beacon of a lighthouse, directing lost sailors in a tossing maelstrom. It had also led me to my absolution. Although my wounds from Harrison's death never fully heal, the strips of repair were growing like scar tissue. That scar was a reminder of my loss, but it *was* healing. I would prevail. I would not let this world break me. Like the world, I would rise from the ashes.

Finn had not been the one lost. It was me. Somewhere along the way, I'd found myself again. A stranger who hardly knew me had restored my faith and brought the flicker of life back to me.

I didn't know what twists or bumps awaited me on my parenting journey with two special boys. I would be okay. Will and Finn would be okay. We would not fade away. I wouldn't allow it. Just like our world would not relent in the wake of modern man's largest natural disaster.

Unlike many of the roads we'd traversed to get to Colorado, I saw not one hitchhiker on the drive today. The disorder had settled, for now. Almost three weeks had elapsed since the eruption. The big dig had begun. People were now transitioning from shock to relief efforts and cleanup. Much to everyone's relief, the panic that had pressed our country to the brink of anarchy had not resulted in a complete breakdown of the country. Our government, our military, and the goodness of mankind had held it together. Stories filled the newscasts. Stories of hope and humanity. Together, we would rise from it all.

A long stretch of open highway lay ahead. Completeness radiated through me.

Before long, I spotted a lone person traveling along the road, walking. His gray and red plaid long-sleeved shirt was unmistakable. His pack looked lighter. He, too, had unloaded his burdens in Colorado.

"Mom! Look!" said Will, his voice light and happy. "How great is that? We have his bike!"

I slammed on the brakes without hesitation, the gravel spitting beneath the tires. Luck, hope, my keen navigating skills, or fate…I don't know which it was. I found him. My heart thumped. I rolled down the passenger window. "Hi," was all I could manage. How could I convey my apologies for my own unkind ways?

His richly colored eyes smiled at me. I'd once heard Susie tell Will that his eyes smiled. I smiled myself.

"Hi," Reid said.

Will leaned through his opened window. "Don't you live in Colorado?"

Finn said, "Hi! Got any of those lollipops?"

Reid pulled two from his upper pocket. "Last two, buddy. I was saving them for you guys." He handed them to Will, who then gave one to Finn. He added, his look upon me, "If I ever saw you again." His face shone with hope, with regret, and with his natural sincerity I had grown to appreciate. And I had missed it. It said what neither of us could say with words.

A swaying voice danced in my ears. It was a voice I had not heard since before finding Finn, for I had finally let him go, for my own good. *Love again. It's time. Make a new home.*

*Yes, Harrison, I will. Thank you.*

"Are you going home?" Will asked.

"Yes," I answered for Reid, leaning over to open the passenger door.

## A word about the author...

Jean is a scientist and a mom to two active sons. She currently resides in Massachusetts and draws from her interests in history, science, the outdoors, and her family for inspiration. She writes historical and contemporary romances and women's fiction.

She enjoys writing nonfiction articles for family-oriented travel magazines, and aspires to write children's books while continuing to write novels.

Jean enjoys working in her flower gardens, tackling the biggest mountains in New England with her husband, and playing with her sons, while daydreaming about the next hero and heroine to write about...

Find out more about her books by visiting her website:

http://www.jeanmgrant.com

Thank you for purchasing
this publication of The Wild Rose Press, Inc.

For questions or more information
contact us at
info@thewildrosepress.com.

The Wild Rose Press, Inc.
www.thewildrosepress.com

To visit with authors of
The Wild Rose Press, Inc.
join our yahoo loop at
http://groups.yahoo.com/group/thewildrosepress/